Praise for
A Shadow All of Light

"Magnificently executed."

—Matthew Hughes, author of the Luff Imbry series

"Sword and sorcery escapades with Shakespearian panache."

—*World*

"More than the sum of its parts."

—*Locus*

"The humor, inventiveness, and suspense are top-notch, and the concept is as sly as Lewis Carroll's Cheshire."

—*Citizen-Times* (Asheville)

"Chappell has a deft touch for comedy and for capers, and his witty, elegant prose shows a poet's deep love for words."

—*Publishers Weekly*

Praise for
Fred Chappell

"Chappell reminds us of the almost forgotten phrase 'man of letters.'"

—*Los Angeles Times*

"A master storyteller."

—*Miami Herald*

A SHADOW
ALL OF LIGHT

Fred Chappell

TOR

A TOM DOHERTY ASSOCIATES BOOK

NEW YORK

A SHADOW ALL OF LIGHT

Copyright © 2016 by Fred Chappell

"Thief of Shadows," "The Diamond Shadow," "Dance of Shadows," "Shadow of the Valley," and "Maze of Shadows" all first appeared, sometimes in different form, in The Magazine of Fantasy and Science Fiction. "The Creeper Shadows" appeared in Cat Tales, edited by George H. Scithers.

Designed by Mary A. Wirth

A Tor Book
Published by Tom Doherty Associates
175 Fifth Avenue
New York, NY 10010

www.tor-forge.com

Tor® is a registered trademark of Macmillan Publishing Group, LLC.

The Library of Congress has cataloged the hardcover edition as follows:

Chappell, Fred, 1936– author.
   A shadow all of light / Fred Chappell.—1st ed.
     p. cm.
   "A Tom Doherty Associates book."
   ISBN 978-0-7653-7912-2 (hardcover)
   ISBN 978-1-4668-6613-3 (e-book)
1. Thieves—Fiction. 2. Shades and shadows—Fiction. I. Title.
   PS3553.H298 S525 2016
   813'.54—dc23

                                                                  2016287129

ISBN 978-0-7653-7913-9 (trade paperback)

Our books may be purchased in bulk for promotional, educational, or business use. Please contact your local bookseller or the Macmillan Corporate and Premium Sales Department at 1-800-221-7945, extension 5442, or by e-mail at MacmillanSpecialMarkets@macmillan.com.

First Edition: April 2016
First Trade Paperback Edition: July 2017

Printed in the United States of America

0 9 8 7 6 5 4 3 2 1

The whole of this is dedicated,
at the request of Susan Nicholls Chappell, to:

Louis
Sparky
Eugenia

PART ONE

The Dealings of Shadows

I

Thief of Shadows

"You know who I am?"

"Sir, I do," I said. "You are Master Astolfo. Everyone knows."

"You know then something of my station?"

I had to think quickly. An ill-chosen word might be an insult. An insult could well be fatal. "You are the Maestro Astolfo of the shadow trade, the most highly respected dealer and most knowledgeable appraiser of shadows in the city of Tardocco, in the province of Tlemia."

"You have me at a disadvantage," he said, "for I know nothing of you."

I could not see what advantage I might have, backed against the wall of a dim corridor of his great manse, with the point of his sword at my throat and a hulking, silent hireling at his side. Astolfo seemed no murderous sort; he was a stocky, almost pudgy, man with an air of deliberate nonchalance and a relaxed gaze that betrayed no particular animosity. Yet his blade had come to my guzzle with swift efficiency when the bulky one had led me to him from his garden.

"My name is Falco," I said. "I am of an honorable family in the southern provinces."

"You are most likely from Caderia or thereabouts, as I judge your accent. That is a country of small, muddy farms. It is not long since you left off trudging a furrow behind the nether end of a mule. Hay wisps protrude from your ears."

I made no reply to these calmly spoken truths. I was not surprised. Astolfo's reputation was that no one knew more of the world than he and that few were wiser in the usage of that knowledge. These were reasons sufficient to make his acquaintance, I thought.

"Furthermore, Falco is a name you have bestowed upon yourself. 'Clodpoll' or some other clownish appellation is your true name. You are a bumpkin trying on the airs of a town bravo and you have stolen over my garden wall in the dark of night, intending to do me grievous harm and to take property that is mine."

"Not so, sir," I said. "I came a-purpose to meet you and to talk with you."

"Why could you not come by the light o' the sun and knock at the gate and make yourself known in honorable fashion? This midnight sneakery must harvest ill."

"I tried the honorable practice," I replied, "and your man here turned me away like a louse-ridden beggar without a word. I believed I would gain more careful attention entering by stealth. I believed you would apprehend me and be curious."

He lowered the point, but did not scabbard his blade. "So you formed a plan and it has worked as you hoped. You must feel proud of your cunning."

"Do I look proud to you?"

He surveyed me with a glance almost desultory. "Well, let us see. Pied hose you wear and a greasy leather doublet that I judge a hand-me-down, and black harness-leather shoes with the out-of-fashion square toes. You very wisely chose to enter here unarmed, but the two steel rings at your belt show that you habitually wear a broadsword or a long sword which is now doubtless in the hands of a tavern keeper who holds it to secure a gaming or wenching or toping debt. In fine, you are a hot-blood lazybones who has run away from a dull farm and a phlegmatic, thick-handed father. You are one of scores who seek each year the streets of Tardocco to hinder the foot traffic of the honest citizenry and to play mischief when the moon is risen. This is you, Master Rustic Lumpfart, and a hundred like you."

This pretty speech succeeded in its purpose of angering me and it was well that I had not carried my sword hither. If I had drawn upon him, Astolfo would have skewered me like a piglet on a spit. "If all you say is true, then I must acquire more urbane ways," I said. "And that is why I have sought you out."

"You think me to be a mincing dancing master, some type of finger-kissing courtier?" He cocked his head to his left side. "No. You believe me to be a great thief, a felon who steals the shadows of the gentry to make himself wealthy thereby. You believe I have acquired all the arts and skills of shadow-taking and you hope I will impart them to you so that you may go abroad and plunder and pilfer and ruin my trade and pile up riches for yourself. You would pay me to make you my prentice, though all you possess in the way of fortune is but one eagle, four coppers, and a pair of dice."

I was so startled that I patted the waist of my doublet to confirm the absence of the pouch I saw in his hand. His name as a pick-purse was legend, but how had he done the trick? I had kept my eyes upon him the whole time. I felt now more strongly than ever that I should acquire his tutelage. "I will admit that I formed some such fancy. You find me naive, I expect."

"I find you backward," he said, "and probably incurably so. Here is your purse."

He tossed the pouch toward me, but when I reached, it was not there. It had returned to his hand.

"That is a childish trick."

"Its purpose was only to demonstrate how very backward you are, and it has succeeded. Now how shall you argue your case?"

Racking my brains for a stratagem, I concluded that only the truth would deliver me; there was no point in trying to deceive or cozen or blind-bag this man. I would tell him all, not omitting how I had rapped my older brother Osbro on the noggin with a spade and robbed his pockets and stole a candelabrum from a priest-house and arrived at Tardocco hidden in a manure cart headed to the municipal gardens. Perhaps by amusing this Maestro Astolfo I could bring him round. Whatever was shaming to me would be risible to him.

So I told him the whole of it, even the part where a scullery maid named Hana thwacked me in the cullions with a skillet for placing my hand where she had given no warrant while at the same time I was attempting to steal a wheaten loaf from the windowsill. And he, Master Astolfo, nodded gravely, as if he had forethought everything I said and found it banal.

But then when he gave me a straight look in the eyes, piercing and unblinking, the question he asked surprised me. He gestured at his manservant and said, "What color are Mutano's shoes?" And added: "Do not look."

I responded immediately. "A purplish black with gilt buckles."

"Clean or soiled?"

"A little mud on the edges of the soles."

"From what source?"

"I know not. How should I know such a thing?"

"By observing. Do you not think it important to know?"

"How, then?"

"If you had noticed that your own footwear bore a trace of that same mud, what might you think?"

"That we had been sometime in the same place and I might have seen him there but did not recognize him here."

"And also?"

"That he saw me and remembers me."

He looked me over again, bottom to top and back, and nodded. He hummed a snatch of music. "Tell me what you think: Is he to be pitched on a dung heap or can some use be made of an imbecile?"

"If the imbecile be a willing and faithful fellow, he can be of great use," I replied.

"And the lunatic, what of his case?"

"If his lunacy can be kept in a narrow space and brought to purpose, he could be of use."

"And if this person were both lunatic and imbecile together?"

"Then," I said, "I would have not one but two handsome chances to stand improvement."

"Perhaps, but only if you are the sort to follow orders without question and without delay." He hummed again that snatch of song and returned his sword to its sheath.

It was this gesture that decided me once and for all that I had come to the right place, to the right master. He slid his blade into his sheath, which hung loose in ordinary fashion, without looking, without fumbling, in one smooth motion. I had seen swordsmen of tall repute, duelists and fencing masters, triumph in match upon hard-fought match, and with all of them, even the most expert, there was always that moment of awkwardness when they fitted the sword back into the sheath, just a minor gracelessness of no importance, yet minutely out of character. Nor did Astolfo guide the blade with the thumb-web of his left hand, as stage actors learn to do. Without glancing down, without hesitating, he slid the weapon home, and thus, so far as I was concerned, our pact was sealed.

Master Astolfo, I thought, you do not know it yet, but you have gained the best, most ardent pupil of your arts that you shall ever have instructed.

⊷═◉═⊶

Well, that was a time ago, and the ordeal of my training was every bit as difficult as I had imagined it would be.

The first task was to persuade him to accept me. I made so many promises, told so many overripe lies, pleaded, begged, and groveled so assiduously that I blush to recall the episodes and will not retail them now. After that, it was drill after drill: plunging my hand into a small velvet bag prickly inside with fishhooks to bring forth the piddling coin he had placed there; boxing with the voiceless Mutano who always thumped me soundly; learning the use of the quasilune knife to cleave shadows from their casters (iron posts in the beginning, cats at the latter stages); blindfolded to feel cloth of every texture; tasting lush wines I was not allowed to swallow.

Always and ever, I was set to practice with various swords, the usual broadsword, the rapier, the saber and scimitar and the others, but most often and most carefully with that swift, slender graduated crescent blade Astolfo called the Deliverer which can sever from even the most agile of performers his or her fleet shadow.

If you are one of the curious, make this experiment: Choose a bright, windy day in springtime, attach to a head-high pole a banner of flimsiest blue silk to flap in the breeze, and slice it in two with your shiny Deliverer. Do not mangle it. The cut must be as clean and straight as if sheared by a keen-eyed tailor perched cross-legged on his cushion. This you must learn to do if your desire is to heap wealth by being a thief of shadows.

Of course, Astolfo denied that he was a shadow thief at all, much less the acknowledged master of the art. "I deal in shadows," he explained. "Clients come to me. I do not seek them out. Let others purloin as they will—I traffic only in commodities."

And it is true that I never saw him take a shadow by stealth except in the process of a training exercise. His thieving days were behind him. Yet they left a long trail of legend which was vital to his legitimate enterprises. If he were not the hero of scores of tavern-tales and beggars' gossip, he would have attracted fewer clients. To traffic within his sphere was to gain a warrant of security for any risky venture at hand.

Most tedious of all the parts of my training were the mathematics and the treatises of theory. I am no lover of brain-toys, and to spend a long rainy day poring over Teteles's *Primeval Shadow Theory* or the *Liber Umbrae Antiquitae* of Carnesius is not my ideal of entertainment. I disliked geometry too, though I could see the sense of it. If you plan to cut away a shadow where it is splayed across a wall nook with three irregular corners, you will be glad to know of angles and arcs and degrees. But if you find any use at all in the worm-gnawed pages of the anonymously written *Speculum Mundus Umbrae,* you are a scholar far superior to Falco.

The training seemed never to leave off; it was continual, and part of the discipline lay in his deceiving me as to what was an actual theft and what was only an exercise.

Consider the most recent matter, for example. Here we stood at the side entrance of a gloomy harbor warehouse. Astolfo gave the weathered, strap-hinged door a coded knock, two-one-two, and we were admitted by as large a pair of dusky ruffians as you would ever care to accost in the greasy alley called Rattlebone. One of them led the way through the mazy corridors to a small door with no window. The other followed us. At the moment Astolfo rapped upon this door, I felt the unmistakable prick of a sword point between my shoulder blades.

In such circumstances, the apprehensive body allows no rational thought. I dropped to the floor while snatching my dagger from my small-boot, curled like an ingratiating cat around the feet of the large fellow, and clipped in two his heel tendon above his pretty yellow shoe. He howled in a tone surprisingly high-pitched for one so hirsute about the chops, dropped his cutlass, and staggered against the wall. I sprang to my feet and swept out my sword, ready to defend myself and Astolfo. I assumed that we had been led into a trap. Astolfo's wealth was fabled and attempts upon it—and upon his life—were not infrequent.

With a gesture he calmed me. "Hist'ou!" he said. "What are you doing?"

"The fellow threatened my life," I said. "His point was in my back."

The door opened and a wizened, yellow-faced old man peered out and took in the scene with a single glance. "What, Astolfo? Have you brought some assassin upon me?" His voice was that of an elderly man accustomed to the use of authority.

"Look to your man there, Pecunio. He attacked Falco from behind. He is fortunate to escape with a gizzard complete. Why does he draw steel upon an invited guest?"

The old man gave Astolfo a searching look before nodding assent. He signaled to the other lummox of a servant, who helped his companion to stand and supported him as he limped away into the dimness. I watched them go, thinking it would require some space of time before the one who had so rudely poked me would be leading the dancing floor in a quadrille.

"These are perilous days, Astolfo," Pecunio said. "I have made it a practice to hold strangers at blade point when they enter my little counting room."

"Anyone with me is no stranger. You have long had my surety upon that."

Pecunio nodded. "My man Dolo is large, but he is not a giant of the intellect. Let the matter rest and come in."

When we entered I saw by the light of a dozen candles that our host was smaller than I had thought and that he carried a hunchback. He was dressed in black, tunic and hose and footwear, with white laceless linen at throat and wrists. He took his own good time looking me over, and his expression gave nothing away. Then he turned to a tall cabinet, brought forth a decanter and three small gilt-rimmed glasses, and poured a measure for each of us.

I followed Astolfo's lead, raising my glass in salute and draining it in one swallow. It was fiery, and cloyingly sweet, and I knew it too costly for my purse and too genteel for my taste.

"It is good to see you again, Pecunio," Astolfo said. "I hope to be able to do you better service than chopping off the feet of your servants, as my hasty prentice is so eager to do."

"We will come to terms about that when you name a price," Pecunio said, "for the service I have in mind is but a modest one. I only desire your opinion about a certain piece of property."

"An appraisal?"

"Call it so. I have come into possession of a shadow. It has been represented to me as a curious and valuable object. And so might it be, if it is genuine."

"What is its provenance? Can you not trace down the owner?"

"I dare not come anywhere near him, if the provenance is as reported," Pecunio said. "Perhaps you too, even the adroit Astolfo, would think twice upon the matter."

"Perhaps. Just what is this marvelous shade supposed to be?"

"Let us have a look." Pecunio crossed the room to a huge oaken closet with a heavy door that reached to the beamed ceiling. With a small silver key he clicked one well-oiled lock and then another and then finally swung open the silent door. He gestured to Astolfo.

The plumpish shadow master slid his arm carefully into the recess and brought out one of the most opulent umbrae I have ever seen. Midnight its color was, the midnight of a deep forest, with the wind brushing the leafy boughs overhead so that starlight arrowed through in bright streaks. There were colors in its deep blackness, a quick threading of silver here, of scarlet there, and now and again a dull mauve glow hard to distinguish pulsed in the general texture. If 'twere cloth, it would be heavy velvet, but it was shadow and had no weight—mass, of course, but no weight. I will forbear to cite at length the *Testamentae gloriae umbrae* and all the other beetle-nibbled volumes on this point. Anyone who has seen shadows bought and sold knows all that is necessary.

Astolfo's touch with the stuff was so light, he might not have been holding it at all but only allowing it to drape about his half-opened hands. That is the proper way to handle shadows, but skillful experience alone makes it possible. At that time I had yet to attain to that level of skill.

He gestured slowly, turning his hands over as if warming them by a brazier. "This is excellent material," he said. He put his face near and inhaled gently. "A complex aroma, but with pronounced salt. This is the shade of a quondam seaman, perhaps of someone who no longer follows the sail." He closed his eyes and considered. "If he be such, he has fought many a battle and sent many a poor tar to swirl in the deepest currents." He put his tongue out briefly, tasting the air like a serpent. "I should not like to have the owner of this shadow as my enemy."

"You believe that the caster of this shadow is still alive?" Pecunio asked.

"I know men now standing in their flesh less lively than this shade. Whoever stole it from its caster had best beware."

Pecunio replied quickly, his tone apprehensive. "I did not take it and I do not know who the thief might be. I bought it only for its fine qualities. How it came to the seller I do not care to know."

"Very well," Astolfo said. "But in that case, I fail to see how I might be of service."

"It was represented to me as the shadow of Morbruzzo," Pecunio said.

"The pirate?" Astolfo asked. There was an unaccustomed hint of surprise in his voice. "The sea raider infamous in broadside and ballad? The villain who razed the port of Lamia and ravished the queen of the Dimiani clan? If this be his, it is a rare treasure, but its price may be higher than you are willing to pay."

"I have already parted with a smallish treasury for it."

"I do not speak of gold."

"My life, you mean?"

"He is no squeamish breed of pirate, by all account."

"What if it is not Morbruzzo but only some other felon?"

"Then the value of the object decreases, yet you are still in danger."

"Can you determine for me the lay of the situation?"

"Let us be clear," Astolfo said. "You would have me first affirm whether this shadow really is that of the man-slaughtering Morbruzzo; then I am to find out if he has sent or is sending agents against you; and then I am to advise you whether you may guard yourself or if you should rid you of the property as soon as may be."

Pecunio hesitated, then nodded.

"If I undertook this commission, I should put myself in mortal danger."

"To which you are no newcomer."

"In fact, you have already exposed me to such by inviting me here."

"There are already those with designs upon your life by day and by night."

"If I accepted this little chore, my fee would be a tall one."

"Your fees are always exorbitant."

"You shall have answer two days hence. I know that Falco and I will be followed when we leave here today, but I shall take pains to ensure we will not be followed when we return. Now if you will bid a servant guide us out of this labyrinthine storehouse, I will make certain that rash Falco here will refrain from puncturing him."

Pecunio smiled. "Of course."

Astolfo placed the shadow back in the great dark closet and

Pecunio turned home the locks upon it. Then he crossed to the table and raised the decanter in invitation. "Shall we seal our compact with another sip?"

"I have not yet agreed," said Astolfo. "But when our business is concluded, a glass would be welcome."

"I understand." Pecunio reached to a shelf above, took down a hand-sized copper bell, and rang it. Almost immediately the door opened and a serving man stood there, a slender, yellow-haired fellow who wore incongruous high boots. He was fair of countenance, and his person might well have been thought attractive by helmsmen as well as seamstresses. His feet, to judge by the boots, were outsized, even larger than my own.

"Be so good, Flornoy," Pecunio said, "as to show our guests the way out."

As we followed this figure through the corridors, I was surprised by the aggressive way he stepped along, but Astolfo seemed to take no notice, peering in one direction and another along the clammy walls.

⤙⊷⊷◉⊷⊷⤚

When the warehouse door eased to behind us and we were alone in the malodorous alley, I started to ask one of the hundred questions that bubbled in my head.

"Not yet," Astolfo said. "We shall be followed, and we must discover by whom. At the corner next, we shall part. I shall cross the cobbles to the tavern opposite. You turn to the right toward the wharf, then cut back through the little passage there and come round behind our pursuer. Find out everything you can, and we shall rejoin at the manse."

I followed his orders and took advantage of the occasion to gain some knowledge of this port of Tardocco upon which the well-being of the city depended. The bay was one of the most tranquil, protected from the wild storms of the Rodantic Sea by two peninsulas that curved round like the claws of a crab to form an inlet. The harbor that lay within was extremely deep, unfathomed at its centermost, so that its waters were more black than blue, so black as to give credence to old wives' tales of a sea dragon that dwelt below. It was called the Mardrake, this dragon. The old fable with its monster was a favorite among the gentry and nobility, who recalled the legend as a handy terror with which to correct mischievous children.

"The Mardrake adores to gobble up wicked little boys like Ricardino." There were Mardrake toys of various shapes and forms to amuse children.

The hoary legend was no hindrance to trade. Tardocco was a busy and prosperous port but not well guarded by civil or military arms. The possibility of pirate attack was a source of continuous concern. Part of the lore of the Mardrake was that it was guardian during the direst circumstances. When the enemy came, it would rise from unsounded depths to fall upon their vessels and tear them to flinders. It was a jolly tale, but it did not serve so well as would a warship.

I wandered about for a space, trying to appear to be aimlessly idle as I kept my eye out for any figure that might be following me. At last I turned my steps toward Astolfo's town villa, which was now my home.

—◦—

When I got back there Astolfo had not yet arrived. Mutano, his dumb but not at all deaf servant, allowed me the largess of the pantry, including a hunk of buttery cheese, a handful of black bread, and a tankard of ale to obliterate the taste of Pecunio's sickly-sweet wine. While I was making good use of these eatables, Mutano signaled to me that Astolfo had returned and now awaited me in his library—the small one with the fire grate, not the great glum one with all the musty books and their eye-murdering tiny print.

Seated in his leather armchair, Astolfo motioned me to the splint-bottom across. "Who was't dogged us, think you?"

"I saw no one," I said.

He thought. "That means there were not two hounds on our trace. You would have spotted two. You might well have spotted one who was inept. So either there is none or there is one who is sharp in his craft. We shall of course proceed on the latter assumption."

"Proceed to what end?"

"Why, to preserve our skins and to plate them with gold; that is, to stay alive and make a profit. Here lies the shape of things as I surmise. Pecunio did not come by this shadow in the way of ordinary trade. It was offered to him by someone close enough to Morbruzzo, or whoever the shadow's owner is, to be in the confidence of the robbery victim so that he could betray him. This would be someone well skilled, with an expensive price on his head. His first thought might have been to sell the shadow back to its caster for a goodly sum and then to renege on the bargain and afterward sell it to Pecunio. In this way, he could make two profits at once. But there may be other motives involved."

"Who is this overly sly one?"

"He has to be an artful shadow thief. Three well-known adepts have lately dropped from sight. The red-haired Ruggiero with the scarred right hand has not been seen in a fortnight. Perhaps he visits his sullen uncle Pedrono, from whom he hopes an inheritance. The canny, silvery woman Fleuraye and her carefree lover Belarmo have made off with many a prominent shadow over the last few years. Their latest theft, of the Countess Tessania's shade, has made them conspicuous. Rumor hath it that they now lie low in the neighborhood of the western marshes. Those are three possibles for Pecunio's seller. And there are others, but there has been some delay. For some reason, Pecunio has kept the shadow too long by him. He feels dangers mounting."

"How so?"

"Pecunio must have had in hand a second buyer with a heavy purse, or he would not have undertaken so perilous a prospect in the first place. He was to turn it over as soon as he got hold of it; the price would be paid; his buyer would have departed for his distant home place, leaving no track. Those who came sniffing around Pecunio would find nothing. But once he had it in his store he was loath to let it go. He kept putting off his buyer. And now this buyer has become fearful and has wisely absented himself. The longer the shadow stays in one place, the easier it is to find."

"Whatever could Pecunio want with the thing, if not to reap profit as the middleman?"

"Let us consider," Astolfo said. "What are your thoughts?"

"Well, he is no footpad to use the shadow to lurk for prey at night. He is no diplomat to veil with it the intentions of his words. Nor is he sculptor, painter, or composer to use it to tinct his compositions, adding nuance and subtlety. He is no—"

"We shall both molder in our tombs before you list all the things he is not," Astolfo declared. "What was his own shadow like when you saw it in his place?"

"The room was dim," I said, "but meseemeth his own was but paltry, thin, and malformed and palsied when the candles flickered.

Just such a shadow as I'd expect to find companion with a miserly merchant."

"Do you think he would describe his shadow in these terms?"

"You have told me that people rarely form true pictures of their own shadows, but he must have some notion that his is not the handsomest."

"His temptation, then?"

I thought for a while. "To try it on."

"To cloak himself in the shadow of one who has faced a hundred dangers in the heaving waters, who has peered laughing into the noose's mouth, who has crossed sabers with four opponents at once, who has abducted princesses and caused them to adore him—would not that be a seductive temptation?"

"For a daydreaming schoolboy. But Pecunio is elderly."

"Old, and with little opportunity remaining for a life not bound to the counting house, the tax summons, and the accompt ledger. With the shadow folded about him, he feels the vibrancy of that other life; the sounds and smells of mortal conflict thrill his sluggish blood; the swathe of the shadow around his thighs is like the caress of a woman."

"So he shall keep it as a plaything?"

"It is too lively. The emanations will give it—and him—away. But his one foolhardy prospective buyer has deserted. Pecunio now believes he has but a single choice left."

"He is holding it for ransom? Is not that the most foolish of choices?"

"It is. But he can try to misdirect those who would corpsify him to retrieve the shadow."

I dreaded to ask. "How shall he misdirect his pursuers?"

"By employing us. We shall have been seen visiting Pecunio. His goings and comings are watched every hour. Those who have seen us will take us for middlemen arranging a sale on his behalf. We shall be watched even more closely than he is. They expect that sooner or later we must transport this shadow to the buyer with whom we have made arrangements. At that point, they will attack. They will slash our throats, thrust pikes into our tender guts, and chatter like jovial monkeys as they bear away the prize."

"We are but decoys in the old man's plan," I said. "Let us go now to his rat-ridden warehouse and remove his liver and spleen and feed them to the alley curs. I do not like being made a dupe."

"What then?"

"We shall be revenged on his insolence."

"Revenge will not make weightier our purses."

"We shall have the shadow."

"And along with it those who will kill us for it. Are you satisfied that it truly is the shade of Morbruzzo the infamous pirate?"

"You described it as the companion of a daring privateer."

"Yet I think if it belongs to Morbruzzo we would see lying at the mouth of the bay two of his three-masters and his attendant sloop cruising the harbor. He would not scruple to torch this city of Tardocco if he thought he would regain his shade by doing so."

"If it is not Morbruzzo's, then—"

"Then we must think upon the matter dispassionately. We must meanwhile guard ourselves closely. Mutano and you and I had better stand four-hour watches until we more clearly comprehend the situation. I will stand first; Mutano will wake you for the third."

⊷═◉═⊷

In the bare little room of the manse Astolfo had allotted me I sat for a while musing at the wall. I stared at the rhymes he had ordered me to carve into the thick headboard of my bed—*Bumpkin lad, Protect thy shade; As in this life I come and go, The hardest task myself to know*—but they were too familiar to have force upon my mind.

Was I really so bloodthirsty as I boasted? Would I kill an old man in cool revenge? I had never killed anyone, though I had broken pates and cracked bones in rough combat and left a few ostentatious scars on the hides of the unmannerly. But I had never felt an urge to draw blood for the sake of it, even to revenge myself.

Then I realized why my temper had grown so short. I was unsure whether this affair of the pirate's shadow was an actual piece of business or only another training exercise. Astolfo had set me upon several ventures before, escapades involving intrigues, espials, petty thievery, forgery of sale documents, and so forth. Then, when things were just coming to full boil, he'd stopped me off, saying, "You have done none so ill. But when the actual business is afoot, you must not talk so freely or so loudly, you must not be so hasty to unsheathe, you must listen to the words and even more carefully to the music of the words." And so forth. I had felt duped as a child is duped, and if this affair with Pecunio was but another lesson in the trade, it seemed a vain waste indeed.

Sometimes I fancied I could see my sweet and zesty youth disappearing like a gourd of water poured on desert sands, and I would wonder if learning the craft of shadows was worth the toil. How had I ever thought of doing it?

In part, my brother Osbro had helped me to decide. He thought himself the clever son, the one quick with ciphering and plans. Claiming to be a reader, he loved to lord over me by quoting some cloud-minded poet or graybeard sage and then asking with an expression of cool mockery, "Now what do you think about *that*?" And my reply would be a shrug, for I never comprehended a word of what he had said.

At Astolfo's direction, I have read shelf upon shelf of antique tomes to learn the lore of shadows and the history of that lore. This newly gained knowledge led me to suspect that all those wise saws and pithy remarks Osbro uttered were actually senseless strings of words he linked together himself and that he could not read even one written sentence. That his pretense of ability masked a keen yearning to be a lettered man.

Me he regarded as a backward mud-wit, and his superior airs grew so intolerable that I determined to make my way in life by the use of my mind. I had heard much of those who dealt in shadows, men who stole them and sold them to artists and criminals and politicians and suchlike, men who bought shadows and fashioned them to the taste of pampered women and subtle nobility, men who kidnapped shadows and held them until their proper casters crossed their palms with currency. Such a craft seemed a sort of magic—to transmute a thing so filmy and unsubstantial as a shadow, something almost not there, a thing that was barely a thing, into gold and silver, into acres and houses, carriages and servants. If I could do that, it would be proof that I was not the stone-brain Osbro made me out. Let him poke holes in the dirt and set in his turnips and chop at weeds and counterfeit false sagacities; let him grub out the rest of his days under the rheumy gaze of our taciturn father. With subtle and daring schemes, with swift and nimble fingers, I would amass out of the air itself a fortune as solid as a mountain.

⁘⟰⟱⁘

After Mutano with no gentle hand had shaken me awake, I found myself patrolling the winding, silent corridors of the manse, listening to my own footfalls over the slate floors, seeing naught but the moonlight rubbing through the horizontal slits below the ceilings. No rodent, no death-watch beetle, was stirring; no nightjar sang outside.

I searched the cellars with their huge wine casks and stone jugs of oil and bins of grain and meal. All was in order, so I stepped through a small door and sidled up the steps into the south garden. The moon was beginning to set and shadows were long and still. The breezeless, warm hour left the trees motionless.

Nonetheless, there was another presence here, I thought, and in mid-thought saw a heavy form bulk over the top of the garden wall, squeeze carefully around the spearheads mounted there, and begin its descent. This encounter was too easy, and one of Astolfo's sayings muttered in my head: *Where one is seen with ease, Two will be in place.*

I slipped off the flagstone path into the dark shelter of an arching willow. My presence would have been spotted by the thief on the wall; he had the advantage of height. But maybe his confederate had not discerned me and would come from hiding to join the other if I stayed still.

No such luck. He was here among the swarm of the drooping withies with me, and when I heard the whisper of leaves against leather behind me, I grasped a handful of the stringy branches and swished them about. By this means I located my man, and I had my dirk in my left hand on the instant; no space for sword-use in this tangle of greenery.

The skulker grunted in surprise and, since the sound would bring his colleague, I thought I might set them upon each other. Shaking the bunched withies as hard as I could to cause confusion, I uttered a doleful, loud groan, as if I had been thrust through. This noise brought the other swiftly into the swirl of branches, and as he came blundering through on my left-hand side, I kicked with all my might the place where one or the other of his knees ought to have been.

He crashed through the willow leaves, falling directly into his comrade's chest, and this other, finding himself so rudely attacked, choked out a curse and buried his fist in the clumsy one's face. If his sword had not been so entangled in the willow, he would have taken the life of his friend. But he only laid him cold at his feet.

He leaned over him now with his blade freed and prepared to do him in.

It came to me to say what I imagined Astolfo might say: "There is little sport, Mister Thief, in dueling a fallen man."

He spun round and thought to bring his sword up, but my point was already set upon his heart-spot.

"Too late for that," I murmured. "Best let it drop to the ground."

He did so.

"Let us go speak to the master of the house," I said. When he gestured to the form prone on the ground, I added, "Leave him as is. The gardener may desire to manure the roses with him."

I prodded him round to the back entrance and we entered the antechamber there, where Mutano awaited us. He ran his fingers over the big man's tunic and sleeves and belt and, finding him weaponless, led us into the kitchen, where Astolfo was perched on the heavy butcher's block, swinging his legs like a farm boy sitting on a stone bridge with a fishing pole. There was a low stool in the space between the brick oven and the long counter and Mutano thrust our guest roughly down upon it.

Astolfo looked him over. He closed his eyes for a moment. Then he said: "A cousin, I think, and not a brother. There is some small resemblance to the one whose heel you nipped with your little blade, Falco. See what nuisance you have brought us. This one came to avenge us on your trick of rolling on the floor like a dog in excrement. . . . Is that not so, intruder? I see you are a Fog Islander like the other, so there must be some bond between you. The only question of moment is whether Pecunio set you upon us. Did he do so or is this invasion a notion of your own?"

The man stared at the oaken floor. Then Mutano pulled his head back by the tangle of crisp black locks so that he must look into Astolfo's face. His expression was impassive.

"The hour is late," Astolfo said. "The morning slides up the eastward and I have missed my proper sleep."

He nodded at Mutano, who pried the man's left hand loose from the seat of the stool and broke the little finger.

The fellow did not cry out, but his eyes bulged wide, sweat suffused his forehead, and his complexion went from blue-black to dullish ebony. "I am Blebono," he croaked, "Dolo's cousin. My cousin is injured in his leg and will lose much wage by the knife of that man there. I come to get money for lost wage. Dolo has children, much to feed."

"Falco is young and somdel rash," Astolfo said. "He has a deal to learn. . . . For one thing"—he gave me a straight look—"if he ever tries out that rolling-in-the-dirt device on a seasoned blades-man, he shall be pinned like a serpent and left to wriggle his life away."

I started to speak but thought the better of it.

"You came by your own advisement? Pecunio is faultless?"

Blebono snuffled and nodded.

"Tell us a little about the old goldbags. Are there any new folk in his employ? What visitors has he lately entertained?"

The islander shrugged.

"Well," said Astolfo, "I must think of more questions. I have only three or four in mind and you have fingers yet unbroken. . . . Tell us about the visitors."

When Mutano took up the man's hand again and grasped the thumb, he said, "I work for the old man, no. Only my cousin, he do work for him."

"Even so, he will babble and gossip all the secrets of the miser's house. Tell us of his guests."

"Dolo told of one to me. Young fellow—skinny, secret fellow. Talked not much."

"Did he bring a shadow to sell to Pecunio?"

"Bring, no. Talked some about shadow. He talked big. Said he had good shadow, very fine shadow."

"Tell me about the feet of this shadow-seller."

Blebono stared at Astolfo in pure incomprehension. Sweat dripped from his nose. He shook his head.

"Big feet? Big feet on a small man?"

"Boots, Dolo said. My cousin Dolo, he laughed. Big boots up to the thigh of quiet fellow."

Astolfo rocked back and forth; he seemed to be thinking of many things at once. Then he slipped nimbly down to the floor. He said to Mutano, "Bind the broken finger of this imbecile. Give him a copper coin and ale to drink. Make certain he knows never to come again where I can lay eyes on him. Toss his comrade into a barrow and wheel it down toward the wharf and dump him in an alley. Fetch me mutton and bread and a flagon in the small library in the late afternoon. Hold the house quiet until then. Falco is to sleep and afterward read through three swordplay manuals in the large library. When he finishes those, take him to the courtyard and practice him with wooden swords. If he begins to squirm around in the dirt, stamp him like a blindworm. Signal unto him that big boots may disguise delicate feet."

At this penultimate command, Mutano nodded and grinned. He enjoyed nothing more than to drub me with dummy weapons until my flesh swelled like bread dough.

⊶⊜⊷

I rose next morning late and sore-ribbed and broke my fast on wheaten bread and fruit and a mild white wine I recognized of old. The vintage came from near my farm home and the taste reminded me how different my life had become. It had been long and long since I had seen an honest dung heap or one of the ungainly stone barns so common in the south. Yet the wine did not rouse in me any desire to return to the ducks and geese, the cattle and asses.

Only our sour-visaged cook Iratus and the other under-servants were about. Mutano and Astolfo had departed, though a folded note in Astolfo's precise hand told me to ready myself for another call upon Pecunio. I used the unexpected dutyless time to lounge in the sun and think about a certain wench in a tavern in the Hamaria district. Maiden's Sorrow this tavern was called, a pleasant place for a twilight tipple and a midnight tumble, if ever again I got my hands on a silver eagle. . . .

Then I began to muse more seriously, berating myself as a fool to squander hours and silver upon sweetmeats when I should be developing my martial skills, studying the biographies of famous shadows and their casters, training my eyesight to discern outlines in deep haze, and testing my patience with mathematical puzzles. It seemed unlikely that Astolfo had wasted his youth and money in idle pursuits. I had never considered that the rigors of thievery would so closely resemble those I had heard about in the priestly vocation— for which I considered myself supremely unfitted.

⊶⊜⊷

This my second meeting with the ancient rich merchant was to be different. We had spoken about it beforehand and Astolfo had given me a few brief instructions. He wanted me to be very particular in observing Pecunio's physique, to see if I could discern differences from the way he was two days before. I was to watch most closely his shadow.

Now when we were ushered into his dim little office, it was by no lumbering, dark-skinned Fog Islander but by the slender slip of a lad who had shown us out before. For some reason he had now painted his face to resemble the fleering Jester of the fair-day comedies, Bennio. He was so vividly made up that his personal features were hard to discern. Most distinctive was his gait in the tall, black boots.

He strode in an exaggerated, aggressive fashion, as if to convince the timorous that he was a daring young bravo indeed. Yet he wore no sword—an oddity. His manner seemed risible to me, the more so because it was not so long since that I carried myself in much the same fashion, probably for the same reasons.

When he brought us into the room, he bowed and departed, backing through the door in an unwontedly servile way. I looked to Astolfo to gauge his reaction to this strange creature, but he seemed scarcely to take note of him.

Pecunio offered us wine as before. I started to decline the syrupy stuff, but the raised eyebrow of Astolfo caused me to accept. He was also correct in surmising that the old man might have changed in appearance. He had been no tower of brawn at our first meeting, but now he was frailer, much shrunken upon himself, I thought, and the palsy of his years was more pronounced, as was his hunchback. His hand trembled the decanter almost violently, and not trusting himself with the tiny glasses, he allowed us to take them ourselves from the yellow lacquer tray.

"Now, Master Astolfo," he asked, "have you made any conclusion about the shadow of Morbruzzo?" He rubbed his hands together as if to warm them.

"Not all my conclusions are firm ones," Astolfo replied, "so I thought we had best make the conditions clear."

"How so?"

"If I see fit to affirm that the property is genuinely that of the pirate, my fee will be seventy eagles. If I decide to find that it is not genuine, the fee shall rise to three hundred."

"I do not follow."

"You may discover that you prefer to pay the higher fee. But before the bargain is struck, I must gather some information. The more you tell me, the more you will have to pay and the better you will like it."

A thin, wry smile stretched Pecunio's wrinkled face. "You are well known for your games, Master Astolfo."

"My best games are in earnest. What I surmise is this: that you were offered this shadow of Morbruzzo by someone who claimed to have been in his employ, one of his murderous crew, an officer perhaps. First mate? I see by your expression that I have hit it. This person told you that Morbruzzo had done grave injury upon this person's dignity or honor or purse or corpus—an insulting slap or sneaking blow or deceit at the gaming table, or in the division of booty. The latter? I see."

"How do you know what was said to me? Even if you had spies in my household, you could not know, for we were alone."

"Now this person assures you that he is not a follower of the art, that he is no thief of shadows but only an ill-fed seaman who this one time, to assuage his wounded pride, undertook to steal the shadow and purports to sell it to you for less than a fraction of its true value. He wants to be rid of it, not to be held responsible. He has said he fears Mrobruzzo will come for it and, having got it, will depart, leaving a lagoon of blood behind him."

"That too is just what was said."

"Let us make examination of the property again."

Pecunio went to the armoire and after fussing with the locks opened the tall door and drew forth the shadow.

"Yes, bring it to the middle of the room, please," Astolfo said. "My man Falco will arrange the candles in the way I have taught him is best to appraise shadows."

At this signal I went about the room, collecting the candles from their niches, and arranged the twelve together at the corner of the table where the decanter sat. Astolfo watched me carefully, then took the shadow gracefully in his hands.

I had disposed the candles so that the light fell full upon the figure of Pecunio, and now I looked at the shadow he cast on the floor. At first I could not find it and supposed that I had placed a candle wrong so that something stood between. But then I managed to make it out, woefully changed from what it had been. It was a mere wisp of shade now, wavering, and crooked as a twig from a crab apple tree. It was so thin and tenuous it was nigh invisible, and it seemed barely to cling to the old man's heel. It looked as if it might blow away like the last leaf on a winter oak.

"Let us look closely at the selvage," said Astolfo. He brought it close to the light and I saw that it too had changed. The mauvish-greenish glow that had smoldered within it now pulsed, throbbing

like the heart of a speeding runner. The whole seemed to have
gained bulk and the thin streaks of silver that hovered there before
had broadened and vivified. I could feel on the skin of my face that
an extraordinary power emanated from it.

"See this edge?" Astolfo ran the tip of his finger through the
space surrounding the shadow's margin. "That is skillful cutting
indeed. Falco, have a look. What implement would make such a cut,
think you?"

I examined it closely and found no sign of raggedness, no tearing, no place where it might begin to ravel. "I would say a quasilune."

"One such as this?" From an inside pocket of his broad belt with
its leopard's-head buckle, Astolfo produced a small, shiny, quarter-
moon blade. "Of silver, honed and polished in a workshop of
Grevaie?"

"If so you say."

"Friend Pecunio," Astolfo said, "your excellent sweet wine of
the south has brought a thirst upon me. Could you prevail upon
your servant who at this moment stands without the door there
spying upon us to fetch a flask of water?"

Startled, Pecunio crossed to the door and swung it suddenly
open. There stood the slender fellow with the large feet and tall
boots. Though plainly revealed at his transgression, he did not lose
composure. He gave a slight smile, bowed, and said, "I shall bring
water."

"It would be welcome," Astolfo replied, and when the fellow
had hurried away turned to Pecunio. "The instrument that took the
shadow you have purchased is of use only to those who traffic in
shadows as a profession. It is a special favorite of thieves. Your servant is better acquainted with cutlery than you have been led to suppose. He was wearing no sword when he left us just now, but when
he returns he shall be armed."

The old one frowned. "What is taking place?"

"Don't fret. This may be the first opportunity we have to see
how our Falco handles himself against artful swordplay. He is entrusted with protecting us from your counterfeit servant. If you had
told me at first that he was the purveyor of the shadow, I could have
saved you time and coin. But now we must see the affair through
in a less efficient manner."

When the servant returned with a flask and clay tumblers, we
three watched in silence as he poured the water. He was now wear-

ing, as Astolfo had predicted, a sword, the short, broad-bladed cutlass favored by naval warriors.

"Before you return to your duties, I should like to ask a question or two. Curiosity is a dire fault in me," Astolfo said to him.

The fellow stood at his ease, the slight smile still playing upon his lips.

"By what method did you poison the shadow you sold to Pecunio? There are several ways of doing so, some which ruin the property forever, others from which it can be restored to some fairly useful measure. We must needs know—*Falco!*"

His warning was timely, for though I had seen the fellow's fingers twitch toward his hilt, I was surprised at the celerity with which his sword was out and ready. But I was ready too and leapt between and warded off the thrust that was intended for Astolfo's belly. Then there we stood pressed against each other, hiltguard upon hiltguard. With my left forearm I pushed him back and then gave a quick shove. He was light-framed and I figured I would have good advantage of strength.

But he was nimble as a dragonfly. He slipped backward easily without losing his balance and fronted me with an insolent grin.

Then we were at it in earnest, thrust and parry, slash and sidestep, overhand and underhand and backhand. It was warmer work than I had anticipated. I struck the harder blows, but my opponent's forte was the art of evasion and I spent much strength upon empty air. He had a smooth, swift, sidelong motion that a stoat might envy, and by the time he began to breathe a little more quickly I was panting heavily. Finally he made a quick, twisting thrust aimed at my shoulder and in avoiding it I tangled with a table leg and went down on my back, my sword clattering away into a far corner.

I thought my hour had come as I lay helpless, seeing his sword point descending toward my nose, when he disappeared from my view. Where he had been there stood now a dark mist. I could see nothing inside this dimness. But I heard a sharp, high-pitched cry of distress.

And then Astolfo's voice, jovial and mocking, sounded: "Falco, this dueling tactic you cling to—falling down prone—will never be praised in the arms manuals. Why you persist in following it I shall never learn."

I got up quickly. I did not want to look at Astolfo. Instead, I watched the cloudy mass that had appeared above me. From this angle I saw it was the shadow of Morbruzzo. It roiled and heaved like steam that might rise a little above the mouth of a pot and hang there, working furiously within itself. Out of the mass of this shadow came little gibbers and yips, as of someone being nipped by a pack of terriers.

Then with a broad, gently sweeping gesture Astolfo removed the shadow.

The art of shadow-flinging is a familiar conversational subject of those who trade in the commodity, of thieves of every sort, of warriors, of courtiers, of tavern-sitters, of priests, and of scribblers. I had read many an account in many a dusty page, but I had never witnessed it before. Even in the observing I was not sure what I saw, only that the roundish, shortish, baldish master of shadows held his body at a certain angle, extended his right arm and drew it in a wide semicircle, and held his hand relaxed with the fingers bent slightly inward. I could see that if I were to try such a maneuver, my hand would tear through the fabric of the shade and I would be holding nothing.

But Astolfo brought it away to reveal Pecunio's servant standing there in a vastly altered condition than formerly. In the first place, this was no man. Her blonde hair was cropped, and most of her clothing was in scattered rags and giblets, as if eaten away by acids. The tall boots remained intact, but the thighs that emerged from them were fair and smooth, not mannish in the least. Her figure was lissome and small-breasted but undeniably female and her face, now that the greasepaint was mostly removed, was that of a piquantly attractive woman.

She struggled to speak but could not. Her eyes were filled with confusion and fear.

Astolfo spoke to Pecunio: "If you had but told me you had taken this woman into your household, you would have saved yourself much grief."

The old man hung his head and shook it regretfully. "I thought it wise to keep her secret and all for myself. I am not the man that once I was."

"Your vanity and venality have cost you dearly, not only in gold but in the matter of your health. Did you not know that she is one of a famous pair of shadow thieves? This is the notorious Fleuraye."

Pecunio was visibly startled. He looked again at the woman with his mouth amazedly open. "I did not know that."

"She and her consort, the silken-mannered privateer Belarmo, have been partners in many a merry escapade. They have cozened and cheated and robbed and stolen with profitable success for some few years now. Much of their success may be credited to the fact that she is most pleasurable to look upon. Is this not so, Falco?"

"Umm . . . Yes. That is true," I said, and at last tore my gaze away from her true blonde charms and her large gray eyes, which were now filling wetly.

"Pay no mind to her tears," said Astolfo. "She can pour them out at will, as if from a canister."

At once the welling stopped and she gave Astolfo a stare of scarlet enmity.

"We have crossed paths before, a few seasons ago, and Fleuraye saved her Belarmo from the fate I designed for him by means of a diverting ploy I may sometime whisper to you. But I believe they must have fallen out with each other now. In fact, I am certain that the shadow you purchased from her is that of her consort."

"It does not belong to Morbruzzo?"

"That savage pirate would have retrieved it by now, wherever it was hidden and whatever the cost to him. No, this is the shadow of Belarmo." He held it at shoulder height before him. "And you see what decadent state it is in. Fleuraye has worked upon it so as to make it a poison thing. This you can observe in its colors, the nauseous tints and tinges of corruption."

"Poison . . ." Pecunio's weak murmur sounded like an echo of itself.

"Did she not implore you to cloak yourself in it? Did she not tell you how brave and stalwart it made you appear when she came to your bedchamber? And yet the anger and jealousy that rages within it fed upon your manhood and shriveled all your virility. Is not this true?"

"True as the summer sky," Pecunio said. "And now, if you will but hand me her sword where she dropped it from within the shadow—"

"No no," Astolfo commanded. "Nothing of that. I have saved your life and you are indebted to me in the amount of three hundred gold eagles. I shall collect another three hundred from Belarmo when we rescue him from whatever grim place it is where he is being tortured."

"He is yet alive?"

"If he were dead, if his lover had dispatched him, his shadow would be a poor, pallid thing almost lifeless. But it stands in strong sympathy with him. As its condition is, so then is his. I suppose that this all fell out as it did from the beginning because of a lovers' quarrel. Jealousy will be in play."

Flueraye spat her words. "A low tavern wench. A slattern with teats like harbor buoys. An arse like a refuse barrow."

He spoke to her. "And so you suborned some of his men with gold and they turned on him and you are exacting your revenge. At the same time, you thought to acquire a coin or two and increase the humiliation of Belarmo and of my friend Pecunio here."

"I am not of a mood these days to coddle the coxcomb sex," she said.

"Yet your only hope to escape the gallows is to tell us where to find your lover. Rescuing him, you rescue yourself. For your other crimes a prison ship bound for the sultry latitudes may suit. But now is the moment to tell us, for he is after all little more than a pirate himself and his life may not weigh greatly in your favor. Yet if he die, that fact will weigh large against you. And I think you would not long be able to endure being cloaked again in Belarmo's shadow. The rage within his spirit as he lies bound and tortured makes his shade a cruel garment to don, does it not? I am of temper to fling it about you on this instant."

And so she told where Belarmo lay in the cellar of a warehouse near Rattlebone Alley and gave clear directions how to reach him. Then she added, with the most baleful of looks, "I daresay we shall encounter again, Astolfo. Perhaps next time you shall not fare so lucky."

"Perhaps by next time Falco shall have learned the proper use of a sword."

So Pecunio was rewarded with his life and some restoration of his health; Astolfo was the richer by hundreds of eagles; Belarmo was to be rescued from his agonies. My reward was to undergo more practice bouts with Mutano, my bruises black as onyx and purple as sunset. This discipline for the craft of shadow-taking is a harsh one and I do not lightly recommend it to anyone whether or not you may have thought of taking up the trade and art of shadows.

But if you are attracted to this occlusive way of life, you will find the demanding disciplines salutary. Some individuals come to attach to them for the challenges they present. If I had relied upon my previous martial skills, I might have been slain a dozen times. If I had not turned over so many musty pages, I should never have known of the hidden associations that shadows share with echoes, with cats, and with certain types of jewels, such as the one belonging to the eccentric Countess Triana.

II

The Diamond Shadow

The heavily gilded carriage that brought us hither halted before the side door of this elegant château with its air of slight desuetude. The silent footman opened the carriage door, let down the stair for us to descend, signaled to the driver, and the conveyance rolled away.

Astolfo and I stood alone, he taking a long moment to survey our surroundings. Then we entered without ceremony into a dim, long hall. Why had no one come out to greet us? I trusted that the maestro had made a prior arrangement that I was not privy to.

We walked slowly, tentatively, toward a door at the end of the corridor. A streak of light shone at the sill beneath the door edge.

"We were fools to come to this place," I said.

"This place," said the right-hand shadows.

"Disgrace," said the left-hand shadows.

"We were fools, Falco," Astolfo said, "before we were bidden here. You must not lose courage."

"Courage," said the dexter shadows.

"Outrage," said the sinister.

"I am none a-feared," I said. "But I mislike these shadows that mock my phrases."

"Phrases."

"Mazes."

"The shadows do not speak," Astolfo said. "They stand silent in their long corridors. Only a peculiarity of the construction of this dim hall makes them seem to speak. When we are silent, they will be silent. They own no breath."

"Breath."

"Death."

I said nothing more. It behooved me, I thought, to observe wordlessly until speech became necessary. I felt honored to accompany the maestro to the court of this small domain within the province of Tlemia. I felt also a little puzzled, for I knew well I had not acquired manners and graces proper to the situation. I was satisfied that I had been making fair progress in attaining the skills and knowledge of swordsmanship, shadow-taking, geometry, shadow-history, and so forth. But polish and finesse had not blessed my social encounters, especially with those of elevated rank.

So I held my tongue when we pushed open the heavy door that blocked the corridor and swung it shut behind us. It almost seemed that these doors had been hung to keep back the shadows, for the space we entered into was bright with ensconced torches and batteries of flaming candles that swathed in a soft glow each object here.

There were a good two dozen people ranged about—grave courtiers, expensively appointed ladies with their maids and young daughters, quick-smiling lads in silken trunks and with curiously sheathed short swords—and though they made the noises a pleasant company makes, they now fell silent and looked upon Astolfo and me with undisguised curiosity. I felt as if I had come into a court of petty royalty, though our hostess was no more than a thrice-widowed countess; so Astolfo had informed me.

A countess then, yet she sat in her high-backed chair of dark oak with its carvings of gryphons and lions' heads and fleur-de-lys with seat and back sumptuously brocaded. There was no dais, but a respectful space surrounded this chair as the men and women kept proper distance. On her right-hand side a standard displayed on a white background two interlocking rings. In one of them three crossed lances signified the county (formerly the duchy) of Trevania; in the other the Mardrake symbol of the Tlemia Province was black upon scarlet.

These courtiers watched closely as we approached, as if they had gathered there for no other purpose than to observe Astolfo and me. The maestro made a graceful obeisance, I a clumsy one, and he addressed her in a confident, easy voice: "Milady Triana, we have come at your bidding."

"At my invitation, Master Astolfo. I have no power to order you about."

Was it the bulk of her chair that made her look so petite? Though her face showed her to be a woman of handsome middle years, the way she was perched upon her seat caused her to appear no larger than a child. Her voice, however, possessed the sound of old age, not quavering, but with an uncertain timbre and a lightly suggested crackle. Her hair was blonde streaked with white and it seemed to shiver in movement with a liquid opalescence. Her eyes were fixed at a point somewhere between herself and the person she addressed, as if she looked inward more than outward. This gaze gave her a distracted air, though her words were clear enough.

"We are honored by your kind invitation," he replied, and bowed again, pulling back his stiff linen cape with his left hand and sweeping the right before him like a violoncellist drawing his bow.

"May I inquire into the health of your wife and children?"

"I have none," said Astolfo. "As an unfortunate, I live alone with my mute manservant Mutano and with this man, Falco"—he nudged and I bowed—"and with such house servants as I require. It is some- times a cheerless existence, almost eremitic."

"But perhaps this way of life has allowed you to gain the skills and arts you need in your cult of shadows. I have been informed that your craft requires stringent and constant application."

"I have labored in my discipline, but maybe to a quick-witted chap it would come more easily."

She said nothing for a moment and paused to take in the figure of my plumpish, balding master with his swift hands and uncus- tomary finery and mild gray eyes that never threatened.

It seemed to me that she knew already much about Astolfo, and perhaps about me also, and that her questions had been put merely to give her time to form impressions. I was a little surprised when she said, "I think that we have met aforetimes."

"I believe we have not met, milady. I am certain I would re- member someone so gracious and charming."

Her tone sharpened as suddenly as a gust of wind off a frozen peak. "If I say that we have met, then so it has been. It is true that my mind is not so agile as in former days, nor so integral in its work- ings, yet I must recall Astolfo the thief who filched the shadow of the assassin Torrodo and delivered it to his mortal enemy to ravage at will."

"Those stories of days long past are more rumor than history, milady."

"'Twill do no good to set at me crosswise," she said. "If I say we have met, we have met. If I say you have done such-and-such, you have done so." She drummed her heels under her broad skirt of figured white silk against the stretcher of her chair, as an impatient child might do.

"Milady." He bowed once more.

"I do not much like shadows," she declared. "Creeping, sneaking things they are. People say that you are a thief who steals shadows for profit. I do not understand how anyone can steal a shadow. But if a shadow is a thing, I suppose it can be stolen. There are thieves everywhere. I am continually missing rings and gold and silver bangles, tiaras and suchlike. Some of the thieves are in this room at this moment."

"Milady."

"Not you, Astolfo, but these others. Oh, I might tell you histories about this crowd that you would scarcely credit. Fine lot they are, very fine indeed."

Many of the assemblage must have heard her words, but none showed response. They continued to amble about and chat together in low voices. I received the impression that they were accustomed to the countess's cross outbursts and took little account of them.

"Perhaps there are misunderstandings," Astolfo said. "We are surely in gentle company among these nobles."

"Never believe it," she said. "Why do you insist on contradicting my observations? Think me a fool, do you?"

"No, milady. Never."

"Sometimes I am a fool, of the worst sort. A cloud comes into my head so that there are hours when I cannot say who I am. I am not myself and lose all placement in the world. That is when these betrayers and whisperers take advantage, perceiving that I am not all that I need to be."

I looked the crowd over again, but they remained to my eye placid and unconcerned.

"Why," she asked, "would anyone wish to purchase shadows from you? Nasty, slithering, lisping things they are, always dogging one's heels or clinging against the walls with sullen faces, ne'er a cheerful countenance among 'em. Tell me why."

He answered lightly. "Oh, I am often surprised by the various usages people find out for them. Generally they are employed only to lend coolness or the impression of coolness to an interior atmosphere. They promote intimacy of discourse and soften the edges of social interchange. Harpists and lutenists may be hired to play softly at a gathering, furnishing a pleasant background; shadows can serve the same purpose. And there are a myriad other uses. Perhaps you have heard that winemakers often steep wines in certain tints of shadow to add subtlety and depth to vintages that lack sufficient character. To darken silks and linens ever so slightly, to support the mood of a love letter or ballade . . . Do not you yourself employ a coterie of umbrae in the hallway that leads to this salon? I assume you placed them there to unsettle visitors of unknown purpose, testing those who come to visit here."

"I do not desire them. They have flocked to my walls unbidden. Unless"—she looked about at the company with bitter eyes and continued—"unless some one of my betrayers has brought them in to do me evil. Since my mother died, I can no longer say who is my loyal friend and who my secret enemy."

"I am unhappy to hear of your loss," said Astolfo. "When did this happen?"

"It might have been yesterday. Or perhaps some years ago." Her eyes blinked wide; her expression was a startled stare. "It might have been tomorrow."

"It is a sorrowful loss at any time."

She waved a tiny, heavily bejeweled hand at me. "Why does your young friend stay silent? I am suspicious of those who watch and watch and say naught."

"Falco is newly from the ox-furrow," Astolfo said. "He is uneasy in polished society and fears to show himself a dunce. But as an aide to me, he does well enough."

"In your business with those shadows."

He nodded.

"Well, it is about filthy shadows that I bade you come."

"I am honored by your kind invitation."

"Why must you continually abrade? I say I bade you come at my deliberate insistence. Did I not dispatch my carriage to Tardocco to transport you? And did so much against the advisement of my councilor Chrobius. I do not know you well enough to invite you. Few there are these days whom I invite. I can trust almost no one."

"You have no one to confide in?"

She clapped her hands, making a surprisingly sharp report. At once the murmuring of the company desisted. They fell all silent as an elderly man rose from a curve-armed bench against the wall, stepped slowly to a large table with a white runner-cloth, and lifted from it a small casket of embossed leather bound with iron straps. As he was bearing it to the countess, she waved him aside toward Astolfo.

"Please examine the jewel that Chrobius carries," she said. "I would know your thoughts upon it."

Astolfo took the casket from the old gentleman and opened it to disclose, lying on plush purple velvet, a diamond that looked to be as large as a crab apple. Though I stood a good seven paces away, I could see how brilliant was the light it gave off, gleaming in the candlelight. It seemed to capture those mellow flames and make them one within itself and then to disperse that glow in a thousand warm points throughout this broad salon.

Astolfo looked at it for long moments and then said to the countess, "Have I permission to take it up?"

She nodded.

Between thumb and forefinger he held it before his eyes, peering closely. Then he wheeled slowly on his heel, bringing the stone around in a complete circle and turning it over and over to expose every surface. Polished but uncut, it throbbed as the torchlight and candlelight pierced its cool center. Then he laid it carefully back in place and bowed to the old courtier, who returned it to the long table.

"Well," said the countess, "what do you see there?"

"I am not certain," Astolfo answered. "At first I thought I saw a flaw of the mineral, but then it seemed more a smudge. Nothing mars the outer surface. If only I had brought hither my enlarging glass to examine it more closely."

"No," she said, "no magical glasses. I do not trust 'em. What is to be seen must be seen by the unaided eye. You shall say if you see what I see."

"I see a shadow."

"So!" She clapped her hands again, startling me and all the company. "I too saw the shadow, a horrid, dark, oozy, smoky thing wriggling in the very core of my stone. It was never there before. My diamond was formerly all clear, as bright and sharp in its glitter as starlight. Now it has gone yellowish; it has goldered. I do not like that. Each hour it loses value, does it not?"

"It is an immensely valuable stone, milady."

"No, I tell you it is forfeiting its worth even as we speak. Why will you always quarrel with me?"

"If it is not so bright as formerly, it may be damaged. But I do not know the cause. May I ask where it was found and how it came into your possession?"

"You may not. I am weary of debating every point with you. Chrobius will give you such history as you may need to know. My head hurts insufferably and my mind slips like a donkey on greasy cobbles. I am done with our audience. When you find out the problem with my best diamond, when you have discovered a remedy for its illness, you must return and inform me and I shall reward you generously. I do hope that you will not quarrel with me about this commission I have laid upon you. I am sick of your controversies."

"Milady."

The old man came to us, bowed, and padded away to a door at the farther end of the salon, and we followed at a befitting distance.

This small room off the main salon lay quiet. A single bowl-shaded lamp on the table between four chairs in the center gave off a genial glow and Chrobius set the jewel casket beneath it. He wore a thin, silvery beard that came to a point below the V of his soft collar. His voice was gentle, weary, and he displayed the slender, ivory fingers such as might grace an accomplished harpist. He seated us and offered refreshment, which Astolfo declined. I followed his example. Then Chrobius sat in the chair between us and told us that almost nothing was known of the provenance of this diamond that so concerned the countess.

"How now?" said Astolfo. "So handsome a jewel must have a voluminous history."

"It will be a history of which we are ignorant." Chrobius's voice was extraordinarily calm, almost hypnotic with its measured cadences. "It was discovered among the effects of the countess's second husband, Tyrin Blanzo. The Blanzi were a family of merchants quite powerful in former days but latterly fallen upon scanty luck. Like many another trading company, they had ventured ships into the perilous seas northward, seeking for trade among the woodland tribes of Justerland and with the fisher folk of the Aurora Isles. But tempest and piracy dealt severe and at last mortal blows to the Blanzi enterprises, and then their finances rested upon the rents of their estates. It has been supposed by some that this stone was derived from the profits of trade, but no record of its provenance has survived."

"How long after the death of Blanzo came its discovery?" Astolfo asked.

"A good two years," Chrobius replied. "The countess had remarried by that time and considered that for purposes of economy she ought to make an inventory of her late husband's possessions. In going through his sea chests, she found the casket with the jewel."

"Was it then in the same condition as now?"

"I know little of the lore of precious stones, but meseemeth it has changed since that time. Perhaps it has dulled somewhat. The countess says it has *goldered,* and that is as apt a term as may be."

"And the countess herself? Has she changed since the advent of this diamond?"

He hesitated. "I should not like to say overmuch. She speaks of certain misapprehensions to which she is prey; you heard her speak of these. Whether this jewel has connection to her condition, I cannot affirm. It appears very unlike, but 'twas at that time she began to complain. Some who have long known her claim to have noticed a change, but she was always somdel bewildered in the world."

"Are there those who wish her harm?"

"You see our little orbit here, so much like a court of rural royalty. There is hardly anyone who is not wished some degree of harm by another. The countess is subject to arbitrary humors and peremptory demands, some say. Injured feelings follow in her train."

"Have you ever felt the brunt of her impulsiveness?" Astolfo asked.

"Not I, no. But it is well known that all women are prey to changeable moods. Her position is precarious and demands perhaps more will-call than she may possess."

"You use an odd term: *will-call.* What doth it signify? I am unfamiliar with it."

Chrobius smiled in the manner of an indulgent schoolmaster. "It would rarely occur in your mode of business, I would think. It is a philosophic term, meaning something like 'fortitude' or 'bravery of spirit.' 'Manliness' may come closest to its purport."

"Would anyone design the countess bodily harm? Would anyone be bold to take her life?"

He rubbed the point of his beard with thumb and forefinger, as if feeling the texture of cloth. "I do not know. I should think it not likely. Her last husband, the third, that count of some vague area he called Ondormo, was a dark and bitter man who never showed real love for her. But he has been banished by the countess and lives in exile."

"So she is not thrice-widowed."

"She accounts him as dead."

"Where might he now inhabit?"

"Again, I do not know. Some have said that the rugged coast of Clamorgra is pierced with caves and that he coils within one of them like an adder in its hole. There are other rumors also."

"What were the points of contention?"

"There are whispers only, something about a division of property. But I credit none of that. He was headstrong, willful, arrogant, and she is, as you see, sometimes distracted and of sudden waywardness. There may have been little other than a conflict of personalities."

Astolfo took up the diamond and held it against the lamplight, turning it slowly. "I regret that she will not allow close inspection with a jeweler's glass," he murmured.

Chrobius smiled. "As to that . . ." he said, and produced from his sleeve pocket a silver loupe, intricately enchased, "I can see no harm in your looking at it and cannot say why she objects. It may be only one of her personal superstitions. In these days, she lacks all proper and confident will-call." He handed the loupe to Astolfo.

I took for granted that the shadow master was expert in the knowledge of precious stones, as he is in so many other matters. He converses easily with savants and tradesmen in regard to objects of every sort. But as he studied this stone, bringing it closer to the light and then withdrawing it, revolving it over and over, his expression troubled into perplexity and he began to hum to himself singsong. This was a sign that he had struck upon an intriguing puzzle.

Finally he laid it back, almost reverently, upon the casket plush. "It would be shameful if such a prize should be an instrument of harm," he said.

"Do you think that it is?" I asked.

He turned to Chrobius. "You, sir, do you believe that it could be harmful?"

The old gentleman gave his beard a short tug. "Today all my replies are but professions of ignorance," he said. "I do not know. I cannot say how it might be."

"Falco and I must consult our sources," Astolfo said. "In the shelves of my libraries at the manse there may be helpful folios. If you will guide us, sir, back to the corridor of whispering shadows, we can find our way from there."

"No need for that nuisance," he replied. "There is another way, speedier and more pleasant, to the entrance."

"Thank you for your kindness," Astolfo said. "Yet we should like to retrace our steps. Those shadows appear to have secrets they desire to share."

"I think you can gain little from them, but I shall be glad to accompany you the way you came." He set off slowly, then paced lightly through the salon. The countess was absent and her tall, throne-like chair had been set against the wall. A few murmuring late-stayers stood about and seemed to take no notice of our passage. At the door to the corridor Chrobius made a final bow and bade us farewell.

⟢⟐⟢

My mount at this time was a dapple-gray cob of complaisant temper. My heavy-handed colleague, Mutano, had chosen this horse called Torta from Astolfo's stable and handed her to me with that fleering, sardonic smile that signified he had picked out an easy mount because he considered her suitable to my abilities. As to that, he was mistaken, but I accepted the reins with good grace and resolved to take excellent care of the animal. I could see that this Torta had her points: not swift but powerful and of steady courage. She would not shy during a set-to.

Astolfo had turned off on the way back to the town villa with a salute signaling that he would return in a short time. I could see that he was headed into Tardocco, but what his errand might be I could not know. It was late afternoon and the sun was just at the roof edges of this busy city, now settling out of its workaday bustle, readying for the pleasures of twilight and early evening.

I stabled Torta and looked to her welfare and then went for a stroll about the grounds. Early summer gladdened the grasses and trees and some of the rare flowering shrubs Astolfo was partial to. It occurred to me that he might have gone to consult in the town with one of his friends, perhaps an astute jeweler, and I thought I might gain a little credit in his eyes by some quick study. I went into the house, into the great, quiet library, and strolled to the area where the volumes on valuable trinkets were shelved. By this time, I had achieved some familiarity with his extensive collection of books and maps and manuscripts, though I knew the maestro would not agree. He held me as being only a little more learned than a runt beagle.

Even so, I knew enough about the subject to begin by looking into a late edition of the Grand Albertus and to follow its hints into Rhodius's *Gemmae liminosae et lucidae,* thence to Cassurio's *Lux opali et carbunculi.*

It was in these latter pages that I came upon the story of the Lady Erminia. This antique baroness always wore a dazzling opal in her hair. The resplendently milky stone closely matched the character of its mysterious owner, sparkling brightly when her mood was lightest, spitting out red gleams when she angered, clouding like a wheel-parted lane puddle when she wept. In her later years, when her heart was broken by a perfidious suitor, the opal cracked into five pieces, spilling its various, shattered colors upon the air and extorting from the miserable woman her dying breath. When her spirit passed from her, the five fragments of the stone crumbled to a dull gray powder, as did the shrunken form of Erminia herself.

I wondered if the legend of this opal could suggest fruitful application to the case of our countess. When I mentioned the possibility to Astolfo, who had now returned, he did not instantly reject it. He professed pleasant surprise at finding me at search in the library but warned me that the study of precious stones was a complicated and uncertain matter. "Superstition collects around expensive gems as thick as rumors around a beautiful woman," he said. "And, as with the woman, the more pure and powerful the virtues, the darker are the conjectures that swarm. The brightest and clearest diamond will be accounted the most perilous to its owner."

"How does this come about?" I asked.

"Partly because of envy," he said. "If thou hast not the means nor the fortunate luck to possess the fine sapphire that your rival possesses, thou'lt impute every dire quality to it and find ready credence among your rabble friends."

"But is none of the hearsay true? Ominous tales about jewels are thick as the winter fur of an Aurora wolf."

"Some knowledge is certain. I for one would never wear a black pearl," Astolfo said. "And I would not allow a mumbling priest with his stinking smoke and his murky sprinklings to come within half a league of any topaz I might have in store. But ware you of anyone who says a sard has been tainted by the poison of a dragon who guarded it in his hoard."

"Are there any so gullible as to believe?"

"There is many a merchant sharp-eyed in accounting, in the surveying of lands, in the lading of ships, and in the interest rates of lending who will lose all compass when he comes to the subject of gems. Those small bits of gleam seem to have been created to drive men's wits astray. Here is another quality they share with women."

"Is not the countess right to be concerned? Her diamond seems of no steadfast state. It is changing from its former condition, is't not?"

"'Twould seem so. But what have you observed of the countess? We had but short time in her company, yet I found her a striking figure."

"She is a conundrum," I said. "I could not even judge her age."

"Tell me of her shadow."

"The flicker of torches and candles made examination difficult, but I thought she possessed a double shadow."

"Two primaries, you mean—apart from the many penumbrae caused by multiple lights."

"Two primaries."

"Describe them."

"Both were small," I said. "One was a playful, gray shade, lively in its motion, with flirting, fluttering outlines. The other was of a cast much darker, its shape somewhat crooked, the edges crabbed and ragged. It was bent in upon itself, reclusive, where as the first shadow was an outgoing thing, ready to engage with any surface or slant of light."

"Which of these two would you say matched the countess herself both in body and in spirit?"

I hesitated. "Neither of them. Maybe both combined in some way I cannot explain. Yet not even such a combination would well connect to her."

"And the diamond?"

"From where I stood I could not well see. Its size is it salience. 'Twould be shameful if it is damaged, for a jewel of that size, be it perfect or not, might bring a small realm as its price."

"And the velvet?"

"Velvet?"

"It was placed upon the casket's purple cushion. What saw you there?"

Long I thought, closing my eyes. "There was a little space where the nap was depressed, just next the stone."

"Good." He nodded. "Perhaps this estimable gem had a companion in its casket."

"May we conjecture that the diamond may have some spiritual bond with the countess?" I asked. "For I have read how a certain Lady Erminia was so closely soul-yoked with an opal that—"

"Enough of that old tale," Astolfo said. "It is as moldy as a cave for cheeses."

"Is it not true?"

"Even a truth, if too often cited, may lose some of its savor. And that antique instance carries us too far from our present one. We must keep close our attentions upon the countess herself. What kind of person will cast two shadows?"

This was a question familiar to apprentices in our profession. "One whose twin died at birth. Or one who has been loved, adored beyond all measure by one who lies in the grave. Or someone whose mind is distracted, split into two minds, so that the man or woman is twain. Or a mother or father who early lost two dear children. Or—"

"Good enough," he said, and gave me a calm look. "You are not the blockhead that once you were. Now tell me, what manner of person will cast three shadows?"

"I am not certain. I have heard it said that priests who serve three gods or a triple-god-in-one may drop three umbrae, but I have not actual knowledge of this."

"Sometimes there are born," said Astolfo, "certain persons who embody the spirits of three others, being themselves but vessels. They will be triply shadowed, but none of the shades belongs to them personally and those shadows are only evidences of the entities that inhabit them. Among women, however, there occur figures who are themselves three-in-one and embody the three great powers of womanhood: the capricious candor of the child, the copious beauty of the adult, and the age-wise, humorous, secret lore of the crone. These triple figures are rare in the world and much revered by members of the female gender when recognized. I believe the Countess

Triana to be such a figure. As such, she will be a remarkable, strong leader of her people, if she is not debilitated in some fashion."

"She is a beautiful woman," I said, "and it is easy to find in her much of the child, the spoiled brat. But I saw no trace of the crone about her. And I saw only two shadows."

"She complains of being distracted in her mind, of not being at one with herself as formerly she was."

"If she lost one of her shadows, that might mean one-third of herself was missing."

"Lost? Stolen?"

"I cannot say."

"I will suspect theft," Astolfo declared. "Chrobius has warned us that there is something not right about our little 'orbit,' as he called it, of her great hall. We need to pursue further. I am particularly interested in the diamond that was shown us. We must examine it at leisure, with our library of jewel lore and history at hand."

"How is that possible?"

"You will have to steal it," Astolfo said. "But only as a temporary stratagem. Being honest gentles, we could not plan to keep it."

"Steal it? I? I could never—"

"Are you eager to learn the art of shadows or not? This is but one simple early step."

"Very well," I said, but my heart lurched within my breast like a skittish horse balking at a leap.

⋅─▬◖▬─⋅

I had made no long-drawn vocal objections to Astolfo's statement that I was to purloin the diamond from the countess. He and Mutano, who was my constant and ever-vigilant drillmaster, would surely spend some weeks educating and training me for this unsavory and dangerous exercise.

So I thought. But once again I had failed to apprehend the design.

The theft was to take place on the second night from today— or rather, in the second morning, for I was to enter the grounds of the countess's petite palace two hours before daybreak and to make my departure just as the earliest dawn-light brushed the rambling brick walls surrounding the edifice.

"We must be brisk about this business," Astolfo said, "for I believe that the countess stands in danger to herself and to the little realm that is loyal to her. The task is not so difficult as it may first seem. This is no iron fortress high-perched upon some vulturous peak but only a small habitation of many doors and corridors, many adits and exits. Formerly it was a religious institution with the great salon as its principal place of worship and the outlying rooms and buildings serving as quarters for the clerics and devotees. 'Twas never constructed to keep out intruders, expert or clumsy. Mutano will attempt to subtract some of your natural clumsiness, but it is unnecessary for you to gain the handiness of an experienced burglar. The place is not well guarded. The wealth of the countess is comparatively small—though I would not say meager—and her palace holds no strategic position."

"What if I am apprehended?"

"'Twould be a sour business," he replied, "for you will be recognized and the surmise shall be that you have come for the diamond."

"As will be so."

"And then they will attempt to discover if you have entered there at my order and whether I am involved in some intrigue against the countess."

"What is to be my answer?"

"Why, that you came to thieve out of your own cupidity and that you have betrayed my trust in you and that I will be in a fury upon you when I am told."

"Will they be satisfied?"

"After some period of torture, you would undoubtedly reveal all."

"I do not savor this experiment."

"Mutano will supply you with a delightful drug. The first moment you are threatened with torture, you have only to swallow this bolus to die an immediate and rapturous death."

His gray-eyed gaze never clouded in its mild steadiness. When I looked at Mutano, he gave me a broad smile and held up a little sphericle, as carmine in color as a pomegranate seed.

"Very well," I said.

Since the enclosing walls were of brick and stood at a height no more than half again my own, my scaling apparatus would consist only of a light horsehair rope attached with a small three-pronged hook of iron. The claw ends were naked; the rest of the hook was sheathed in leather to deaden its sound against the brick. My weapons were to be a short sword with a blade three hands in length, a poniard to tuck into the breast of my chamois doublet, and a short-steeled dirk hidden in my left boot.

"This is but feeble armory," I complained. "If I am caught, there will be more than one to come at me."

"If you bear more weaponry, you shall go clacking about like a pelican," Astolfo said. "Your only true advantage is a stealth that more blades would diminish. Graceful stealth, that is your only method. And for that, you shall have the concealment of a shadow."

"Indeed?" I was enheartened by the prospect. Astolfo had not yet trusted me to wear a shadow. I was too fumble-footed, he said, too sudden in my movements. The sturdiest shadow he drew about me would soon disintegrate to tatters and giblets, lose all its dark luster, and grow foul with my sweats and farts.

But now I was to don one, and I began to think that here was a real engagement, after all, and not another mere exercise drill to sharpen my skills and deepen my education and provide Mutano occasion to drub me. Of course, that would mean that the scarlet suicide dosage was a true and earnest poison and that the prospect of torture was not a figment of fancy. I was experiencing a creeping uneasiness of mind, but there was no turning back. I had given my yea and could never live down changing to nay or shill-I-shall-I.

One sandglass before daybreak was my time to enter the palace compound. "Late-reveling courtiers do not rise at cockcrow," Astolfo explained, "and so there will be early light, fore-dawning, and then full dawn. A black shadow would be as noticeable as a camelopard and a gray one as visible as mist. So we must resort to colors, Mutano. What tints should we drape about our daybreak thief?"

Mutano replied with a swift twittering of his fingers. I had puzzled out much of the sign language in which master and manservant conversed and had learned that they communicated in three different gestural dialects. What they signaled now I could not fathom.

Astolfo smiled humorously and told me that Mutano thought I should have the choice of colors since I was to be the wearer. "What do you choose?"

The study of shadow color is long and intricate and I had barely touched upon it in my reading. Since whatever tints I named would be declared mistakes, I made the obvious choices. "If the day is to be fair and bright, the early light will be purple changing to yellow and silver. Perhaps a dun color might pass without note."

As I expected they grinned at my blunder.

"So now, Falco," Astolfo said, "it is time for a hasty lesson in the hues of shadows." He signed to Mutano to draw the curtains of the tall library windows so that we were standing in a dimness close to darkness. Then he went to a small oil lamp sitting upon the smaller table, lit the wick with a single striking of flint, and set a concave, brightly polished mirror behind the lamp. He motioned me to step to his position at the table. I came to where he stood. He laid out flat before us a blank sheet of snowy paper.

"How many kinds of primary light have we in this room?" he asked.

"Two," I replied. "A strong white one from the mirrored lamp and a duller, softer one that seeps through the linen curtains."

"Very well. Now observe the shadow upon this paper. What do you see?" He took up a small dagger from the tabletop, customarily kept there to break the seals of documents, and held it perpendicular to the surface with his fingertip.

"I see two shadows. The one produced by the lamp is bluish; the other, a dusty yellow, comes from the window light."

"So you believe you see," Astolfo said. He signaled Mutano to draw the heavy satin drapes over the curtains. "What see you now?"

"The blue shadow made by the lamp has turned black."

"And the edges?"

"They were somdel indistinct before. Now they are sharp."

He nodded and Mutano opened the drapes. Astolfo doused the mirrored lamp.

"The dagger shadow now?"

"It is a thin, gray wash, dim, with withered edges. A common shadow, I should name it."

"There are no common shadows. This lesson you have been taught many times. The lamplight and the curtained light are complementary and result in a falsity of vision. Your eyes deceive you because of this commixture of lights. When you are at your business in the palace of the countess, there will be two kinds of light. The early light of the east will commingle with the retreating darkness of the rest of the sky, a dark gray shading to mauve. The shadow you wear must be of a complementary color that will not be invisible to sight—that is not possible—but only deceptive to it."

"What color, then?"

"I put it to you."

"I can do no better than the evidence of my senses, deceived though they may be," I said. "This mild blue is complementary, is't not?"

"It is one of the complementaries, but do not forget that as the hour toils onward, the light will change in intensity and hue."

"So then . . . ?"

"We shall have a parti-colored shade of several tints," Astolfo said. "They shall flow in and out of one another like the shades in a rainbow where a waterfall pours into the pool of a forest stream. In this wise, you may go from place to place and seem to be only a part of the natural changes of morning."

It did not seem plausible. "But will not so many colors present a garish, anomalous sight in a peaceful dawning?"

"Do you trust already the depth of your knowledge in this lore?"

"I suppose I must not. From what person did you gain this shadow of many colors?"

"From the renowned actor Ortinio. A man who has portrayed many characters with true and convincing manner will have a various and variable shadow. But this particular shadow lacketh strong texture. It is a consequence of the actors' trade that they have but pallid personalities themselves and must rely upon the playwright to supply them with character. The shadow must be suggested by an undergarment. You shall wear a many-colored tunic of several light fabrics to help to sustain the delusion. The correct stratagem with colored shadows is to cause men to see what they already believe that they see."

"Very well. How am I to enter the grounds of the palace?"

He laid down the dagger, took up a sharpened stick of charcoal, and began sketching a series of squares upon the paper, elaborating upon the small sketch I had studied. "Here is a rough plan of the palace and the grounds. How shall you proceed? Where do you think you should try entrance?"

"That depends on where the stone is kept," I said. "Best to come as close as possible to that place unless it be heavily guarded and most closely watched. If it be so, then better to enter at a more distant point and make way to it by degrees."

Mutano and Astolfo traded gazes, nodding agreement.

"And where will the diamond lie?" Astolfo asked.

"I cannot say. I think the countess will want it close by her, but now she has begun to mistrust her faculties. Perhaps she entrusts it to Chrobius or another councilor for its safety. Perhaps it is in a separate room by itself and under armed guard."

"Will you then steal into three places at once?"

"Time is lacking. On succeeding nights I might do so, but the choice to begin with is easy. I would try the room set apart for it where I would stand less chance of being recognized."

Again they nodded agreement.

"Can you find this place on our little map?" Astolfo pushed the paper toward me.

His sketch showed a long north-south rectangle with the large palace building against the east wall, flanked on both sides by a dozen adjoining squares. In the middle of the whole he had drawn a square divided into two, and this I took to be an armory and barracks for the guards. He had not indicated entrances there, but I supposed it to have four, faced in opposite directions.

"Here." I touched the third square on the left side of the main palace. "I can go over the wall, onto the roof, and then along here to the left."

"Well enough," he said. "I believe that to be a sort of dormitory for the bachelor courtiers. I picture them sleeping in their cots, giving off wine-sodden snores, as you tiptoe catlike above them. Only look below when you come to the corner to begin your descent and make certain that guards are not hiding out of sight in the several doorways to lay hands upon you."

"I shall be wary."

⊶═◉═⊷

His warning was a prediction.

The night passed tediously and as soon as I had made my cautious, finger-straining descent of the terra-cotta drainpipe at the corner of the building, eight burly guardsmen appeared as if summoned by a silent bell. Beyond them a group of twenty or so stood in close order in the great courtyard. Six of the eight ringed me with drawn blades while a seventh sprang to pin my arms behind my back. The eighth, a villainous, scar-faced captain every inch as large as Mutano, searched me over efficiently, tossing away my short sword and dagger and fishing from my boot the favorite little dirk I had thought so cleverly hidden.

"Your name?" he asked in a voice that was accustomed to transmuting the blood of new recruits to cold cat piss.

"Osbronius," I said, pronouncing the full name of the brother who had tormented my earliest years with his bullying.

"Doubtful," he grunted. "Your occupation?"

"Thief," I said.

"More doubtful still," he growled, and his brothers-in-arms seconded this statement with derisive guffaws.

"How came you here?"

"I say no more. Do your worst."

"So we may—and without your permission. But please, I entreat you, answer one thing further. Why do you come clothed in this ridiculous, gaudy motley? A man, be he thief or sea cook, will be seen in it seven leagues off. Do you think to celebrate by yourself the Feast of the Jester long before its proper moon?"

I looked down at myself and was astonished. No subtle shadow of slowly shifting tints and flamy shapes enwrapped my shoulders, torso, and arms. Instead, I wore a filmy, light mantle or robe of ungainly cut all pieced together of vivid ribbons, with colors of lime, azure, scarlet, emerald, ember-gray, and inky purple. No self-respecting harlequin would ever don such an outfit. Now that I saw it plain I could feel its weight upon me, slight but palpable.

"See his face," crowed my chief captor. "His mouth hangs slack like a gate unhinged. Is he not the very paragon of ijjits? Should not our countess take him just as he stands for her court jester? . . . But hold. He is too tall for the Jester's office. We must subtract an ell or so." He drew his sword and came close upon me, garlicky breath and all. "Where shall we lessen you, Sir Jackanapes? Shall we take from the bottom?" He thwacked me across the knees with the flat of his blade. "From the top?" He scratched a horny thumbnail across the knob of my throat. "Or from the middle?" He traced the sword tip across my chest, tearing open the flimsy contraption of ribbons.

All his smug japeries brought forth unbounded hilarity from his whiskery, overfed troop, and I vowed that if ever I enlisted in a guard troop, I would choose one whose leader did not fancy himself a humorist. But at this moment I was so abashed by my capture and by my beribboned motley that I could form no response but to repeat my former challenge: "Do your worst."

"Our worst?" He laughed a gravel-throated long minute. "Sir Harlequin, you would not beg for the worst if you could conceive what it might be."

With this sentence, the troop parted ranks and Astolfo came ambling toward me. He was dressed in his military best, a sea-colored caftan belted with a broad sash of cloth-of-gold, a short-sleeved red cloak, and a tall, broad-brimmed black hat with a white plume. A sword hung from his left shoulder in a brightly jeweled sheath and he bore a tall lance in his left hand. He stood directly before me and said again, "The worst is mine." With that he balled his right hand and delivered me such a blow to the neck that I fell backward to the ground. The dawning sky, the roof of the building, and the faces of Astolfo and the soldiers twirled round in my sight like fern leaves circling the mouth of a drain.

I tried to speak, but the blow to my neck, just at the base of my throat, had made words impossible. I could not cough or croak and heaved for breath like a fresh-landed carp.

"Stand him up," Astolfo commanded, and when the captain gestured, two obscenely grinning troopers jerked me to my feet. If they had not gripped me on both sides by elbow and shoulder, I surely would have toppled again.

Astolfo strode round in a circle, striking the dust with the butt of his lance and seeming to plod in deep and furious thought. Finally he halted and addressed the guards at large:

"Gentlemen! Behold the spectacle that treacherous ingratitude and sneaking rebellion may make of a man. This Falco, when first I took him into my employ, was but an unlettered, unmannered peasant boy still aromatic from dunging the stony fields of his father. Like many another trusting man of elder years, I believed his innocence and gave him a berth in my household and a place at my table. His only duties were to better himself with study and to perform some light labors under the guidance of my faithful manservant."

He ground the lance into the dirt and paused. "But—see him now. He has wantonly entered your palace compound, intent on I know not what villainy. He came armed, and that is always a sure-proof of evil purpose. He has clothed himself in this tatterdemalion rag-taggery for no reason I can put a name to. This outfit once belonged to my young sister, who wore it to Midsummer Eve festivals when she was a child of twelve years or so. Perhaps he dreamed 'twould serve to excuse him as a madman if captured, rather than the perfect natural he shows himself to be."

The soldiers laughed in hearty appreciation and Astolfo came to accost me again. "It was a happy accident that led me to discover, by means of certain papers found in his quarters, that he planned to come here tonight and steal what valuables he could lay hands on. Then he would hide them away in my own domicile and one night before the last quarter of the moon, on the eve of the Feast of the Jester, he would slit my throat as I lay sleeping, ransack my meager belongings, and join with the infamous pirate Morbruzzo to plunder all the city of Tardocco, murdering and burning."

He lifted the butt of the lance and thrust it sharply into my belly. My knees went water. My gut surged with pain. "As soon as I found these darksome, infernal papers, I hurried here to warn your good minister Chrobius of Falco's miscreant plans. That is why you were all turned out for the successful capture. The countess will be pleased with your dutiful performance."

He turned his back upon me and lifted his voice, which, though still mild in tone, carried with powerful strength. "Look upon him and ware you," he declaimed. "See what the low taverns and fleshpots of the town have wrought upon a lad too simple to withstand the easiest temptations, too weak to learn a skill, too cowardly of mind to take stock of his own character and embrace proper discipline. Your wise Chrobius proposed that we hang him from the scaffold yonder at the far corner of the wall, but I have persuaded him that certain interrogations must first proceed, for we know not what other designs he hath formed nor which confederates might be leagued with him. We shall lead him back to my house, gentlemen, and put questions to him in such manner that he shall plead with tearful eyes and broken bones to be hanged with all dispatch. Your good captain has offered a detail of men to guard us homeward, and I have gratefully accepted."

With this sentence two men fell into rank on either side of me while Astolfo and a shaggy corporal posted themselves before. Then we were off on a dolorously sluggish march out of the compound as the soldiers rattled their weapons in derision. Through the gates we went, over the road through the fields of knee-high grain, and into the highway to Tardocco. The pace became a little brisker,

yet still was slow enough that early risers—the farmers carting eatables to market, the night watch returning sleepily homeward, unsteady revelers ceasing their rounds—had a good long view of the
sorry spectacle of dejected Falco trudging the streets in soiled and
bedraggled motley.

When we reached Astolfo's manse he unlocked the gate to the
east garden and led us to the springhouse there under the great
hemlock. Into that cold, dank space he booted me, wrapped a chain
around door-slat and jamb, and secured it with a massive lock.

"There he'll cool his senses, gentlemen, and my manservant will
come shortly to guard over him. Meantime, let us go into the house
and try what the larder might supply to break our fast. I seem to recall
a platter of kidney pies and a small keg of new country oat ale."

They responded to this invitation with ready good cheer and
marched off, Astolfo leading them while whistling a merry martial
tune. I heard him say, "I should not be surprised if your generous
countess and the sage Chrobius do not reward us handsomely for
this morning's labor."

I sat down weakly on the edge of the spring run where jugs of
fresh milk, oilskin packets of cheese and butter, and jars of wine were
set to cool. As I was rubbing my tender belly and nursing my throbbing noggin, my eye fell upon a basket of woven willow in the corner
by my left boot. I dragged it open to disclose a pewter mug, a loaf of
black bread, a knuckle of boiled beef, and some table cutlery.

I had realized, from the first moment of Astolfo's appearance,
that my attempted burglary was only a staged mummery, a stratagem designed to force attention upon myself and away from some
other occurrence, but I could not fathom what that might be. For
the time being, I did not care. Despite my knocks and aches, I was
perishingly hungry and fell upon the victuals like a gryphon tearing asunder an ox.

Afterward, I took thought whether the rough, damp stones of this
springhouse might serve as a bed. I was much a-weary and though
food had restored my spirits somewhat, my pains did not desist. The
little players' scene before the soldiery was but sham, but Astolfo's
blows had been authentic.

⊷═◉═⊷

The stones made no easy pallet, but they must have afforded some
portion of comfort, for I had to be awakened by Mutano's kicking

of my boot sole. When I opened my eyes I was startled. I knew the
dumb man to be of unusual proportion but had become accustomed
to his bulk. Now I looked up at him as I lay prone and he seemed
as tall and solid as an astrologer's tower.

I rose shakily and with much groaning followed him through
the full morning light into the kitchen of the great house. Astolfo
was there, seated, according to his wont, on the large butcher block
in the center. He swung his legs idly and hailed me at my entrance:
"How now, brave Falco? How like you the life of the thief? Is't not
a jolly existence, replete with surprise and unlooked-for reward?
Have you determined to follow its ways to riches—or to the gallows?"

If I showed ill temper, his sarcasm would only sharpen. "When
I take up thievery," I said, "I shall make certain that my colleagues
are trustworthy and do not betray me at whim."

"Do you truly find me a whimsical man?"

"I must suppose that the painful blows I took and the embarrassment of my soul were parts of a design you had in hand. You
will no doubt name them necessary parts."

"We had to convince a skeptical guard troop and the cautious
Chrobius," he replied. "We may be assured that he was watching
our playlet from a high window, trying to discover any trace of
deception."

I rubbed my rueful ribs tenderly. "He shall have been convinced,"
I asserted. "And I am curious to know what Mutano brought away
with him while all eyes were feasting upon my wretched plight.
When did you cloak me in this clownish ribbon-dress? When I set
out in the fore-dawn, methought I wore a shadow of subtle tints
and colorations invisible in dawn light."

"And so you did," he explained. "This frock of giblets and
flinders, which no sister of mine ever could wear, if ever I had a
sister, served as undergarment to the shadow we cast over you at
the last. But that shadow possessed some of its rainbow qualities
because its genesis was in moisture. 'Twas the umbra of the actor
Ortinio standing in mist with the light bright behind him. As you
went along, throwing off animal heat from your exertions, and as
the morning grew warmer, this mist-shadow dissipated, leaving you
all checkered in parti-colored motley."

"I hope you are content with the spectacle I made, for it could
not have been completer."

"Let us see how content we are to be, for I am curious about this prize myself." He signed to Mutano, who nodded and with a grave smile unlaced a white leather pouch from his belt, fingered open the mouth, and poured into his left palm four small stones. I recognized them as black opals, ominous gems of grim reputation. They are warranted to bring ill fortune to whoever possesses them.

Astolfo counted them over. "Here is the sphericle; here the mandorla; here the small lozenge; here the larger cartouche." He pointed out each shape as he went, then looked at Mutano. "It is the tiny arrow-leaf opal, then?"

Mutano smiled more widely and from the cuff of his ocher leather sleeve plucked forth another opal, even blacker than the others, which had been cut at one end into a sharp point.

Astolfo clapped his hands slightly, then rubbed them together. "So our surmise was correct. The piercing form had been chosen, though there is only superstition in the choice and no science whatsoever."

I began, "I do not—"

"You no longer need to appear so ridiculous." Astolfo reached out casually and ripped away my robe of ribbons, crushed it into a ball, and flung it on the flagstone floor. I stood now in a knee-length robe of coarse linen. "You will learn more thoroughly without reliving your embarrassment. Let us sip a mug of ale to help wash down the dusty matter of explanation." He dropped from his perch lightly to the floor, rummaged three mugs from a cupboard, and poured them foaming from a stout stone jar. He, and then Mutano and I, raised our mugs in salute and tasted the brew. Such an ale would cheer even the glummest hour.

"Do you remember when Chrobius showed us the diamond and the things he said then to the countess?"

"He lauded her generosity," I answered, "but lamented the late infirmities of her mind."

"Good. And do you remember how he termed these debilities?"

"He said that she began to lack sufficient and proper will-call."

"Yes. *Will-call.* In your wide and profoundly thorough perusal of the writings of sages and mages, have you ever encountered this odd word?"

Something nibbled at the rearward of my memory like a mouse in the corner of a meal bin. "Is there not a school or maybe a cabal of philosophers who have formulated certain notions about the nature of authority, about who should be allowed to rule, and how succession of princes, counts, and other nobility should be arranged and that . . . that . . ." The memory of the fusty, worm-eaten manuscript crumbled away in my mind-sight.

"Perhaps 'twill aid your recollection to note that this gabble of thinkers is sometimes denominated by their deriders as the Prickalists or Pricktolists."

"The *Masculinists*," I said. "Yes, they who believe it is graven by the stars upon the tablets of fate that only men are to bear sway over other men and over women. That, they believe, is the true and natural order of things. Any female who occupies a throne or any other seat of power is reenacting some ancient and illicit act of usurpation that has brought the world into its present state of degraded confusion."

"Now you have got it," Astolfo said. "Those who follow this course of thought will not allow that it is legitimate for a woman to rule or to have power over any others, excepting her children, her animals, and her female servants."

"So, if Chrobius subscribes to this way of thinking—"

"He may desire to overthrow any woman in a seat of state. Yet what sort of woman, what exemplar of the female mind, will he distrust, fear, and perhaps envy most?"

"The woman who is three-in-one," I said, "the triply endowed, triply powerful woman who is child, beauty, and crone in one." The thought of it so fired my enthusiasm that I drained off my mug and held it out to be replenished.

He pretended to demur. "We are not to the end of this knotty length of string. You had better keep your wits clear to think the pattern through."

"You are in fee to me for another ale and many another after that," I said, "because of the ugly drubbing you laid upon me at the palace."

He grinned, and Mutano poured me full again.

"But I cannot cipher how Mutano's stealing of that small black-opal arrow can hinder the schemes of Chrobius."

"He stole nothing; he traded for the opal. You have studied the lore of precious stones. You have read how jewels, and diamonds in particular, partake of or share into after being long in their possession, the spirits of their owners."

"Yes. I recalled to you the instance of Erminia, whose jewel crumbled when she died, but you dismissed the tale."

"'Tis worn thin from too much wear, but 'tis applicable. I have no quarrel with its kernel. Now you have read also that the nature of one stone can be transformed by keeping it in proximity with another and that the black opal is an especially debasing companion."

"In Maxilius's *De gemmae et spiriti mundi,* there is a lengthy—"

"Yes, and in Bertralius, Ronio, Militiades, and many another. Chrobius had paired the countess's diamond with a pernicious opal while the casket stood nighttimes in her bedchamber. By little and little, it drew one part of her tripartite spirit into the diamond, the opal serving as conduit. In due season, the other sides of her nature would also follow and the diamond itself would cloud to dull gray and finally to black. She herself would be left a husk, without memory, without spark. She would be lifeless in her mind, her body deteriorating like a drift of snow melting in the first heats of springtime."

"And Chrobius would then seize her state."

"No, he hath no lineage of blood. The people would not countenance the usurpation. But her third husband, the count with whom he is leagued, would return from exile, pretend to care for the countess in her infirmity, and bring all power to himself."

"This diamond found in the sea chest, this legacy of her second husband, has not proved the happy largess she thought it."

"It was no legacy. Chrobius or some accomplice secreted it there to be found."

"But why does Mutano hold not one but five black opals?"

"We do not know the design of the one Chrobius paired with the diamond and were forced to surmise, choosing the most often favored designs in which that gem is usually cut. Fortune was with us."

"But now Chrobius will see his opal absent, will think upon my stupid burglary attempt and its childish farce, and know that you—"

"He will not find the opal missing, for Mutano substituted a harmless bit of obsidian in that shape to lie in the casket by the diamond. It hath no occult powers and in time the countess's spirit will escape its imprisonment and she shall be three-in-one again, and whole."

"Yet he shall observe her transformation, her renewal, and know—"

"He will know that we know his scheme and that if he move against her we can reveal all upon him."

"Why not do so at once?"

"Better to watch and wait. Hath he confederates in the palace? Has he formed secret alliances with other princes, other provinces or forces? He shall be aware of our gaze, and if he does attempt any hidden plan we shall detect it forthwith."

"So we do nothing for the present."

"We watch and wait. You may improve the time by further study of gems, and Mutano will begin your preparation for exercises in the wearing of shadows—how to don them without causing damage, how to choose the best for the task at hand, how to fit them to your form, how to move within them so that you seem a play of light and dark and not a peasant clopping through a murky fog."

"This is a more entertaining exercise than any you have set me to undertake so far," I said. "There may be enjoyment in it."

"As may be," said Astolfo. "Yet this too is a discipline requiring rigor. And has Mutano ever disappointed you in a policy of rigor?"

I looked at Mutano's broad smile, and did not much like the cast of it. "No," I said, "he has not."

⊷══◉═══⊶

We had arranged for the unmasking of Chrobius to take place in three stages in our next and final visit to the court. The first stage was for me to be brought before the countess in chains and shackles, bearing the marks of ungentle treatment. I was to make confession of my dastardly fictitious crimes and she was to conceive and pronounce punishment.

This little prelude was to afford us opportunity to observe the countess, to see whether or not we could discover changes in her demeanor, in the movements of her mind, in the health of her physic. We were also to observe Chrobius for any hint that he had found out Astolfo's replacement of his conduit opal with an innocuous shard of obsidian, or for any change about him that might betoken danger to the countess or to us.

Our audience with her this time proceeded in the beginning similarly to the first one. We were received, as then, before her imposing, elaborately carved chair in the large salon. Now Mutano was present as guard over me, and he found it his part in the acting to cuff me about the jaw from time to time and to give my ankles an occasional contemptuous kick. This part he played with unfeigned relish.

I stood before the countess, Mutano on my right-hand side, Astolfo on the other, and Chrobius off to the left behind us. I mumbled out the rigmarole Astolfo had rehearsed me in: how I had planned to steal the great diamond, keep it secret till I could use it to buy my way into the good graces of the bloody pirate Morbruzzo, and then join with him in a campaign of pillage, enslavement, and destruction of the city of Tardocco. But now, following the shadow master's minute regimen of iron discipline, I had become a miserable and sniveling penitent content to live or die in any fashion at the countess's desire.

She spoke to Astolfo. "What think you, sir? Is his penitence genuine or only a further sham with which he hopes to escape the severest sentence?"

He inclined his head, his expression ambiguous. "I believe that at this moment he is sincere, in this hour of the day. But who can read what thought will come tomorrow to such a viper's-knot of a mind?"

"You have him securely in hand?"

"Yes, milady. My man Mutano looks to him closely."

At these words Mutano fetched me such a sharp slap that blood dripped from my nose. This, I thought, was overacting the part. I longed to take his place in our drama; I would devise any number of painful cranks and pinches that would send him reeling—if we but exchanged roles.

"Then I leave final judgment to you, Astolfo," said she. "If he is reformable, well; if not, mayhap the world should be unencumbered of him."

"Milady."

"Now as to the diamond," she said. "In what condition will you say it stands?"

"It has been polluted by some means or other," he replied. "You were correct to observe that its shine had somewhat muddied and its brightness occluded. Yet it is such a grand diamond, such a valiant one, that I believe it must possess inherent strong virtue to regenerate itself, to purge the darkness from it."

"That would be a joyful event."

"My advice is, *Bright to bright and never night.* That is to say, milady, 'twould be best not to shut it away in casket or box or vault, surrounded by black gloom and tomblike silence. Better to bring it to its own likeness and let it breathe and find itself again. Your own physic may strengthen along with it, milady, for it is well attested in the accounts of history and the writings of sages that the health of the possessors stands in close relation to the condition of the stones they possess. I could furnish many a treatise and pluck from memory countless examples."

He paused and cleared his throat. "Perhaps, if you have time and patience, you might hear the little-known story of the Lady Erminia and her opal. It so closely was attached to her thoughts and moods that it changed hue and, some have said, even its shape as her own thoughts journeyed and her moods shifted. . . ."

And then Astolfo went on to tell at length, with intriguing detail and in high-colored language, that tale of Erminia of which he would brook no syllable from my lips. I found this most irritating and might even have preferred another of Mutano's blows to Astolfo's elaborate account of the Lady Erminia's opal. I rattled my chain and Mutano, as if to oblige my unspoken thought, delivered a solid kick to my shin.

Astolfo was concluding: "So, as you see, the connections between possessor and possession are intimate and enduring. For the sake of the stone and for the sake of your own well-being, I would pray you to place the diamond upon a sheet of the snowiest linen on a table in an open room, with two lamps set about it day and night to shed upon it the warmest and most lucent light. I am certain that you will then see it returned to its former brilliance."

"It may be as you propose," the countess said, "but I mislike exposing my diamond in such a public area, so prominent to the eyes of all, with everyone passing by and about. Why, 'tis to welcome thievery with a handwrit invitation delivered upon a salver."

Her doubtful remark brought us to the third part of Astolfo's scheme.

"It will be broadly approachable, milady. So it must be constantly guarded and its care must be given over to the responsibility of one who is completely—nay, slavishly—devoted to your welfare. It must be guarded by a person whom no taint of suspicion can ever join to, one who has served you faithfully for many a long season, someone you have learned to trust without stint or reservation."

"You intend my minister Chrobius," she said.

"But milady—" Chrobius stepped forward and made as if to remonstrate.

"Our Chrobius hath many a weighty matter already in his charge," the countess said. "There are affairs of state which pluck at his attention like hungry children at their mother's apron. Matters of finance bedevil him, rumors of armed revolt, whispers of intrigue and conflict. Every day his hours are so overfull with such considerations that they spill out of their allotted times like oat grain pouring from a torn sack."

"If't vex not your forbearance, milady, let me plead," Astolfo said, "for I believe there is no charge in all your affairs so urgent as this one. It touches directly upon your health and therefore upon the safety of your lands and dependents. I would urge you to create a special, particular office. Let Chrobius become 'Master of the Jewel.' If any stratagem advance against it, he shall find it out, though it be hid like an adder coiled in a cave in the cliffs of Clamorgra."

With the mention of Clamorgra, Chrobius's change of expression showed that he understood the allusion to his ugly scheme. He came forward with unexpected quickness for an elderly man. "Milady Countess, I feel I must turn away from this sudden and injudicious honor. There are affairs of—"

The countess giggled merrily and clapped her hands like an excited child. She drummed her heels on the rung of her chair. *"Master of the Jewel!"* she cried. "Oh, that is a dear, a precious title. I do love the ring of it."

"Yet it is a grave responsibility and much hangs upon the office," Astolfo warned. "If anything were to happen to the Great Countess Triana Diamond, as the gemologists now name it, all the consequence would be upon the head of the Master of the Jewel, and Chrobius must stand to answer."

"It is grave—but also jolly," she said. "It is done. I now declare thee, my good and faithful minister Chrobius, 'Master of the Jewel.' It shall henceforth be your sole duty to guard by night and by day, in peace and war, in foul weather and fair, the welfare of the Great Countess Triana Diamond. You shall be well rewarded for your service."

Chrobius did not quiver an eyebrow. "Yes, milady Countess." He bowed and stepped backward into his place behind our trio.

"You too shall be fitly rewarded, Master Astolfo. You have but to name your fee, be it not too burdensome to our treasury."

He made one of his unhurried, elegant bows. "The service was too trifling, milady, and I am still embarrassed by the perfidy of my once-apprentice, this verminlike Falco. I could expect no reward."

"You should. You must."

"If it please you, milady—no. But I shall return from time to time to see if all is in order, that no other gem has been brought to proximity with the diamond, that it is kept in a bright, bare place all its own, and that no shadow is stealing into its heart like some arrant villain crawling into a secret cave in Clamorgra."

This second mention of Clamorga would be, I thought, Astolfo's repeated warning to Chrobius that that his alliance with the countess's third husband was foreknown and that we were alert to any threat from that quarter.

"Well then," she said, "I fear not that I shall find some way to recompense your good effort. And now, as his last duty before he attendeth only to the jewel continually, Chrobius shall lead you the way out."

"Milady." Astolfo bowed once more and we departed, with the wretched, battered, peevish Falco shuffling along in chains and devising in his furious mind many little revenges upon his friend Mutano.

Chrobius preceded us through the great salon, through the corridors where the shadows no longer whispered ominous threats, to the wide hall at the front doors of the palace. Here he stopped, turned, and gave each of us a level, uninformative gaze, signaled to the footmen to open for us, then turned and padded his way to his task of nursemaiding to the end of his days that immense diamond.

Outside, we climbed into the carriage provided by the countess and set off toward Astolfo's manse. I slouched in the corner of the vehicle, weary and resentful, yet pleased withal. Master and colleague sat across from me in high good humor.

"A stout piece of work, methinks," said Astolfo. "We need no gold in our pouch for't. We stand to flourish in the countess's favor and gratitudinous goodwill. We have the treacherous Chrobius in our power. A happy day's labor, eh, Falco? And none so onerous, either."

"Easier," I said, "much easier for you than for me." I clashed together my shackles.

Astolfo and Mutano grinned at each other. "Ah, lad," said the shadow master, "when I consider how far you are from proper attainment, how much you have yet to learn, there swims into my brain a vision of the wide and starry sky."

I received this cheerful insult with the best grace I could muster. If my mental instruction and physical training kept on at the rate they were now progressing, I should one sudden day become as wise as any sage and as strong as the swiftest stallion. These were attainments to enjoy, for the time being, in rosy prospect.

III

Dance of Shadows

The array of the knowledge of jewels—their kinds, conditions, styles, and histories—that the maestro brought to bear in the matter of protecting the Countess Triana and the renewal of her diamond did not surprise me. Our trade is often an ancillary one, our business to design, produce, and provide *qualities* that are added to objects of value. To a stiff canvas fabric we might add an almost unnoticeable shade of gray that will increase, when the artist renders his subject upon it, both definition and subtlety. For a woman whose face has been marred by accident or intentional violence, a mixture of shades and tints of certain gradations can cause the flaw to seem to disappear. When a diplomatic letter must be dispatched that is intended to convey a paucity of substance and a plenitude of ambiguity, we can admix several umbrae to the ink with which it is written, producing a sort of locutionary fog over the meanings of the phrases.

To these instances Astolfo brings his practical knowledge of painting and drawing, of cosmetics and fashion, of the chemistries of writing fluids of every sort. Underlying all these particular sciences and the many others that are related is a confident grasp of the nature and properties of light.

I have often wondered if the ancient sages who penned the crammed volumes I was required to read knew even half as much as my master who compelled me to read them.

It is no marvel then that Astolfo is sought out by collectors of all kinds of valuables to judge, appraise, estimate damages, suggest repairs, and so forth. Indeed, a good half of our custom was in dealing with wealthy collectors.

But the maestro had affected to disdain what he called the vice of collecting.

"For it *is* a vice, you know," he said, and looked at me with that gray-eyed gaze that so rarely gave away the true cast of his humor. "I have known many a man to waste his substance upon trifles. He may bestow a fortune upon a heap of essence-bottle stopples, upon elegant sword-hilt pommels, upon coins of fabled cities in fabled ages past. Then these connoisseurs expire and their descendants scatter those spurious treasures to the round of the compass for a fraction of the amount expended. This collecting, Falco, is a costly vanity."

"I take it that you make an exception for the collectors of shadows."

"Shadow collectors may be the worst of the lot," he replied. "For not only do the objects themselves extort fat prices, but a discriminating taste for them is expensive to acquire. And then there are the further costs of proper care and storage and restoration when that is necessary and possible."

"Yet you derive some large part of your income from collectors."

"Ah." He sighed and blinked. "I lead a superfluous existence. I cannot fathom why you feel attracted to such an inutile way of life."

I might have talked at length of the fascination that the trade of shadows held for me, why it stood in my mind as one of the subtlest, cleverest, most demanding methods of maintaining oneself. But I knew better than to give my lash-tongued mentor reason to ply me with sarcasm. I only inquired what he thought he might occupy himself with otherwise.

"Why, I should retire from commerce," said he, "and devote myself to the close study of the ancient mages. I would delve into the unexplored hinterlands of reality. I would strive to achieve equanimity of mind and equability of temper. I would exercise to be always cheerful in this world of futile strife. And I seek always one particular object, a thing that embodies within it a complete purity of spirit."

"I cannot imagine what that thing might be," I said, "but most who know you would say that you have already arrived at the other goals you aim at. You are equable and balanced, hardly a melancholy man."

"A long face discourages custom," he declared. "If my clients see me downcast, they may suspect I fret over an unsound business and carry their trade elsewhere."

"So then, your talk is not pure philosophical disquisition. We have a venture in hand?"

"We do." He had not objected to my use of the plural pronoun.

"And it has to do with the pursuit of shadow-collecting?"

"As soon as you have made your appearance presentable to polished company, we shall go to the house of Ser Plermio Rutilius," Astolfo said. "I shall tell you about him as we travel."

"Will Mutano accompany us?" I asked. If Astolfo felt the need of our colleague so fierce in combat, we might be entering a situation of some danger.

"No," he replied. "If our host saw the three of us together he might doubt of my capacities. You shall answer well enough as a diverting companion, and no more than that. He will see that you are harmless; Mutano does not readily present that aspect."

I agreed.

⊷⊜⊶

Our travel was accomplished in handsome style, for Ser Rutilius had sent a well-appointed coach-and-two to Astolfo's mansion to fetch us the two leagues to his château. As we rolled smoothly through the green springtime countryside, Astolfo informed me that our host was the scion of an ancient race of warriors who had hired out to duchies, principalities, and great estates to protect them from marauders, enemies and friends alike. Since our province of Tlemia had very recently blundered into peaceful times only occasionally troubled by rumors of pirates, there had been naught to occupy the hereditary skills and services of Rutilius. And so, as a young man, he had entertained himself with dissipation, gathering from cellars their sumptuous wines, from tailors their most costly and elaborate cloaks and doublets, and from respected families their comeliest, most complaisant females.

"In short," said Astolfo, "he led such an existence as you have dreamed of leading, Falco, a life of idle pleasures following upon one another like raindrops in a springtime shower. And do you not dream of it still?"

I would not reply, but my thought was that such an existence would not be wasted upon me. Youth, strength, and high spirits would guide me through the vale of rainbow temptations.

"But Rutilius is an intelligent young noble and in due season he found these pastimes to pall. He has educated himself in the sciences and the arts. He raised the farming practices of his lands to extraordinary levels; he has renewed and refined his martial skills; he has become a knowledgeable connoisseur of painting and tapestry, statuary and architecture. His senses and apprehensions having become so acute, it was perhaps inevitable that he should come to pursue shadow-collecting, for no other cultivated attainment is so difficult to achieve. But, as it is the most expensive of such follies, so is it the most rewarding, for, as you have discovered, umbrae are infinite in interest and delight."

I would assent to this latter assertion while envying the fact that one in Rutilius's station could become an adept of shadows without enduring the physical discomforts the discipline was inflicting upon me.

Astolfo seemed to have overheard my thought. "You must not think him some soft-handed, sweet-scented dilettante. He is an expert swordsman, an avid huntsman, a canny and alert man of affairs, and a fearless pugilist. Of his prowess with women I have heard nothing. Perhaps one of your town wenches has whispered to you thereof."

I shook my head.

"Well then, we understand that whatever commission he may propose to us must be a tangled one, because the man himself is so very able and has such deep resources to command."

"Yes," I said, "and from these resources he can well afford whatever toplofty fee you may ask."

"It is for that reason we have come," Astolfo said, "for I am past the age when mere difficulty itself is an attraction. . . . And so, here are we."

The carriage rolled to a stop, the driver opened the door and assisted us down the gilt steps he had deployed, and we stood in a pleasant greensward before the great oaken doors of the château.

⤙═◦═⤚

We were brought into the presence of Rutilius in a foyer almost immediately inside the doors. The foyer spread large, with a high, arched ceiling of cedar wood, and enclosed a circular area three steps below the main floor. This sunken space contained a small pool lined with blue tile in which red and silver carp wafted long, gossamer tails. Flowers and trailing vines spilled from the mouths of sand-cast urns. From an adjoining room a lute not visible to us was being played with gentle and pensive hand.

I had thought that the mansion of Astolfo, where it stood with its gardens and lawn and stable near the center of the port city of Tardocco, must be close to the apex of luxury. Now I knew that however large the fortune Astolfo had amassed, it was to the fortune of Rutilius as a sower's handful of seed is to a granary.

Rutilius showed himself, however, as no pompous or overbearing sort. A slender, sandy-haired man in his late thirties with a manner easy and open, he seemed sincerely pleased to acquaint himself with us, though he did not offer his hand. Yet his ease in his bearing was so confident that this oversight bore no hint of arrogance. A footman approached to offer the customary welcoming glass of wine, as fine as any I have tasted since.

The preliminary conversation consisted of our host and Master Astolfo trading reminiscences and guarded confidences about mutual friends and acquaintances. Ser Rutilius was sounding out Astolfo for his society connections, inquiring about the health of Princess A and the new foal in the stable of Count Z. The shadow master bantered his way through this testing, showing familiarity with the persons and affairs of one and all, but without giving impression that he gossiped.

Rutilius broke off these preliminaries. "Have you some inkling why I desired to meet you?"

"I have supposed that you wished to acquire my services."

"Do you know in what regard? You must answer this question truthfully."

"I have no slightest notion," Astolfo replied mildly.

An expression of relief passed over the face of the baron. "I am pleased to hear you say so. I have feared that my comportment of late has given me away. There are those unfriendly who observe me closely for any sign of weakness."

"Ah then," said Astolfo, "now I shall suppose it is some affair of the affections. I must tell you straightway, Ser Rutilius, that I am no mender of broken hearts. Nor, come to that, am I a broker of mended hearts."

"In neither case could I use your skills," Rutilius said. "But come along with me to another room. Let me fill your glasses once more and you shall fetch them with you."

"Thank you. It is a inspiriting vintage," Astolfo said.

Rutilius led us from the foyer down a long, tapestry-hung gallery and brought us into a small salon. Intricate carpets smothered large areas of the parquetry floor, ensuring a sleepy degree of quiet. Large windows admitted southern light and gave an impression of openness to the room. But it was the walls that we had come to see. Paintings and drawings covered them in close profusion. Some paintings were life-size portraits; some drawings were not much larger than the leopard's-head belt buckle that clasped Astolfo's broad belt.

I marveled at them. Portraiture of shadows is one of the most demanding and delicate of the pictorial arts and the most skillful of artists might labor an arduous season to produce even a mediocre rendering. Here every example was a masterpiece. One or two I recognized from engraved reproductions in books, but all the others were new to my eyes and this first impression of them all together made the hairs stand up on my wrists.

Astolfo, though his constant watchword was *nil mirari,* gave over to rapt admiration, going from one frame to another, stepping forward and back, cocking his head to one side, and shading his eyes with his left hand. I had never before seen him so avidly engaged and wondered if this display might be partly a show of manners, a way of complimenting Rutilius on his taste.

I also noted that the baron observed Astolfo attentively and seemed gratified when the shadow master kept returning to one drawing. Among the other, more imposing pictures, this one at first looked none so remarkable. It was no larger than a sheet of foolscap, a rendering of the shadow of a female in graphite and chalk. But the more I looked at it, the more it unfolded not only its artistic beauties but also an ineffable, intimately personal charm that must have derived from its subject.

In spite of all the instruction Astolfo had set me to—the examination of scores of paintings and drawings in the collections of his clients, the volumes of prints and engravings, the crabbed treatises on the pictorial art—I have not sufficient knowledge to speak with any wisdom. I believe anyhow that pictures speak for themselves and much that is said in their presence by ink-smeared daubers and chalky schoolmasters is so much vain bleating. I would rather hear a goat fart than to listen to doddering know-alls speak of composition, impasto, contrapposto, and the other drivel.

From Astolfo's scattered remarks, however, I learned some good, practical sense, especially in regard to the picturing of shadows. First, he told me, your shadow artist must learn how to show *volume,* the dimensions of bodies in space. It is a childish error to see shadows flat, as unlit two-dimensional strips adhering to surfaces. The first task is to see that for all their seeming insubstantiality, shadows have volume and extend round in three dimensions, to which—unlike solid bodies such as stones and trees—they add another surface borrowed from the ultra-mundane source to which they are allied. At the time, I could not see what he was asking me to see, but to this simple-seeming drawing his words fitly applied. The contours of the figure seemed to rise from the sheet on which they were limned. The shadow was modeled on paper as if it were a study for a sculpture in bronze or glass.

Astolfo spoke to Rutilius in a voice even milder than usual. "I take it that these works represent properties in your possession."

"All but a few are renderings of shadows I have gathered," Rutilius replied. "There are one or two works I acquired for their excellence as art. Some of those are quite old."

"Indeed," Astolfo said, "for I see that some were signed by the artists. There is a Manoni by the door and in the painting next to it the little salamander scrawled into the corner of the canvas is the sign of the celebrated Proximo. But the newer ones are unsigned."

"Shadow artists discovered that noising their names abroad was unsafe practice," Rutilius said. "They are bound not to disclose the identities of their models, but some viewers who become obsessed with one image or another would not scruple to extort this knowledge by violence, even by torture."

"Yet there are some so skilled, so deep-thoughted, so individual that their work speaks their names. For instance, that drawing of the young female's shadow must have come from the hand of Petrinius. He is our contemporary genius of shadows, and his touch is unmistakable."

"You are correct."

"I see too that this drawing is fresh. You must have come by it recently."

"He completed it only a sennight past."

"And the shadow itself is in your possession?"

"It is."

"I congratulate you. That shadow is a treasure to make any collector proud."

"Proud, perhaps. But not entirely happy."

"The reason?"

"I have a great, an overweening, desire to know what woman cast this shadow and where she is."

"Did not your purveyor tell you these things?"

"He did not know, for the one he got it from did not. It is possible that it passed through many hands before it came into mine."

Astolfo stepped forward and leaned in for a closer view of the drawing. "Perhaps. It is difficult to tell from a drawing. If I were to see the original—"

Rutilius said, "Before I chance showing the property I shall need to know if you accept my commission and what your terms may be."

"You wish me to find out about the person who cast the shadow?"

"I want you to find her, the woman herself, and tell me who and what and where she is."

"I can accept your tender only provisionally," Astolfo said, "because I cannot foresee what may be involved. A tedious, long search might be necessary, and might well prove fruitless."

"True enough. Yet you are the most experienced hound in the kennel to set upon the trace. Your renown must have been well earned. And you should be fitly rewarded."

"Provisionally, then—yes. Let us see the original. Then I may say more."

Ser Rutilius unlocked the heavy door with a key he kept in his sleeve and we entered.

In this other smaller salon that opened off the collection room, I watched Astolfo to try to discern how he judged the way in which Rutilius tended his shadows. Many collectors and dealers believe that shadows should be put away in secret recesses—closets, armoires, and cellars—so that the surrounding darkness might keep them fresh. But darkness drains them of vitality, gradually absorbing a little of their natural vigor. A dim light is best, light that is not a steady glow but a fluctuating or flickering convergence of beams.

These varying conditions keep the shades exercised, furnish them tone, and lend them suppleness. Their odors keep cleaner in a light like that of an overcast morning, and their edges are less likely to lose definition than if they are stored away in some dank hole.

For his most dearly prized shadow Ser Rutilius had ordered the construction of a special cabinet. It was a hand taller than myself and its glass sides enclosed an array of lightly smoked mirrors, together with bright ones, wherein the shadow floated in an ever-changing, vague light. These mirrors revolved slowly by means of a clockwork mechanism attached to the side of the cabinet. The shadow hung amid their surfaces like the carp wafting in the tiled pool in the foyer.

Astolfo walked three times around this cabinet, leaning this way and that to see the different angles. I could tell that he was considering how he might improve the construction of our storage mirrors in the manse. I noted too that his gaze often left the glass box and its shadow to take in Ser Rutilius.

The baron must have looked upon this sight some hundreds of times, yet now he stood transfixed, again devouring it with his eyes. He had hooked his thumbs into his brocaded linen sash and his fingers played restlessly, hungrily, upon the band of cloth.

Ah . . .

It drifted there in ineffable beauty. There was about it such refinement and grace, such a lilting freedom, that it lightened the heart. Astolfo has described some of the most beautiful of shadows as being music, and, to speak in that vein, this one was a cool, clear soprano aria of purest tone. I was not so deeply enamored of it as our host; my taste is for the darker shade, the more satinlike texture, and the deeper fabric. But for those who prefer the shadow that verges on the edge of disappearance, an image that is but the whisper-echo of an image, this shade was paragon. And it required some moments well after Astolfo had finished his examination before our host was able to tear himself away.

"Any collector," Astolfo began, "of the greatest wealth or noblest blood, would consider this shadow his crown jewel."

"And so for me it is—and more than that," Rutilius replied.

"Your love for the object has persuaded me," Astolfo said. "I will accept the commission, as long as I am not bound to guarantee favorable result."

"And your fee?"

"I cannot tell that yet, but it will not discommode you."

⟡

In the coach as we rode back to our manse, Astolfo said, "This is to be a delicate business. We must tread gently. Perhaps we shall require from Ser Rutilius a bond for our safety from his hand."

"Why should he wish to harm us?" I asked.

"Because lovers are madmen and may do violence in a passion. Did you not see how he looked upon the thing? He is in love."

"With a shadow?"

"In his mind he sees beyond the shadow."

"How so?"

"He has imagined the woman who shed upon the air so graceful, so lissome, so lyrical a shade, and this picture he has imagined has fastened upon his heart like a kestrel taking a sunfish."

"You make him out a blushing virgin," I said, "but someone of his position—"

"A man who has had his fill of women in the flesh, who has tired of their jangle in his ear, their depletion of his purse, their weight upon his loins, may perhaps seek a different and nobler experience with a shadow-woman."

"The caster is no shadow. She is flesh and bone like the rest of us."

"Flesh and bone, yes—but not like you and me."

"How do you mean?"

"What sort of person will cast so delicate a shadow?"

I pondered. "Some saintly lass, maybe. An ascetic student or a devoted temple maiden."

Astolfo nodded, but his expression was dubious. "Or a prophetess—except that those figures rarely attain to gracefulness and when they do, their grace is in a strongly individual, eccentric mode. The movements of this shadow have a high degree of finesse unavailable to the temperament of the hermit."

"You speak as if you have formed conclusions as to the identity of this female."

"A thin conjecture, no more. Let us try to lure the artist who drew the shadow to our dinner table for tomorrow eve."

"Petrinius? He will not come. He is said to disdain all company but his own."

"And even with that he is none too pleased. Yet I think he might make an exception for our invitation. At any rate, we shall send it round."

⊶═◉═⊷

The silent, broad-shouldered Mutano ushered Petrinius into the large library where Astolfo and I stood by the great fireplace awaiting his arrival. It was too warm an evening for fire so Astolfo had ordered the hearth-space cleared and had installed small agate flamesprite statuettes within. From various rooms and corners of the mansion he had brought all his best works of art—paintings, drawings, tapestry screens, ceramic fooleries, ornately bound books—and distributed them around the room. He evidently thought it worth trying to impress our distinguished artist guest.

He even began, after the usual greetings, to make a witty speech of welcome, but Petrinius cut him short. "I came to wolf down your meat and swill your wine and to hear what sort of business you have with me, Astolfo. Let us not waste the hour with rhetorizing."

He was unperturbed and held Petrinius in one of the mildest of his mild gazes, unruffled by the artist's calculated gaucherie, a commodity he seemed to possess in abundant store. Petrinius was a short, almost dwarfish man whose gestures fluttered swiftly and jerkily. I could imagine him as a marionette whose strings were manipulated by a palsied puppeteer. He abounded with nervous energy; it crackled from him as from amber rubbed with lynx fur. His fingers twitched, his feet stuttered on the worn carpet. When he spoke his words flew like darts, and when he was silent his face betrayed his every thought and impulse in a succession of grimaces. One of the common sobriquets bestowed upon him was "Candleflame," and he did indeed flicker with a fiery spirit, every motion animated.

"I am pleased that you have come to taste my wine," Astolfo said. He poured from a dragon-spout flagon a draught of aromatic inky wine for each of us.

Petrinius tossed his portion down his gullet and at once held forth the glass to be filled again.

"I feel no urgency to broach my question," Astolfo said as he poured the proffered glass to the brim, "for I believe you already know what I wish to ask."

Again, Petrinius drained the draught with one noisy swallow

and put forward the silver-enchased goblet. "This will be in the matter of the drawing commissioned by Ser Plermio Rutilius. Am I correct?"

"You are correct," Astolfo said. He smiled gently as again he filled the glass.

"I do not think we can content each other. I have no real knowledge of the shadow to impart and the little I do know must come at a cost to you. I believe you already divine what I shall demand."

"A certain shadow," Astolfo said, "or, more accurately, a portion of it."

"Yes."

"It must be that you are still designing your great mural. What is the title you have given this long-planned masterwork?"

"At present it is called 'The Dead Who March to Shame the State.' Tomorrow it may take a different name. What do you offer me for the bit I can tell?"

"Of the shadow of Malaspino a cutting two fingers' length in breadth. More, if your replies answer to my desire."

"What, then?"

"Do you think Ser Rutilius says true that he knows nothing of the provenance of that shadow you so brilliantly sketched?"

"*Brilliantly?* Do not spend your breath upon flattery. I am aware of my capacities. It is in the interest of Rutilius to tell the truth. Why should he deceive you, his hireling, in the matter?"

Even the mean term, *hireling,* did not discompose Astolfo. "The way of shadow-dealing is as crooked as the shaft of the Great Wain. Did you form any surmises about where it came from?"

"Let us bypass catechism," Petrinius said brusquely. "These things I know from observing the object itself: It passed through few hands before it came to Rutilius; it is fresh and without wear or soilure; it maintains its essential character. I would think the thief entrusted it to a middleman with Rutilius in mind as the sole buyer."

"The one who took the shadow was no thief by vocation or the middleman would have gained the name of the caster from him as a means of protecting himself."

"Of course, of course." Petrinius waved an impatient hand. "It implies too that the price the middleman obtained was of secondary importance to the taker. He wanted chiefly to be rid of the thing."

"Yet not from fear, for the shadow is that of a young woman who could offer little harm."

"Unless she had a lover, brother, or some other protector who would pursue the taker."

Astolfo nodded. "And yet—"

"And yet sufficient time has passed and no one has appeared. And I have some conceit that the lass might be an outcast or orphan."

"A slave girl, mayhap?"

"She is no clumsy bumpkin like your man here," Petrinius said, with a quick contemptuous gesture in my direction. "She has a grace not entirely inherent. She has been cultivated after some fashion."

"As I thought also."

"You have thought already all the things I have said to you. Did you call me here merely to annoy me? Lead me to the table. I will eat my fill and depart." He held out his goblet again.

Astolfo complied, saying, "We shall dine on trout and sorrel, lamb and flageolets shortly. The cook must set his own time to bring us to table. I promise you will not regret his tediousness in the matter."

"Even the most savory of meals is but fuel for the body's brazier," Petrinius said. Then he looked directly into my face and I saw for the first time that his eyes were of different colors, the left an opaque, steely gray, the right a brilliant ice blue. "Has this briar-muncher learned the difference between mutton stew and oat straw? He would seem to be ill fitted for your machinations, Astolfo."

"Oh, Falco does well enough. He only requires a bit of polish."

"As does mule flop, but polish never improves its nature."

"At what weight would you estimate the shadow's caster?"

"No more than eight stone. She will be right-handed, though in walking she will favor her left side. The bones of her arms and especially of her feet will be prominent, her instep a high arch. She is capable of swift movement and also of holding a set pose for a long while. The carriage of her shoulders is almost military in its steadiness and serves to emphasize a long, graceful neck. Her hands are puzzling to me; sometimes I think them too small for her body, sometimes too large."

"How was the shadow stolen from her? Forcefully, with a sudden violence? Or slowly and carefully, when she was unaware?"

"Not by violence. And yet not gradually either. The edges are not abrupt, yet neither are they vague in boundary."

"I will give over three finger-breadths of the shadow of Malaspino. And now we have done with this subject and you may speak at length of the plan of your mural."

"It is to be dark, gloomy dark, in its center. Only the shadow of an evil man taken from him as he stood upon the gallows will supply the necessary blackness. You were on the scaffold with Malaspino, were you not? I have heard the rumors."

"Since all excepting myself now are dead, I can affirm them. I bribed one of the hangman's prentices to keep at home. I wore his robe and the filthy hood he lent. It was his duty to bind the feet of Malaspino just before the trap was sprung, and when I knelt to the bonds, I slipped the shadow away at his boot soles. I had never at that time seen so black a shadow. The doomful poet Edgardo has been using minute parts of it as an admixture to his inkwell for some time now, and his lines grow ever more ominous and sardonic."

"You allude to his poem 'Chance,' of course. 'Bow down before the daemon of the world—This monstrous god, half idiot and half ape.'"

"And to other poems he judges too bitter for auditors of our generation."

"Methinks he too much prides himself," Petrinius said. "His horrors are but apparitions. The ones I portray may be found in council chambers, in courts of law, in the streets of this greasy city. My horrors are the more frightening by far."

"A point well made. And since your appetite is so keen, let us go in to dinner," said Astolfo. "My nose tells me the dishes are ready. We must speak more of your great mural."

He was not loath to do so. Between bold goblets of wine and weighty forkfuls of lamb loin, Petrinius spun out at length his scheme for his beloved project. The name of it kept changing as he warmed to the subject. Sometimes he called it "The Triumphal March of Justice Upon the Contemptible Species"; another time it was "The Furies Well Deserved, or Look Upon Us for What We Are." It was to be his revenge upon history as he knew it, upon life, regarded more as a crime than an affliction. "There shall appear upon my wall figures who will recognize their shames and wail in anger."

"'Twill be a most passionate masterpiece."

"Passion, yes, passion!" Petrinius sputtered fragments of lamb.

"I shall put into it all my brimstone heart and all my skills of hand and eye."

"Will not the images you thus produce work ill upon the actual subjects?" Astolfo asked. "For I have heard it told of Manoni his art was so powerful that when he drew in ill will a person's likeness, that one fell sick. Some, they say, came near death."

"Pah." Petrinius took a generous swallow of wine. "Those are legends merely. Old superstitions. And I am not certain that Manoni deserves all his musty repute. I can show you clumsy passages in his best work."

"So then, it is not true that an artist's portrayal may alter the condition of his subject? I had always heard otherwise."

"It is not true, though many of the brotherhood promote the falsity. But of shadows, however, it is a truth. It can come about that the portrait of a shadow can affect the appearance of that shade, for good or for ill."

"I see. Is it the passion of the artist which effects this result?"

"That is one of the things, but now I perceive you work to worm secrets from me. Yet I am no longer thirsty or hungry and so will depart."

"Mayn't we tempt you with one thing more? A sweet wine of the Sunshine Isles? A fresh melon?"

"Useless to squander fine manners on me, Astolfo. I bid you good night."

⋅→═◉═←⋅

After Petrinius had taken his brusque and tipsy leave, brandishing happily above his head a moleskin packet containing his patch from the shadow of Malaspino, Astolfo proposed that we go into the small library for a last glass to invite slumber. Mutano was already there and sat at his ease by the writing table. A decanter of sherry and three small glasses stood ready.

At first Astolfo and Mutano conferred in one of their finger dialects with which I was unfamiliar and I wondered what their discussion concerned. Astolfo poured and we sipped in a momentary, contemplative silence. Then he turned to me: "What did we discover this evening?"

"That this Petrinius is eager to have his ears boxed," I said. "His artistry, however estimable on paper and canvas, does not extend to courtesy."

"Yes, he too referred to you as a cowherd chaff-brain. You are recognized in every place."

"Under your tutelage I shall become an urbane scholar, a polished wit and silken murmurer of vain compliment," I said. "You shall yet be proud of your creation."

My little sally must have caught him unawares, for he paused to consider. "There might be something in this widely held apprehension to your advantage. It is rarely a mistake to appear less able than you are. The more willing others are to think you a fool, the more you should strive to appear so."

I nodded. His words strengthened my hope that our association might continue for a while. I now counted four years in his service and calculated—or hoped—that four more would establish me in an independent enterprise.

Astolfo went on: "What physical attributes did you observe that would contribute to his power as an artist?"

"I am surprised at his comportment. He is a creature of jerks and starts, wriggles and itchings. He contorts his body as continually and absurdly as his facial expressions change, yet his drawing is easy and gossamer; it seems to have been breathed upon the page."

"We cannot suppose that the man who swills grape and engorges flesh at table is the same as he who stands before the easel. Once he engages the discipline of his craft, his demeanor and personality will change. The priest who expounds a pious and arcane theology in the morning is not the same as the identical priest you encounter that evening in the drunken brothel."

"He coils and uncoils like an adder in embers."

"To aid his way of seeing. Did you not take notice of his eyes?"

"They are of different colors."

"The clear blue is quick and precise. The left eye, colored like the iron of a dagger-blade, was shattered blind in a street brawl. He has to move his head continually to see things in the round. The loss of sight in one eye has given him an advantage in depicting shadows."

"He has, then, acquired a valuable infirmity."

"He has made it valuable. His infirmities and eccentricities are avidly cultivated. His aloofness of manner and careless speech signal an independent spirit free of sycophancy, and this bravura elevates the fees he commands. Where another might eat toads to gain favor, Petrinius spits venom and is the more prized. His great mural when finished will stand as one of the most powerful of misanthropic statements. Many in this city shall be furious to recognize themselves therein. If he includes representations of their shadows, those will suffer sad decline. The scrap of shadow from the felon Malaspino has lent him more power. Some high-placed persons will be savagely drawn in his panoply of rascality."

"'Tis risky," I said. "Some there are of the nobility would have him taken off the planet if he set them cross-grain."

"He depends upon his genius to protect him. Did you note what he said about how the shade was thieved in the first place?"

"He did not know. He said it was neither taken by force nor eased away quietly and subtly."

"You know the first two ways in which shadows are taken?"

"By stealth," I said, "and that is called *severing*. By violence, and that is called *sundering*. The third I do not know, as you have not yet informed me."

"Yet you might easily think it out for yourself. How do you acquire a possession of another and leave no trace of theft?"

I was momentarily perplexed. "Well, I suppose if I purchased it, or if someone gave the thing to me—"

"If you voluntarily allow someone to take your shadow, it leaves no trace of theft or even of the act of taking. This act is called the *surrendering*."

"People do not lightly give up their shadows," I replied. "Under what circumstance would anyone do so?"

"That is the question I shall put to myself as I sleep. If my pillow is as informative as I hope it shall be, perhaps the three of us may need to wander about the city tomorrow," Astolfo said. He and Mutano began their silent colloquy again, their fingers busy as a flock of sparrows in a mulberry.

I left them at it, retired to my solitary, almost barren room, doffed my clothing, bedded myself, and slept like a sentry relieved from a six-sandglass watch.

⊷══◉══⊷

On the next morning, after my customary lone and frugal breakfast, I was standing in the east garden. My eyes were closed as I turned round and round, judging the placement of the shadows there. It is an error to suppose, as I had done before entering apprenticeship, that comprehension of shadows is exclusively a matter of the eye. All the senses are engaged. I listened to the breezes as they mingled darker and lighter tints together; I smelled the differences between those plants that were in the shade of wall or tree and those that stood in full sun; I tasted the perfumes of the air with the tip of my tongue; I felt on my face the dapple that fell upon me through the newly leaved plane tree. I heard with special pleasure birdsong, how when it pours from the interior darkness of a thick bush, it lightens and rises minutely in pitch as it trills out of the foliage into the bright day.

I thought that I was aware of all around me, but this illusion was rudely dispelled by a sudden, solid, but not vicious kick to my arse. Mutano, my comrade and the maestro's bear-sized manservant, he who looked as if he would shamble when he walked, could move as silently as any midnight wraith. I was grateful to him for his boot up my backside. In another, similar situation an actual opponent could have buried a dagger in my spine.

He beckoned me to follow him into the small library, where Astolfo sat in a worn leather armchair. He seemed half asleep when we entered and spoke in a lazy, almost slovenly drawl. This was his mode of speech when his mind was occupied with a problem. "My search has not been fruitless," he said, "but its results are uncertain. We shall go within the hour to the workplace of the ballet master Maxinnio. Before we leave, you must drink the pot of tea which has been prepared for you. That will give you excuse and opportunity to examine his establishment. Mutano shall serve as our protector, if need be, and also as observer, for, to say truly, I do not know entirely what to expect of this visit. My surmise of the matter may be correct or it may err. At any rate, you and I shall go unarmed, but Mutano will bear his short sword. . . . And so, prepare."

As bidden, I went to my room, performed brief ablutions, put on a clean doublet, and downed in hasty gulps the pot of bayberry tea that had been set out. Then I joined Astolfo and Mutano in the front of the main hall and we departed. Astolfo, I noted, had changed attire and was dressed in the customary gold-and-green trunks and doublet of a spice merchant. If he hoped to disguise himself, this clothing would not suffice. Master-of-shadows Astolfo was recognized by everyone in the city of Tardocco.

⊷═◉═⊶

The door to Maxinnio's establishment was a shabby, unvarnished affair of oak boards with a small square cutout to see through. It was opened by a girl of ten or twelve years in a gray scullery smock;

she was unremarkable except for the great, dark, almond-shaped eyes set in her young, impassive face. The solemn eyes seemed older than the smudged face, a feature apart. Silently she showed us up the stairs to the studio salon.

Here were a half-dozen young girls stretching legs and torsos, clothed in the traditional white tights and frilly short skirts. Ranging in age from perhaps twelve to sixteen years, they leapt and pirouetted under the cold eye of a gray-haired chorus mistress. Maxinnio sat upon a campaign stool, looking without much interest upon the girls. The bored lutenist in his spare, wooden chair did not so much as glance at them.

Nor did Astolfo, as he hurried over to bow to Maxinnio and to press his unenthusiastic hand. Mutano and I gave each of the girls close and furtive examination, as we had been instructed to do. For me, such instruction was superfluous. These were remarkably pretty girls, in the very dawning of their beauty. I tried to ignore distraction, to concentrate on what I was looking out for.

"Strange colors for a shadow thief to wear, Astolfo," Maxinnio said. "Why such a gaudy getup so early in the day?"

"Is it not jolly? I am happy that my thieving days, if ever there had been any, should lie behind me so that I can sport such livery as this. Today my green-and-gold signifies that I am just now in the service of another, a wealthy spice merchant who does not care to have his identity bruited about."

"What have I to do with spice merchants, whatever motley they require you to wear?"

"He is wealthy, and that datum must interest you."

"How so?"

"Because he is considering whether he may wish to invest funds in your company of dancers."

"Did you bring this mass of gold with you, Astolfo, so that you require two ruffians to guard the treasure? Your dumb manservant I have seen before, this Mutton, or whatever he is called."

"Mutano," Astolfo said. "He is the most discreet of persons."

"Let him keep so. But who is this clay-foot ox-goader by his side? He looks as if grasshoppers might spring from his codpiece."

"He enjoys to be called Falco and I perceive he is in a state of discomfort. I think he may have been swilling ale even at this early hour, and if so shall not be in my service by this afternoon. Perhaps there is a place here where he may relieve himself."

"Out the door and down the long hall to the end he will find a pissing room. If some girl has engaged it, he must hold his water until she leaves," he said, and added: "I do not like the look of this Falco."

"I plan to improve his appearance," Astolfo said, and waved me away.

Mutano's bitter tea had worked its way with me so that I fairly trotted down the gloomy hall to an open door within which stood a row of four stoneware pissing jars. No female was in the room, so I closed the door and went about my business, making sure, according to instruction, that my urination would be audible even through the walls. Anyone set to watch me would be satisfied with the legitimacy of my need.

Afterward, I stood listening for a moment, then stole to the door and opened it gradually. The hall was deserted and I went into it, going along slowly and silently, stopping by each of the doors to listen for any sound within.

At the end of the hall was a stairway, and I fancied that music sounded from the floor above. I mounted quietly to the door that closed off the stairs at the top. Here I heard distinctly the soft strains of harp music. When I tried to ease the door open, I found it locked. I was gratified. To pry back this lock with a short strap of stiff leather was the work of brief moments. Anyone inside would be unlikely to guard closely a locked door.

When I inched it ajar and peeped through I could see clearly because a panel of the roof was drawn back and daylight poured down upon a lank, abstracted youth with curly locks who sat playing his harp as if rapt by the music he produced. A girl dressed all in white tights to her neck danced in the sunlight. She did not wear the usual pleated dancer's skirt.

She could not be above sixteen years and so slender within the white sheath she wore that she looked like a spiral curl of silver as she made a slow turn with her hands held aloft. On her toes she barely touched the floor and so weightless-seeming were her motions that a puff of air might have carried her up and away like the downy dandelion seed. She looked upward, following the line of her arms to her small, long-fingered hands, and her blonde hair hung long and free down her back. She would be the principal dancer of Maxinnio's troupe, and she danced in the shaft of light as the spirit of loneliness. She moved as if she were the only being in a separate world. I felt that in looking upon her I looked upon my own spirit as I sometimes conceived it in melancholy humor—alone and un-companioned in a moment of halted time, in a place that could not be reached from ordinary space. If every human soul is an orphan, as Astolfo once averred, this young girl embodied the soul of that soul.

I watched her, transfixed for long moments, before I recognized one of the things that caused her to emit such an atmosphere of soli-tude. Although she danced within a wide beam of full daylight, she cast no shadow on the polished maple floor. Shadowless, she seemed to burn in her space, a cool, silver flame as pure as starlight frozen in ice. The absence of a shadow attached her more closely to the music; she seemed a part of the music, as if when the harpist gently rippled his strings, he was caressing her figure with his fingertips, bringing from her, and not from his instrument, the strains and measures that fell upon my ears.

With difficulty I brought myself away down the stairs and re-turned to the salon where Maxinnio and Astolfo held conference among the other dancers. All the way back again through the dim, grimy hallway the sight of the silver dancer floated before me. When I came into the room with the harsher light and the different music and the prancing girls, the sensation was disagreeable. Everything, and especially the dancers, seemed tawdry and dull and clumsy. Afore-time I had found the room pleasant enough, but now it was im-mediately stale, flat, and tiresome.

Astolfo greeted me. "Well, Falco, you have been gone a good long time space. I must congratulate you on your bladder capacity. Perhaps we shall engage for you in a pissing tournament."

"It was tea and not ale that I had drunk," I said. "My innards are not so avid to entertain mere tea."

"Must we spend more time hearing how your oaf makes water?" asked Maxinnio. "I hold the subject a shallow one."

"Perhaps we have overstrained your hospitality," said Astolfo. "Now that I have learned from you that you have no desire and no need to open your company to the investment of my client, we may decide our business is concluded."

"It is well concluded, Astolfo," Maxinnio declared. "I do not know why you have come knocking upon my door, with unsavory fellows at your heel, blathering some suppositious story about a spice merchant. Whatever underhand affair you have under way, I am to be left out. And there's an end on't."

"I am sure you know best," Astolfo said. He bowed and then Mutano and I bowed and the gray-smocked, great-eyed girl showed us down the stairs to the street. The lute music grew louder behind us.

When I told Astolfo about the dancer I had spied upon, we were sitting in his large kitchen. He enjoyed this room, with its enormous oven, its walls glowing with copper pans and kettles, its smells of breads and spices. He drew himself up backward and perched on the huge butcher block. We drank new ale from clay tankards and chewed on black bread and sour goat cheese.

When I finished my account, he closed his eyes and nodded. "The dancing master must have been asked to prepare an important entertainment for the municipality and has designed a particularly gratifying dance. You glimpsed her in rehearsal, Falco, and were transported. The full spectacle shall surely glow famously."

"It is a sight worth living to see," I avowed.

"Maxinnio will not be eager to give over this paragon of dance to Ser Rutilius."

"He will not give her over," I said. "Nor would you once you had set eyes upon her."

"You are certain it is her shadow in the Ser's cage of glass?"

"It can be no other."

"Then we must find out our choices. What would Rutilius do if we delayed a while and then reported to him that we could not trace the caster of his shadow?"

"He would pay others to discover her."

"How might they do so?"

I thought. "He would tell these others that we had failed. Then they would follow in our footsteps, seeking any sort of intelligence. By that time our visit to Maxinnio's dancers would be known and they would find the silver dancer and inform Rutilius."

"When once Rutilius knew that we had seen her, he would consider that—"

"That we had betrayed him, having designs of our own. He would not be pleased."

"What of the girl, once he knows where and what she is?"

"He will abduct her, despite all that Maxinnio can do."

"And then?"

I shrugged. "I cannot say. He shall have attained his desire. He shall possess the girl."

"The consequence of this possession?"

"I cannot say."

"There can be but one consequence. Did you gain any impression of her? Not of the dancer, but of the girl apart from the dance?"

I waited, but nothing came to mind. "I think there is no girl apart from the dance."

He blinked his eyes and nodded once, gravely. "Because she casts no shadow. Like the music itself, she casts no shadow. She has been changed like those boys lopped of their coillons to become soprano singers, pure vessels of the art. Apart from her dance, she hardly exists. Petrinius understood this matter. His drawing of the shadow has more vital spirit, more spark of the soul, than does the shadow itself. And the shadow has more breath of spirit than does the girl who cast it."

"How does this fact serve Rutilius? I see advantage in it only for Maxinnio and the spectacle he is planning."

"'Twould serve him ill," he said, "and ourselves also. We must look for some other avenue of success or of escape."

"How so?"

He shrugged. "I am a-weary of pondering and drawing up schemes. My wits are not so nimble as formerly. Why do you not tickle the ribs of your ingenuity and produce a plan for us to follow?"

"I shall attempt to do so," I said. I sounded my words out light and eager, trying to disguise my unconfident apprehension.

"We will await with indrawn breath your masterpiece of machination," Astolfo said. "You shall deliver it mid-morning tomorrow."

Well, I would have to prepare some scheme or other for the morrow, that was certain. Certain too was the fact that it would be dismissed by the shadow master as harebrained, lackwitted, and impossible of execution. Therefore I did not trouble myself deeply about the matter and took his words to imply that this evening was mine to consume in whatever way I desired.

And so I stepped out across Tardocco to The Heart of Agate, these days my favored tavern in which to re-create body and mind.

It was there, between bouts of tankards and bed-thumping, during one of those floating moments when I began to doubt the healthful value of such dissipation, that a glimmer of a notion entered my head and I abruptly and unsteadily betook me homeward. It was no thunderbolt conception, but even so I did not want to drown it in ale-swamp forgetfulness.

⊶⊷

I rose late, only just before the appointed hour, composed my corpus as best I could, and went out of doors to greet Astolfo where he sat in the springtime splendor under the great chestnut in the east garden. He eyed me with humorous disdain, shook his head, but said nothing. Mutano, standing by a small rustic table, poured a foaming beaker of ale from a pitcher with a cracked spout. I tried to turn from the sight and smell of it, but he thrust it upon me and I drank and began to feel a little better. He had infused it with some sort of spice that so inflamed the palate I had to fumble for speech when Astolfo put his question.

"You cannot gauge with what eager anticipation we have waited your proposal," he said gaily. "Speak out at once and dispel our anxiety."

It hurt to swallow, but after I had done so, I said, "Did not you tell me that Ser Rutilius spent much of his youth in headstrong dissipations and carefree frivolities?"

He made no answer, so I plunged on. "He must have sown wild seed during this time. Perhaps he has fathered one or two that he knows nothing of. Perhaps he could be persuaded that the dancer is one of these, his own daughter."

"What then?"

"Then he can have no use for her as bedmate and will leave her to stay as she is, where she is."

"Yet he already adores her shadow to distraction. Will he not be proud to acknowledge the work of his flesh, seeing what dear loveliness it hath brought forth? Will he not be more avid than ever to have her within his house?"

"As his daughter—that is, as his supposed daughter—she may prevail upon him to accede to her wishes."

"And will not a young girl of no fortune, apprenticed to a stiff-willed tyrant of the ballet, be pleased to find a wealthy and doting father and enter into a life of luxurious ease and well-being?"

"Not if she be wedded to her dance and its music," I replied. "And that is what I saw when I watched her. It is difficult to imagine that she would give up the art willingly."

"Willingly she gave up her shadow."

Now I began to falter. "But that—that is different . . ."

He spoke as if from the depths of lassitude, uttering the very phrase I had foreknown. "This will not serve. The risks are too threatening." But then he surprised me. "And yet, there is something in't to ponder on. Let us befriend our thoughts a while longer. You can be meditating upon it while Mutano instructs you in the brave art of the whip. The whip is a way of taking shadows you may not yet have considered."

⋆⋰▤◖⋆⋰

Three days passed in which Astolfo seemed to neglect the entire affair: the commission of Ser Rutilius, Maxinnio, and the shadowless dancer. I kept busy, of course; my training seemed never to abate for two hours together. Now the emphasis was on drawing. I had been ordered for a space of time last twelvemonth to draw the shapes of shadows splayed across irregular surfaces: the shadow of Mutano as he stood at the corner of the clay-walled springhouse in the back garden so that it appeared halved on both walls, the shadow of the black cat Creeper where he crouched by the rough stones of the outer wall, the shadow of my own left hand as it fell upon a clot of harebells.

It was soon discovered that I possessed no talent as a draughtsman, but Astolfo explained that the case was of small moment. This exercise was to train my discernment of the shapes that surfaces can make of umbrae; it was a study in recognitions.

But this new assignment of drawing was less a geometry exercise and more in the vein of art. I sat with a sheaf of paper, trying to render likenesses not of shadows but of their casters: garden urns, hyacinths, a quince bush, the sleeping form of Creeper, the huge hands of Mutano. Now and again Astolfo would stop by, leaf through a handful of my drawings, and with a finely pointed length of graphite make swift corrections. Each of his strokes was a revelation and, though I learned much in a short time, it was clear that I was destined to be no Manoni or Petrinius, and I felt, as I often had before, that many hours were misspent.

I was pleased, therefore, when Astolfo informed me we were to

pay another call upon Maxinnio and that I should prepare to answer certain questions that might be put to me. "I do not foresee
that he will query you," Astolfo said, "but it is ever best to prepare.
You are to recall each detail about the dancer you saw who has no
shadow. If you are asked, you must answer truthfully."

"He will not be glad to find we know of her," I said. "If he offer
to fight, shall I combat him?"

"I do not think you would fare brilliantly in swordplay with a
dancing master. We must soon lesson you in dancing to lessen your
pudding-footed lubbardness."

"But if he offer fight?"

"He will not," Astolfo said. "Go ready yourself. We leave within
the hour."

⁘

Yet when we set out again Astolfo had buckled on that sword he
called the Deliverer. This time he did not bedeck himself in the cut
and colors of a spice merchant, all green and gold, but wore his
ordinary habit of russet doublet and trunks, and soft boots whose
floppy tops concealed ingenious pockets. He carried now a rolled
case of pliable leather, of the sort used to transport largish maps.

We walked at leisurely pace into this seedy square of town with
its sleepy shops of tailors and shoemakers, tinkers and tapsters. When
we knocked at the street door of Maxinnio's establishment, it was
opened again by the young girl who had attended us before. This
time, at Astolfo's suggestion, I observed her more closely, but she was
only as I remembered: a thin little thing of medium stature, with
the jet hair and great dark eyes that shone like wet onyx. Of her
figure in the dingy, gray scullery smock I could tell little.

When she led us into the rehearsal salon, the scene was as before, with the severe ballet mistress yapping crossly at her charges,
the weary lutenist fingering along in rote fashion, and the lanky
Maxinnio on his leather campaign stool, rapping the floor rhyth-
mically with a short silver-headed cane.

He did not weep for joy at our appearance. "Here you are again,
Astolfo," he snapped. "It seems you feel bound by some compul-
sion I cannot fathom to honor me with your presence and with the
company of your overgrown henchmen."

"I bid you good morrow," Astolfo said in his mild voice.

"Have you auctioned off all your store of spices? I see you fitted today in a more customary livery."

"Today I come in my own interest and not in that of the merchant."

"That merchant who did not exist in the first place."

"That is true," Astolfo said. "But you must not complain of being deceived. You did not credit my tale from the beginning. I had not really thought to deceive someone so perspicacious as Maxinnio."

"Now I sniff arrant trickery," he replied. "I warn you that if I grow impatient with your pitiable ruses, I shall have my troupe of young girls pitch you through the window onto the cobblestones. They will likewise defenestrate these two footpads that hang to you like baubles on earlobes."

"Cry you mercy," said Astolfo. "The day is too shiny new; a shame if violence should mar it. I came only to acquaint you with some intelligence that may not yet be in your possession."

"You came to monger gossip? I think you will not expect to be paid for this intelligence, as you call it."

"Only look upon these drawings I have brought. I am curious to know your judgment of these works." Astolfo untied the laces of the leather case and began to unroll it.

"The only artworks in which I am now interested are the designs for my new ballet," Maxinnio said. "The preparatory sketches are useless and we must begin them anew."

"But only glance at this bit of handiwork." Astolfo unrolled a drawing on fine-wove paper and held it up before the dance master.

When Maxinnio blinked his eyes wide and gave a start that shook his whole body, I edged around to see what image must have produced such a reaction. I judged it would be in our interest for me to give but a lackadaisical, cool look at the drawing, but when I saw the figure there I too was surprised and intook my breath audibly. Maxinnio did not notice, staring fixedly as he was, oblivious to all else.

Here was the dancer without a shadow, the girl I had spied through the cracked door on the floor above. This was her face uplifted, her figure weightless and elongated, her arms raised above her flowing hair, her slender hands thrusting into the light of day.

My late exercises in art, clumsy as they had been, gave me to appreciate, to savor, the achievement that lay on the sheet Astolfo upheld.

When Maxinnio turned his eyes from the drawing to the shadow master, his face was full of rage, every feature contorted. He looked for all the world like one of those small statues of demons that are set out to fend away evil spirits from temple gardens. When he spoke, his voice was low, choking with fury. "I would have your life for this."

"My henchmen, as you name them, will answer for my safety," Astolfo said. "Anyway, why do you threaten? I have brought this exquisite picture as a gift for you."

"This dancer is my secret. She is the guarantee of my success with the new entertainment. I do not understand how you come by her likeness. She has not been seen abroad. I keep her close. No one is to see her until the ballet of *'The Sylphs of Light'* " is presented in the new season."

"She will not appear in your dance of sylphs. She will never dance in public."

"She must. All is settled and cast as in stone."

"You have rescued from a meager and grudging life many a young girl," Astolfo said. "You have made the pliable ones into dancers and found employment for some of the others. But your interest in them reaches only so far as the boundary of your professional purposes. You know little of where they come from or who they are or may have been."

"I maintain neither orphanage nor almshouse," Maxinnio said. "The girls learn to be not persons but only dancers. They learn to live solely for dance, as I do live."

"And that is why you do not know even the true name of this girl. That is how you could with impunity strip her of her shadow, sell it away so she could not retrieve it, and present her onstage in perfect purity."

"I could easily rid them all of their shadows. But only this one embodies the ideal I search for. It is not shadow-lack that composes her perfection."

"But I have found that she is the natural daughter of a great and powerful noble who does not care to have her prance before the garlicky, mutton-gorging rabble. You are to hand her over to me to deliver to him and thus spare your own life and the lives of those in your employ, at the same time preventing the razing of this place to smoking embers."

"Who is this giant terror you threaten me with?"

"You shall not know that."

"How do I know that he exists?"

"Because I tell you so and have the picture of her. . . . Here, look you upon this other likeness. What do you observe?" Astolfo rolled up the drawing of the dancer and gave it to Mutano, who secured it with a black satin ribbon. Then he unfurled another drawing and held it up as before.

Maxinnio gave this new image a puzzled glance, then leaned forward in his little chair and peered closely. "I think I know this shadow," he said, "but I cannot say how."

"It is the shadow of your silver dancer, the shade you bartered away."

He shook his head. "No. Her shadow is a thing of unparalleled grace. There is something askew about the drawing of this one. It is impaired. It looks as if some wasting disease has befallen it, some distemper that racks its shape."

"That is the condition it has acquired since it left your hands. This drawing depicts how the shadow now looks at this moment. I shall deliver it to the girl's father. From this picture of her shadow he will draw certain conclusions about how she is being treated here. When his anger is at its flaming peak, I shall tell him your name and show him where to seek you out."

"You would play me false and destroy me and my work. . . . For what purpose?" Maxinnio demanded. "There has been no enmity between us. I hold you in perfect indifference. If you go to ruin me, it will be only in order to fatten your purse."

"The father will reward me when his daughter is restored to him. There may be payment also for you."

"I care not." Maxinnio clenched and unclenched his hand, rapped the floor with his ebony cane. "Heap your coin till it drown you. My concern is with my *'Sylphs of Light.'* If I could spare my silver dancer, she should go to her father on wings of wind. But the entertainment cannot afford her absence."

Astolfo gave the picture of the shadow to Mutano, who rolled it up and secured it with a red ribbon. "And now, if you will examine this third rendering." He unscrolled before Maxinnio a last drawing, a likeness of another young dancer. The pose was the same as in the picture of the silver girl, but this girl had black hair instead of blonde and the eyes that gazed sunward were of shining onyx. Though not so tall as the other girl, she was equally graceful, a creature of calm and guileless movement, with the ease of brook water.

Maxinnio looked at it with grave care. "This is an interesting fantasy of what a dancer might aspire to. No one but Petrinius could have drawn it so, but it is not a study from life. If 'twere, I would find the girl and put her to use."

"The drawing is not taken from life, but the girl is real enough. You may be acquainted with her. She is called Leneela."

"I think not," Maxinnio said. "The one Leneela I know is but a little servant girl in our household. She has been sweeping stones and scrubbing floors and pots for three years now since her mother died."

"This is she."

"If it be she, how could I not recognize her in this guise?"

"She is so customary to your eyes that she became invisible."

"She is no dancer, only a scullery maid."

"She can be trained."

"In time, perhaps, if she have ability. But time is short."

"You speak as if you had choice in the matter. The father will claim his silvery daughter. I have offered you another to take her place. There is no cost to you except a delay in presenting your 'Sylphs.' You can bargain a deferment."

"That will not be simple and will incur further expense."

"Expenses will be compensated. Again, I tell you that you have no choice. A carriage will call for the girl at first twilight. You will ascertain that she is in the best of condition and will hand her into the carriage yourself. To join a child with its parent—that is a handsome thing to do."

"Handsome or foul-featured, it shall be done. Yet I will not forget this tiresome japery you have turned upon me."

"I have saved your life," Astolfo said.

⊶⊜⊷

It was early evening before the three of us came together again, sitting at a table laid out in the kitchen, dividing an enormous beef and kidney pie Astolfo had got from the cook Iratus. A cask of aged cider stood ready to ease down the meat. The shadow master had traveled earlier in the day to the château of Rutilius and arranged how the girl was to come into his household.

"I hope this will prove a fortunate event for the lass," I said. "'Tis a sorrow, her loss to the art of the dance."

He nodded gaily and said he was obliged to me for a happy thought.

"How so?"

"I have told Ser Rutilius that I believe her to be his natural daughter and pointed out several similarities of feature and physique. You suggested some such thing. We may well have preserved both of them from destruction."

"Destruction?"

"One who falls in love with a shadow loves an image of the ideal. No woman can approach to the perfection of such a fond delusion. When disappointment and disillusion set in, a rank distaste for the fleshly person follows, for she will be seen as a betrayer of the ideal, a spoiler of the perfection that once gloriously existed. In a passionate man, revenge will come to seem a necessity. The blade, the noose, the poison goblet stand forth in the mind, palpable and inescapable. There is none so desperate, none so dangerous, as one whose ideals have crumbled."

"It is well to deceive him then, in the matter of blood ties," I said.

"If indeed we have deceived. It is yet plausible that she is his own."

"Will he not go now to seek the mother and verify your story?"

"Alas!" Astolfo cried. "In my vivid account, the mother was strangled by a jealous lover and thrown into the harbor. The sea laves her sorrowful bones ceaselessly."

"And this lover? Shall not Ser Rutilius look for his track?"

"Alack! He has repented himself and lives in exile in the Fog Islands, leading a solitary, miserable existence lamenting the excesses of his former life."

"A pretty fable. But there are yet matters I do not comprehend. How was it possible for Petrinius to make the three drawings? He had seen neither of the girls and he had no way to observe how the shadow had deteriorated."

"I knew that he would have made for his own collection a copy of the drawing he made for Rutilius. I asked him to make another, only altering it as if the shadow had started to deteriorate."

"And the girls? I do not comprehend how he could have seen either of them without his presence at Maxinnio's establishment being remarked."

"Petrinius did not see either girl."

"How then did he make their likenesses?"

"He made none." Astolfo swallowed heartily from his mug of cider, set it down, and wiped his mouth with his wrist. "But there are others in this land who can draw besides that vain and impertinent artist. In fact, I have been known to dash off a sketch now and then, sometimes in the manner of Manoni, or the Anonymous Citadel Master, or even in the style of Petrinius himself."

"You produced those fine drawings? But you did not see the silver dancer. You were in the salon below, distracting Maxinnio from my prying."

"I made attentive note of your description of her," he said. "And then, of course, there was Petrinius's rendering of her shadow. Look you, Falco, if a person may cast a shadow, why may not a shadow cast a person?"

"A shadow may cast—"

"Can cast the *image* of a girl, at least. Think upon your own lustful and lurid fancies. Do they not drive you out into the town in fair weather or foul? Do they not compel you to deceive yourself that a sooty tavern wench is the ideal of grace and beauty? The shadow-ideal in your mind casts Greasy Joan as the rose-cheeked handmaid of Venus. The shadow is the engine of your conception of the actual."

Mutano nudged me with his toe. He carved in air the hourglass shape of a voluptuous female. He rolled his eyes and licked his lips and panted heavily, miming Uncontrollable Lust. Never before had I disliked him so earnestly.

The continual rites of physical punishments and spiritual rigors had at last become too cumbrous to be borne. I resolved to request— to demand, if need be—a commission that I could fulfill under my own volition and by my own, personally conceived means.

IV

The Creeper Shadows

Haughty, hard-eyed, horse-faced: I formed no favorable impression of this tall woman in her long gray smock the slender young footman had summoned forth. I was not tuneful in temper anyway and when she inquired my name and station, I handed her Astolfo's letter of introduction without other response. She swept away, leaving me alone in the foyer.

She had reckoned me a servant like herself, but I took pride to stand as confidential aide to Astolfo, especially upon this occasion when a possible venture had been entrusted to my hands. I had dressed with particular care in forest-green doublet, tawny trunks, and shining black calf-length boots still spotless of mud, even though I had walked from Astolfo's mid-town villa across Tardocco to this manse of the Esquire Sativius on the outskirts. Red gloves with silver piping I had donned and my wine-red cap sported a brash white plume. It should be obvious that I was no menial, yet that equinous woman had taken but cursory notice of my finery. I was overdressed, but in that time I still suffered from the embarrassment of the ridiculous motley I was forced to wear at the palace of the three-personed Countess Trinia. I had resolved henceforth to present a more fashionable appearance.

She did not hasten to return, and so I took leisurely stock of my surroundings. The house was a rambling two-story edifice of weathered gray brick. A bay window checkered with glass and alabaster panes fronted the protruding second story that overhung the portico with its sturdy oaken columns. The foyer floor was of unpolished flagstone and the door that led to the farther rooms was of lightly varnished chestnut. In short, here was just the sort of domicile one would expect to enter when visiting the wealthy merchant rope-dealer Matteo Sativius.

I drew four deep breaths, anxious because this was the first commission of any true import that Astolfo had entrusted solely to my care. Five swift and crowded seasons I had spent in his employ: five seasons of grueling training under the large and horny hand of Mutano, five years of scanning closely printed books and manuals, of undertaking grubby, piddling tasks and assignments, of enduring unending if cheerful contumely and admonition. This harsh period had steeled my disposition, I fancied. It was a course of life much like preparing for a priesthood, except that at the end of it, I hoped to amass wealth in golden hillocks instead of an airy bower in a painted paradise. I had learned a great deal, though not as much as I would need to know. But I had finally acquitted myself satisfactorily in the business with Countess Trinia, and I had shown some spirit in dealing with the puppet shadow that threatened the existence of the puppet master Drolio, and I had exhibited, according to the maestro, some power of reasoning in the matter of the Mardrake toys that cast such gigantic umbrae over the children to whom they had been given.

Astolfo had told me little of this present affair in hand. " 'Tis some difficulty concerning the umbrae of offspring," he said. "I am otherwise occupied just now and so I leave all to you. There may be a plumpish fee. This Sativius is reputed generous."

"Will Mutano accompany me?" I asked, thinking that if there were danger involved I should be glad of the presence of my over-large drillmaster.

"Mutano has in train a serious personal business," Astolfo said. "He may require your assistance as it progresses. He is already enlisting the aid of Creeper."

"Of Creeper?" I was not easily surprised these days by what I learned from Astolfo, but now I was astonished. Creeper is the largest, oldest, and blackest of all the sixteen cats that haunt the grounds and outbuildings of the manse. Mutano had never evinced fondness for Creeper or for any other of the feline troop.

The shadow master shrugged his rounded shoulders, spread his nimble hands in a dismissive gesture, and said, "They are spheres unto themselves, the man and the cat. I know only that Mutano is engaged with the animal for endless hours, and I know the nature of the task he has set himself and that he holds it to be of the greatest importance."

"He wishes me to aid him?"

"So he has signaled."

That was another imponderable conceit, that my master in the art of the sword and of the shadow-sundering blades, of purse-snipping, lock-tickling, and so forth, might desire, even perhaps require, my assistance. He had always fixed me in sardonic regard.

The train of my suppositions broke sharply when the gangly gray-smocked woman returned. She handed me unopened Astolfo's introductory letter and with the crooking of a finger bade me follow her through a large salon muffled with carpet and darkened with wall hangings, up the stair, and around a gallery into the room of the bay window. She ushered me into the presence of the Esquire Sativius and his spouse, Funisia, and retreated toward the doorway, making me feel rather as if I had been deposited before the older couple as a lump of merchandise to be considered for purchase.

It did not suit me that the light from the bay window flooded their figures from behind, making their faces dark, so I began to sidle little by little, making a leg here and a bow there, in a half circle until the light was more in my favor.

Making much show, Sativius broke Astolfo's seal, unfolded the heavy page, and took his own good while perusing what would have been only a short message. When he had done, he gazed upon me with a frown that almost knit his bushy white eyebrows together. I judged him to be of sound middle age, with his salt-and-pepper beard jutting over his wimpled collar and his smooth hands emerging from starchy, frilled cuffs. He wore a ceremonial short sword.

"I had expected your master to come to my summons," he said. His voice was soft but held reserves of authority.

"Maestro Astolfo tenders his regrets," I replied. "A mortally urgent business closely touching upon his person prevents his presence. I am his confidential secretary Falco, as I think his letter informs you. I am authorized to act on his behalf in every particular."

He turned to look at his wife Funisia. She was somdel younger than her man, with a face that retained much of its youth, a comely countenance. In figure she was not tall, but there was a grace about her that suggested height. Her dress was modest, with a full skirt, dark blue silk bodice open only at the clavicles, her dark hair worn in a braid coiled around the crown. Her only jewel was a small diamond set in a wedding ring. Demurely she met her husband's gaze with a smile and a brief nod.

"You will make report to Maestro Astolfo complete with all detail?"

"Assuredly."

"In brief, then, the case is this: Funisia and I are the parents of twins, the one a boy and older by less than an hour, t'other a girl. Except for the difference of the sexes, they are identical. They are devoted each to the other and are reluctant to part company for any reason, even for those of necessity of nature. They never argue or quarrel; even their sharpest disagreements are sweetly couched. We have doted upon them perhaps too closely, they being the offspring of our middle years. Yet, tightly as we kept watch, we failed to note a fault in their two physiques and were astonished to find it out. It came to our notice only this sennight past."

"Is it not a defect a medico might reflect upon?" I asked.

"Only one of our children possesses a shadow," Sativius said. "The other is quite bare of any umbra whatsoever."

I stood silent for a moment, trying to fix the conceit in my mind. "One shadow only between them?"

"Yes."

"To which of them belongeth the shadow, lad or lass?"

"We cannot say. When they are close together it seems to attach to both of them at once. When they are separate, it will go to one or other as it seems to choose."

"And you first took stock of this debility only these seven days ago?"

"'Twas but five days," he said. "Funisia first took note when she was reading to them from a book of fables."

"They were standing before me as I sat in a chair by the table there," she said, indicating with a nod the table behind me that was placed before the bay window. "They remained stock still, as always they do, to attend the tale of the jolly cobbler and the shoeless witch. The candles stood on the table by my right hand and when I looked up from the page, I saw what I saw."

"May the children come forth?" I asked, and after they dispatched Mistress High Horse to fetch them, I requested that candles be set along the table. There was good light from the window, but more would be useful.

The candles were arranged and lit and Graysmock led in the children. They came forward to stand before me with Sativius on one side and their mother on the other. I gazed upon them curiously, for they made a striking pair.

They were pale of complexion, almost nacreous, like the pearly oyster shell. Slim in figure with blond hair verging on silvery, they were clad in black knee breeches and black jackets and stockinged in shining white silk. Large silver buckles were set upon their black, square-toed shoes. The boy's hair was longer than the girl's, and only this single distinction marked them apart, for otherwise they were as identical in appearance as any two raindrops. They looked up at me fearlessly, their bright gray eyes seeming as large as doorknobs in their delicate faces. They were wraithlike. I discerned with my first glance that they would be taciturn younglings. Expectant silence hung about them like that preceding the onset of a nocturnal snowfall.

I smiled and said my name and they did not reply.

Their silence was perhaps of no great concern, for I was employed to look about their shadows, or the lack thereof; yet I tried to take stock of all that I could, for I knew that Maestro Astolfo would query me closely.

They stood before me, a hand-span apart, and behind them lay a single shadow of ordinary appearance, except that it was darker in tone than I might have expected. Considering that this darkening might be an effect of the darkish carpet on which they stood, I requested their parents to part them, widening the space between by another hand-span. The shadow did not alter its shape, though it should have begun to split apart where it joined the feet of the children. Farther and farther apart we posed them until an arm's length separated the pair and still the shadow did not split, though it became difficult to discern where its nether attachment was located. At last, Sativius and Funisia placed their children a long lance-length apart and the shadow, without a motion visible to my observation, no longer attached to the girl but only to the boy. Behind her, light held all the floor-place where shade should lie.

"You seem to have lost one of your valuables, little mistress," I said. I gave her the most gently ingratiating smile I could muster. "What is your name?"

She gazed at me with those great luminous eyes and remained as silent as a melting snowflake.

"She is called Rudensia," her mother said. "Her brother is Rudens."

I bowed to the children. "I am honored to make the acquaintance of so unusual a brace of youth," I said, though the phrases sounded clumsy. In fact, all my efforts at playful diplomacy sounded lame and gauche and I discarded the notion of trying to become friendly with the strange children.

We repeated the experiment three times again, with the result that Rudensia lost her shadow once to her brother while he twice lost his to her. I was unable to see how the transference occurred, yet the motion of it—if there had been a motion—was neither swift nor gradual. At one time it was simply there, stretched out behind the lad, and next time it fell behind the girl.

"What is to be done?" Funisia asked softly. Her eyes were fearful.

"I must study upon the phenomenon," I said, "but I have every confidence that all shall be resolved in happy manner."

"I do wish Maestro Astolfo had seen fit to answer my call," Sativius said. "You may tell him I am vexed."

"I shall make full report to him concerning every aspect," I replied. "It may be that he can postpone some part of his business and make a visitation."

These words did not mollify the rope merchant, but I had not expected that they would effect any change in his temper. Still, I could not allow such awkwardness to put me out of countenance; this, the first task to be delegated to my own counsel, I held too important to be disfigured by trifles.

I took my leave, promising to return soon with the best and most fully detailed prognosis I could mount. Both parents received my pledge with dull grace. Making my manners, I edged toward the door. Graysmock opened it and escorted me down the stair, through the foyer, and out into the cool midday, where a threat of rain was steadily increasing. I hastened my stride, hoping to arrive beneath Astolfo's roof before the clouds let go.

⊷══◉══⊷

Astolfo was absent from the kitchen, the first place I looked for him, and he was not in the large library. He was not in the smaller one either; but in this cozier room, with its book-strewn table and leathern armchairs and friendly small hearth, I chanced upon Mutano.

He gave me a noncommittal salute and returned to his disport with Creeper, pursuing a game that any babbling child might play with a cat, teasingly jigging a scrap of paper tied to a thread and whisking it away when the animal pounced. It was but an idle pastime. Where was the grave business with Creeper of which Astolfo had spoken? I settled into an armchair to await the shadow master's arrival. Rain had begun to lash the ivied walls of the villa and nothing else seemed so pleasurable as to sit at ease for a spell, finding pictures in the flames and hearkening to the fray of the elements.

The fire comported itself in no ordinary fashion. It brightened and dimmed and sent a roiling, misty smoke out over the hearth, a vapor that retained a defined shape and had not the formlessness of familiar hearth-fire smoke. Against the gently leaping flames, the smoke-shape was difficult to define precisely, but the longer I observed, the more knowable it became. Then I realized that its writhings and saltations, its turnings and toilings, were like those of a cat at play. The mist-form creature was aping, as if it were an image in a mirror, the motions of Creeper as he cavorted, twisted, and feinted in merry chase of Mutano's dancing scrap of paper.

I rose and drew closer, trying to discover of what substance this active shape consisted; it was so airy and light and agile that it must have been composed of the most aethereal of stuffs. Soon I knew it to be a shadow, the true shadow of Creeper, even though it was not attached to the green-eyed cat at any point of the body.

Here I beheld a marvel I had only heard rumored. When a shadow is taken from its subject, be that caster ever so active, ever so fluent with sinew and *vis vitae,* the shade, as a rule, loses all inner spirit and lies or stands or hangs inert. It retains its volumes and textures, its tints and tones, and something of its flavors and aromas. Astolfo is capable of detecting certain sounds belonging to a severed shadow, small noises like distant echoes from a lost valley. He is the master. But animation of the shade requires an amplitude of art I was certain Mutano did not possess. Astolfo must have had some hand in this accomplishment.

While I sat down again and pleasured in the music of rain-sweep against our walls, Astolfo came sprightly into the room, paused briefly to smile at the antics of Mutano and Creeper, and beckoned me to follow him into the kitchen, where he poured for both of us a generous drop of sweet, resinous wine into thick glass beakers.

Thus he commenced: "How went the discussion with the rope merchant? Have you learned to escape the wiles of the rope-maker's daughter?"

I was mystified; the pale Rudensia was but a child. Then I understood that he used thieves' language; *the rope-maker's daughter* is an alehouse term for the hangman's noose. "I learn some new thing every day," I replied.

"Tell me then of your dealings with Esquire Sativius."

In slow and careful words, I gave him as minute an account of the encounter as I was able, trying to omit naught that might be worthy of notice. Seated on the butcher's block with his head inclined toward me, he almost seemed to twitch his large ears as I spoke. When I concluded, he sat silent for long moments.

"How many years of age hang on these children?"

"Thirteen."

His expression grew grave. "This matter may be of a darker character than we have suspicioned. Would you describe their shared shadow to me again? Come as close to the object as may be."

When I repeated my impressions with some slight enlargement, he still seemed unsatisfied.

"You say this shadow that lay between them was darker of tint than you would otherwise observe in the circumstance?"

"So it appeared there."

"Was it uniform of its darkness or was the center of it perhaps a little more dark than its flanks?"

"It lay upon a wine-colored carpet of thickish pile," I said. "I could distinguish no gradation."

"Close your eyes. Envision all again."

I did so, but with no result. I shook my head.

"The mother and the father spoke, but the children spoke not?"

"Yes."

"Suppose that they had spoken. Which voice would be louder, that of the boy or of the girl?"

I considered. "They would be equally soft," I said, "with something of the timbre as of the pealing of little silver bells. But they did not speak."

"How did you form your conjecture as to the sound of their voices?"

"I do not know. Yet the soft bell-peal comparison cometh vivid to mind."

He nodded. "Now close your eyes and envision the shadow where it lay on the carpet. Only do not think about it."

I closed my eyes, deepened my breathing, and relaxed the concentration of my mind. Then I recalled what I had seen but had not noticed. "The center of the shadow is indeed darker than the larger body of it. Yet that center bears the same outline as the greater shadow. It is like an inner shadow of the greater shadow."

"Doth this dark one rest content where it lies?"

I did not hesitate. "It is a shadow," I said. "The ways of its thought—if it is capable of thought—I never could describe."

"Could you declare if the parents are affectionate of their progeny?"

"I believe them so."

"Might one of them be more so than the other?"

"That is possible," I said. "When they turned them about-face to depart the room, the mother Funisia rested her hand for a moment on her daughter's shoulder. Sativius did not bestow that small gesture upon his son."

He hesitated long before he spoke again. "I have given this piece of business over to your care and it belongs to you to conclude successfully. But I will tell you somewhat of similar circumstances that I have heard in my years. I do so to be of some aid but not to direct the affair myself. It is in your charge. I desire also to impress upon you the gravity of this state of things.

"These children now approach that time when 'swift-wing'd desire,' as the poets name it, first makes its trembling advance within mind and body. Those who have been innocently affectionate as childhood playmates commence to look upon each other with new eyes. They may join in amorous union. This act brothers and sisters ordinarily will not perform, but even without doing so they may draw together more tightly in mind and spirit than ever before and at last become almost a single entity. These pale-souled children of Sativius already share but one shadow. Soon they may possess only the one soul between them. If this annealment does take place and then at a later season they happen to be parted by some circumstance, one of them will surely die. Both may perish."

"What would be the case if they were separated now, before the tumult of early desire comes upon them?"

"With only one shadow between them, one or t'other would pine away to sickness and live out a life of pallid misery."

"I can foresee no happy result for the dilemma," I said.

"Have you no glimmering of a notion? I thought when I found you in the library that you might be setting out upon a course of research."

"I had thought I might pursue the genealogical line," I said. "Perhaps this strange malady has been recorded of the Sativius family in time past. If such a case has been recorded, perhaps a remedy may have been noted down. I have also conjectured that an ancestral curse might have been laid upon the family by a rival family or by an unknown foe."

"Beware that you do not mire in superstitious notions concerning inimical spells of witches and warlocks. Keep to our science of sciomancy. There may be something in the genealogical tables; you know where the records are shelved. But I will also suggest that you thumb some way through the pages of Morosius."

"Morosius? *Annales tenebrae antiquitatae?*" This was a tome I held in especial disfavor, a dull, bulky volume of confused accounts from every era and territory of miraculous or preternatural phenomena: fairies that infested bakeries, toads with jewels in their foreheads, flying anvils, drowned monasteries, and so forth. Morosius was particularly fond of peculiar rains falling out of clear blue skies— pebbles, emeralds, thimbles, goats, hay carts, thunderstones, powdered wigs, etc. All this farrago of hearsay and cloudy testimonial was flung upon the pages artlessly, so that one had no indication how to join related details.

"I seem to recall there was some story of a statue and its shadow," Astolfo said. "But it has been long since I perused the book."

"I shall look into it," I said. My promise was reluctant.

"Let us hope these children are not victims of some angry plot," Astolfo said.

"We shall have enough dealings with a vengeful opponent when Mutano brings his quest for justice into full career."

"What is happening with Mutano?"

"'Twill be a sober amusement," Astolfo said. "You shall know all of it that is needful sooner than you may desire . . . But do not let me keep you from the library and its family trees and from the learned sentences of Morosius."

Mutano had departed the library, but the hearth-fire needed only a
little encouragement with a poker and a taste of unseasoned oak to
set it crackling merrily. I fetched the requisite volumes of genealogical history to the armchair by the fireside, piled them in a stack
of five, seized the topmost, and set to tracing the mainstream and
tributaries of the race of Sativius. Soon enough I discerned that there
would be little of interest in these histories. It was the old story of
a race of yeoman farmers descended from soldiery. There once had
been a great estate, but it had divided into smaller and smaller par-
cels as inheritors multiplied. The offspring of the former landown-
ers joined the mercenary armies that formerly ranged the countryside
or they went to sea or entered into various trades in the newly
burgeoning towns. Our client, Matteo Sativius, father of the twins,
had first followed the sea, where he studied the gear and tackle and
trim of ships; he then borrowed money from his father when he
abandoned the sail, and founded a rope-making enterprise which
incorporated certain improvements in hempen tackle he had devised
when a sailor.

Of the mother's lineage, little was recorded. I traced a few
branches of farmers, petty tradesmen, and undistinguished warriors
and let the book drop from my hand.

The rain had increased its force—the windows creaked as the
storm beat upon the panes; drops sizzled as they fell down the
chimney into the flames. The pleasure of the hour was so calm
and somnolent I did not desire to distress it by reading in musty old
Morosius, but duty impelled me to return the genealogical tables
to their appointed shelves and again drag down the heavy folio of
the *Annales* and lug it back to my seat. I predicted that it would work
its soporific powers so efficaciously that three leaden paragraphs
would put me slumbering.

But it is the way of certain books to present a different character to us each time we open them. The rain, the tall stillness of the
room, the hearth-fire with the clump of massy shadow there in
the ingle: These surroundings caused Moroisus to seem for the first
time an appropriate companion.

I searched first for any story about a statue, since Astolfo would
surely rogate me upon the point. But all I discovered was a tale

concerning a certain well-loved priest, Prester Vonnard, who enjoyed in his lifetime such high esteem among the populace of his little village of Zenoro that they decided to erect a statue to him and perform an unveiling ceremony lavish with encomious speeches and the solemn chant of a children's chorus. But when the canvas was swept away from the bronze figure of this paragon of virtue it was seen by one and all that the shadow the statue cast upon the paving stones was of a vivid scarlet hue and seemed in texture almost as viscid as blood. A prudent, close investigation of the life of Vonnard was ordered and in a short time the statue was removed and the bronze melted and fashioned into armor. The shadow remained, however, an immutable stain, and any traveler to Zenoro still may inspect it. Morosius is, however, silent about the location of Zenoro.

Turning a few idle pages, I chanced upon a speculation by an unnamed philosopher who conjectured that if a lion eat a man, the shadow of the lion will contain, as an envelope contains a document, the shadow of that misfortunate and that this shadow, though indistinguishable, will not be part of the lion's shadow but a thing separate from it. The man is a spirit superior to the lion, saith this sage, and therefore can never be truly assimilated by an inferior spirit. Here was an interesting thought, but I reflected it must provide but small comfort to the man.

One overladen chapter was devoted to the Specter of the Summit, a phenomenon of northern latitudes that I had heard Astolfo discourse upon. A walker approaching the peak of a mountain cloaked in cold mist, and with the obscured sun behind him, will see a shadow advancing toward him and growing larger in its progress. Then, if the mist lighten but a little, he will see his own shadow, darker in hue, cast upon—within—the approaching shadow. At a certain point, depending upon the light and the density of the mist, both shadows disappear. Some travelers have tumbled into gorges trying to gain closer acquaintance with this phenomenon.

These were the passages that teased my attention. Other pages excoriating Morosius's rival philosophers or speculating whether the shadow of a rose truly possesses an odor or only the memory of one, etc., etc., I passed over with scant interest. But these instances of shadows-within-shadows seemed to point in a favorable direction and as I reflected upon them I fell into a contented doze.

My sleep was shortened by a difficulty in breathing. There was some obstruction to inhalation, at first so subtle I thought it part of a dream. It grew thicker about my mouth and nose and when I opened my eyes the room with its windows and candles was darkened as by a pall of smoke. I'd raised my hands to my face to claw away this weave of fog when it went from me suddenly. It gathered into a ball and then elongated to a ferretlike shape and streaked grayly over the worn carpet to the door. Now, of course, I recognized it as the shadow of Creeper.

Mutano was in another room, directing the movement of the large cat. He had found some way to position the animal so that its palpable shadow here in the library had covered my face and hindered my breath. Mutano was fond of vexing me with jests of a corporeal nature and after so many of them I had grown impatient. I called down curses on his square-jawed, shaggy head.

That is, I attempted to mutter these imprecations, but found that no sounds came from me. I tried again and then again, but all I could manage to utter was a raspy whisper that lacked any trace of my normal timbre. A brass ewer of water stood on a near table and I poured a beakerful and drank it down in three swallows, but there was no aid in it. My voice had departed my voice-box.

Everyone is familiar with the superstition that cats can steal away the breath of sleeping children and cause them to perish by suffocation. That is an old wives' tale foolish in every respect. Yet now the shadow of a cat had thieved away my voice. So I supposed the case to be, at any rate, and went in angry search of Mutano.

⁘⟁⁘

I had not far to look. The kitchen was occupied by Mutano and Astolfo and Creeper. Astolfo had taken his seat on the butcher block, while Mutano stood by a long counter beneath the west window. Creeper was crouched on the window ledge, but, at a sign from Mutano the big cat leapt from the ledge and covered a boule of wheaten bread on the counter with his body. I knew that in whatever other room his shadow was, it too was leaping down upon an object and embracing it closely.

Mutano gave a wide and happy and infuriating grin when he saw me watching, and my impulse was to return his japery with an arse-kick, but Astolfo held up his hand to restrain me.

"This is no inane trickery, Falco," he said. "It is instead a demonstration of part of a plan Mutano has formed to take his voice back from his mortal enemy."

I tried to speak but only buzzed like a cicada.

"Sit you by the oven," Astolfo directed. "Quaff a glass of ale. The tale is soon told and you must hear it before you accompany Mutano upon his mission of restoration."

I did as told. The light, nutty ale soothed my throat and calmed a little my disposition.

"It is the old story of rivalry for a woman's favors," Astolfo said. "This was the Lady Stellina, a bright, beautiful woman of petite figure and immense charm. Have you not noticed how these broad-beamed bravos, thick-necked and huge-handed, are so often attracted by small females doll-like and delicate? It is not always true, of course. Tastes may change as experience is gained and the attractions of a sturdier breed of woman are acknowledged. But often in the beginning, it is the doll-like creature they prefer."

I watched Mutano stroke Creeper and saw in my mind's eye how the cat's shadow, wherever it was, would be writhing with delight. Astolfo's description of his manservant was a just one: broad-beamed, thick-necked, and huge-handed. He might have added knuckle-scarred, excessively muscular, and, as a drillmaster, too joyfully severe.

"Stellina, the daughter of the Count Orlando of the Lovoso Marches, had harbored a taste for the large and horny-palmed lads since she was a child. Now that she had come into her eighteenth year, she was able to inform her taste with a wide experience and, after trying the pleasures of a strong dozen specimens of manhood, settled upon Mutano as one of her two favorites. The other was a tall, lean, hawk-featured young felon named Castilio from one of the western isles. He was a stranger to the garrison town of Rupz, where Count Orlando maintained a private militia. Quick-tempered and sharp-tongued, he was ready to battle man or beast as his whimsy dictated. Such recklessness appealed to Stellina's mineral heart. She had not heard the accounts of his abducting maidens of too-tender years and despoiling them with brutal handling.

"Yet she also favored Mutano, who, though less quick-witted than Castilio and less blade-eager, showed an easy good humor of sardonic cast. He feared nothing. In particular, he showed no fear of Castilio, and only deigned to acknowledge his rival's existence when Stellina bestowed on the lean fellow some mischievous epithet of high praise. In those days, Mutano was known for the quality of his voice—resonant, mellifluous, and compelling. He might have made his way in life as a minstrel had not the martial exertions claimed his allegiance.

"I will abbreviate this long romance of the foolish young. The rivalry developed to such a fevered heat that Castilio, in a fit of jealous imbecility, challenged Mutano to a wrestling match. Almost any other kind of combat might have favored the challenger, but Mutano has an especial liking for stuffing the elbows of his opponents into their ears and twisting their spines into sheep's-head knots. The contest concluded in the space of time it takes to sing one of Zandrio's ballads."

I sipped at the ale and tried my voice once more. It was beginning to return a little, a soft, froggish croak.

"Castilio was as vengeful as he was foul-tempered, and he vowed to take from Mutano one of his proudest possessions: his beautiful voice. So he invited our friend to a drinking contest at a villainous inn whose proprietor was his crony. This occasion was supposed to mark a truce between them and I believe Mutano expected his rival to renounce upon this hour all claim to Stellina, the golden object of their rival desires.

"Mutano mounted the steps to a small room, as had been arranged. The room stood in dim light when he arrived, but when he fed more wick to the lamp on the table, he wished that it had been submerged in blackness. There, bound to a chair across the room, was the naked body of Stellina. Her throat had been torn out. Her features were contorted in agony and her body bore dread, gaping wounds."

"Horrible!" My voice sounded, a raspy whisper.

"Yes. You can imagine the great shriek that Mutano uttered. All his strength was behind the force of his voice, and in that moment it was taken from him, captured. Castilio was in the room with a trio of cruel rogues and he had with him a device that enabled him to steal the sound of Mutano's melodious voice. He took it from him, and now he holds it captive still. Mutano is resolutely determined to repossess his voice. What other designs he has upon the fate of Castilio, I do not know."

"But—"

"Oh yes," Astolfo said. He smiled and shook his head. "That was no corpse of Stellina bound in a chair, but only a waxwork effigy of the woman, disfigured and maimed. The only purpose of this waxen mammet was to extract a great shriek of grief and outrage from Mutano so that the voice might be captured."

"How can one make captive of a voice?" I asked, pleased that my own was at last returning. I drank the ale cup dry and poured a smidgen more.

"With an ingenious series of wooden boxes, nested inside one another, there being sufficient space between their neighbor walls that the echo of a voice rebounds within, again and again, until in the final, smallest box it is reduced to the essence of itself. You understand that I must speak in metaphors. Truly to describe this complicated device would require a long string of geometrical demonstrations, as well as some discourse upon a theory of sound as being transferred from one place to another by a succession of aerial waves. For our present purposes, it is enough to know that Castilio holds Mutano's power of speech in thrall and that our colleague has laid a scheme to gain it back."

"But how may a voice be preserved over a period of time? It consists of breath and must soon fade back into its airy elemental state. No wonder box, ingenious as it may be, is capable of preserving it."

"Correct," Astolfo said. "Your studies are bringing you to sound ways of thinking. The voice must be given over to another entity with some power of speech. It must lodge within an animal that possesses a voice-box of its own. A magpie might be useful in this regard, or a pet monkey. Mutano believes that Castilio has preserved his voice in the throat of a lazy, red-orange cat he hath named Sunbolt."

"Why does he think so?"

"I know not how he came to this conclusion. He is privy to some intelligence I wot not of. It may have to do with a set of verses Castilio dispatched to Stellina, comparing some portion of her anatomy to one of the nobler virtues of his cat."

I drank off the mug and wiped my lips with the heel of my palm. My voice had returned to its normal state and I was regaining my composure. It is an unsettling business, to be struck dumb in an instant, to be incapable of speech for no fathomable reason.

"I have a glimmering," I announced. "This method of capturing a voice recalls to me the conundrum of the twin children. Is there a treatise on the subject from olden times or is this a new-minted conceit?"

"An amalgam of both is likeliest," Astolfo said. "You might look into Lariotti's little monograph on the geometrical diminishments of the musical tone *re*. That is all I can recall that might be of the slightest help."

"Thank you," I said. "I will inform Mutano that I stand ready at any time to aid him in his effort to reclaim his voice."

"You need not trouble," Astolfo said. "He counts you his accomplice already."

⊷≔◉⊜≕⊶

I had read and mused and questioned and I began to believe I could make some progress toward a conclusion. Now it seemed probable to me that the twin children were not lacking a shadow that ought to be present, but that the shadow already was present and was only concealed. Maestro Astolfo must have suspected this to be the case when he inquired whether any part of the visible shadow was darker or more pronounced than the other portions of it. I had observed that the central part was of a darker tint and that it exhibited the same general outline, in smaller state, as the outline of the whole.

The two children possessed two shadows, only one was contained within the other. These shadows must have clung together, then fused inseparably, shortly after the birth of the twins. My task would be to cleave them, to set one apart from the other, causing two to stand where one had stood.

I began to reason upon the undertaking, pacing up and down the flagstones of the library, then going out into the chill, damp weather the storm had delivered and tramping about in the wet grasses of the courtyard. I desired that the cold air would sharpen my wits.

Some shadows are uncleavable from certain objects. If a thief take the shadow of a man on the instant of his being illuminated by a stroke of lightning, that shadow will ever seek out the presence of iron and fasten into its grain irremovably. The fashioners of ceremonial shields often elaborate these shadow-shapes into fanciful designs highly prized by their clients. Almost equally impossible is the task of cutting away the shadow of a carefree maiden standing in the shadow-dapple of a cherry tree. Yet it can be done by masters such as Astolfo.

As I pondered upon the lightning-bred shade's attraction to iron, I recalled also the device of the nested boxes which had stolen away

Mutano's voice. I remembered too the shadow-stain of the statue of Prester Vonnard and how it clung to the cobbles of a plaza. A scheme came to mind then and I determined to trace it out on my own, telling Astolfo little until it came to conclusion. But since Mutano required my aid to further his design, I would entreat his aid on behalf of my own.

⊷══◉═⊶

The morrow broke bright and watery, sunlight gleaming from every grass blade and leaf tip. The dawn birds were hilarious and did not lessen the volubility of their choruses till mid-morning. Mutano was in an easy temper too; he anticipated the regaining of his voice. My part in his plan was small, but it might endanger my person. I was to deliver to Castilio at his lodgings in the Haywain Inn an ugly insult and a jovial but urgent invitation to meet Mutano on the field of honor, where they would settle all insuavity between them with the clash of sabers.

This much Mutano communicated to me in one of the rapid finger dialects that he and Astolfo habitually conversed in. I had gathered enough of it to comprehend instructions and simple explanations, sometimes with the aid of ear-boxings to intensify my attention. The only real peril, so stated his thumb and third finger, was that Castilio might insert a dagger in my windpipe upon hearing my rehearsed insult—a complicated phrase involving his mother, his uncle, a goat, an ape, and a pig—without staying for the challenge to duel Mutano.

I asked him about his odd choice of weapons, for of all the choices open to him—long knives, clubs, maces, broadswords—the saber was the least advantageous; this was the blade he was least agile with. For answer he gave me one of his ear-wide, many-toothed grins.

In return, I requested his aid in a bit of simple carpentry to my design and also in transporting my devices to the house of Sativius. After momentary reflection, he agreed to fall in with me.

⊷══◉═⊶

The hour in which Mutano insisted that I deliver his messages was deepest twilight. Uncommon gloomy 'twas, this tavern room of the Haywain, with its scant half dozen tallow candles disposed diversely. Besides the object of my attention and myself, the only other persons here were a raddle-haired serving maid and a baldpate dotard seated by the cold fireplace, opposing himself at a chessboard. Castilio sat on a bench, sipping at a tankard and playing idly with an ivory-handled dirk of modestly ominous proportion. I sat at a table with a glass of canary, waiting for him to grow tired of his game and sheathe the blade. Finally he thrust it back into his sleeve.

I advanced to stand before him and he looked up into my eyes with a gaze that was challenging but also incurious, the gaze of a man determined to fear nothing that fate flung in his way. When I reeled off the insult entailing his complex ancestry and his dubious amatory practices, his expression did not change at first. Then he laughed, and when I heard that soft, insidious chuckle with its flat intonation, I understood why Mutano so loathed him and why all the world gave wide berth to his presence.

"You are but a parrot sent to prattle words not your own," he said. He looked away from my face into the far corner of the room. "Which of my foes has dispatched you here? Torpius? Scudator? Mutano? Master Thistledown?"

I handed over the document and he broke the seal. Murmuring the phrases as he read, he went through it carefully, poring over each syllable.

Now I took advantage of his distracted attention to lift the left edge of my cloak with its moleskin pocket and let drop onto the table behind me the shadow of Creeper, the coiled mass which had traveled nested in my cloak as I walked half across the expanse of Tardocco. Shadows, though they possess mass, are weightless, yet when Creeper's umbra slipped away I felt that a burden had departed my body.

Castilio laid down the challenge missive. "How is it that Mutano delivereth not this foolhardy piece of effrontery in his own person?" he asked. "Why must he send forth a hireling?"

The truth was that Mutano, even now while I engaged the thoughts of his nemesis, was in Castilio's rooms above, searching for any receptacle that might contain his purloined voice. I sought to occupy his enemy's attention as long as possible. "I am no inconsequential menial," I replied, "but the confidential aide to Maestro Astolfo, whose name is widely known."

"He is known as a prating, elderly thief who has narrowly escaped the gallows a score of times. I care not what title he has hung upon you, for a glance tells me you are but a furrow-slave with the mud of the turnip field still clinging to your soles—and to your spirit."

"Mutano conceived that a challenge when delivered by a third party acquires more dignity and weight."

He rose abruptly, and I knew his suspicions had been alerted. He suspected me of acting as a distraction. "You may tell Mutano that his challenge has been accepted in all particulars, including those of weapons choice, field of honor, and hour of combat."

I bowed. "I will say what you have said."

"Do so, though it may be I shall see him myself before you do." With these words, he brushed past me and strode toward the stairs by the entrance door. I knew that he expected, perhaps hoped, to find Mutano in his rooms.

"Is that the whole of your message?" I shouted.

He did not reply but only bounded to the door at the top and flung it open and rushed into the corridor. I was pleased to see that Creeper's shadow leapt down from the table behind me and glided along up the stairs, following Castilio's heels.

The time seemed opportune for me to depart also. If Castilio found his lodging ransacked, he would speed back with naked blade and unpleasant demeanor. I laid down coin for the canary, went out into the dark, wet street, and betook me to the safety of Astolfo's manse. There I waited in the armchair, watching the dim orange pulse of dying hearth-fire embers until I dozed away.

⋯➡︎◯⬅︎⋯

His search had proved fruitless, Mutano told Astolfo with a flurry of finger-waggling. He had looked into the three small rooms of Castilio's lodging and found no place a voice might be stored away.

"No stoppered flasks or bottles?" Astolfo asked.

Mutano signed no.

"No small boxes or casques, as for jewels or coins or gilt buckles?"

None.

"Tell us, then, what you did see there? Omit nothing and try to recall all."

Mutano named articles of apparel, various deadly blades, some toiletries, handkerchiefs, a few gold eagles and lesser coins, spurs, boots beneath the bed, a woman's scarf draped over a chair back.

"Naught else?"

Mutano shrugged and signed unenthusiastically that a large orange cat of melancholy, surly mien had watched him plundering about without so much as a tail twitch.

"This cat," Astolfo asked, "was he not disturbed by the shadow of Creeper that you deposited in the room?"

I was surprised. I had not known that we had set two of the black one's shadows upon Castilio. The one that Mutano let free would be a secondary, since I had brought the primary shadow into the tavern room. Whatever the purpose of this secondary, the conceit of the two shadows was clever, I thought.

Mutano signaled that the orange cat had seemed to take no notice of the shadow. In fact, it had behaved, in not behaving at all, unlike any other feline he had met in his long acquaintance with the race.

"A human appurtenance, the voice of stout Mutano, has been affixed within its physiognomy," Astolfo said. "Having stolen your voice, Castilio has managed to lodge it in this cat; I know not how. Such an addition to its nature will change the character of the beast at its foundation. For long and long, philosophers have conjectured what a cat might say were human vocality conferred upon it. Many of the graybeards averred that it would say nothing at all, lest it reveal some of the secrets of its mysterious race. It seemeth—in the instance of Castilio's cat, at least—that their suspicion proved true."

"How then may its human voice be captured?" I asked.

"Oh, we have already prepared our voice-trap," Astolfo said. "It is constructed along the pattern of Castilio's nested wooden boxes, only ours is an intricate horn of silver and ivory, in appearance like a twisted ear trumpet. There is no doubt that it will capture the utterance-essence of a voice and keep it safely."

"I mean, how will Mutano take back his voice if the cat does not speak?"

They exchanged glances. Mutano seemed a trifle apprehensive.

"Risks must be run," Astolfo said. "In the first place, Castilio's cat now possesses two voices, one of them proper to itself. If its own voice is dominant within it, then it will make only sounds ordinary to a cat. But if Mutano's voice has gained—so to speak—the upper hand, then it will speak out in his voice and that one will become prisoner of our trumpet-device."

"But why should it speak at all, since its best advantage—or Castilio's—lies in keeping silent?"

"We will put to it the question that, when asked directly, every feline must answer by force of its inner nature."

"What is this question?"

"We shall ask this Sunbolt if he be truly the King of the Cats. If he is King, he will rise hissing, all hackles and claws, and bound away in a flash, leaving behind a smell as of brimstone and burning roses. If he hath not been designated the royalty of its feline world, then he is constrained to respond, 'Nay, not yet.'"

"This is but an old tale to amuse children in the chimney corner," I said. "I was no taller than a milking stool when first I heard it. Even the most unlearned hay-foot villager is wiser than to credit it. 'Tis moldy stuff indeed."

Mutano's wide grin forewarned me I had overstepped the bounds of my knowledge.

"Apply your noddle," Astolfo said. "When has it come about that the hay no longer graces your footwear? If every instance of the elder lore were false, the land would have been depopulated generations ago. Why do you doubt what I tell you?"

Since I had lately been reading in Lord Verulam's *Novum organon,* I ventured to speculate that this interrogation of cats must have been rarely put to the test; otherwise, there would be voluminous testimonial in the writings of the sages. "By making experiment we discover truth and falsity," I said. "There must be by our time many thousands of younglings who have put that question to their dear pusses and have received for reply only uncomprehending disregard."

"Too easy an interpretation to offer," said Astolfo. "How many of the felines so queried have been gifted with a human voice?"

"Few," I admitted.

"Do you not think it likely that cats communicate among themselves with recondite signs and significations?"

"Perhaps."

"Would you be able to cipher out the language of a cat's ears and tail?"

"I could not."

"Then you may ask, for all the remainder of your years, of every animal you meet whether it is King of the Cats and receive continual denials and never know of it because you lack the key to their language. Is this not so?"

"It may be so."

"Let us hear no more of the foolishness of the old tales. We owe much of our new medicine to the simples of farm wives and much of our knowledge of astronomy to watchful shepherds. Since you desire to experiment, after the manner of Verulam, it shall be your duty to put the question to Castilio's cat."

"My duty? How can that come about? Castilio knows me and will take care that I do not depart a next encounter unscathed. How am I to evade his enmity?"

"Tomorrow at the noon hour he will be engaged in a duel with Mutano in the graveyard atop Mount Windscaur in the northern precinct of the town, a good half league distant from the Haywain Inn. Then you may enter his rooms, put the question to Sunbolt, and bring away with you Mutano's voice which you shall have captured in the chambered spirals of the silver trumpet. Also, you are to gather the two shadows of Creeper which ought to be present there."

"Shall he not have suspected a design against him and have posted a confederate to guard his belongings?"

"That would present a difficulty your ingeniousness must overcome."

"I do not comprehend why we have set upon him two shadows of Creeper," I said. "Our plan as it stands does not require their presence."

Astolfo said, "If 'twere only to train them to an exercise, that would be value enough."

"Well, I will perform this commission," I said, "but I should like to exact some payment for it, some just return for my trouble, so that I can fulfill my obligations to the family Sativius, for I have formed, I believe, an artifice that may help to resolve the affair."

"What have you struck?"

When I began to list my necessities—the blue mirror, the sheet of transparent glass, the vials of silver salt, and so forth—I saw that Mutano looked at me with an expression of full surprise. I considered it a victory to have startled my raw-knuckled tutor, who so continuously regarded me as an addlehead ploughboy. Astolfo smiled knowingly, however, and murmured an unintelligible phrase about "membraneous effluence." He acquiesced to my requests for materials and promised that Mutano would aid me in my endeavor.

Just before noon on the morrow I placed myself around the corner across the cobbles from the Haywain so that I might see while standing concealed. In time a groom led round a black, mettlesome mare with black leathers to the front and Castilio came out. He snatched the bridle from the lad and seemed to wish to bark at him an imprecation, yet no sound issued when he opened his mouth. He was in foul temper, all out of sorts with the bright day that had followed the rainy hours. He mounted and jogged crisply away, his saber flapping against his thigh as he plied more spur than necessary.

I tarried a while longer, observing all that I could, and then entered the inn and made my way unhindered to Castilio's rooms. All was just as it had been before, except that the female scarf was absent. No drawer was locked, no door bolted. The man seemed to invite inspection of his every article and, finding things thus, I went cursorily about the business, then turned my attention to matters feline.

First I ascertained the whereabouts of the two shadows of Creeper. The primary dark one had nestled beneath the neatly dressed bed; and the lighter secondary had crouched inside an overturned boot. In a cushioned chair by the window sat the orange Sunbolt that Mutano had found here and described in detail. There was no mistaking this large tom with his subtle stripes of slightly yellow tint. He dozed, with feet tucked under and eyes almost completely shut. But the movement of his ears indicated awareness that I was in his presence.

Here now was the moment of revelation. I had always been curious to conjecture what Mutano's voice would sound like, he being so large of corpus and saturnine of temperament. Would it boom out like a tympanum? Or might it thunder and reverberate like an empty barrel rolled down a tall flight of wooden stairs? Perhaps in issuing from the voice-box of this cat, it would roar forth like some tiger of the night.

I placed myself before the animal, produced our trumpet-device, and turned the wide bell toward it, keeping the cork-lined round of parchment stopper in my right hand, ready to seal the aperture once the sound entered into the tapering silver labyrinth. Then I put to it the question it could not evade:

"Art thou King of the Cats?"

It opened its green, agate-hard eyes and elevated its hindquarters and gave a mighty stretch with its forepaws, seeming to extend to the lengthiest every ligament and fiber of muscle in its thorax. It yawned its widest. Then it resettled itself into its former posture, turned its wedgy face upward, and said:

"Nay. The hour is not yet."

I clapped the stopper in, wondering already if I had held the device in horizontal position aright and in sufficient proximity to the cat's mouth. I had tried to make no sound that would obstruct the passage of the words through the aether or adulterate them with an unwanted noise.

Naught was left to do now but to gather the two shadows of Creeper into the inner folds of my shagreen cloak and march back home across Tardocco. I set a leisurely pace, for there was much to think on.

Mutano's voice was not orotund and commanding, as I had supposed, but rang out a clear, lyrical treble. Astolfo had avouched that he was a musical man, but that disclosure had not prepared me for the peculiar sweetness of tone and the light, reedy vibrato that were so winning in timbre. Had the cat's vocal physiognomy altered Mutano's own, to make it so dulcet? I have endured the amorous lays of cats in the midnight hours with small patience and have found none of them seductive. To appreciate the music they create requires an amount of education I did not yet possess. Whimsically, I pictured Mutano in a form feline, slinking out under a great buttery moon and entreating his lady love to his rapturous embrace with a harmonious cadenza and then receiving as her melodious refusal his own terse, traditional rebuttal:

"Nay. The hour is not yet."

⤙▭◉▭⤚

"These duels consume a tiresome portion of the clock," Astolfo said to me when I returned.

The three of us had lately formed the habit of occupying the small library. In time past we had gathered most often in the great kitchen, but the scullery staff and Iratus complained that we were too often present when he had tasks in hand. For his part, Astolfo would rarely gainsay his favorite cook; that artisan was necessary, he claimed, for the conduct of financial affairs, supplying as he did a sumptuous table when clients were invited.

"I had not expected that Mutano would return till near twilight," I said. I leaned forward in a strap-bottomed chair and watched the two shadows of Creeper gambol together in the far corner of the room. He, the caster of the umbrae, was nowhere to be seen. Lately, Creeper had been known to sleep for days on end, rousing only to tend to the demands of gut and bowel. It was explained to me that the drawing off of two lively shadows from his form depleted his store of *vis vitae*; long sleeping aided return of it.

"These two, Mutano and Castilio, are acting without seconds," Astolfo said, "and there is no need for elaborate protocol—and yet they will be long at the business, though the combat itself shall prolong for only swift-flying minutes."

"I marvel at his choice of weapons," I said, "for Mutano knoweth well that the saber is not the steel to which he is best accustomed."

"Perhaps his challenge is to himself, as well as to Castilio."

"He hazards his life. Is it not too risky a venture to gain so small a point of honor?"

"The rules and limits Mutano establishes for himself are unknown to me. It may be that if we apprehended the rules, his comportment would display a logic."

"'Tis well beyond my fathoming."

"I see there in the corner the two shades of Creeper," Astolfo said. "I conclude, then, that you have brought off your part of the affair successfully."

"I cannot affirm yea or nay," I replied. "I followed my instructions to the letter. Whether I managed to regain with our little trap Mutano's voice, I cannot say. If so I did, then it is here." I reached behind my chair and produced the trumpetlike contraption.

Astolfo then required me to give a full account of all that took place but broke off my narrative when I told of entering the room. "Pray do not leap to the middle," he said. "Did you take heed that Castilio had already departed?"

I hastened to assure him that I had kept watch until he had mounted for his appointment and had kept at my post for some little time afterward.

"You observed him to come out and take the reins?"

"I did."

"How did his demeanor appear to you—in comparison, I mean, with the way you found him two days ago in the tavern room?"

I closed my eyes to bring the picture clear to mind. "He seemed restless of spirit. In the tavern he looked all a piece of easy insolence, but coming out to meet Mutano, he looked somdel apprehensive. Certes, he was irritable, for he was harsh to his groom."

"It appeareth, then, that Creeper's shadows performed well their offices," Astolfo said. "They were set there to obstruct his breathing in the night, thus to prevent sound sleep. You have experienced this obstruction of inhalation by the cat's shadow, have you not?"

"I have."

"Out he came then, ill tempered and nervy, not so well fit to go at sabering. . . . And when he had mounted?"

"Off he cantered, after a sharp spurring of the stallion's flanks." I went on to tell, at a calm pace, everything else that I had heard and seen and done, expressing my surprise at the sound of Mutano's voice as the cat spoke its sentence to me. I tried to describe the peculiar sweetness of timbre and melodiousness of cadence.

"Have you ever stood in a wintry grove of trees with a cold wind scraping and rattling the bare limbs together so that they creaked and squealed?" Astolfo asked.

"Yes."

"That is how I recall the sound of Mutano's voice. None of this consort of musical tones that you speak of, but an eldritch grating almost to stand one's neck hairs on end."

"I will avouch for what I heard. You told me before that he was a sometime minstrel."

"His speaking voice was quite unmusical. It may be that this is a peculiarly musical cat and that his native talents wrought a happy change upon Mutano's vocal qualities in his ordinary speaking. We may hope this to be the case, for the other explanation is less sanguine."

"How so?"

"A man who performs so audacious a theft as that of another man's voice will not be content to perform the deed a single time only. It may be that this o'er-sugared voice you heard belongeth to another than Mutano and that his is placed in another receptacle. Would you think that the voice you heard from the cat might have been purloined from a woman?"

I thought upon it. "I should not say so. For all its harmoniousness, it lacked a certain softness we associate with the fair."

"We shall not know what is certain for some small space of time," Astolfo said. "Perhaps you will tell now what progress you have made in the affair of the Sativius family."

"I shall describe a contrivance I have imagined, a complicated arrangement of mirrors and sheets of glass. I cannot effect the portage of these elements alone and will ask Mutano's aid."

"He is in your debt."

"So I have expected. I shall desire him to help to move and position these glasses." I rose and walked to a long library table and returned with a large square of paper. "Here I have drawn out my plans, if you should care to see them over."

Astolfo took the crowded page with an air of lazy amusement, looked at it, and began turning it sidewise and topsy-turvy. "You make up your designs with great enthusiasm," he commented. Soon, though, he commenced to study my scribbles and hatchings with care, humming a tuneless ditty. He spent a goodish deal of time examining the sheet before rolling it into a cylinder and laying it across his lap. "These conceits you have laid out here—do they originate in your brain or found you them in some treatise tucked away in our shelves?"

"They are mine."

He nodded. "The pride of your tone assures me. I ask the question because of the coincident nature of your imaginings."

"In what way?"

He held up the page. "The designs you have made are similar in many respects to the methods that Mutano and I employed to animate the shades of Creeper."

"I have no knowledge of how that was done and, as you can see, I have no ambitions to create shadows of independent force and motion. I would not care to animate the children's umbrae, only to separate them one from another."

"It is your notion then that the twins do each possess a shadow and that one is contained inside the other?"

"Yes."

"And you propose with this arrangement of glasses to separate the two shadows so that they will then attach to their proper casters?"

"That is my plan." I waited with some wariness for his sentence upon my constructions. I could hardly expect him to applaud them, but if he disallowed Mutano to work in my behalf, I would have to begin over once more, and he had warned me that time was rapidly shortening before a sad fate befell the young ones.

"It seems sound so far as it reaches," he said. "I might suggest a few improving touches, if they will not injure your pride or damage your project as you see it."

"I welcome any advice of Maestro Astolfo." I made a teasing half bow from my seated position.

"My advice must wait," he said, "for Mutano has returned, I believe."

In strode he. His complexion was flushed, his eyes glary, but he wore one of his monstrous, wide-mouthed grins.

A line of spattered blood dotted his tunic from the collar down to the last button. It was not his own.

"Welcome," said Astolfo.

In reply, Mutano tossed upon the small table between us a blood-soaked codpiece I recognized as belonging to Castilio.

⊷⚬⚬⊶

Astolfo and I were not to hear the sound of Mutano's voice—if indeed he had acquired a voice—for some little time, because he took himself aside to spend long hours in company with the capturing instrument, inhaling or imbibing his own voice from the mechanism. We surmised that vocal experimentation engaged him, that he was exercising his throat in private, and that he would reveal the result when he thought most proper.

It was with surprising good grace in the meantime that Mutano submitted to my desires in service of the Sativius family, helping me to transport my apparatus across the city, into the household, and up the stair to the room with the bay window's light. Horseface Graysmock watched us arrange the pieces with undisguised disfavor. I rather hoped she would bestow some disdaining remark upon Mutano. He had no patience with females of her strain and would send her sprawling with the back of his hand did she once overstep.

The schema was disposed as thus:

I) The long table before the window was removed and the children brought forward toward the light;

II) the pair stood close together to cast a shadow behind;

III) directly posterior to them a large sheet of transparent glass was mounted, so that the shadow of the children fell on it complete;

IV) this glass was framed all around with a molding of purest copper;

V) the glass itself had been dusted over with a light coating of a silver salt that allowed the shadows to pass through

VI) to a mirror behind the silvery glass:

VII) which mirror was made of a peculiar glass tinted dark blue that had the power of absorbing images deeply, pulling them far into itself.

Sativius and Funisia gazed with apprehension upon this trifold arrangement. The father was very particular in inquiring whether Maestro Astolfo was aware of what I had projected and if he had approved. I assured him that Astolfo knew all and had contributed wise advice of optical nature. Funisia welcomed any venture that might benefit her brood.

As I instructed the twins that they must stand very still for quite a little while, they only stared mutely into my face, as if trying to read not only my intentions but any trace of doubt my mind might harbor. I murmured softly as I stood them in compliance with my design. When I was satisfied that the images of the shadows passed through the dusted glass into the mirror, I made a finger sign to Mutano where he stood at the side of the glass. He produced a piece of amber about the size of his palm, took from his belt pouch a small patch of lynx fur, and rubbed it over the amber. When he had rubbed for a short time, he touched the electrum to the copper molding of the mirror. This action he performed continuously as I observed. I stood to one side, facing away from the light, watching the shadow of the pair as it fell upon the dusted glass and seeing the image of the children as it entered the blue mirror.

This process required the better part of an hour and I tried not to allow my apprehensions to ruffle my demeanor. If the children grew restless and moved about, the silvered shadow would be blurred, the darker core more difficult to distinguish from the outer penumbra. If Mutano grew impatient, flung the lump of amber at my head, and stalked from the house, all would be ruined. If my scheme proved ineffective, if the spark from the rubbed amber did not transfer itself through the salt across the pane in sufficient force to animate the more passive shadow that was absorbed as the core of the other, I would again be a figure of ridicule to Astolfo and Mutano and must endure their humors and rude satires for a long time to come. And when again would Astolfo entrust me a commission to work upon by myself?

At last there occurred a change in the shadow in the glass. The dark core grew lighter in tint and extended its shape until it was almost identical in size with its envelope. In the blue mirror the images of the twins grew more distinct, their outlines more sharply defined. When the inner and outer shadows verged close to identity in size and density, I sharply bade the children to stand apart, to go quickly to the places I had marked on the carpet with two linen handkerchiefs.

When they did so, the shadow on the glass divided into two and at that moment, following my signal, Mutano smashed the glass with the pommel of his knife hilt. The shards dropped to the rug, clinking upon one another like counted coins, and across them and stretching beyond lay two shadows separate and individual. Mutano hurried to the blue mirror and turned its face to the wall. We could not draw from the children any more of their *vis animae* than was necessary for our task.

I was jubilant at the success of my experiment, but my joy immediately gave way to chagrin as the boy Rudens became even paler than before. His face drained of all color and he fell to the floor. I rushed to him, arriving at his side even before his mother, and put my ear to his face. His breath came but faintly and I asked for water to bathe his face and hands. He stirred a little at the touch of the water but did not open his eyes. Seeing this, Funisia gathered him up and bore him away.

Graysmock ran over to accuse me. "You have killed him! You have murdered the young master!"

"Silence your tongue," I said. "No real harm has come to him. Go prepare a strong effusion of ginger root and give it to him when he wakens from sleep."

She left in silent fury and Sativius knelt to Rudensia. She appeared to me much less affected by the splitting of the shadow than her brother had been, yet it was obvious that she had felt a change rush upon her. Her father peered into her eyes, then clasped her tightly to his chest. "Is it so?" he asked. "Have my children each a shadow now?"

"It is so," I replied. "The effect of the division is less strong for Rudensia because what was taken from her was not correctly hers in the first place. For the boy, the sudden accession of his shadow overpowered him with a feeling that something long lost had been wholly returned. His was the lesser, darker umbra that Rudensia's had absorbed in their earliest hours. We have been fortunate in our day of restoration. Had it occurred later, we might have lost one or both of the twins." I went on to explain, as Astolfo had explained to me, that if once their souls entwined, they must face the doom of either madness as their spirits melted together into one or of physical death if ever they had to be separate one from the other.

He stood, still embracing the girl in his right arm. "I do not comprehend these matters," he said. "I am but a blunt man of business and all this spiderweb machination with shadows perplexes me."

"That is because you are unaccustomed. Think with what bewilderment a ploughboy looks upon a ship as it weighs anchor and steers from harbor. All will seem but arrant confusion to him, with sailors darting here and yon and the masters bawling orders and the sheets tying off and the cables laid by, but to your practiced eye all the commotion is of a pattern and every action is demanded by a necessity. It is the same with shadows. One must learn the ropes."

"I believe the fee you set was two hundred eagles," he said. "If my son revive in sound health, as you say that he shall, I will add another fifty."

"That is unlooked for," I said. "*The fee is set and to be met,* as the saying goes. Only do make certain that Horseface carries out her duties in good order and all shall be well."

"Horse—?"

"Please pardon me. I meant no offense. The term rose unbidden to my lips."

"As it sometimes has to my thoughts." He smiled. "Yet she is fitting in her office, however imperfect in manner. Nevertheless, she shall see that you are offered wine and cake before you depart."

"I thank your kind courtesy, but I must hasten to other duties. Maestro Astolfo always has several affairs in hand and I seem always to lag behind the order of his requests. If you will dispatch the eagles to him by messenger, along with a letter favoring or disfavoring my labors here, as you see fit, we shall be obliged."

"That is soon done," he said, "and again I tender my gratitude. I shall fully commend your execution of the matter."

With the usual bows and flourishing of my short cloak, I took leave.

⋅⊷══◉══⊶⋅

There was to be a petite fete of celebration for the three of us, marking a success in my first unguided excursion into sciomantic venture. We hoped also to be celebrating the return of Mutano's voice, but he had so far kept silent in our company. He had, in fact, kept apart from us for long stretches. We surmised that he was exercising his throat; the voice of a man of his make, confined for a long period in the voice-box of a cat, must have suffered diminution, if not deterioration. Astolfo suggested that he might be practicing an aria supple and trillful and difficult to execute to amaze us.

The cook had told the steward to lay out our supper on a corner of the long table in the dining room, but Astolfo would not have it. The rains had returned and he desired the closeness of the kitchen, with its oven heat and lamplight glancing from the surfaces of burnished copper and polished crystal. He was punctilious upon the victuals too: turbot and cold veal, varied herbage, a roast of venison, and then an apple tart with a great wedge of cheese from my native province. Topery would include cider and beer and a bottle of wine, aged and heady.

He and I sat at the table the steward had brought in and sipped at draughts of cider whilst we waited for Mutano to appear.

As I expected, Astolfo used the time to ask sharp questions about the Sativius children and my procedure in dividing the shadows. I described in detail every stage of preparation, every step of the process, and every piece of apparatus. During my peroration, he smiled at certain passages, closed his eyes, and appeared to meditate during others. When I concluded, he pressed his fingertips together and considered silently for a space. Then: "I will say it is to your credit that you appear to have discovered, by strength of your own wit, another of the traditional methods of taking shadows."

I tried not to show that I was a little crestfallen. "Then this method was known already?"

He blinked his gray eyes and slowly rested them upon mine. "The world was here long before you and I scuffed its soil with our boots. There were mages of great mentation who came in the centuries before, rank on rank. Much of the lore they gained has been devoured by time. If we had it in its greater bulk, we should feel ourselves as small in comparison to them as scurrying voles."

"Hath this method I thought mine own a name?"

"*Severing* you know as the term for the thieving of a shadow surreptitiously, without its caster being aware. *Sundering* you know as when a shadow is taken by violence, raped away from the parent object. *Surrendering* we call it when a person voluntarily gives over

a shadow to the purposes of another. You have discovered without
the aid of instruction the process of *seduction,* wherein the shade is
lured from the parent object and leaves it gradually by force of
attraction to another object or under its own volition."

"You have before now hinted that shadows might possess minds
and wills independent," I said. "I do not see how this can be."

"Yet you might have tried another 'experiment,' as you call it,
and then come to a different turn of mind."

"How so?"

"Your procedure is so ingenious and so complicated that I hesitate to describe this one other method. After your machinations, it
will seem but puerile."

"You think I will scoff at Astolfo?"

He smiled more genially. "You might have separated the children, placing one in a room completely dark and the other in a room
with good light. Sitting in a chair opposite the one in the dark, you
might have whispered, *Shadow, find your own.* They hate and fear
the dark, do our umbrae, for it obscures them completely. In the
dark they fall into a state nearly comatose. They flee it to swim to
the light. But then other sages hold that they enter darkness as into
an ocean and swim about in it, keeping to their accustomed forms
by some unknown power they possess."

"How do you know which subject to place in the dark when
you lure them forth one from another?"

"In the instance of children, that one most confident in the love
of its parents, or of one of them, will have the stronger shadow and
it shall absorb the weaker. You yourself observed that Rudensia's
mother gave her a caress habitual, without thinking. Her shade was
the stronger."

"That is a simpler and less expensive method of division,"
I admitted. "Still, I believe that mine would more impress the
paterfamilias."

"I must agree," Astolfo said. "But yours had a large element of
danger. When you profused the shadow in the silvered glass with
energetic spark, you were fortunate that it did not acquire enough
vis to escape on its own and leave our child bereft."

"That is why I told Mutano to smash the glass upon the precise
instant."

He nodded. "Yes, you had that forethought, at least. . . . And
having spoken of him, we have summoned his presence."

Mutano entered the kitchen with something of a swagger in his march, strode to the table, and gazed down upon the viands with hearty pleasure. He smiled upon Astolfo and me, as beamingly as if he first saw us upon returning from a wearisome journey.

"Now we are complete," Astolfo said, "and the occasion is meet for the proposal of toasts. Falco, if you will but pour Mutano a healthy measure"—I poured the good beer into his mug—"I will begin by congratulating our younger friend upon his triumph in an enterprise of his own."

We drank and refilled and I raised my glass in Mutano's direction. "And Mutano must be feted," I said. "He has made it certain, without taking the man's life, that Castilio will never again despoil young maidens or steal away the paramours of others. I present also my grateful thanks for his aid at the house of Sativius."

We drank and refilled and Mutano pointed his glass toward Astolfo and me in turn. He cleared his throat officiously, took a deep breath, and spoke in three melodious tones:

"*Miaou.*"

PART TWO

⊷⊶⊷

The Gathering of Shadows

V

Shadow of the Valley

Among the most avid and wealthiest of the collectors of rarities who apply to our establishment is a small group of the nobility who name themselves the Green Knights and Verdant Ladies. Theirs is a cult of gardeners. Upon their spacious estates they roll out smooth greenswards and carve parterres tier upon tier; they shear topiary into curious shapes, heraldic, and allegorical and obscene; they plant gaudy exotic flowers rank after rank. They vaunt themselves upon the magnificence of their grounds and comb the world to search out curiosities.

To speak more accurately, they send out mercenaries like myself and my colleague Mutano to make their searches for them, after having first consulted with Master Astolfo. Trusting to his knowledge of all that has to do with shadows, they gape their purses generously to acquire plants that will throw fantastically contoured shadows upon the ground, shadows to complement their fountains and statuary, shadows to cool an enclosure or adorn an open space. They are confident that Astolfo shall deliver happy result. Trust is justified, for in matters where he lacks informancy and skill, he declines commission. The enterprise of shadow-dealing is sufficiently dangerous, he declares, without adding to it the perils of attendant ignorance.

His ignorance would soon be detected, for the cult numbers within it a clutch of learned antiquarians. One of these, a certain Ser Alverius, was refreshing his acquaintance with Pausanias, that ancient encyclopedic travel writer, accompanied by his cat, hearthfire, and wine, when he came across a passage that must have slipped his attention before.

The pages record an account of the Dark Vale in Arkady, an area that stretches southward from the eastern slopes of Mount Lykaion. Pausanias records that even though he had heard the tales and partly credited them, the rebel general Dousonious dared to march his army of seven thousand men through the valley, attempting to surprise his enemy's rear guard in the Lykaionian Meadows. On his bivouac deathbed he ordered his ministers to write down in the chronicles that the loss of his army was caused by plague. But the truth was known. The name of Dousonious now stands humiliated forever.

What seized the imagination of Ser Alverius was the detail that the plants of the Dark Vale are supposed to be sciophages—shadoweaters. He communicated his discovery to his cult colleagues and they were immediately greedy for these mythical plants and unwilling to believe them fanciful. They in turn communicated their desires to Astolfo, and I was sent upon this perhaps useless mission.

⊷═◉═⊶

All this substance I communicated to my host, the hill-country bandit Torronio, as we sat around the hungry small fire in this cave where he and his band had brought me as captive. They had taken me as I traveled the steep path through the pass below and offered violence if I did not follow them to their smoky lair and there deliver to them my gold.

This was an odd proceeding, I thought. Why did they not attempt to chop me down where I stood and lighten my quivering corpus of valuables? I discovered they were avid for news of the world beyond their hill. They would have had difficulty in putting my silver to use, exiled to the wilderness and with tall bounties prominent upon their heads.

Torronio passed to me a companionable jug of sourish ale and informed me that they would be taking my purse, as a matter of course.

"Let us negotiate," I said. "I will hand over six eagles—one to each of your men and two to you. For this amount, I shall expect you to feed and water my horse, share your eatables with me, and lodge me here by your fire for this night."

"Do you take me for your groom?"

"Signor Torronio, I do not. But my mount is thirsty. I should be pleased to spare a coin or two that we might be looked after."

"You but invite us to take all your coin and your makeshift nag also."

"The mount is not mine to bestow. I was reluctant to bring my own horse, the placid Torta, upon this journey and so hired this gelding whose name, I was told, is Belus. I have heard that there are bandits in this wood that prey upon travelers. Some, I understand, are so penurious they would make a meal of horseflesh."

"Do you not think the five of us can work our will upon you?"

"Mayhap," I said. "Yet the struggle would cost you sweat and hard breathing and at least two lives. Why should you suffer such exertion when I would share a few eagles willingly?"

He stared at me long, as if to judge of the soundness of my wits. Then he laughed softly. "Well, thou'rt no coward. It is also to your credit that you are so mindful of the horse. Yet five upon one make the chance strong in our favor."

I looked where the others sat together on an uneven ledge of stone and studied their shadows where the fire threw them upon the cave wall. "I should begin by skewering that beanpole fellow in the patched hose," I said. "He has no fight in him and his quick dispatch will undermine the courage of the others. Then I should look to the fate of that shifty little man there, he with the twitching squint. He only enters a fray when he sees the opponent already hotly engaged and he tries then to sneak about to the blind side. The red-haired lout with the vile laugh fancies himself an accomplished duelist and he does possess arm strength; but his feet are large and clumsy and are not always upon conformable terms with his intentions. That other gent, the dark, silent footpad, will pretend to engage with the sword while looking for opportunity to fling the dagger from his belt into my thigh. I should take pains to press him hard, so that he gaineth no space to ply his trick."

Torronio's smile withered. "And I?"

"Thou art the ablest. If you were of a mind to spare lives, you and I might try our steels in a private set-to."

"The night is long and you are travel-weary. You must sleep sooner or later and then we, having traded watch, will undo your head at the neck and count your gold. But this Belus seemeth too aged to make a palatable stew."

"You would not play me such a scurvy turn."

"Why say you so?"

"Your shadow belieth you." I pointed to its shape on the

moisturous wall. "The outlines of your colleagues are vague and hazy. These jacks lack true character and so might take my life underhandedly. But your lines are firm, and in the center of your shade there is a straight line so black it tendeth to a purple. Uprightness of character produces such a figure. You, Signor Torronio, are no bandit by nature but an upright man fallen upon stingy times."

"These things you know by looking at mere shadows?"

"Let me unfold myself to you a little," I said, and after telling him something of my situation in the port city of Tardocco and describing briefly some aspects of the shadow trade, I told him the story of the ancient Dark Vale and about the similar one in our province, about how men were reputed to lose their shadows there and how the herbs and flowers and shrubs and trees of that place would be in sharp demand among the obsessive wealthy and how I now traveled with the purpose of transporting some of these fabled flora out of their obscurity.

"And will you be well paid for this rooty plunder?" he asked.

"We shall all be well remitted—you and I the more handsomely, of course."

"All?"

"You five and I would make up a competent troop. By all signs, you do not flourish grandly. As I came up the hill path, I observed that none hath traveled here since the rains of last sennight. Scant must be your takings. You will be highly desired by guard troops and shire-reeves if you squirm into such a hole and feed upon vermin like that stoat turning there upon the spit."

"My history—our history—is no affair of yours."

"Indeed not," I replied, "nor of any interest whatsoe'er, unless you might wish to better your plight."

"You speak," he said, "as if you had expected to be waylaid by us. You give out your sentences as might an actor upon a stage. You came a-purpose to recruit."

"If I know of you and your whereabouts, so must others. They only wait till stravation brings you out of hiding. Already the noose prefigures your neck in its hungry oval."

"What is't you offer to better us? Only the opportunity to meet a death more spectral in your Dark Vale. Can you assure us that it truly exists? It resembles the matter of tales for children."

"I have taken it on faith," I replied, "the way I must accept many things I have not personally witnessed. We all know of the Mardrake;

it is the sign of Tardocco. Yet no one living has seen it. And as for Arkady, that country is lost to the historied ages. I go up through the hills to the Molvorio Mountains. In their midst lies another Dark Vale said to snatch shadows and to put forth plants of great value. We can make up a company and seek a fortune, or you may stay hunched in this smoking hole to wither away. In any case, six eagles are all you shall gather from me this night."

"Let me think on't till morn."

"Think then. But meantime you should advise that dusky little hop-o'-my-thumb to stay his hand free of his dagger. From where I sit I can place mine in his ear before he turns toward me."

He gave the fellow a look and quietly spoke his name. "Rinaldo."

The man shrugged, assenting, and turned his attention elsewhere.

"Six eagles be it, then," Torronio said. "We'll give thee meat and sup, poor though they are. We will water and provender your nag. Tomorrow we shall take consult upon the matter of your shadow bushes." He put forth his hand for the coins. "Count out six."

I did so, pleased not to have to cross blades. Torronio was of medium height, lithe and tawny, and his black eyes brooded with intelligence. I would have had difficulty blooding him without slaughter and I wanted sleep, that healing balm the poets prate of.

He gave over the jug again and I drank and it tasted less sour than before.

⊹—◉═⊹

I woke to the sound of their jawing as they debated my offer. My sword was in my right hand and when I sat up, I took care they should see I had held it ready through the night. They looked me over incuriously, then took up their jangle again. I found a dented tin ewer and took a swallow of water to spit out and splashed my face and wrists and inspected what weather I could see through the cave mouth.

Then Torronio beckoned me to join the group. "We would put to you some questions."

"I will answer four," I said, "be they brief."

The little dirk-flinger spoke. His voice rasped like a saw-blade over flint. "Do you know how to find the Vale or must we wander on the slopes like shepherdless goats?"

"I have a map."

"I should like to see this map."

"It is invisible," I said, and touched my forehead. "Count two."
I did not tell that I carried upon my person two maps, a true one
and a false.

"How can we know you do not draw us into a trap to reap the
bounties?"

"What need for that? If I were intent upon bounty gold, my
colleagues would surround us now. Count three."

The red-haired louty one: "How should we provision us? Your
supplies are as invisible as your map."

"Are we not a merry band of cutthroats? We shall denude the
sheepish we find in our way."

He began: "But there are few who—"

"And so conclude," I said. "Four are four."

"I do not like the look of this," said the tall, mopish one. He
fingered the hilt of his hanger until I rested my gaze upon the
weapon. Then he withdrew his hand.

"Thou'lt like it less till the success of the venture persuades thee
otherwise. Thou'rt of a sour mien and henceforth shall be addressed
as Crossgrain. You"—I gestured toward the dark, small one—"are
to be known as Sneakdirk. Tall yellow-hair shall be named Goldenrod and Rinaldo shall be Squint. Accustom these names to your
persons. Use them habitually. In the heat of affray, do not allow your
former names to escape your lips. From this time forward, we are
secret men."

"And I?" inquired Torronio. "What insulting cognomen will
you try upon me?"

"Thou art Torronio, since that was never your true name."

"Thyself?"

I thought for a trice. "Call me Stalwart," I said, "though by
rights I should be called Quartermaster."

"How so?"

"I have arranged to break our morning fast in a handsomer style
than you are used to. If Sneakdirk and Goldenrod will take my horse
down the path for about a mile the way I came, they shall find a
little gray mule tethered by a stream in the grove. That mule is laden
with provisions and weapons and maybe a pannier or two of stout
wine."

Torronio laughed aloud. "Well, we have been foreknown," he

said. "You have made it foolish to do else than follow your direc-
tives."

"It is good to meet a man of sense."

He replied jocularly: "And what shall be the name of the mule?"

"'Woman' I call her, because she hath a mind all her own and
will never learn by being beaten."

⋅⊶◉⟨⋅

Goldenrod and Sneakdirk returned a little before mid-morning.
Their brightened faces told that they had searched through the
bundles Woman had carried and had been pleased with what they
found. Some of the implements and instruments would mean naught
to them, but the dozen quick-edged swords and the array of smaller
blades had struck their desires. They had discovered the brandy too
and had a pull or two at a bottle that I did not begrudge them—a
guard-troop customarily plies new recruits with strong waters as a
means to fellowship. They had broken out the loaves of brown bread
and Goldenrod brandished one of them above his head as he trudged
along behind Sneakdirk on Belus, with Woman in tow.

We ate and drank a while and then I began the oration I had
written out in my mind, telling them that the crimes for which they
were hunted were no worse than what any ordinary men might
commit; that is, upon finding a shipwreck perched on a reef on the
coast north of Tardocco, they had undertaken to plunder it, according to the custom of salvagers. They could not have known that
the murderous pirate Morbruzzo and his men had lured the *Silver-
een* to ruin with false lights on the beach and then hid away till
nightfall. Our four petty plunderers had been sighted bearing away
some silks and casques by townsfolk, who described them to the
local guard troops. They fled, abandoning their gains. These events
had placed them in their present pinched circumstances.

"Better for my purposes were you of a more criminal breed," I
said, "for what I have in mind will require steady nerve in the face
of dangers you have never bethought. Yet you may bring yourselves
to the point if desire of gold can spur you."

"Gold is ever a reliable spur," Torronio said. "Tales of gold are
ever unreliable."

"We shall be mining gold from shadows, as I explained. We
shall be gathering plants to carry from the Dark Vale to be sold in
Tardocco. I will demonstrate how to transport this herbage with as

little damage as possible. You will be astonished to see how much a single *Herba umbrae supplex* can bring."

"In the supplies you loaded on Woman were no sorts of agricultural tools," said Goldenrod. "No spades or shovels or mattocks to dig with."

"We shall trust to the Fates to throw such things in our way."

At these words they declined their polls doubtfully.

"How much?" asked Squint.

"Two hundred eagles at the least—fifty for Stalwart, thirty for Torronio, the rest divided as you see fit."

"If so much gold accrues to mere husbandry—digging plants and carting them away—why do not venturers flock to the place and make themselves wealthy with ease?" This was Torronio's pointed question.

"Reasons three," I said. "Few know the location of the ancient and fabled vale, and fewer still have heard of these strange flora. Foremost, though, is the danger. We may lose our lives and the manner of our deaths, while mysterious, is reputed most unpleasant."

"Whom must we fear?" asked Goldenrod. He thrust his chest forward to signify bravery.

"I know only that they are shadows."

They gazed at me, then at one another.

"I fear no shadow," Squint said.

"Then naught stands in our way."

Torronio shook his head. "I stay doubtful. You have not told us all. Something in this matter conturbeth me."

"I say again: Dangers abound."

"Well," he said, "we shall go to this vale. We have long since left a life of safety behind."

⋅→═◉═←⋅

Torronio was wise to doubt, for I had told them only so much as might persuade them to fall in with me. I had not told them that a great deal more gold than I spoke of was at stake and that some part of it, should we end happily, must go to Maestro Astolfo, by whose commission the enterprise was undertaken. It was he who would inspect these plants, pass on their authenticity, and market them to the vanity of that circle of nobility who named themselves the Green Knights and Verdant Ladies, they who harbored such passion for their sumptuous and curious gardens. It was Astolfo who had outfitted me for the venture—and not me alone.

This horticultural task was not only a commission, it was a test of skills. I had been now six years in service to Astolfo alongside his manservant Mutano. Ours had become a companionable rivalry which lately had risen to such a pitch that Astolfo proposed this present quest for us as a matching of our abilities. He told us of this particular Dark Vale, described its treasures, spoke of the attendant perils, and then set this trial of judgment: "Which of you first delivers to me handsome specimens, truly desirable plants, shall possess as much as seven parts of our profit. From the remaining portion I will pay all accrued expenses and keep for myself only what is left from the rest. If all goes well, one of you shall amass heaping chests full."

His proposal suited. I had been gaining skills and knowledge, laboring in the craft, and had scored successes by my own efforts, prompting Mutano to become jealous of me; he found me mounting the ladder of Astolfo's esteem while he remained in his accustomed station. Too, he had suffered a mishap. In attempting to reacquire the beautiful voice that had been robbed from him by violence, he had acquired instead a voice not his own at all. These days he could speak only in the voice of a cat, a voice that had fastened to him like a disease of the throat. He burned with fury—not against the maestro or myself, but against the unjust circumstances that sometimes betrayed him to ridicule and scarlet embarrassment.

For these reasons, I thought I might have an advantage. Mutano was eager to shine; he would be impatient to make a start; he might neglect some point of thoughtful preparation. If he misstepped, I must seize opportunity to repay some of the knockabout, kick-arse treatment he had visited upon me in our early days together. Here lay a chance to make myself his equal.

Accordingly, I gave myself to long study of certain of the villa's library of books, manuscripts, codices, and maps. One edition of Mandeville's *Travels* was inlaid with many a map, richly colored and decorated with mermaids and mardrakes, but I soon thrust it away as untrustworthy and inspected more recent cartography in the *Collecteana* of Gaius Junius Solinus and in the anonymous *Imago Mundi*. In short, I examined every source with any least promise down to its last majuscule.

Meanwhile, I studied also Mutano, marking in my mind the pages and maps he most often turned to and gauging what sheets most keenly roused his interest. When the day came that he decided to desert the company of ancient authors and strike toward the northern mountains, I was confident I knew what route he had inscribed in his mind.

Over and again he had studied De Casa's *Mappae Mundi Magnae,* and he had copied out one page on a sturdy vellum that could withstand the rigors of hard journeying. He must have been pleased with his thoughts because he began insensibly to emit a feline purr so resonant that it filled the silence of the room like a bowed viol string. He had even been so neglectful of his best interest as to trace out lines on the page with his thumbnail, so that I was able to follow the projected course of his route with ease.

Keeping that track in mind, I consulted the newer maps and journals of the region by Duclessis, Filomorio, Amerigus, Getzner, and the brothers Muzzino, among others. I had hoped I might discover a swifter and more efficient path to the Vale than Mutano's, a path that might cross his own at a farther point so that I should be ahead of him on the track.

My hope was fulfilled. I hit upon a more efficacious trail to the valley, one less littered with obstacles, and made a serviceable map. I also made another map, a feigning one of no use to a traveler, of the kind ship captains wary of pirates preserved, along with false logs. If one of my maps were to fall into the hands of others, this false one must be it.

Then it was necessary that I should try to confirm some of the rumors I had heard in the street-stalls and taverns about the flight from justice of a luckless quartet of fishermen who plundered the vessel that Morbruzzo the pirate had lured to reef-wrack. They had afterward leagued, it was said, with the dispossessed scion Eleazar del Binnoto, also a fugitive, though not from public justice. He had become embroiled in a tiresome family squabble over estate property, had boxed a cousin's ears, and had offered to duel. His father had disowned him—or pretended to, for the sake of propriety—and Torronio, as he now called himself, had exiled his existence to the savage wilds, there to bemoan his fate to the trees and rocks like a lovesick shepherd.

Holding all this matter in mind, I depleted my small personal treasury, gathered weapons and other usefuls, provided my pouch with eagles, and set out to be captured by the Wreckers, as the towns-people named the ill-starred five. In the rumor galleries of Tardocco they were reputed a fearsome group. I did not credit such report.

These were the reasons, therefore, that on our second day of the journey toward the Dark Vale, I gave my band of illicit dependents certain orders.

"In a short while, we shall come to a place where the path widens to receive the jointure of another trail to the west. We shall go past this fork two furlongs or so, then we shall return to efface every trace of our coming there. No pebble, no hoofprint, not a displaced leaf shall show disturbance. Then we shall go back to the farther point, set up a cold camp, dig holes to cache supplies in, and await our guest."

"Who is this guest to be?" Torronio asked.

"He is our provider," I said. "He bringeth the spades and other implements we must labor with. And if I mistake not, he will be supplied with wine, cheese, salt meat, and bread. These stuffs will provide for our meals into the Vale and back again and on to Tardocco, where I will merchant our prizes."

"He must be a generous soul, so graciously to charitize."

"He is as yet insensible of his munificence. You must employ persuasion."

"*You*—and not *we*?"

"You will have an easier time if he see me not. The sight of my visage would redouble his fury and he would fight like twelve devils."

"How furiously will he fight with you viewless?"

"Be well prepared," I said, "for you must not take his life or wound him in any serious fashion. If he come to real harm, we are all done for."

"How so?"

"He hath powerful friends. In particular, he claims one friend whose reach is long and whose grasp would be merciless."

"Who is this all-powerful eminence?"

"You need not know. Sufficeth that I have provided easy tak-ings necessary for our enterprise."

"The more I learn of you, the more I find to mistrust," Torro-nio said.

"Your misgivings are natural. But do be mindful of this man's person. He will be of use to us in other ways at a later time."

"If so you say." He shrugged and turned away.

→═◦═←

The business went almost as planned. Attentive to my request that Mutano not be harmed in any serious way, they decided to overpower him rather than to brandish steel. Sneakdirk shinnied up into an oak which overhung the trail and knotted a rope to climb before dropping it to Squint. There in the leafage they made seats as comfortable as they might and then Sneakdirk climbed out to the tip where he could overlook the trail behind.

I stationed myself in a thicket to eastward where I could observe unseen and hoped that I had calculated with some accuracy the pace of Mutano's passage. He had taken the shorter route as it was laid out on his favored map but neglected to search into the condition of the track. Washed away in places, with two bridgeless streams to cross, hindered with fallen timber, it was the slower way. I computed Mutano at about seven hours in arrears of me and, if I proved correct, he must be nearing us now.

And here he was, pat on cue like the cat i' th' adage. Sneakdirk clambered to his lower perch and told groundlings Crossgrain and Goldenrod that our man approached from the west, mounted on a roan horse and leading in train two mules laden with boxes and chests lashed with diamond hitches. Squint uncoiled his rope, saw to the loop knot, and snugged into the leafage so closely I could hardly make out his form.

Along came Mutano, careless under a cloudless sky, thinking no doubt of the profit he would soon turn with easy spadework. But when Squint dropped the loop around his shoulders and began to spin the rope about him like a spider enwrapping a hornet, Mutano let out a ferocious roar, loud as any lion waylaid by pygmies in the Hyrcanian deserts.

I had heard Mutano's feline voice only in domestic setting, when he would purr to himself or meow to me in hopes I might begin to decipher his cattish dialect. This great, hoarse roaring startled me. One would not think that a man's breast held breath sufficient to give it utterance. The hairs stood erect on my neck.

The sound startled his mount also and it bounded from beneath him and galloped up the trail ahead. The mules, being loosed, ran off into the bordering woods, for they took fright equally with the horse. If Squint had not already twirled two loops around Mutano, the large man would have landed on his feet, ready to defend himself. As it was, he swung there in the air for a short space, time enough for Crossgrain and Goldenrod to emerge from the bushes and tether more rope upon him.

Mutano growled and spat and hissed as loud as a lynx caught in a forester's net. If I closed my eyes, I might declare it was not my colleague there but a large, dangerous animal bristling with fight.

In fact, this description fit Mutano at this moment, as he gave battle with legs and feet and tried to wrest his arm free to get at his sword. He was beginning to make some headway out of his toils when Goldenrod wrapped his arms around his legs and pulled Mutano down as if plucking an apple from a limb. Then they bound him tightly, Sneakdirk and Squint dropping down to aid, and all taking care to keep clear of his boots and his teeth—for he snapped at them as he spat and hissed and his eyes glowed greenish-orange, tiger-wild.

Crossgrain tied Mutano to a sturdy ash tree and stood by to keep guard. The others set out in search of the mules and I struggled to the other side of my thicket and stalked up the trail in pursuit of the horse.

In about half an hour, I found Defender, Mutano's mount, cropping grass beside the trail. This horse knew me of old and did not gallop away as I came to take the reins and lead him a little farther still, to where we had set up camp. There I awaited to hear the approach of the Wreckers with Mutano in tow, and when I heard their voices and the shuffle of the mules on the trail I slipped away into the surrounding wood where I could observe the doings in camp.

So far, all had succeeded as I'd I planned, except for the leonine roar that had cost us some bit of trouble with the mules. And my makeshift band of hapless highwaymen followed my orders in regard to Mutano. They made him a place by the fire, which they now set spark to, not knowing that he had exchanged his own tongue for that of a cat.

In a while Torronio strayed casually from the site and sought me out. "Well," he began, "it has taken place as you said it would. I may now be willing to believe these miraculous tales you tell of man-eating shadows and gardener nobility and easy wealth."

"'Twill be none so easy. We have but made a start. We will push on tomorrow sunup and make the longer part of our journey."

"What of our captive?"

"Before we set out, you shall give him his freedom, leave him sufficient eatables, and tell him that you shall return to rescue him from the wilderness. Also you must hide away, in the hidden cache-holes we dug, food and drink to enable us to march back to Tardocco from here. Tell him also that if he have patience, he shall possess his mount again."

"Should not you deliver these tidings?"

"He must not spy me."

"As you say, then. Shall I fetch bread and water for you here?"

"Thank you," I said. "Do so discreetly. In the morning, join with me about half a league farther on. I will ride Mutano's horse. Sneakdirk may ride my hireling mount and bring along Woman. He showed a capable hand in taking our captive."

"He has a fisherman's wrist for casting rope," Torronio said, departing.

⋅→▬◉═⟪⋅

They made a late start from camp; the sun was over the treetops when they joined me on the trail. We went on, the six of us with three horses and three mules, making slow progress, with Cross-grain quarreling over his turn to ride and Goldenrod complaining that he, being lifelong a jolly sailor, was not suited to stony trails in thickety hills. When we came to an open space at ridgetop, I halted our train and gestured toward the forward vista. "Behind yonder mountain lie our fortunes."

Though it was a league from us, it looked to stand as close as the wall of a castle and seemed as sheer in its slope. Green and pleasant shone its foot, but the incline darkened to a misty blue and then to purple and along its topmost ridge a fringe of frost silvered the peaks against a bright blue heaven. Our trail meandered from our vantage through a grassy, unpeopled plain, then disappeared into the mountain's lower forest.

"This day's march shall bring us to the foot," I said, "and there we shall make camp for tonight and all next day. We shall be climbing that eminence for two nights, lying doggo during daylight. We must accustom ourselves to moving in darkness and we shall not enter the Dark Vale until the dark o' the moon."

"Why so?" asked Crossgrain. "The Vale does not retreat. Let us make haste and reap its lettuces and sell them off and spread our blankets on massy heaps of coin."

"Daylight is too perilous in that place," I replied, and did not explain, though I saw by his expression that impatience sat restless on his mind like an unhooded falcon on a hunter's wrist. "Alive you may sleep on coin; dead you can sleep as comfortably on stones and thorns."

⋯⋰≡◎≡⋱⋯

So on we went at leisure. The sky was pleasant, the verdure appealing, and by the foot of the mountain ran a river where we filled our two casks and watered the beasts and refreshed ourselves, bathing in the cold water.

We found an easy glade a little above the plain and set up camp and lazed and ate. When night fell, I went to my supply chest and brought out four lanthorns fashioned to my particular design.

"You see how this lanthorn is made," I said, "with top and all sides but one so tightly enclosed that no ray of light can escape its innards."

They looked on gravely.

With a scrap of tinder and a quick steel spark I lit the oiled wick inside. "You see?" I closed the black tin door so that no light showed, opened it again to let light shine out, then clapped it shut quickly. "You see?"

They stood silent. Squint shrugged, and I called him forth.

"Stand here," I said, placing him between the lanthorn and the thick, whitish trunk of a plane tree. I opened the lanthorn blind, then snapped it closed. To the others: "You see?"

"What is there to see?" Crossgrain said. "Anyone can open and shut the blind of a lanthorn."

"His shadow on the tree trunk—what did you observe?"

"That without the lamplight it does not appear and when you loose the light upon him his shadow darkens the wood. "'Tis but a child's game."

"How long does his shadow stay on the wood?"

"Briefly, of course."

"What else did you see of the surroundings?"

"Little. The light went away too quickly."

"This then is our exercise," I explained. "In that brief space of

time while the lamplight is loosed we must each learn to see and
locate the objects about us accurately and remember where they are.
And we must not allow our shadows to lie on any surface for more
than the swiftest of moments."

"Why so?" asked Torronio.

"If our shadows be not visible, they cannot be taken from us.
Yet in the dark we cannot find the objects of our desire. So we must
learn to place them in our minds as if by the flash of a lightning
bolt and then go to them in the ensuing blackness. If we are deft at
this sleight o' hand, we shall take our prizes."

They gazed at one another for some moments and then laughed
softly.

"We are fishers," said Sneakdirk. "We work our boats and nets
at sea when no light from landward shows. We float silent in the
darkest night."

"That is one reason I have enlisted you," I replied. "But fishermen labor in moonlight and starlight. We enter the Vale in the dark
of the moon. Have you seen your shadow cast by starlight?"

"Faintish to discern."

"Too faint, too flimsy, we shall hope, to be snatched away from
us. We shall toil when the moon is absent in a place where little
starlight enters. If we work quickly, our shadows shall be secure."

"Shadows are often stolen from men and women," Torronio
said. "I have heard that in Tardocco town there dwelleth a master
thief named Astolfo whose trade in shadow-filching is profitable as
well as venerable. Yet I never heard that they who lose their shadows to him perish afterward."

"Those shadows still exist in our world," I said. "They only go
to serve the purposes of others. But shadows forfeited in the Dark
Vale are destroyed utterly—so all the sages agree. It has been said
that they are devoured. Such a destruction must bring the end
of life."

"This is but a tale for the idle chimney nook," he said.

"We shall take precautions," I stated firmly, and with that we set
at it again, opening the lanthorn blinds quickly and clapping them
shut. We advanced so well in this practice that in the time required
for the least gray glimmer of a shadow to appear on the tree trunk, we
had thrust into memory much detail of the surroundings.

When this employment began to wear the aspect of sport, I
called a halt and we made ready for sleep.

"By tomorrow midday we shall reach the limits of the Vale," I told them. "There we will stop and observe. In the dark we shall enter."

"Well," said Torronio. The others said nothing. Solemnity had crept upon them.

⸻

"Stalwart, where are you?"

It was Crossgrain inquiring, but his voice lacked its customary querulous tone. There was no reason to whisper as Sneakdirk did, since we were going not among men or animals but only plants. The Dark Vale, it was said, was void of animal life. Only plants throve there, as in that happy age of the world before humanity arrived to sully creation.

"Here I am," I said.

"I cannot see you. I can see nothing."

I grasped his shoulder from behind and, startled, he made a tremulous half leap.

"Gods!"

I had wrapped myself in a thin black cloak, muffling the green-forest colors of hose and doublet and eclipsing the glitter of buttons and silver buckles. My colleagues were outfitted less prudently and I could just make out their forms, dark against the dark.

We had made our way in the gloaming down the disused trail through the hill cleft and had paused till full dark before descending into the Vale itself. I had spent the daylight on the hilltop, scanning the area with my glass, trying to distinguish the more valuable plants and locating them in memory. This was a vague undertaking. The terrain would be much different at the lower levels than it appeared from a height and the darkness made of this landscape a different world.

Commercing with shadows, as I had done now for a half dozen seasons, I had experienced darknesses of every shade, texture, and smell, but this night in the Dark Vale brought forth a voluminous atmosphere aggressive in blackness. Here might be one of the world's origins of darkness, I thought, and there was writing to the effect that great earth-mouths in the Vale opened to a world below and that visible darkness poured forth from these orifices like streams gathering themselves to rivers from woodland springs. It had been conjectured by Albertus and Lullius that the precious flora of the

Vale had first developed in these local subterranean caverns and over their long generations had progressed gradually to the surface, braving the light and changing their pallid mushroom hues to dark greens nigh black in their flat dullness. It was proposed by some half dozen wise herbalists that these plants—ferns, flowers, creeping shrubs, and low bushes—fed upon shadows to replenish the obscure powers they had derived from their underworld beginnings.

But books are never so accurate or so wise as their authors claim and here we had to trust mainly to our own wits.

We had fared middling well so far. Squint had proved the aptest among us for facility in opening and closing the lanthorn blinds and Goldenrod was most capable at locating specimens in the black intervals. But the farther we penetrated into the depths of the Vale, the deeper the obscurity thickened, and this had caused Crossgrain to lose all sense of where I was and where the others might be.

"All goes well," I told him. "I am here at your side."

"I can see nothing. I feel this dreadful darkness pressing upon my eyes like dusty cloth."

"'Tis thick," I admitted.

"No! My eyes—"

"Light us," I told Squint. "Be quick."

He unblinded the lanthorn and shut it again and in that instant we saw that Crossgrain's eyes had been taken from him. That was our swift impression. Then when the dark returned and the glimmer-echo of the light had faded from my eyeballs, I understood. A great black moth had lit upon Crossgrain's forehead—the size of a saucer, this insect—and its velvet wings spread over his eyes.

"It is but a bug," I said. "Cast it from you. The gleam of your eye-water drew it to you."

"'Tis monstrous," he said.

"There will be more. We must take all care."

"There was to be no animal in here. So you said. What else might there be?"

"Our business is with plants. Did you not glimpse a night-bloomer just now in reach of your right-hand side?"

We heard him step away and heard the rustle of his hand amid foliage. "Yes," he said. "I feel a huge blossom here. Moist and pulpy, like the tongue of a young heifer, though not wet."

"Feel below where its stem joins to the main stalk. Snip there and place the blossom in your pouch. Then follow the stalk to the ground and find whether you can lift it out or we must dig."

We heard him fumbling with the plant and breathing hoarsely as he stooped, though not from exertion. The black moth had quickened the breath of each of us.

Then he swore. "The ground is covered with—"

We waited. "What is it?"

"Light!"

Squint complied, and we saw that the ground about Crossgrain's feet writhed as if with throbbing vines. A network of ebon vines undulated, shiny and repulsive. When he closed the lanthorn, we waited a space to try to comprehend what we had seen.

Goldenrod spoke first. "Black serpents. They are all around us. I can feel them over my boots and crawling upward."

"We are undone," said Crossgrain.

"Courage," I said. "If they were noxious, we should already be shrieking with pain. But there is nothing here for a poison serpent to strike. The plants consume the shadows of anything that moves."

"These serpents move most unpleasantly," said Goldenrod.

"But they cast no shadow, being so close to the ground."

"What if they be attracted to eye-gleams like the moth?"

"Did you not note that they have no eyes? They are harmless to us. Let us set about our tasks."

"What is that smell?" asked Torronio. "It much clingeth."

We made sounds of disgust nigh unto sickness. A passerby in this deep night, if any such person could be in this place, would surmise that we had all fallen foul of spoilt oysters.

"It smells as of an ancient offal pit, filled with excrement and diseased corpses."

"It is odorous as a hundred turnip-fed bum-blasts."

"A devil has shat here and been proud of his work."

Squint ascertained the source. "It is those cursed blind serpents. They exude an oil that smears upon the skins of things. They need not fangs to repulse their enemies. Their perfumery is more daunting than the sharpest bite."

"Take heart, lads. Let us cleave to our purpose. Keep in your mind's eye the picture of gold coins stacked into a tower. Let it glow before you in this foul darkness like a beacon on a promontory."

They answered not, but Squint was busily opening and closing the shutter of the lanthorn and the Wreckers were gathering leaves, buds, roots, and blossoms as quickly as they could. They were not discriminate in their collecting, but I had no heart to admonish. I longed to depart this noisome hole as avidly as did they.

⊷═◉═⊶

We were at this tedious work for the rest of the watch. The Wreckers tried to lighten their burden with common shipmate raillery, as when Goldenrod said to Crossgrain, "Had'st not thou once a wife who smelled as of this place?" and Crossgrain retorted, "If you say so, then thou know'st more than is well for thee." But there was more determination than true humor in their chat and when the east began to lighten they were glad to hear me give order to depart.

"Take care to tie up the bags and keep the vial lids tight," I said. "We must not cast our shadows on our prizes."

They mumbled assent and we turned to go back up the slope, but I had miscalculated the hours and more light was spread through the sky than was healthy for our welfare. A saving grace was that clouds thinly veiled the east; we did not cast dark shadows with sharp edges but only ghostly emanations, the tinges of shadow that the pulpy leaves rubbed against and the questing tendrils of vines touched searchingly.

Wrapped in my black cloak, I was less affected than the others, but when a great black leaf that looked something like a burdock swept against my tinge-shadow my forearms went gooseflesh and my neck hair prickled. I urged them along more quickly, and they did not hang back. They struggled upward as fast as they could.

When we arrived at camp on the crest of the ridge the sun was almost ready to peer over the horizon, and I ordered them to cache all our goods in the holes we had dug to store them and to cover these over with canvas and brush.

This done, we looked to one another. Squint must have caught the worst of it. His pupils were enlarged and unfocused, gray sweat bathed his neck and forehead, and his face and arms and hands had taken on a sickly, blue-gray pallor, as of a consumptive shut long away indoors.

"Brandy," I said. Goldenrod reached for the bottle in our chest of potables and Squint dosed himself with three liberal swallows. His eyes became calmer, but his complexion remained gray.

"How goest thou?" I asked.

He considered. "It felt like something was being pulled out of me," he said. "Out of my chest, from between the ribs."

"Like a knife withdrawn?"

"No . . . like a length of wool-stuff slipped through the fingers."

"Painful?"

He shook his head and tottered and his mates settled him to the ground, where he put his head between his knees and coughed dryly.

"Is anyone else affected?"

"Here, cap'n," Sneakdirk said. "Naught but only a twinge, like the passing of a dead woman's hand over my front." He wiped his forehead. "'Tis away from me now. . . . I will take brandy for it."

"Better conserve," I said. "We know not but we may have need."

"Let us all take a sup now," Goldenrod suggested. "I am certain it hath power to ward off evil aforehand."

I let them jolly along with such talk, then put it to them: "What think you? Shall we try the Dark Vale again tomorrow night? We have learned that it is indeed the danger it is fabled to be, though we know not what causes it to be so."

"But we have learned," said Torronio, "that our precautions are good defenses, if we take pains to follow them aright. We were only tardy in taking leave, so that our palest shades betrayed us. If we approach in full dark and depart while the dark still holds, we shall be secure enough."

"But we would not return to the same place," objected Crossgrain. "If we go back, we must thrust farther to gain a different variety of herbage."

When they looked at me, I nodded. "He says true. There will be more profit in a wide selection. But are we willing to face those slime-snakes and their dire stenches again? Maybe we can ablute ourselves with a substance to keep the ooze from us."

"But look!" said Sneakdirk. "The slime is drying."

So it was. Goldenrod had been most thoroughly covered with the ooze, and I asked him to stand forward against the sunrise now full on the horizon. As we watched, the black oils whitened like campfire coals embering, gathered to a gray dust, and fell from him like flour through a sifter. He shook himself like a bear that has forded a cold river, and all that substance dropped away.

"I am game to return," he said.

When I put it to them that we must capture some of those black serpents to bring out of the Vale, they were displeased. The hour was drawing toward twilight and it would soon be time to reenter.

"Wherefore?" scolded Crossgrain. "I do not relish going again amongst these smelly slime-worms, but I will do so to obtain plants. Yet I see no profit in the serpents. No sound mind would purchase such ugliness."

"I have not become enamored of them," I replied, "but I have had a thought. The slime that covered Goldenrod changed to white powder when the sunrays struck it. Upon examining, I found it to resemble that generative fine dust the ancients called *pollis* or *pollen,* necessary to the propagation of all flora excepting the ferns. I think that if we carry our Dark Vale plants away, they will not propagate without the aid of those black snakes."

"So you think," retorted Crossgrain, "but you do not know."

"True . . . Can you conjecture another purpose for such animals?"

"They exist," said Sneakdirk, "in order to sour the innards of anyone who attempts to uproot those plants. Their guardian purpose is to sicken by putridity, in the fashion of vultures that protect themselves by vomiting."

"I will perform this task myself," I said, "since none else hath heart for it. If the rest of you will gather the flora, I will collect the serpents. I may take as my reward a slightly larger portion of profit."

"And welcome to it," said Goldenrod.

So we returned to the Vale, following the track as before but pushing a little farther into the valley, where the darkness seemed to grow thicker and more malodorous with every pace. Squint had acquired a swift skill in unblinding and reblinding his lanthorn and the others grew defter in plucking, snipping, and uprooting. I judged that we would have a broad variety of plant life to take away.

My duty with the serpents went none so pleasingly. I grasped them up, dropped them in disgust, found others, and thrust them into a leathern bag. Though eyeless, they struck at my hands and legs as would any of their breed, but they had no fangs. It was something like catching eels, except that people make dishes of eels.

The man who would eat these serpents must be a starving omnivore, capable of ingesting iron, stone, and the burdens of privies.

Yet again I had miscalculated the amount of time our expedition must consume, and my error cost us grievous. There being no birds in the Vale, there were no fore-dawn songs to warn of daybreak and, too, we had penetrated farther and would require more time to leave.

The light came on sooner than we were prepared for, and on this return our shadows were more substantial than before. Torronio advised his Wreckers to keep close to one another, reasoning that in a group they would cast but one large shadow instead of five smaller ones and the plants would not be able to tear such a large one away.

It proved a sound stratagem until Goldenrod gave in to his terror, broke from the pack, and struggled up the slope past me as I led them. There he stood plain against the light that slanted over the ridgetop. He had climbed some six paces before me, panting, stumbling, and sobbing. I saw that his shadow, though not solid, had sufficient body for a black, spiny bush to catch its edge with a thorny twig.

There was an instant when his shadow seemed to stretch like a woolen stocking pulled from the leg. And then came a sudden *chuck* of sound, as of an arrow striking into an oat-straw archery target. The tall fellow uttered no more than a squeak; a mouse in the claws of a tabby would make a louder sound.

His shadow I could not see as the bush enveloped it, but the effect on the plant was evident. The ebon thing shuddered from ground to top leaf. It wriggled within itself, enlarging its shape, and the pulpy leaves rubbed against one another with a motion like a butcher washing his hands after a slaughter.

Goldenrod—or rather, his corpus, for he was no longer a living man nor even the same man now dead—pitched southwise off our track like a statue toppling. As life left him, I could feel the serpents in my bag suddenly roil and tumble together. The other plants around set up an inward commotion. All about us there was a change in everything, even in the soil. Everything *shifted*.

Now the Vale gave birth to an eerie music, a moaning dirge mingled of the voices of scores of men, a chorus of those who had died here, their shadows absorbed into the bodies of plants as red wine is absorbed into a swatch of linen. What mouths produced this music we never discovered. I have conjectured that the sad chords emitted from animals we had not seen, but Torronio proposed that the blind serpents sang out when a shadow was taken by the Vale.

There was no time to debate. We redoubled our efforts, straining every muscle to haste us out of that place. Each of us felt a mucid clutching at his shadow, a sensation we would feel in our sleep for long nights to come.

⊷══◉◉══⊶

We climbed at last out of the reach of the Vale and no more of us were stricken fatally, yet none was soundly whole. Each had lost some part, though small, of his shadow and of his *vis vitae.*

We stored last night's gathering quickly and then flung ourselves to the ground in silence and lay like shipwrecked men cast ashore. I felt strengthless, as after a long bout with grippe, and strength did not return to my limbs for some part of an hour.

My case was not the worst. Crossgrain lay perspiring in rivulets, staring sightlessly at the high blue sky. He heaved for breath and his teeth chattered. We rose to our feet to gaze down upon him but offered no aid, for none knew how to minister to one whose shadow had been half devoured. Squint thought to pour brandy into him, but his chattering teeth and the convulsions of his breast prevented that succor. Sneakdirk thought to allay his anguish somewhat by holding a blanket between him and the light, so that his sadly torn shadow did not lie in the sun, and this did seem to alleviate his suffering. In a while he quietened and closed his eyes in unpeaceful sleep.

Though none had stomach, we moved ourselves to eat and drink. Afterward we sat silent, looking sorrowfully at one another. In time I said what all waited to hear: "We must bring Goldenrod out of the Vale."

"Why must we?" demanded Crossgrain. "He lives not. He has no wife nor child to mourn. His elder brother died off the coast of Clamorgra in a great tempest. There is scant reason to risk ourselves."

"He is our friend and comrade fallen in the enterprise," Torronio said. "This duty bears upon us."

Crossgrain objected. "I would not call him friend. We were ill sorted."

"It matters not," said Squint. "It is our duty regardless."

"Our time there would be better spent in collecting more herb-age," Crossgrain said. "We have much expense to make up for now."

"As to that," I said, "we shall gather no more. I spoke before-hand of the perils we might meet, but this mortality is too sorrow-ful. We must return to bring Goldenrod away and bury him with proper honor."

"We have no honor—" Crossgrain began, but he was shouted down. I believe that each felt that any of us might have failed of his nerve and broken rank and suffered shadow-loss and died dread-fully in an alien place. We did not wish to live unreconciled. I pictured my lifeless corpse lying in a black hell apart from all other humanity forever, my life taken by gruesome, foul agency.

We decided to put our gatherings in order, go back after dark to the Vale, bear Goldenrod away, and depart on the morrow for the bivouac where Mutano stood abandoned.

⊷══◉══⊷

Events did not fall in so orderly a succession.

As soon as it was securely dark we made our way back down the ridge slope, our estimation being that Goldenrod's body would lie about halfway to the valley floor on the overgrown path. We had to steel ourselves to begin the lightless decline and our spirits were sorely battered. I tried to assure Torronio and the remaining Wreckers that our shadows would regenerate from their damaged states and, over a healing period, make themselves whole again.

I did not know if this conjecture would prove true. Shadows damaged by clumsy thieves or by accident or combat or otherwise will indeed return to their earlier conditions or near, but a shadow devoured must be lost, I thought. Yet I said naught, for it was best not to dishearten my fellows.

Nor had I been wholly truthful in the matter of Goldenrod. In a different circumstance, I might have let him lie to decompose into the evil soil of the Vale or to be eaten by whatever tenebrous scav-engers ranged therein. My hidden desire was to examine the corpse, in order to determine if the manner of his dying left marks by which I might discover some method of defense against the deadly flora of the place. If I could find such a thing, a fortune lay before me.

Down the pathway we struggled, keeping close company and

hearing all around us the succulous leaves rubbing one against another and feeling, more than hearing, the blind black snakes crawling about. We made ourselves silent as the night and place demanded.

Then we could not ascertain the spot where Goldenrod must lie. The track had overgrown notably during the brief time we had come away from it. There was an abrupt steepness of the slope where our comrade had fallen, but he was not near it.

"I misremember it being so close-knit here," Sneakdirk whispered, and we assented silently as we scattered out to search.

We were sufficiently diligent, I am sure, to have turned him up, but that tall, lanky body was nowhere to be found. He seemed to have melted into the surrounding Nature as a pinch of salt will melt in a pail of water. Squint unblinkered our light more times than was safe, but naught was to be seen.

"Come away, lads," I said. "There are mysteries in this place we lack resource to comprehend. Our friend is gone from us, taken by peril, as I forewarned you."

They agreed readily, except for Sneakdirk, who averred that Goldenrod had owed him some small amount he wished to reclaim from the corpus. His objection was swept away.

The starry midnight had passed by the time we returned to camp. We composed ourselves for sleep and lay in our places, keeping well away from the pallet where Goldenrod had lain. My sleep was uneasy with nervy dreams and, to judge by the muttering and restlessness, so was that of all.

⤖⊙⤖

In the morning we were brisker, boiling up tea and munching the biscuits and salt beef we had found in Mutano's store of victual. We spent a goodish deal of time putting our samples in order to travel, and it was then that my bagful of a dozen or so of the black serpents disclosed itself as a clutch of inert vines or roots.

They had been snakes when I thrust them into the leathern bag—slime-sheathed, offal-smelling, writhing, and blindly striking. But when I brought them out into the light to place them in a wicker basket, they had changed into solid, woody lengths, so stiff as to be almost rigid. Except for the general shape, there was little to recall their former serpentine nature. An indentation here might suggest a mouth or some lichenous mottling elsewhere might recall scales, but these details seemed but accidental as the early sunlight fell upon them.

The others gathered round to gaze and wonder, but only Torronio supplied a useful thought. "Your adders," he said, "must share something of the nature of the Vale's flora. We have guarded the health of our plants by hiding them away from the light. Try if darkness will restore them to serpents."

I placed the lengths of root and vine in the bag, but no change transpired.

"Perhaps," he said, "a momentary darkness is insufficient. It may be that the deep nighttime only will reveal what they are."

"Perhaps," I said, shaking my head over this conundrum that but added to our store of ignorance.

We finished our preparations and departed the place of this mount that walled off the Dark Vale from the rest of the world.

I had anticipated encountering Mutano at the place where Torronio and the Wreckers had abandoned him. He did not know of my connection with his situation and of my small but sweet retribution for his overly strenuous methods of training me in the shadow trade. I had pictured myself riding into his bivouac with Torronio at the head of our band of makeshift plants-men, exhibiting with dramatic flourish the specimens we had obtained, and flaunting my triumph with pretended nonchalance.

We made good time on the journey back and our spirits lightened as we came farther away from the Vale. No rain had fallen in recent days and we could follow backward our track with ease for a long while. Then at one point in our trace that seemed most familiar, all evidence of our passing disappeared. Our surroundings seemed less well known here, and I wondered if we had strayed. I spoke my misgiving to Torronio.

"There was one spacious width in this road I am sure I would recognize," he said. "It cannot be far ahead."

I reflected then that Mutano had been keeping a solitary watch for three days and nights and might have devised a way to recover his losses from the Wreckers, if he expected them to pass this way again.

We trudged around a slow bend and Torronio pointed and said, "There we made our camp. I recall how wide the space was and what refreshment that hospitable canopy of leaves offered. Yet there is no sign of our encampment. That man—Mutano, you call him?—must have moved along to where he came from, trusting to fortune for shelter and direction."

"He is not one to joy in a long journey afoot," I replied. "Something is amiss. Let us keep keen watch for trickery."

As soon as I spoke, that cooling canopy of leaves came falling down upon us, covering us over, men and beasts, with a coarse, tatterdemalion netting of rope and rags and thongs all interlaced with foliage. It offered an obstruction that the five of us ought to have made short work of, but I think our wits as well as our bodies had been weakened by our recent struggles. Boxes and baggage went tumbling; my comrades swore and wrestled against the tatty netting, even as it grew tighter around us.

And then there was Mutano, of course, with a short staff in his left hand and a rope that served as drawstring for the netting in his right. With the rope he pulled the reticulate mass close about our ankles; with the staff he poked and belabored us in every undefendable place our carcasses presented. All the while, he was howling in the way that cats do, with a wailing that sounds like angry grief to men but signifies ardency of erotic joy to the claw-foot race. As soon as I saw the happy smirk on his face, I knew that Mutano had understood that not only was I involved in the waylaying of him but that indeed I must have planned the whole business. My surmise was confirmed by the severe drubbing his staff laid upon my ribs.

We were too pressed upon one another to unlimber our blades, but Sneakdirk managed to squirm a small dagger from inside his doublet. He began sawing at a joint knot, but Mutano spied him and with a sharp stroke broke the blade and, to judge by the outcry, one of Sneakdirk's fingers into the bargain. Then, with expressive motions of his hands and contortions of his features, he made known that we were to divest ourselves of iron and push all weapons onto the ground outside our leafy cage. He encouraged us heartily with licks and pokes and as a matter of course I received the most and the heartiest.

Further expressive pantomime indicated that we were to thrust our hands through the netting, and when we did so he bound our wrists and set us free one by one. He stood us in a line and stalked back and forth before us, purring like any fat house puss sated with cream. Now and again he paused and with a knock or two brought our stances to more erect, military postures.

Here was another sad moment for poor Falco. Pleased with myself as we had come back along the track, I had been spinning fancies of the commendations I would receive from Maestro Astolfo, of the coin I would collect from my herbalizing, and of the trinkets and cates and amorous companionship I would purchase. But now again I was under Mutano's thumb, or beneath his heel, and must bow to his will.

Forward and back again he strode, looking us over severely, taking close views of Torronio and Squint. Myself he hardly deigned to notice, until with a smart rap to a shinbone he directed me to follow him apart. He seated me on the scabby butt of a fallen plane tree. Pointing with his staff, he indicated which boxes, bags, and canvas-wrapped vials he desired Squint to bring forth and place on the ground before me.

Then commenced the most awkward and intense lesson in grammar a backward schoolboy could ever have endured. I had gathered some smattering of Mutano's feline dialect over time, but now I was to learn in earnest what the different growls and half growls, the purrings hoarse or mellifluous, the quiet or importuning meowings intended to convey.

He thumped a box of stoppered vials with his staff, a stout green length of ash with a few leafy twigs dangling, and uttered what was unmistakably a question: *"Mrowwwr-mirr?"*

When I shook my head uncomprehendingly, he boxed my ears. His notion seemed to be that I understood him well enough but pretended not to. I was accustomed to such blows from Mutano. What vexed me more was the laughter it drew from the Wreckers where they stood all in line by the fallen netting. It was good to note, though, that Torronio did not join in.

In fact, I did perceive what my shadow-trade colleague wished to find out, but the situation confused me. Did he expect me to answer him in the cat language? A slap to my forehead brought me around.

Yet I could not return answers I did not have. "These plants we gathered in dark of deepest night in the darkest of valleys," I said. "We worked quickly and crudely, more by sense of touch than by sight. We only gathered in the mass and have had no opportunity to examine our findings."

"Mrr mrr-mrr mrrieu?"

"Yes, I believe them to be of sound value," I said, after puzzling for long moments. "I could not set a price. In a sense, they are beyond price, for our man Goldenrod gave up his life to find them."

Mutano's eyebrows rose and his expression grew pensive. This was something he could not have known.

"He was forewarned," I said.

He touched one of the oblong boxes with his green staff. *"Murr rr."*

"Best not to unseal the baggage here. Sunlight has a deleterious effect upon this flora of the darkness. We have already lost several fine specimens."

"Mir?" He gave me a skeptical look but let the matter go. He brought from an inner pocket of his doublet a square of soiled vellum and thrust it at me. It was the map he had made from study of the old books, the map that had brought him here by a toilsome, hindrous journey.

I shrugged and he pushed it into my face. Then he flung it down and held out his hand, demanding my more helpful map to take him back to Tardocco.

Here was a point requiring careful judgment. If I handed over the false map immediately, he might suspect something amiss, knock me over, and ransack my clothing. If I held back for long, I would be inviting bruises purple and yellow. I decided to chance three blows before pretending to give in and present the deceptive document. But Mutano was no tyro in the skill of tendering punishment, and one solid thwack upon my shoulders sealed my decision.

Groaning and swearing, I brought out the counterfeit, with all its elaborate notations and whimsical instructions. Mutano examined it front and back, then turned about for the advantage of better light and pored it over. I retained all confidence in this map wherein I had mingled the true and the misleading with judicious balance. Many of the features he would know from his travel or by hearsay; others were in plausible relations with those he knew; still others were but mere brain-wisps and shared likeness with no place on the round earth.

After long study, he tucked it inside his doublet. Then he turned his attention to the Wreckers. His grin broadened as he surveyed them, and I surmised that he was proud to have caught the five of us in the same trap we had laid for him, dropping from the trees. At length he tapped Crossgrain on each of his shoulders, like a prince knighting a worthy squire, and motioned him forth, always keeping his staffless hand near his sword hilt. Under his direction, Crossgrain began gathering up the containers and loading them on the mounts and mules. Goaded by the staff, Squint aided in the task.

Mutano looked at the sky to ascertain that a half day's light remained, then mounted Defender and departed, taking with him not only our herbal treasures but all our weapons and almost all the food we had robbed him of.

We watched him out of sight, then all eyes turned upon Falco.

"Now, Stalwart," said Torronio, "Thou'st brought us to a pretty pass. Are we to starve in this wilderness or have you another lamewitted scheme to bring us to destruction?"

"Be of better cheer," I said. "Let us find our former camping ground; it cannot be far down this pathway. You will recall that we made a cache of provisions there to replenish us homeward."

This sentence struck a more pleasant note, but Sneakdirk reminded me that now we had no horse.

"After we find our provisions, we shall have but a five-day march to Tardocco."

"Why go we there?" he asked. "The noose awaits us, and this Mutano will anticipate our coming."

"If my cartographic skills stand good, we shall arrive before Mutano by some hours if not days. Then I shall make arrangements."

"Arrangements?"

"Let us stir along," I said. "I shall enlighten you as we go."

※—◎═◄—

We did arrive before Mutano's advent and I brought my companions directly to our town villa.

When I introduced Torronio to Maestro Astolfo, the shadow master looked him over side to side, bottom to top. Then he spoke in his calm voice: "I know the set of these features. Are you not of the family Binnoto? There is a certain length of jawline—"

"My name is Torronio. That is all the world need know."

Astolfo's gaze rested on him still, those mild gray eyes never roving from his face. "There was a story of one of them who fell into disfavor with the clan and fared into the forest to live as a celibate hermit and ponder the ills of life."

Torronio sighed. "Celibate I am, and for a long while. But the ills of life thrive stoutly without my thinking on 'em."

Astolfo nodded. "And you are confederate with Falco in this scheme to gull his friend and cohort, my man Mutano?"

"If Stalwart be Falco, then I am bound with him. As for gulling, are we not the parties injured? We have not the herbal treasures we labored after and this Mutano, wherever he may be, enjoys their possession. I am no coney to cheat and delude; if I rob, I rob forthrightly, in order to keep spirit and corpus united."

Astolfo turned to me. "I must inform you, Falco, that lately such exotica of greenery has dropped from fashion. You will recall Ser Marchiotti, who prided himself on his great collection of noxious plants. He hath fallen prey to a peculiar, miasmic lily and his health is much shaken. The exotica mania may be running its course."

"Have we then no buyers?" asked Torronio.

"Have you any wares?" Astolfo inquired.

"We shall have within three days or fewer such oddments of nature that even the most jaded of the Green Knights and Verdant Ladies will vie anxiously for them," I said. "These specimens follow behind us by messenger."

I did not say that the messenger was Mutano and that I had stationed Sneakdirk, Crossgrain, and Squint a half league above Tardocco on the Via Auster to waylay him and once more lighten him of his precious burdens. I counted upon my delusive map to bring him down from the mountains by the Via Auster and not the Via Boreas to eastward.

"Perhaps you overvalue this cargo," Astolfo suggested.

"I think not," I said, and went on to describe the character of some of the plants we were bringing forth. The march from the mountains had made us dusty, weary, and footsore, but its tediousness had given me time to think on our travails in the Dark Vale and upon the things we found there. I recalled the silence that was thicker than silence, with the whispery sibilance at its heart; I recalled the mucid, velvety leaves and blooms of the shrubs and how they rubbed upon our clothing and how the vine tendrils sought for our patches of bare flesh. I pondered the fetid gum that clung to us and sublimed to white powder in sunlight and thought long upon the black adders that changed their forms to become hard roots and vines.

"I believe the flora and fauna of that valley to league in convolvement together," I told Astolfo. "Their mainstay food is the shadows of animals, though they doubtless derive some nourishment also from rain and soil. It is not that they eat shadows as donkeys munch down hay. They take into themselves the shadows they capture and within them are preserved the living shades of passersby— of the troops and caravans and robber bands and solitaries who come that way. Undoubtedly, they also hold captive from early times the shadows of bears and boars and deer and suchlike. All these shadows are interwoven into a single entity through the roots and vines underground and above. It is a thing like—like a fisherman's net." I'd almost said, *Like the leaf-net that Mutano dropped upon us from tree-top,* but bit my tongue in time. "They propagate by means of an evil-smelling slime that blind snakes exude, crowding amongst 'em. And all this dark herbage, together with the serpents and some invisible flying creatures like black moths, make up, all of them at once, a single intelligence, darkly knowing, ravenous in its need for animate shadows."

As I was speaking, Astolfo closed his eyes, the better to comprehend my meaning. He was silent a long time. Then: "All this matter, if't be true, will be a discovery to the world. Such plants would have a value beyond any price that might be set."

I agreed.

"But," he continued, "there are dangers attending, known and unknown."

Again I agreed.

"If one of these plants, be it set in soil and nurtured, grow to maturity, may it not snatch away the shadow of its possessor or of some other?"

"It may."

"Will this taken shadow join to the great knot of them?"

"I know not. The Vale is far."

"Yet the nighttime covereth all the world."

"I take you not."

"The sea hath its currents, as do the river and the lake. Fish and other water creatures know and traverse such flowings. Midnight owns its currents also, which these umbraphagous plants must know and utilize."

"How so?"

He fell silent. Then: "I do not know. 'Twill be a matter of constrained study."

"You imply that our plants are too dangerous for human possession."

Sighing ruefully, he shook his head. "The peril only makes 'em the more precious to those of a certain cast of mind. We shall not lack buyers, but we must be at pains to inform them how to ensure their safety."

"We!" said Torronio. "How are you concerned with the selling?"

"Our expedition was undertaken at the maestro's commission," I said. "He hath vested coin and the labor of his servants, mine and Mutano's."

"If so you say." He took the news with ill grace, feeling deceived.

"Fear not," Astolfo said. "My interest here is more philosophical than monetary. There is an unthought-of world to be known of these plants, if indeed they come into our hands. And it may be that Mutano will return with an entirely different store of specimens and a different history."

"That may be," I said, keeping my laughter silent. "Meanwhile, Torronio and I must go to look after our own."

"Well, then."

⋅•➤━◉━◄•⋅

This time it fell out more easy.

Torronio, Sneakdirk, Squint, and Crossgrain accosted Mutano and his pack animals on the Via Auster a league above the western gate of Tardocco. He offered but puny resistance, Torronio reported. His long and fruitless wandering had sapped strength of body and vitality of spirit. He drew his cutlass but threw it down when the four raised their points toward him. He handed over the reins with the air of an aged prince abdicating a weary throne.

I did not make my presence known to him until I had overlooked the cargo and ascertained it was in good order. I performed certain experiments with lamps, mirrors, and sheets of fine-wove linen and was satisfied.

Our trio of confederates could not enter the precincts of the city on pain of apprehension by the civil guard, so Torronio and I presented ourselves with the containers of roots, blossoms, and so forth before Astolfo and then requested that Mutano be sent for.

When he entered and saw me there, he showed no surprise. He must have understood that in following the circuitous, perplexing routes my false map laid out he had fallen into a ruse. He eyed me with silent resignation, but I heard from his throat, or perhaps from his mind, a small feline growling that promised retribution.

I must keep watch on him, I thought.

Yet he did not go without reward, for Astolfo promised to apportion him a small share of whatever profits might accrue. It would be my duty to study these materials and to turn them to trade. Meanwhile, Astolfo advanced a fat pouch of eagles to share out with Torronio and his comrade exiles. There would be sufficient coin to buy off the bounties that had been set upon them. He suggested also that this little band of former exiles had accrued skills and experience that might be useful to the city in times of crisis, and he advised them to keep current with one another.

"*Mrrir mrrir?*"

"Mutano inquires," I told Astolfo, "about what might happen if I fail to find profit in these specimens."

"Then the materials will be placed in his charge," he answered, "to see if he may do better."

At these words, Mutano grinned cheerfully, and that grin, more than the prospect of coin, gave spine to my resolve. I would research these black plants and their husband serpents and make experiment. I would bring their secrets to light.

As if in answer to my thoughts, the adders fell into a commotion in their leathern bag, tumbling and thumping, and a small, quiet, sourceless music sounded in the room.

Astolfo looked a question toward me.

"Some errant pilgrim has wandered into the Vale," I said. "His shadow is his no more."

VI

Maze of Shadows

Where was he? Mutano had been absent for two days and nights and no word had come from him or concerning him. I was peevish upon his absence, for it meant that all the chores connected with our Nighthouse, the converted stable where we were cultivating the shadow-eating plants taken from the Dark Vale, fell to me. Worse still, when we were summoned by Maestro Astolfo to receive reprimand, I had to bear all by myself the brunt of his displeasure.

"You have told me," Maestro Astolfo said, "that you and Mutano made safe the emptied château of the baron, Tyl Rendig, that you mounted shadows in his halls and disposed them along his corridors and hung them about his stairways and massed them in cellars and storerooms. You wagered a gold eagle that no thief could get into the innermost room and take what was placed there. Do I recall your words aright?" He gave me a severe and piercing regard.

"You do," I said.

"And do you recall the valuable that you set upon the marble chessboard in the center of a close, dim room?"

"A ring of silver, it was, with an onyx stone in a pierced setting."

He stepped to the door of this, the smaller library, and opened the door. There entered a tall, long-faced, gaunt man with a scanty white beard. In his right hand he held a worn hawthorn staff that stood to the height of his ear and his left hand rested upon the shoulder of a girl. She appeared to be about fourteen years of age and was pale as the winter moon. They were dressed in beggars' threadbare robes, the girl wearing an undershift of coarse white linen. The old man wore sandals; she was barefoot and visibly cold. Her expression was strange and haunted, her dark eyes large in her pale face. Whatever her glance rested upon she gazed at fixedly, as if trying to comprehend its meaning.

"You have heard me speak in time past of my friend the Signor Veuglio and you know of his skills in ministering to diseases and ruptures of mind and spirit among the wealthy and the indigent of the city. I have told you of the many kindnesses he has performed without reward. Friend Veuglio, wilt'ou please show to my man Falco that bauble?"

The girl disengaged and stepped before me, gazing wide-eyed into my face. Veuglio reached into his sleeve, withdrew the object, and held it in his open palm. When I raised my eyes to his, I saw that they looked past me, not responding. They were gray, clear and bright, but the man was blind.

"Tell me, Falco," the maestro said. "Doth he present the ring that you and Mutano hid away?"

I hardly glanced, knowing the answer. "It appears very similar."

"Take it up. Examine closely. Let us try to be certain."

I sighed and took the ring from the old fellow's steady palm. This nettlesome prelude was designed to shame me. If the ring were not the same, this exercise would have no point. "I believe it to be the same."

"How can it be? You and Mutano claimed to have set in place a maze of shadows no intruder could penetrate. Yet Signor Veuglio saith he entered the château, walked almost directly to the ring, and came away with it. Is that not so?"

"It is." His voice was firmer and more vibrant than I could have expected in so old a man.

"And so, Falco?"

I said, "Shadow mazes are designed to deceive the eyes. Signor Veuglio, being blind, must have developed faculties that enable him to evade such entrapments. That would not be the case with your ordinary thief."

"Ordinary—meaning that other thieves will possess the use of eyes?"

"The most of 'em," I said.

"Yet may not a person having sound eyesight so discipline himself as to acquire such abilities as our guest possesses? If so, then he too could find his way."

I thought. "Perhaps so," I admitted, "though this feat would require a long and arduous course of discipline. The thief must not be impatient to come at his prize."

"Do you think that you and our other man, Mutano, could acquire such abilities?"

"Mutano is missing from our villa for two days now," I said. "I do not know where he is and I shall not venture to answer for him. As for myself, I think that with time and proper instruction I might attain some of these skills, though never any so keenly honed as Signor Veuglio's. He must have been without sight for many a season."

"Only three years sightless," Veuglio said. "Even so, you would not pay so dear a price. Three years blind seemeth a much longer term."

"Let us make trial," Astolfo said. "Falco, come forth to the signor so that he may examine you."

I stepped to the blind man and he ran his fingers lightly over my face and along the sleeve of my dun tunic. He touched my right hand and then withdrew his. The whole time of his touching me did not consume the space of ten breaths.

"Tell us somewhat of Falco," Astolfo said.

"He is a well-formed jack," said Veuglio, "though not so young these days as he pictures in his fancy. He trims his beard closely so that it will show a little less gray. He carries a brawn that bespeaks the labors of the field and his accent still bears a rustic note. He has been in your employ here in Tardocco for a longish period, arriving directly from a farm southward. He will disport him in expensive finery; only the tailor Gambe-Casserta keeps such close-woven bolts in stock. Yet though he dresses bravely, he keeps company in low taverns and stews, as the smells upon him declare. His bearing is easy and confident; I do not hear him shift about in his boots or twitch his fingers in the air. So I conclude that he is a swordsman of no common practice."

"Falco?" said Astolfo.

"His describing is just," I said, "insofar as I can judge of myself."

"Essay a little further," Astolfo said.

Veuglio paused for a moment, then spoke hesitantly. "There is a certain contradiction in the timbre of his voice. It seemeth complaisant, but beneath sounds a subdued hint of mockery. I might name him as one who desires the learning that his master Astolfo has gained and yet is skeptical of its final value."

"Falco?"

"I cannot know how close is the accuracy of what the signor says," I replied. "Yet I shall not deny his account, for I felt a little abashed as he spoke. He must have pointed up a truth or other I do not wish to own up to."

"Very good," Astolfo said. "Now give me back my silver ring before you lose it again."

I handed it over, thinking how he had risked a costly ring merely to display my shortcoming.

The maestro rose from the big soft-leather chair by the fireplace. He was dressed in his wonted outfit of a green jerkin over tan trunks supported by his broad belt with its leopard's-head buckle. He hunched his shoulders and flexed his hands, then slid the ring into an inner pocket. "Our guests are to sup with us this night," he continued, "so I had better acquaint you. Veuglio I have known for many a season. We have undertaken a number of ventures together, during which I learned a great deal. You will find him a man of various skills and acute probity. His assistant we call by the name of his daughter Sibylla."

The tall, bony man made a slight, grave bow. When he took his hand from Sibylla's shoulder, she bobbed an awkward, childish curtsy, never shifting her gaze from my face. I bowed too, though I judged the gesture lost on a blind man, and muttered a polite acknowledgment.

"It will be well for Mutano to dine with us also," Astolfo said. "I believe that he and thee have much to learn from our guests."

"I know not where he may be," I replied. "As I say, he is two days absent. He must have some private affair in hand."

"Our meal is six hours distant," Astolfo said. "See if you cannot search him out. I will have the servants show our guests to quarters and I will speak to our surly cook in regard to the meal. I take it, friend Veuglio, that you still abstain from the eating of flesh?"

"My diet is spare," he said, "but I think that Sibylla may well have tired of roots and herbs and pulse and may welcome a fatter refreshment."

She did not respond to this comment. All this while, she had been staring at me and Astolfo in a most fixed manner and her gaze did not waver when her name was spoken.

"I will have a word with Iratus, who prides himself on his sallets as well as on his haunch steaks."

"We are obliged," said Veuglio.

"I too have some business in hand," Astolfo said. "And so, fare well until that hour."

As he left the library, a maidservant entered to escort the blind man and the girl through the corridors to the east wing of the villa and I went away to wander the town.

⋆═◉═⋆

Drawn on a map, the city of Tardocco presents a shape something like a chestnut leaf with stem upward. This main stem might represent the River Daia, flowing from various sources in the northward Molvoria Mountains through pastured plains below and into the center of the town, which spreads from it in all directions. The veins that trace out from the main stem might represent the streets and avenues, while the tiny veinlets might figure as the web of alleyways and narrow corridors through which donkey carts and handcarts and barrows transport stuffs from the loading docks, where ships of every design ride at anchor.

Along the upper edges of this figurative leaf will be the graceful, tree-lined avenues where the houses of the grand perch upon the rise that looks down upon the less peaceful parts. The houses become none so prosperous as one descends, and in the center of the town a network of busy streets is interrupted at points by spacious plazas, many of which encircle small green parks attractive to lovers and to nursemaids with their charges. The nethermost area is an extended belt which sweeps alongside the bow-shaped harbor, and here lie the fiddlers' greens, the greasy taverns, the cockpits and bullrings and fighting-dog kennels, the brothels and flea markets and warehouses and tun cellars. Here there be snatchpurses, ratkillers, coney-catchers, footpads, cloak-twitchers, and drunken soldiers and their chuckaroos.

There is one large area a little westward of the center of the city where wide, crossing boulevards enclose tall-treed estates, and at this point of the city stands Astolfo's villa, as proud in its posture as are the houses of the wine merchants, counting-house proprietors, and well-eagled military commanders which are its neighbors. I held it a matter of some pride that this villa was built upon the traffic of shadows and hoped that my life in the trade would be similarly well rewarded.

I had only the barest suspicion where Mutano had betaken himself. In late days he had become more and more despondent, sinking into dark moods that allowed him little of his accustomed cheeriness. I supposed that his disposition might have soured because our enterprise with our shadow-devouring plants was not thriving. Then there was the problem of his voice. He had lost his own voice to the machinations of a foe and it had been supplanted with the voice of a cat. For two long seasons now he had been confined to a cattish dialect. I had learned to comprehend much of it, though I could speak little. The meowing and growling and purring which rose from his throat were bound to try his patience most sorely and the burden of the feline tongue must soon undermine his naturally sanguine temperament.

The thought had come to me late yesterday, as I visited a tavern where Mutano and I used often to repair for long tankards of a wheaten beer we relished, that my colleague might be engaged in trying to recover his voice. He was formerly possessed of a fine tenor, as clear in timbre and nimble in music as a clarino; his voice was an asset in which he took a justified pride and with which he could ardently woo beauty after beauty, supposing each successive one to be a paragon of virtue and modesty and of an ideal comeliness of carcass. A number of bitter disappointments had not halted his quest for his dreamed-of female, but the loss of voice had caused a hiatus.

To the best of our knowledge, Mutano's proper voice was lodged within a great orange cat named Sunbolt. This was a feline peremptory of manner, cool of address, and casually unimpressed with humankind. It would be inaccurate to say that Sunbolt ever belonged to a master, but for a long while he had kept company with a swaggering bravo who suffered a painful humiliation at Mutano's hands and afterward had departed Tardocco to take up, as 'twas rumored, the life of a celibate eremite. Sunbolt was now lost to sight and it was undecided whether that cat kept in his possession Mutano's tuneful voice.

Yet he would try to seek out the orange cat, methought. It would seem a futile essay, Tardocco being a well-catted town, its gentry fond of the feline race and its harbor alleyways plentifully furnished with dark nooks and crannies, wharf rats and mice and scavenging sparrows. A man might spend his life and discover one particular cat no sooner than he would light upon a true sapphire in a street-seller's jewel stock. Even so, desperation is a sharp urgement to enterprise and Mutano had shown the signs of a desperate man—pacing about

nervily, meowing raggedly to himself, and displaying a short temper over such trifles as a misplaced dagger sheath.

He was no featherbrain; he would not roam the pavements.
There are two thriving catteries in Tardocco and I assumed he would
inquire of them first of all and then ask among the well-known
fanciers of the breeds.

At the end of an alley off Chandlers' Lane stood the establishment of Brotero, who captured, trained, and fed cats he let out for
hire. Ratkillers they were, bred to the trade and prepared to live up
to their brave repute. The rats of the harbor environs are often as
large as good-sized terrier dogs and just as eager for combat. A flock
of them can in two nights despoil half a cargo of wheat and eat into
a bale of silk and hollow out a foul nest. The ruin they will make
of a bin of green pears is as unsightly as it is inedible.

Dogs made much less effective opponents than cats, for they
were not sufficiently fleet to keep up when the rats darted along high
rafters or wriggled into narrow holes. They could pinch their bodies so as to squirm through apertures hardly larger than keyholes;
yet when they stood to fight, their bulks swelled like bakers' loaves
rising in an oven. An especially hot-blooded rat would not scruple
to attack a man, first giving warning with a tooth-baring snarl.

This rat, though, would be no match for Brotero's cats, for he
had trained them to work in pairs in ordinary circumstances and in
packs when the odds grew large against them. A pair sent to extirpate
a champion rodent would consist of a large, deep-chested, yellow-
eyed, brawny beast accompanied by a small, lithe, spring-spined
specimen, in shape something like a stoat. Brotero named the large
cats Maulers; the lesser, swifter sort were Worriers. A Worrier har-
ried the big rat flank and tail while the Mauler braced his enemy
froward.

If an edifice such as a granary or molasses warehouse were being overrun with the pestilent species, Brotero would stage full raids
upon the premises, loosing a good two dozen cats of each size within
the premises and letting them scour the walls and niches and crannies
ratless. These squealing, growling, gut-spattered wars made fine
spectacle, and Brotero gained additional copper by charging admission and brokering wagers.

Sunbolt, the object of Mutano's quest, bulked not large enough
to work as a Mauler, nor did he own the quick responses of a
Worrier. Falling between the two types, he would not be enlisted

in Brotero's armies, but the wily ratter could have intelligence of him. It was rumored he knew the name and the pedigree and abilities of every cat in Tardocco. It was whispered he even knew the secret names of many, the names which, given in antiquity by forgotten gods, passed down through each lineage from the times of primal millennia.

Of Sunbolt, however, he could tell me little. He rubbed his spraggle, gray moustache with a forefinger and peered up into my face. He was a slight, restless, narrow-shouldered knave whose corpus throbbed and jerked with tics and twitches. He resembled much more the prey of his animals than the cats themselves.

"There must be uncommon value in this Sunbolt," he said. "Two others have asked already. One was your amicus, that Mutano fellow."

"Who was the other?"

"He claimed to be a steward for a noble, a Baron Somebody. I forget."

"You spoke with Mutano?"

"He spoke and I with difficulty made out his meaning, though I think that someone not well acquainted with cats might find the trick impossible."

"He chooses to converse in the feline tongue. I know not why."

"Nay-nay. 'Twas evident he had no choice in the matter. I conjecture that Sunbolt hath purloined his language. That is a thing that occurs with very young children, but it is nigh unheard of among those come of age. Your Mutano appeared to be of about forty years."

"He is on the trace of the cat Sunbolt and I trace the steps of the cat-speaking man. Otherwise, I know naught."

"As he departed, methought his way led toward the house of Nasilia three streets over. Fortune might show a fairer countenance at her cattery. Here our employment is useful and necessary. Nasilia's business may tend more conformable to his—and to yours. For I know that the two of you are in hire to the shadow thief Astolfo. But mine is an honest trade and forthright."

"Then long may you thrive," said I, "and I am grateful for your words."

But as I came away, heading toward Nasilia's place, I reflected that Brotero lacked the physic and comportment of a hearty man of business. His manner was more that of someone you might trust to filch your purse while he performed his agitated little dance of tics and quivers.

⇢⟶◉⟵⇠

Nasilia's establishment was a squat building with yellow walls of baked clay and a roof of dark red tile, but for all its brightness of color, it appeared sad, with an air of mute misery. I had visited here before, in company with Astolfo when I was early with him. In this place cats were slaughtered to get at the musk pouches. We were closely associated with perfumers, shadows lending influence to scent in countless ways. Nasilia, whose specialties were of the heavier sort wherein muskery was most utilized, was one client for our darker shadows, hues tempering from light mauve to deep purple to the blackness of a midnight grave.

I was long in coming to distinguish such shades of odor. At the beginning, I could smell only the gross corpus, as 'twere, of a perfume and had to spend many hours in a shuttered room, wafting scents to my nose with a poplar-leaf fan, before I learned how a perfume too suggestive of clove can be lightened and freshened by tincturing it with shadow taken from the boughs of an apple tree in bloom; or how a perfume delicate as the scent of an early spring rose may be given keener interest by storing it a fortnight in violet umbrae, from which it will gain force of contrast.

I learned a little too of the character of women, having my suppositions stripped from me by example. The older woman does not always prefer the stronger scent; if she go forth in a dark blue gown, she may tease the senses of males by wearing a perfume as light in texture as the smell of white clover. If a maiden trip about gaily in a white frock bedecked with intricate frills, she may put on the scent of a red, red rose which has stood a while in magenta shadow, bringing an unexpected contrast to her visual appearance.

Such combinations of scent and shade have been the study of fashion since ever the first female enwrapped herself with cloth. In Astolfo's libraries thick catalogues of scents and shades, herbs and humors, stand ready on the shelves and are often consulted. A man or woman who fancies the possibility of taking up a profession in shadows will discover that it consists in a great deal more than sly snippery and sharp sundering.

The knocker of Nasilia's door was of heavy iron shaped like a cat's curled tail. I rapped with it seven times before the door was opened by a tall, broad-shouldered woman wearing a leathern apron over a stiff white linen smock. An almost visible cloud of cloying scent boiled out of the dark room behind her and I stepped back unthinkingly, the way I would avoid the puddle-splash of a passing carriage.

"You are Falco," the woman said. Her voice resounded as if it proceeded from an empty rain barrel. When I admitted to this truth, she told me that my unintelligible friend Mutano had already paid a call here and, receiving no news to his liking, had traveled on.

"Did he chance to say—"

"He did not and I did not stay to ask. I desire no close acquaintance with your unsavory sort, O stealer of shadows."

"And what may you be called?"

"I am Maronda, chiefest assistant to Nasilia, a woman famous in the perfume trade."

"You are Maronda, murderess of helpless pusses," I said. "Let not the black iron pot malign the polished brass kettle."

"A fine polish it is you sport. Know you, Falco, that my brother lost his shadow to such a thief as you. He wasted nigh to nothingness before I could afford to replace it."

"What is your brother's name?"

"He was named Quinias and hath been called Quinny since childhood."

"Does he suspicion some person or other?"

"He believes that it was taken from him at a tavern, The Double Hell. Other than that, he can say nothing."

"If you had applied to Maestro Astolfo, we could have aided in his restoration. We provide many similar services which tend to the good of the citizenry."

"Well, he is hale once more, all praise to Asclepius. And now I have no more to do with thee." She clapped to the heavy door, sealing in the musky, unseen fog that had enveloped us.

I went from that place desirous of a river to plunge into, to wash away the smells that I thought must hang upon me like a woolen cloak. Since no river conveniently presented itself, I thought to repair nearby to The Red Stallion, where a tapster named Giorgio would furnish a basin of clean water and a tankard of clear white wine.

So he did, for one copper, and I carried the basin into the court-yard where a stout bench was set under a spreading white oak and laved my face and beard and then rinsed and finger-combed my hair as best I could before returning the basin and seating myself at a table. I inhaled the fresh, green-grape smell of the wine and im-bibed it in tiny sips, savoring its cleanliness. I had got through a good half of the tankard before discovering that the large fellow at the table in the dim far corner of the room was the man I sought.

I might not have recognized him had I not been seeking. And though he looked directly at me, he seemed not to know me; he seemed, in truth, to take no notice of his surroundings. Mutano sat staring in a black melancholic trance, his gaze fixed upon a mote-less point in empty space, his mind sunken in cloudy thought. When I rose to approach him, his eyes did not follow me, and when I spoke he gave a little start before responding.

"Ah, Falco." He spoke cat speech.

"You seem in a dumpish state, old comrade."

"I have grown tired of this world as it corkscrews. Naught keeps its savor in these drear days."

"So I have heard report. I have followed in your track and your despondency hath been remarked."

"You followed me?"

"You have been sent for."

"By Maestro Astolfo?"

"There is a venture afoot," I said, and delivered a brief account of the visit of Veuglio and the girl Sibylla. "As you would expect, he is an old crony of Astolfo's, a most remarkable personage. You will find him impressive. The girl is new to me. They are to share bread with us this evening and we must be present to receive instruction."

"I have no stomach for food, nor for instruction neither. I have mine own ends to pursue."

"You seek the cat that beareth your voice in its body. I have asked about this beast where you did and received the same empty result."

"I shall not leave off. I detest this cattish tongue I am forced to use. The sound of it curdles my belly juices. It sounds even worse when you essay to use it, as you are doing now."

"I had thought I was finding the custom of it—the music, so to speak."

"If you spoke as born to it, it would still be an ugly brangle, barbarous in every vowel."

"Well, we must away to the villa. The sun hath passed its mid-afternoon mark."

"You shall, if you please, convey my regrets."

"I dare not," I said. "The maestro is already displeased with us for leaving our task at the château unfulfilled."

"How so? We took meticulous pains. All was in order."

"This Veuglio marched through our snares, traps, mazes, and dead ends with less trouble than walking through cobweb."

"Then," said he, rising to his feet, "I should like to meet this signor and to learn of him."

⋅◦═◉═◦⋅

At table, Mutano appeared in a better state than he had in The Red Stallion. There his slovenliness of dress matched his bedraggled spirit, but now he was scrubbed and brushed and combed and togged in a dark green tunic new to my eyes. I had been studious of my ablutions also, washing away the musky perfumes that had engulfed me at the cattery door. I had no doubt, however, that Veuglio would detect the smell of that establishment.

Of the food I made little account, it being fleshless, fowl-less, and fishless. I dutifully made my way through groats, pulse, three different porridges, and an undistinguished cheese. Mutano and I refreshed ourselves plentifully with flagons while Veuglio and Sibylla drank water. Both of our guests fed themselves like herons a-fishing; they sat unmoving for intervals and then would dart their hands into the bowls and platters and take up victual with their fingers. This practice was convenable to blindness, methought, and the girl followed it also.

For a long time there was small converse. If Astolfo had not undertaken a long tale of a princess who had lent her beautiful shadow to a homely lady-in-waiting, silence would have immersed the large dining room and its carmine drapery and ornate silver candlesticks.

At last Astolfo too fell silent and Mutano redoubled his attack upon the wine jug; and then Sibylla spoke: "It is of no use, Signor Mutano, to try to lave from memory the face of a beloved with drink."

Mutano did not reply but only stared upon this white, thin girl as if she had shied a candlestick at him. She gazed at him steadily with her haunted eyes.

I was alert upon the instant. The child was correct. Why had I not thought how my friend's despair proceeded from the fact that his fancy had lit upon a new beauty while he had not the means of speech to declare his passion, much less to ornament it with poems and songs after his custom?

Who his adored one was, I could not know, and it made small difference. In his usual course of love, Mutano would charm some beauty fair of form, delicate of manner, and refined of taste. He would worship her as acolytes of the Spring Goddess worship their deity. Then he would discover that she was no more than a woman like many another and his adoration would turn into indifference and the sweetness of his dreaming hours to bitter ashes. He had followed this path unchanging some seven or eight times that I had knowledge of, and it was likely there had been others of whom he had kept silent.

Now Sibylla had divined his secret and, though it explained much to me about his late comportment, I knew it could not alter Mutano's cast of mind. He would try to regain his voice and if successful would pay devoted court to this unknown female, waylaying her with ballads and springing sonnets upon her as from an ambuscado. She was likely to be burdened with violets and near drowned in roses until some coarse expression flew from her lips or some act of petty treachery betrayed her inmost character. Then my wide-shouldered colleague would sit in heartsore solitude and his ballads would turn acrid and his sugared sonnets degenerate into satires.

This latter stage I secretly welcomed, for his angry lines held four times the wit and savor of his amatory mewling.

"As for Mutano's capacity for wine," I replied to the girl, "there you need not fear. I have seen him down goblets by the dozen without showing effect."

The old man spoke. "What is not shown without wreaketh more direly within. Yet let that pass and tell how you and he sought to set safeguards upon the baron's château with your placement of shades."

I looked to Astolfo, not willing to share the secrets of our trade without his permission. He remained impassive, so I followed my own discretion. "It is difficult to describe. It will be easier and more instructive to demonstrate."

I rose from my place, took up a candelabrum, set it at the end of the table, and advanced to the edge before it. "If a man walk along a corridor with light behind him, he will swerve to a new direction when he sees upon the wall before him the shadow of a mastiff large enough to tear out his throat." With my hands before the candle flame I projected such a shape on the wall. With the fingers of my left hand curled to represent a shaggy mass, I placed my right fist in that palm, wrist bent to form a plausible leonine face. I sounded a growl low in my throat.

Sibylla giggled lightly, but Veuglio frowned. "This is nonsense," he said. "You must be making a shadow-play of the hands that does not deceive even the children whom it amuses. Its effect is lost upon me, a blind man, even though I know what you are doing."

"You must recall the circumstances," I replied. "You are a thief whose life hangs in the balance. You hardly know this dark corridor by daylight and not at all by night. Your senses are overwary and you fear making the softest sound. Suddenly on the wall before you appeareth the shape of a lion. You are in a state of mind easily to be misled."

I bent back my wrist so that the lion head lifted and then bent it forward so that the shape fell. There sounded a heavy knocking upon timber. An expression of puzzlement crossed the girl's face.

"What you have taken to be the shadow of an animal was only that of a sculpted door knocker," I said.

"Your accomplice, Signor Mutano, rapped the underside of the table," Veuglio said.

"True, but your young assistant was taken in, if fleetingly."

"She hath the disadvantage of being able to see. It has betrayed her more times than two."

"If all the world were as you, friend Veuglio," said Astolfo, "my table would lack sorely. No one would buy my wares."

"Do not the olden philosophers declare that most men are as in my case, blind and without true understanding?" Veuglio said.

"The sages are glad to point out the failings of others," Astolfo said. "Upon the subject of sightlessness, they are wont to say that all who shun their particular strains of wisdom are blind."

"Tomorrow Signor Veuglio will accompany Mutano and me to

Baron Rendig's château," I said, "and there he will point out to us our failings in regard to the guarding of the treasure, whatever thing it may be. We saw nothing precious there but the ring we ourselves had placed. Can we not let the matter lie until then and strike upon another theme?"

"Perhaps we shall enjoy to have music," said Veuglio. "Sibylla hath a singular voice for tune."

"Let us hear her sing," I said. "What music, child, dost thou know?"

"I have five songs," she said. "'The Dolors of the Faithful Knight,' 'The Ballad of the Unjustly Hanged,' 'The Queen Who Would and Yet Would Not,' and 'How Jason Came Home from the Thirsty Land.'"

"What is the other?"

"The fifth I do not sing and keep hope that I never shall."

"Thy choice, then," I said.

She sang out in a fine, thin voice like the trembling of a silver wire: "O Jason was a brave seafarer, And none was fairer than he . . ."

Forty verses this song entrained, and they were sufficient to send us to a bed each and all.

⋆═◦═⋆

The commission upon which Mutano and I labored at the baron's château was on a vastly different scale from most of our undertakings. Here we did not dispose dribs of shadow to the allurement of Signorina Millifiore's bosom nor tapered curlicues of colored shade to the ringlets of her coiffure. Large spaces confronted us, walls and ceilings and, of our most particular concern, floors. Stairs we studied and corridors and the great drains of courtyard and kitchen and stables. We investigated the one dry well in the center of the courtyard, Mutano letting me down on ropes to a sort of small chamber at the bottom. We traveled the upper stories with their dim hallways and the under-roof space where a pair of red owls nested. The cellars and larders we went through and we made everywhere extensive notes and sketches.

The edifice contained three secret chambers; these were small, windowless, silent rooms that were barely furnished. One was located off a dank cellar corridor; a shabby little oaken door that looked as if it would open to a little-used storage space was sheathed with steel plate on the inside. This door guarded a room not much larger than the fireplace in Astolfo's main library. In the center of this room stood a small, sturdy table with a low stool beside. The table was bare, but on the single wall shelf opposite sat a short pewter candle-holder. It was empty, but three dirty candle stubs lay beside it, along with flint and steel and a tinderbox.

There was another secluded room like this one on the second floor, and on the third and uppermost floor, still another. These doors looked most ordinary, but they too were steel-sheathed, as if shabby tables and dingy candle ends were handsome treasures.

The one other appurtenance for each room was a small stone-ware bowl set unobtrusively in a corner. Mutano lifted one to his nose. "It hath held cow cream," he said.

This then was the domicile we were to protect from intruders and thieves by arranging and disposing everywhere our deceptive shadows. Baron Rendig would not set a troop of guards in his house. He seemed to rate this unknown treasure so precious that he could trust no one to stay by it. Other systems of trapdoors, tripping wires, suspended broadaxes, and the like had proved as ineffective as the shadow mazes Mutano and I had set in place.

I thought it a useless exercise to go with Veuglio through the château. He and Sibylla had traveled this house before, as he recounted, and had come to the secret rooms without being misled. That had been in the dark o' the night and they had walked as stealthily as any jewel thief. He told us that the girl held a lantern before them as they walked.

"What aid can a lantern lend a blind man?" I asked.

"So that if there be others in the house they may recognize who we are and offer no threat," he said. "Your Maestro Astolfo advised the baron I would be making a midnight trial of the shadow-tangle, so as to prevent my being taken for a thief, my cranium battered and my guts run through."

"Very well," I said. "We have brought one of our lanterns from our Nighthouse and Sibylla must carry it just as she did at midnight, though it is now only forenoon. I will walk beside her to see how you wend your way and Mutano shall follow thee."

"Let us begin," he said, and made straightway for a set of steep stone steps that led to the cellar passageway. I had to go smartly to keep pace with the old man.

Here was a tedious chore. When we had completed our commission at this château, Mutano and I surveyed our work with no small pride. We had laid shadows athwart shadows and overlaid these with others. A thief who trusted to his eyes would find that an oblong darkness he took to be a corridor was a swift exit to the stony floor below; this passageway that opened to the upper balcony was actually an adit to the empty void around a parapet; that slant of light ahead that promised admission to the largest bedchamber was actually a slanted and shadow-applied mirror that would send one tumbling down a flight of breakneck stairs.

One deception in which we took particular pride presented the sight of a gauzy curtain wafting in the breeze at a casement. Yet it was the rippling umbra of the surface of a stream that we had excised from the underside of a bridge and hung beside the large drain that fell two stories to a rock-ribbed culvert. To step through that imagined window was to step to a painful death.

Many another ingenious illusion we had set in corners, at doorways, inside closets, and along galleries, and Veuglio and Sibylla passed by or through or about each one, finding sure footing at every step. He located each of the three secret rooms, advanced to their small tables, and felt his way to sit upon the stools. In the last one he said, "I detect the smell of tallow, but there is no candleholder on this table."

"The holder with the four stubs beside it sits in a shelf behind you," I told him.

"Ah," he said, nodding.

"And now this exercise is completed. Will you return to the villa?" I said.

"Yes. I am beginning to tire."

We were concluded here for the time, I thought, but just as we were exiting the courtyard gate, Mutano gave a quick *"Mrrr"* and spun round in his tracks and lifted his head to look at the overhanging balcony. On top of the balustrade there sat a great orange cat looking down upon us with piercing gaze. Mutano returned this gaze steadily for a moment before following us outside and pulling shut the wide gate. I saw that he was excited but was trying not to show his agitation.

That cat, I said to myself, must be Sunbolt, the beast within which Mutano's true voice was lodged.

⇥━◉━⇤

I did not mention my conjecture for a time, thinking it preferable to let Mutano broach the subject, if he desired. We were sitting in the east garden of the villa on a willow-wood bench beneath a great holly tree, nibbling at stalks of orchard grass, having been denied access to the new beer in the larder by our contrarious cook Iratus. Veuglio had declared that he needed rest and he and Sibylla had taken to their neighboring rooms.

I spoke to Mutano in his cattish language. "Proof that our network of shadows may yet be efficacious is that there were no servants in the château. We have not yet given the baron our plan of the traps, and without it servants would be tumbling down stairways like barrels and dropping off balconies like walnuts from trees."

"It may be that he will reside there almost alone," Mutano said. "He claims no near kin. He seems to live in such fear of losing his treasure that he will abide no other company."

"He is of no ordinary make," I said. "I have conceived a curiosity about this treasure. What is so precious to a man that he will give over a château to contain its secret? Its worth is not to be valued in silver."

"Something touching his very life, is't?"

"It will be of value perhaps only to himself and of little interest to your ordinary thief. But if so, why will he need such protection? We must know more of this baron. What have you heard rumored?"

"Little," Mutano said. "I have not inquired directly, but when he is mentioned a wariness creeps into the tone of the conversation. Some of the dwellers of the lanes and byways know of him and show a fearfulness. He has a troop of armed men who obey his direction. I would call them disciplined and merciless. None of them goes alone to carouse and they do not speak to others than themselves. I have heard darker hints, yet as of now they are but wisps."

"We will follow further. I should also like to know whether Veuglio is the only person with skill in the avoidance of our measures. I am puzzled by his art."

"Some things we may surmise," Mutano said. "Being blind, he is much aware of the differences in the heats o' th'air, the changes in coolness from one place to another. He will also feel the pressures of draughts upon his skin that you and I are oblivious to. Odors he readeth and, as we well know, every kind of shadow bears its own smell."

"All true. Yet mass them all together and they do not account.

He and the girl trotted through our mazes and around our pitfalls as if led by the hand."

"You walked by his side through the château, but I walked behind and could see the shadows of the pair. Sibylla's umbra informed him of perils."

"Her shadow?"

"I observed clearly that it swiftly recoiled, drawing close to her body when she approached a doubtful spot. At this recoilment, she changed the direction of her going so swiftly and smoothly it was difficult to see. Also, her shade would stretch out before her or to either side, as if a light were lowered beside her corpus. The look of it was like a dog sniffing the soil on the trace of a boar."

"He receives intelligence from her shadow?"

"So I believe. At first, I thought this stretching and withdrawing to be illusory, but after watching closely, I was convinced that it was the case. The thought came to me that this ability might be common to the shades of those who guide blind men, for I have seen them make remarkable turns and recognitions, so cleverly done that they are hardly noticeable."

"As have I. Todow, the blind juggler in Daia Plaza, can distinguish by touch one silver eagle from another though they be minted in the same hour."

"And I thought, as we traced through the hallways, that perhaps for such guides their shadows act as do whiskers on a cat, to guard and guide them in the dark. But it is more than that. Some communication passes."

"If such does take place and we could bring to light the nature of it—"

"This theme has much occupied Astolfo of late," Mutano said. "I have suspicioned he hath in hand a momentous project he is not ready to unfold to us."

"If shadows had motion and power of thought, they could be led to act. Imagine us, under Astolfo's direction, commanding an army of umbrae. If the girl's shadow spoke in some wise to Veuglio, perhaps that is what the maestro desired for us to observe," I said.

He rose and began to make a circuit of the garden, stalking along slowly. I walked beside but kept silent, not wishing to disturb his course of thought. He spoke as if to himself, his feline sounds softened to a near purr, regular and unhurried. "I have conceived a hard notion. If we could learn the speech and custom of shadows, we could no longer buy and sell and alter their shapes and inner natures. Such cruelties must not be laid upon volitional beings."

"Animals are such beings," I said, "and yet may be brought under our sway."

"Not all of them. The lion, the pard, the python do not bend to my will."

"Nor did your mount, Defender, when first you encountered him. But by patient stages, the two of you have sealed a silent pact from which both of you obtain much good."

"Yet we do things to animals that perhaps we should not. This thought hath plucked at my mind of late."

"You lost your voice to the cat Sunbolt," I said, "and since that time you have had to speak in the tongue of cats. This has drawn you close to animals. You do not look upon them now as you used to do."

He stopped walking and did not reply for a space. Then he spoke in a tone almost mournful: "That is true."

"And if I mistake not, you saw this Sunbolt at the château, perched upon a battlement."

"I saw a cat."

"And I saw the change of your countenance. You must not dissemble with me."

"It was the one called Sunbolt. But I do not know if he still possesses my voice. I was surprised to see him there, alone upon the parapet. And the thought of him is strange, alone in the château, with all those rooms empty, including the kitchens and larders, which were stocked with only a jug or two of cream. Sunbolt walks a lonely patrol, inhabiting there almost alone."

"Except when the baron and his occasional manservant are present," I said.

"That is but one more puzzle. We know of houses, châteaux, and even of fortified castles built for the purpose of protecting treasures. Many princes and other nobles have built strong houses in which to lock up their gold and other baubles. Many a house has been constructed to keep a female chastely under key. The Lady Aichele has constructed a curious lattice-walled garden that only she could enter and in it planted the rarest of her many, far-brought plants. But what this baron secludes away, I cannot surmise, for the places most secure within his château are mean, dusty little rooms that would not dignify a hound turd."

"We will visit again," I said. "We shall go stealthily and observe what it is like when we are unknown to it. And we shall recover your voice from that cat, who can get no good out of it in any way."

"He may find little use for it, but it is not likely he will willingly yield it up," Mutano said. His tone was as glum as a pallbearer's cloak.

"But I have formed a scheme," I said, "and you shall hear it at length tomorrow morning in the east garden."

⊷⊚⊶

In truth, I had formed several schemes that had to be joined in overlapping fashion, like tiles on a roof, to be effective. As I outlined the steps, Mutano shook his head slowly, his expression a study in doubtfulness. "This plan you propose is more a maze than our shadow-tangle in the château."

"A maze through which a blind man made easy progress," I said. "Let us go at methodical pace, a step at a time. First, if a man were to have his shadow stolen in a tavern called The Double Hell, can we conjecture who the thief might be?"

"'Tis not a dishonest house," he said, "yet sometimes the sly-fingered Mercurius awaits his prey therein. Even so, The Double Hell is where the unskilled go to dice their fortunes away. Thieving, being unnecessary, is uncommon."

"I shall return to the musk-house of Nasilia and speak to the keeper of the door, the woman called Maronda. I shall tell her that I have discovered the culprit responsible for the loss of her brother's shadow. I shall tell her that I will deliver this person to her in return for a vial of the most alluring musk she has in store from a female cat in heat. This vial will cost us a silver eagle, or at least a handful of coppers."

"This suits not," Mutano complained.

"Suit it must, if you are to regain your voice. Unless we are willing to part with a little coin, she may not credit our story."

"For what purpose, this vial of musk?"

"We will come to that. During the while that I arrange with Maronda, you are to take the largest of our lanterns from our herbage workshop, polish the mirror inside it to the highest degree of clarity, and make certain the shutter works easily and quickly. We

must be able to prepare the lantern to emit the narrowest and sharpest of rays and then to snap shut upon the instant."

"I will do as you say," Mutano replied, "but if this flimsy web
you weave ravels under your hand, you must replace my coin and
add more to the sum."

"Well," I said.

We left by the same gate but parted company at the roadway,

⊷═◉═⊶

There is a strangeness about a great deserted house like the baron's
château; the emptiness speaks a light sadness to the senses, a kind of
longing like that of a young wife, perhaps, whose husband is at sea.
The hollowness of such an edifice in this early hour of the night
caused me to fancy that if one would strike it on the far wall with
a club the whole of it would resound like a kettledrum.

We needed to enter no farther than the courtyard. Before coming, I had sketched out a hasty diagram showing that we would place
our vial of musk, embedded in a nest of velvet, close to the project-
ing wall that presented the great doorway to the entrance hall. We
would station us behind the corner there, out of the cat's line
of sight, and trust that the attraction of the musk would mask our
presence.

The device worked as I had hoped. We unstoppered the vial and
waited patiently as the hour grew longer and darker until at last we
could make out the shape of Sunbolt in a lower window and hear
him drop from it to the flagstones. We sensed more than observed
his progress to the vial and then, just as he halted at the velvet-
cloaked tube, I flickered open the shutter of the lantern. Sunbolt's
shadow was starkly limned on the wall behind him. Mutano withdrew from his dark nook and sundered the shadow and clapped it
into a dark, plush portmanteau.

Sunbolt gave a quick howl of outrage, his voice so exaggerated
I could not tell whether it was human or not. Then he scrambled
away behind the château walls.

Now we had the cat's shadow in our possession and came away
to the villa feeling that our task had been neatly accomplished.

⊷═◉═⊶

We ate, slept, and amused ourselves till past noon of the following
day, then returned with light hearts to the château. There we sat

ourselves on the bench by the well curb and waited for Sunbolt to greet us.

"How shall we manage this exchange?" Mutano asked.

"First, you had best engage in conversation," I said, "for we have not yet heard him speak. It may be that he has lost the use of your voice or that it has been taken from him. Then tell him that we will return his shadow if he will but say a word or two into that device that captured your voice in the beginning." The box with the enclosed, many-curled, membranous trumpet sat on the stones before us. I nudged it with my toe.

"I lack skill in trading," he said.

"It will be a simple exchange. You have there the device within which your voice was imprisoned before. You have only to persuade the cat to speak into it and later you may restore it to your own body at your leisure. I doubt not that you shall spout odes and bellow ardent arias within the fortnight."

"I pray it go so easy as you portray."

"He will be wary of the two of us together. I shall withdraw to the farther bench and you shall make your bargain."

As I spoke, Sunbolt appeared from behind an arcade column directly across. He ambled slowly toward us, pausing now and again to display an attitude of nonchalance by sitting and washing his paws and ears and underbelly. This cat carried himself with a posture that proclaimed he knew his worth and held it considerable. If he were a man, he might play the role of a youngish sea captain with a ready and playful sword.

I gave him a courteous nod, then strolled to the yonder bench and sat.

Though the day was mild and sunny with the fleece of milk-white clouds floating here and there in the bluest of skies, the atmosphere of this large, open courtyard, with its marble well curb in the center and its narrow arcade that promised coolness, appeared drab and dispirited, its air in keeping with the general disposition of the château. The light fell openly upon Mutano and Sunbolt as they conferred, yet it seemed to me that they stood at a distance farther than the one that in fact separated them; 'twas almost as if I were reading about them in an old romance poem.

Mutano sat leaning forward, elbows resting upon his knees. He peered into the space before him and took notice of Sunbolt only

when the cat crossed his line of sight. On his part, the cat made no
overt overture but only sidled slowly back and forth, sometimes
sniffing the flagstones and peeping down into a drain grate. This
exercise continued for a while and then at last Sunbolt eased down
upon his haunches before Mutano and stared up into his face.

No language passed between them, neither feline nor human,
but some sort of intercourse must have taken place, for Mutano nodded, placed the voice-box device before the cat, then stood and
came walking toward me.

"Is the bargain concluded?" I asked.

"We are to leave and I am to return in an hour," Mutano said.
"During that time, Sunbolt will seal my voice within the device or
he will not. I am to bring his shadow with me. Then the exchange
will be made—or it will not."

"Well then," I said, "I shall conclude that my part in the affair
is done with."

We went out to the hitching rail and horsed ourselves, he to
ride Defender, surveying the grounds of the château, and I to repose myself at the villa and muse upon the nature of shadows, a
subject of infinite profundity and compelling perplexity.

⊹⊶⊙⊷⊹

Mutano had said that Sibylla's shadow communicated to Veuglio
where objects and free spaces lay about him. He compared the
shadow to the whiskers of cats that brush against obstacles and enable
the animals to locate themselves in the dark. But that shadow as he had
described it was not so passive as cats' whiskers; Sibylla's shade, he
said, seemed to search ahead and behind for perils that might threaten
the blind man. It is well known that the other senses of the blind—
hearing, smell, touch, taste—are keener and make finer distinctions
than do those of the sighted. Did this guardian action argue for some
degree of intelligence on the part of umbrae? If such were the case,
would the intelligence of my shadow be an extension of my own
mind or would it belong independently to the shadow?

I had read, two seasons ago, in a treatise of some woolly-faced
philosopher, the fanciful proposition that shadows did indeed have
intelligence. In those days I sometimes tested the learning, as well
as the patience, of the maestro. I had posed the question to him,
saying, "The old philosopher must have been jesting. If shadows

could think thoughts and possess volition, they would not be content merely to imitate the motions of the casters. They would perform deeds different from those that their casters perform."

"If shadows do think," Astolfo replied, "they believe that they initiate movement and that we gross bodies but clumsily ape their motions."

"How could that be? Doth not the corporeal control the incorporeal?"

"You conceive an incorporeal thought, that it would be gladsome to down a mug of ale," he said. "And, lo! The corporeal hulk hauls the vessel to its maw and guzzles it off, obedient to the incorporeal."

"Yet the thought, being conceived in my brain, is joined to the body. It is, in that way, a corporeal object."

"Where is it, then? Show this object to me."

"The emptied mug is the sign of it."

"If emptied ale mugs betoken thought, our world is o'errun with philosophers," he replied. "Your exemplum is faulty, attempting to demonstrate the existence of an incorporeal by pointing to the absence of a corporeal."

"The ale is not absent," I said. "I have drunk it off and now it resides in a place where it may work good to my soul."

"It hath not unmuddied your brain. There are many recorded instances of the umbrae acting upon their own. Sometimes, it is said, a shadow is attached to a man of such evil nature that it becomes ashamed and deserts him. There is the story of a shadow that conceived such a profound distaste for its caster that it attempted to murder him. A woman of the alleyways once purchased and wore the shadow of a chaste vestal, and it labored to purify her character. There is an ancient account of a warrior whose shadow aged at a speedier rate than did his body; it wasted and shriveled and ended by draining his natural strength."

"Idle tales," I replied. "You will not tell me that any of these instances, or others like them, have fallen within your experience."

"And yet I may," he said. "I was brought to a household where it was thought that a young girl's shadow had deserted her. She was but twelve and always in precarious health. An overwise medico whom they had consulted inferred that the umbra feared for its existence if she died and so detached and went seeking a wholesomer body."

"That could not be."

"It had not happened. Her shadow was yet with her, but it was so wispened and insubstantial it had become almost invisible. She had fallen into a state something like dormancy. I suggested that she be forcibly fed and be kept in moderate light instead of dimness. Her shadow regained also."

"There is a sage who pretends to cure this dormancy and other ills of the spirit, I hear."

"His name is Veuglio. I know him to be honest. It is probable you will make his acquaintance someday. At any rate, I do expect that your interest in volitional shadows will increase."

In that prediction, the maestro proved correct, for now Veuglio was here and the question of umbral volition had become vital.

❦

I had thought Mutano would return to the villa as soon as the exchange with the cat of shadow and voice was concluded, but the afternoon lengthened into a cool, peaceful twilight and he did not appear. Yet I did not lack for company. Veuglio and Sibylla emerged from their rooms to take in the beauty of the hour in the garden where I sat oiling the shutters of a half dozen lanterns. These were necessary implements for dealing with the shadow-eating plants in our botanical house. Mutano and I divided this labor and the other tasks.

The gaunt man proceeded over the grass with the girl at his side, she whispering to him continuously. I could not hear her words but supposed she must be describing the garden and its light.

I invited them to share my place beneath the tree and they assented. As soon as I saw them, I thought to question the ancient upon the apprehending abilities of Sibylla's umbra, but he only frowned and said, "I know not what you speak of."

I told him what Mutano had reported of her shade's behavior, but he only frowned more darkly and shook his head.

"It may be that your friend teases your gullibility," said Sibylla.

"Why so?"

"Perhaps he is abashed that my master found no difficulty traversing your labyrinth of shadows. He invents a fanciful reason to account for it."

"He would not trouble, since we share fault equally."

"Perhaps his eyes deceive him."

"His seeing is keen," I said, "as it must be for all in our trade."

Veuglio was seated by Sibylla on a short bench facing me. He tapped the ground with his staff, as if to break off this discussion. "On another head," he said, "I am curious to know by what means you and Mutano transported such a large volume of shadow to the château."

Ah well, I thought, if you hide knowledge from me, I shall not be free with my own, and so I improvised several unheard-of, unusable methods that would delude not the silliest addlepate. His shunting my inquiry aside had vexed me, and the thought came that I might steal the sensitive shadow of Sibylla to try its capacities for myself.

⊷═◉═⊷

That was the foolishest thought ever to flit through my brain. If what Mutano said was true, to steal that shade would be akin to stealing Veuglio's staff and his guide. Such a breach of Astolfo's hospitality would result in my well-earned banishment.

And the character of Veuglio himself made me ashamed that I had even momentarily entertained such a knavish impulse. How could I bring myself to do even the least harm to such a person? I could name a half dozen religious sects that would regard him as a saint.

Besides, the streets of Tardocco were thick with blind beggars, some of whom actually could not see. I resolved to query among them, though they are a closemouthed lot, jealous of the secrets of their calling.

It grew dark and a servant arrived to fetch us to table, and we partook of this victual in a cool strained silence. Mutano had not returned and Astolfo too was absent until the repast was nigh complete. I sat sipping wine and looking my fill at the gaunt elder and his companion, so white and quiet she seemed almost an apparition. Peaceful thoughts breezed through my mind.

When Astolfo did at last appear, he seated himself abruptly at table head and called for a glass of plum liquor that he drained in one swallow. He was out of temper. Sibylla whispered to Veuglio and he did not respond.

"There has been a gross error of judgment," Astolfo said.

"Who has made this mistake, I do not know, but the possibilities are few."

"What has happened?" I asked.

"Someone has disturbed the valuable the maze was laid to protect."

Immediately I looked to Veuglio and the girl but their expressions were impassive.

"I disturbed nothing," I said. "That is a truth you know already. And just what is this object of world-surpassing value? I have tried to imagine what such a thing might be and can form no picture. It has become in my mind an object unguessable, something beyond the reach of the senses."

"You need not imagine, for you have seen it," Veuglio said. These words were spoken with grave deliberateness.

"I saw nothing of worth in that hollow house. The furnishings of the rooms are meager. The hidden rooms that cost us such pains to enclose in our labyrinth contain nothing. They are empty. The whole place is deserted."

"Those close-kept quarters are not empty," Veuglio replied. "Recollect what you saw there."

"There is naught to recollect—a plain table with a stool beside, a candleholder or two, and a few trifling candle stubs."

"A small, useless-seeming candle-end is what the baron seeks to protect," Astolfo said.

"I do not understand."

"Was there nothing else at all in those rooms?" Veuglio asked.

"Rat droppings," I said. "And Mutano discovered some empty bowls that must have supplied the cat Sunbolt with milk."

"These have their parts in the story," he said.

"I do not know the story."

"The nub of it is," Astolfo said, "that the baron fears for his life. He has attached himself to a notion that will not let go. He fancies that his life, his very being, is dependent upon one or the other, or perhaps upon several, of those shabby tallow candles. Whatever is done to them is also wreaked upon him, in dread measure. When he walks the daylight, he has a sensation that his bones are being gnawed by rats. When he lies abed o' nights, he feels that his brain has been set aflame. He sweats and cries out most piteously."

"He conceives that someone is burning his candle of life," I said, "and that rats are toothing it. This is a brain sickness of the kind our Signor Veuglio ministers to. If these fears left the baron, his agonies would cease. Maybe you might offer your services."

"I could not," said the old man. "I would not."

I heard in his voice a tone of personal animosity, of powerful rage and fury. Veuglio tried not to betray his feeling, but I could hear how control of his voice was shaken. Here was something hidden from me, something utterly out of the character of this peaceful man. I glanced swiftly at Astolfo but was uncertain I saw any response. "One thing we might do is to gather these silly stubs and present them to him to keep safe about his person," I suggested.

"But he trusteth no one," Astolfo said, "and he particularly mistrusts those closest to him. That was the reason for the maze at the château."

"It is as if he had a foreknowledge of his phantasies," I said, "for he set the big cat Sunbolt to guard his candles against rats. I have seen the cream bowls and Mutano saw the cat."

"It is difficult to account for the mind and character of such a one as the baron," Astolfo said.

Veuglio spoke softly but emphatically. *"Yet an accounting must be made."*

"Since you and Mutano know the maze, you shall go to the château and locate all the stubs and scour about for other detritus of this sort, and we will keep all here in safety till we decide what may be done," Astolfo said. "You must also make certain that the arrangement of the maze is as you constructed it. Be sure that it has not been changed."

"Very well. I will try to find Mutano. He may be at the château even now, pursuing negotiations with Sunbolt in the matter of his voice."

"His affair will keep," Astolfo said. "Let us make safe the candles."

"We will go there early tomorrow," I said. "I will instruct Mutano when he returns tonight."

⋆⇒◦⇐⋆

Mutano never arrived. I went to bed in an unfit frame of mind and found myself in no better spirits when I woke. Some vigorous ablution, along with a mug of light morning beer, refreshed me, and I saddled Mutano's horse in the paddock and rode away. If he was content to absent himself from our labors, then at least Defender, his large, mellow bay, might be put to saddle.

I had dreamed of the château and in my sleep I had seen the great orange cat stalking the corridors, eyes, nose, and ears all alert. Now and again he entered one room or another to lap from a bowl of water or to lick a bowl thinly filmed with cream. My dreaming did not discover whether the mazes of shadow we had constructed were noted by the cat. I seemed only to follow after him from place to place, as if following a guide lantern through a dusky forest.

Then my dream showed me that Sunbolt was being followed by the baron himself. My vision offered no picture of his features, for I had never seen him. But I knew that the dark, stumbling form was his as it blundered after the confident cat. He carried a brief candle in a pewter holder, the baron, and kept it close to his bosom. Errant breezes slid through the hallways and he shielded the flame against them with his hand. He seemed to know that he must not allow the flame to go out, yet must not let it continue to burn. He was desperate to live and desperate to die.

This dream had determined me to inspect the château anew. I tethered Defender in the courtyard and made my way unhindered through the great outer door to the long gallery on the right-hand side.

All was deserted, just as before. The baron had posted no guards and a hollow silence hung upon the halls. This house held the air of a mausoleum, and the echoes of my footsteps were disconcerting. I began to tread lightly.

Naught had changed. The great rooms displayed the confused, angular shadows that Mutano and I had set within and the gradations of light that tapered along the corridors to sudden man-traps were all in place. If thieves had taken advantage of the empty house, none had fallen to injury or left other trace.

Yet in both the close rooms where the baron's treasure was supposed to have been hidden, there was a small disturbance. In the dust in the corners and upon the ledges where the candle stubs had lain, I found certain evidence of rats. Paw prints decorated the dust and turdlets punctuated it.

Sunbolt was away, perhaps in the company of Mutano, and the rats were pranking about in his absence. I reflected admiringly upon

Sunbolt's prowess; the whole of the château had been under his guard; all alone he had protected it. The picture of this solitary, golden animal padding silently through the edifice had inspired my dream.

The other part of the dream was unreadable. The nobleman followed a cat through the dark, protecting in his bosom a flame that devoured him. At one point, when he came to an intersection of corridors, a shapeless shadow leapt out of the darkness and snatched at his own shadow, which cowered away from the attack, gibbering with the sound of a mouse squeaking.

Now here was a shade with power of will . . .

But only in my dream—and I place no faith in the revelatory powers of dreams. It is difficult enough to deal with umbrae, entities of fractional substance. To deal with dreams I would have to stretch my intuitive faculties beyond their capabilities. Astolfo shared my skepticism, though he did once remark that dreams have suggestive qualities and murmur to us hints sometimes worth pursuing.

For example, maybe a shadow did not have to be self-willed in order to act. What if it were under the control of someone other than its caster, someone who might train it as a hunter trains her hounds or Brotero his cats? If Sibylla's shadow were actually controlled by Veuglio, it would serve him more efficiently as guide. But why would she relinquish control, assuming that to be possible? What was the relationship between them?

Now I recalled what Astolfo had said of them before their arrival at the villa. Not "she is his daughter" but "she is called by the name of his daughter." I recalled also the marked emphasis Veuglio gave to his sentence: *"Yet an accounting must be made."*

Tightly tangled, here was the central knot of the fabric.

"The rats grow in number," I said to myself. "Shall we bring Brotero to bear?" I had seen little sign in my earlier visits, but now I fancied I heard rats in the walls and in drains and above the ceilings. "It is as if they keep watch, and when they see Sunbolt depart, gather together in the château."

I returned to the courtyard, mounted the patient Defender, and rode slowly back to the villa, thinking aloud.

⋆≡◦≡⋆

Mutano's absence was a subject of sharp curiosity in our villa, but I did not fret. I surmised that if the bargain with Sunbolt had been concluded, the cat now again casting a shadow and Mutano possessing his rightful voice, my colleague would seclude himself for a time. He would be practicing to regain the use of the human tongue and running vocalic scales and singing arias to the groves and skies. He would return to us with his instrument in full glory, ready to bell out "A Boozy Short Leave to My Nymphs on the Shore," as he so often used to do when the bottle held him in its warm embrace.

So I was surprised when I was walking down the corridor to my quarters to hear a familiar *Sssst, ssst*. Before I could react, he plucked me by the sleeve to draw me into an empty bedchamber there.

"How now?" I began, but he signed me to be silent and closed the door.

"*Mrrr. Eewow . . .*"

I was disappointed when he spoke in that tongue. I replied in my own: "So you could not strike the bargain you desired. Do we yet possess Sunbolt's shadow?"

He assured me that the cat's shade was ours still and that negotiations were ongoing, having taken a new turn. In the course of their private business, they had talked of many things, exchanging confidences that neither would have spoken of so freely with another of his own species. Neither would judge the other, since confessions of moral transgressions do not translate, the social codes being so dissimilar, and with cats already holding an opinion of humankind so low it could hardly worsen.

They spoke of this and that and the course of their duologue turned toward the subject of the Baron Tyl Rendig. Mutano wondered at the frigid reclusion of the man and Sunbolt ascribed this behavior to fear. At bottom of the matter were females.

Here the stream of converse grew muddy, because a cat hath no conception how one animal can lay possessive claim to the generative organs of another animal. Small wonder, Sunbolt remarked, that if humans hold to this strange doctrine, they reproduce so infrequently and take so long in the doing of it and bear such puny litters.

The baron was a creature of ugly lusts, according to widely whispered report. He was thought to have abducted more than one young girl, despoiled her in cruelest manner, and ended her life in a way sickening to describe. He had done some like harm to a member of Brotero's clan, to a niece, perhaps, or to her friend. The baron was unaware of the connection when he applied to Brotero for a cat to patrol the château. Brotero deployed Sunbolt to the house, giving out that the feline was the most accomplished and many-victoried ratter in Tardocco, in all the province of Tlemia, and maybe in all of history, if the exploits of Prodicus the Black Island Mauler are discounted as legend. The baron held a vivid and particular fear of rats, that they would devour a secret treasure he had laid up in his château. Sunbolt could not say what this treasure was, but he proved worthy of his task. After a few spirited skirmishes, the rats learned to keep their wary distance.

"This Sunbolt ranks himself a champion," I said.

"Long may he thrive, and my proper voice within him," Mutano replied.

"Yet he never discovered the nature of the treasure?"

Mutano said that the cat told him he had once seen the baron alone in the close room as he fumbled with some dirty old candle ends, taking them up one by one and examining closely, then putting them by and tugging at his red beard. This accidental moment meant nothing to Sunbolt.

"It may be that some of the elements of this affair begin to cling together," I said. I told him what I had learned from Astolfo and Veuglio about the baron's fixed idea that the length of his life matched the length of a candle stub. "But how did these short ends come into his hands?"

"They would be sent him as a gift," Mutano said. "The gift would be a taunt or a threat. The accompanying message would tell that his life and soul depended upon the disposition of these unworthy objects and of the others in the possession of the sender."

"Why would he credit the message?"

Mutano said, "It can only be that he is guilty of some black misdeed which the sender knows of fully. Fearful rumors abound. Sunbolt considers that the baron is a feral animal, unfettered in his acts by the customs of society or the sensible constraints of animal nature."

"We must make inquiries," I said. "This use of the candle ends bespeaks a desire for revenge."

He stretched his arms before him and yawned widely. Then he enumerated three things we did not know that must bear upon this business. First, we knew nothing of the relation between Maestro

Astolfo and Tyl Rendig; we knew little of Veuglio and Sibylla; and we knew not who sent the candles that struck such fear into the baron's soul.

"It may be simplest to ask our questions directly," I suggested. "Why not broach them at table tonight?"

He demurred, saying that we gave too much away upon the prospect of getting little in return. We could not know how well the trio were informed and what their own involvements might be. Better to act discreetly, he said, and to pursue inquiries that he and Sunbolt had discussed.

"Well," I said.

⸱⸱⸱⸺◉⸺⸱⸱⸱

I had readied a fable to explain Mutano's absence from the evening table, but the room in which we usually took dinner was empty, the chairs tipped forward against the table, the tapers unlit, the sideboard bare. The kitchen was servantless and the foodstuffs packed neatly into the larder.

I decided to fodder myself in the town, but as I passed the open doorway to the larger library, I heard the scritch-scratch of quill on paper. Astolfo's back was toward me as he sat writing in a tall ledger. I watched the rooster tail as it bobbed along in his hand and then I stole toward him, curious. I had never seen him write before.

"Come forward, Falco," he said without turning. "I have been waiting to hear what questions you have. Please seat yourself here at the table."

I pulled out a chair. Two unlit lamps stood before him; the room was dim and gloomy in this early evening hour.

"For," he continued, "I have no doubt that questions bedevil your mind."

"A few, if we are to talk about the affair of the Baron Tyl Rendig."

"We shall speak of anything you wish."

"I wish to propose that you may be the one who gifted him with some peculiar tallow candles."

"Why say you so?"

"The only other person I could conjecture would be unable to do so."

"That is insufficient proof."

"I am no magistrate or judge and do not care about legalism. There is much that you conceal from Mutano and me, we who carried out your directions in the baronial house. That is something of a sore point."

He wiped his pen with a tuft of wool and laid it by the inkwell. "What do I conceal?"

"The true identities of our guests, the blind man with his hawthorn staff and the girl. Sibylla is not the daughter of Veuglio."

"Never did I say so."

"I should like to talk to them," I said.

"The pair are not here. Veuglio wished to visit some of his old acquaintance in the town. As they would not be taking a meal, I dismissed the kitchen servants."

"You had surmised that I was beginning to untangle some part of the conundrum and so put them out of reach of my questions."

"Perhaps."

"You know of the baron's object of fear. There is but one way that you could. You must have observed some crime or misdeed on his part."

"That is not exactly so."

"To those miserable stubs you sent to him, you somehow attached a shadow of peculiar sort."

"Peculiar?"

"I cannot describe it, but it acted upon his mind and spirit, and perhaps upon his body."

"In what fashion?"

"So as to increase his natural apprehension to a state of continual, abject fear."

"Why should I do so?"

"Your reason I cannot guess, but you are the only agent I can think of."

"You believe that I desire to harm him."

"Yes. It marks a strange turn in your behavior. You are a man well disposed toward most other men. He must have committed some dreadful act of which you violently disapprove."

"Why then would I put you and Mutano to construct a maze to protect his interests?"

"I cannot fathom it."

"Do you fancy me as an avenger of some wrong I know of? That ill suits my amiable disposition."

"You are wealthy and may pursue any interest as you please. Why should you not avenge some wrong, if it suited your fancy?"

"Our age does not lack for wrongs. Do you picture me choosing among 'em like a butterfly in a flowery meadow, alighting at random?"

I leaned toward him and spoke slowly. "I will say what I think. I think that much of your character, even the greater part, is of a gamesome complexion. I believe that you enlist Mutano and me as players like chess pieces in your games. I believe also that there is an intricate network of these amusements, wherein each enterprise is connected with another in a web so convolute that I never could trace its outline. It may be that you cannot configure the whole of it yourself and that ofttimes you merely improvise. 'Tis likelier, though, that it all hangs together like the arcane philosophy of a deep-browed thinker long gone to his grave."

He gave a gentle laugh. "That would be the vainest of sports."

"There is earnest at the end of it. You make a dark search for something beyond the realm of outward appearance, something at the heart of the world, or within it."

"You conceive that this jumble of a world hath a heart?"

"I can believe you are determined to find out."

"You credit me too greatly," he said. "I am but a tradesman."

"That is a half truth at best. I have busied myself about shadows long enough now to know that close company with them affects the spirit and character of a man."

"Or a woman, think you?"

"A woman also. Such a woman as Sibylla, perhaps, she who tends the saintly Veuglio."

"How would you describe these effects you believe umbrae to produce upon a person?"

"Since you know of this subject more deeply than I, I shall not waste breath. But I have thought it best to tell you my thought. I would not have you suspicion that I am spying upon you. Yet I shall try to discover what you game at."

"Thou'rt an honest fellow then."

"As this world wags, yes."

"An honest man must sometimes fortify his virtue with a glass.

Let us journey to the kitchen and make trial of a cask of canary Iratus purchased yesterday."

"Very well," I said, "and I thank you. But I would like to ask—"

"And we shall speak no more upon this subject."

He rose and I followed him away. But the subject did not leave my mind.

VII

Shadow of Candles

We were at the paddock in the blue light of morning, inspecting the horses. They had been enclosed here for a long time, the stable being occupied by our Nighthouse and its shadow-eating plants. The horses were in need of exercise. Mutano had been absent from our villa for days and now Defender nuzzled him so heartily that he was nearly pushed over.

"How does the affair progress?" I asked him. "Do you still speak only feline?"

In that language he told me that negotiations had taken a different turn entirely. He had found out that the precious treasure, the valuable to which Tyl Rendig had unbreakably shackled the length of his life, was in the possession of Brotero.

When I asked how this impresario of cats had come by it, he told me that it had been brought to him from the château by a huge black rat he had trained to filch and poach and despoil and do dire damage upon the valuables of Brotero's foes.

"Is it not his proper purpose to kill rats and not to league with 'em?"

"Ho now, Defender," he said. "Be still." The horse was always restless when addressed in cattish.

Mutano scratched with his thumbnail along the line of the black mane and said, "Now and again he will choose one rat and train it in infamous trickeries. He plucks more strings than one upon his cithara."

"Do you know what this treasure is?"

"I do not, but we are shortly to find out."

"How so?"

"I made a wager with the man to match Sunbolt in battle against the best of his Maulers. When Sunbolt defeats his champion, Brotero will give over the treasure to me."

"Do you not run a dread risk? Doth Sunbolt agree to such an arrangement?"

"He is avid upon the prospect."

"How may he profit?"

"I have wagered with him also. If he loses the battle, I will give back his shadow. If he wins, we will bargain again on different terms."

"He has the best of it," I said.

"We shall see."

"Have you looked upon this Mauler? He may be of size and strength to kill your Sunbolt."

"Incertitude makes possible the wager," he replied.

"And the contest will be fair? Brotero does not seem an exemplar of plain dealing."

"He may try to take a knavish advantage."

"What then?"

"You shall be looking out for't and, if it befall, I shall pin his carcass to the wall with a sword and possess myself of a cattery."

"You are well fit," I said, "as you already speak the language."

"Make clear your hours for the second night hence," he said. "That is the appointed time."

——◦═◦——

The appointed place was a large, resounding, empty warehouse on Rovers Wharf. A dolorous edifice of crumbling red and black brick, it sat squat upon waterside, poking a rotting pier out over the tides like a twig thrust into a campfire. I arrived early and made a tour of the outer structure but found nothing amiss. I made short work of the lock on a narrow side door and entered the cavernous space. Unlit torches were set about the walls and a low, makeshift gallery had been carpentered around the large, dusty space in the center, the space where the trial of strength would occur.

I examined all closely. The only cause for suspicion was a profusion of rat-holes at the base of the walls; these would be ordinary, except that I formed a strong impression that no rats had infested here for a long period. When I left the building, I took care to set the door-lock back as it had been.

A brothel catercornered eastward offered a balcony with a view of the warehouse, and I stationed there to watch the arrivals. They began to show just before the hour and they made up an expectable crowd of some four score or more: sailors, draymen, panders, cobblers, doxies, grooms, and the like. They were a vocal, excited rabble, already trading lies and offering wagers.

When I saw Mutano go inside, bearing on his left shoulder a large, leather-bound trunk outfitted with numerous small holes, I left my elevated post, pushed through the remnant of the throng, and entered.

No time was wasted on preliminaries. Brotero, dressed in his gray tunic and trunks, brought in his big black Mauler cat on a red leather leash attached to a length of hempen rope. He led the animal to the middle of the floor and announced his name: "Uccisore." I thought "Murderer" a proper name for the specimen.

When Brotero stepped away into the first row of spectators, Mutano approached slowly. His leisurely progress gave me time to look about, paying particular attention to the heavily shadowed rafters. I saw nothing untoward.

Mutano did not speak, of course, but lifted the trunk from his shoulder and set it down eight paces from where Uccisore sat on his haunches, watching closely my friend's every move. The trunk was constructed so that the hasps opened along the bottom. Mutano unlatched them one by one and lifted off the trunk as a whole to reveal Sunbolt. Our fine orange cat was the most colorful object in the room, except for the flambeaux with their swaying red-and-yellow flames.

Sunbolt was lying, with his paws tucked under, upon a fat cushion of bright scarlet silk outlined with yellow piping. The cat seemed to be dozing at first; then he opened his eyes lazily, one at a time, and gave a wide yawn that lasted for a long space. Then he rose and arched his back. Then he crouched forward and, inserting his claws into the cushion, gave himself a languorous, thorough stretch.

All this calculated insolence brought from the gapers and bettors a round of tipsy laughter.

Sunbolt disembarked his pillow in dainty, lethargic fashion, setting one slow paw at a time upon the floor, whose rough planks, laid loosely, showed between the cracks the bay water that flowed and ebbed beneath. The cat took no notice when Mutano came into the arena, took up the pillow, gave it an affectionate kiss—which occasioned more laughter—and removed it.

Of all catfights witnessed by humankind, this one might have been the most extraordinary. The opponents did not rush upon one another squalling in fury, with slit eyes and flattened ears. Nay, they stepped round in circles, their watchful eyes full open, erect ears twitching alertly. They closely resembled two pugilists taking careful stock of the size and style of each other. Their tails curled and uncurled.

Uccisore made his initial assault a quick feint toward the left flank of Sunbolt, but this maneuver the red one had anticipated and he appeared to react in no way, merely continuing his methodical circling and staring.

Uccisore repeated this same tactic but then turned in midair and came straight on to confront his counterpart face-to-face. He stopped abruptly in front of Sunbolt and, planting his feet, arched his back to its tallest extent, giving the aspect of an inky storm cloud ready to release its winds and lightning.

Sunbolt responded in kind, elevating his spine so that his shape was as large or larger. He took the shape of a fireball poised to roll destructively through a landscape.

Now they both backed away and shifted their foci of interest to their surroundings—the smelly warehouse and the red-faced spectators. These folk had been japing, laughing, muttering, and caterwauling, but when Sunbolt delicately lifted a paw and began to lick it, they fell so silent that the wash of tide beneath the floorboards was audible.

As if this ablution were an insult he could not abide, Uccisore flung himself like a falling star. Sunbolt dodged nimbly but had miscalculated his foe's speed. A black paw swiped his left hindquarter, snatching off a thatch of reddish hair that hung for a moment in the air. He squirmed about in a flash and bit Uccisore's tail, to strong effect, as I judged by the outraged howl that ensued. Then they were at it in earnest. The big black cat was the more savage in attack, so wild in his rage of combat that he fought more as a demon than as a feline. His strength was greater than Sunbolt's and when he clutched the red one by his shoulders to sink teeth behind his head, he rolled him off his feet. Sunbolt was energetic too, as quick to pounce and scratch and bite as was his opponent, but his maneuvers were more calculated and he was willing to take blows and swipes and nips in order to conserve his strength and to judge the style of the other. This meant that he was often on the defensive, rolling onto his back and working all four paws furiously in a disembow-eling action. Uccisore could not attack against those flurrying paws, but neither could Sunbolt gain advantage.

The wagers of the assemblage, which had plumped in favor of Uccisore at the outset, now swelled even more heavily in his favor, and the spectators grew noisier.

The fury had continued already much longer than the usual battle and a few of the more observant spectators saw that many of Sunbolt's attacks were but feints and that Uccisore reacted to them in exaggerated fashion, expending strength but wreaking little dam-age. As the combat continued, his ferocity began to abate and he took a more thoughtful approach to his attacks.

But this meant that he was fighting Sunbolt's preferred kind of fight, and he had burned away so much *vis* in his initial onslaught that he responded tardily to the flanking sallies and almost noncha-lant leap-overs. Then it became obvious that Sunbolt was gaining advantage, sometimes toying with his opponent, then rushing in to mark a telling slash upon a shoulder or along the ribs.

The noise of the onlookers subsided gradually and fell into a puzzled muttering. These folk might be regular spectators at the rat-routs and cat-battles that Brotero exhibited, but they had never seen a struggle like this one, wherein one combatant went at it like a brawny, fight-hardened, experienced beast while the other seemed to fore-think his actions, as would a human wrestler or swordsman. The duel—for that was what it had become—had already lasted long past the expected duration and appeared as if it would continue at length.

This lengthiness gave Sunbolt the advantage, and a promise of victory hung in the air.

Now is the time, methought, that if Brotero is going to play an underhand trick, it will be done. I made my way carefully to where Mutano stood at the edge of the arena, and though my attention was mainly upon my forward progress, I saw out of the corner of my eye one of the planks of the floor lift.

Immediately I understood the mistake I had made. The avenue

of interference would not be from the exterior of the warehouse upon which I had kept watch, but from below. There was space enough beneath the floor for a dinghy to come under and for a Worrier cat to be introduced by Brotero's men. I would be the only one who noticed, since I was looking out for foul play and the others were intent on the duel.

This new combatant was about half the size of Uccisore, of a silver-gray color and as lithe and sinewy as any stoat. Whether Sunbolt was aware of its presence, I could not tell. He kept bedeviling Uccisore with feints, buffets, and occasional earnest slashes that drew lines of blood.

The gray Worrier paused for a moment, as if to take in the situation, and then began to initiate the movements familiar to it. It would sidle swiftly to any blind side, then rush in to nip smartly, then leap back before Sunbolt could retaliate with a hind paw.

This was the game customary in their wars with rats and both Uccisore and the gray one had it well by heart.

I watched closely, for I knew that Mutano would stand by his vow to expose to the torchlight the guts of Brotero upon any such impudence. And he did begin to unsheathe his blade and step toward the nervy, smirking little fellow. But, as I had expected, two of Brotero's henchmen approached Mutano at the same time. I waited for the near one to pass me by and just as he did, I placed the point of my poniard behind his ear and told him in a soft but earnest voice that if he came upon my friend but one half step more I would pierce his brain with a piece of intelligence he would not relish.

He stepped away and I disarmed him.

When Mutano unsheathed, the other assailant retreated. He had counted upon the advantage of number and, not having that, was uneager to cross blades with my expert comrade.

And so the feline fight continued in its course. No one wished to try to come between the cats because of the danger of being shredded like a red cabbage. Mutano would have opportunity to exert his justice upon Brotero when the conflict concluded.

It was not going well for Sunbolt. His two opponents had the superiority a wolf pack enjoys, one of them confronting forwardly, the other coming from the sides. Sunbolt was as limber and swift as a serpent in striking and withdrawing, but the incessant attacks were tiring him quickly and his counterswipes became less frequent and less forceful. The exhibition began to wind down.

At this point, Sunbolt gave a great leap backward, almost a somersault, that afforded him open space from his attackers. There he braced his four feet, puffed out his chest, opened his mouth as wide as it would gape, and shouted, in Mutano's most commanding manner:

"AVAUNT, COWARD MISCREANTS!"

Again the smoky room fell silent. The spectators all drew in their breath at once and stared at Sunbolt as if he were something brought down from the skies by a war-god in a flaming chariot.

His battle cry took even greater effect upon the Mauler and the Worrier. The pair of them scrambled back away, looking at Sunbolt in fright and dazed confusion. Uccisore's eyes crossed. The Worrier arched his back and spat.

Uttering another thunderous, though wordless shout, Sunbolt sprang across the whole of the vacated space and seized Uccisore by the throat. Then, bracing his back feet and standing himself erect, he pulled the black Mauler from the floor and, with a quick jerk of his head, flung the heavier beast into the second rank of spectators.

Seeing the unexpected and dismal fate of his counterpart, the Worrier bounded away from the combat area and ran to the farther part of the floor, to the place where the board had been lifted to admit him to the arena. He clawed frenziedly at the wood, but that exit was no longer available. As Sunbolt advanced upon him grimly, he gave a piteous little *"Miaou"* and slunk away with head and ears and tail drooping, into the guffawing crowd.

In this manner did Mutano win his wager with Brotero, and thus he received a small canvas bag containing fourteen candle stubs. This reward he procured by producing a scrap of paper torn in half upon which an agreement had been inscribed. Brotero, with unfeigned disgust, produced its other half and returned it to Mutano. In the matter of the candles, he muttered, "I think thee shall get little good of them. The baron is not right of mind."

I answered the man: "But thou dost know the beggar who laid this tallow burden upon the noble's spirit. And you shall tell us how we may trace him out."

He shifted anxiously in his boots. "Who can tell that? He is no doubt known among the beggary, but I am not of the brotherhood."

"Tell us something of his appearance and manner of speech," I urged.

"He was roundish of corpus, with delicate, clever hands. He

wore the brown, patchy robe common to his station, but his voice was mild and reasonable and hinted that he was lettered, a man of knowledge."

"Did he tell you his name?"

"Nomio or Nurmio or Rumino or some such. I cannot recall."

"Was he accompanied by a girl of fourteen or so years, a silvery slip of a thing with a fixed stare?"

"No. When he went away, he gathered to him a tall, thin blind man with a hawthorn staff whom he guided along the lane. They did not speak to each other."

"How did you come to commerce with him?"

"He came to me," Brotero said. "It was an unhappy hour, for I think Uccisore may be broken in spirit now and useless. He offered then to tell me where lay the baron's treasure and how my band of trained rats might fetch it for me."

"Having got it, you were to sell it to him at a price you would set?"

"Yes. I had thought to demand a handsome fee, but my rats brought back only some paltry candle stubs. I set a fee of two eagles which I expected him to reject."

"But he paid without complaint?"

"He did, and how do you know of this? What is its concern to you?"

"I know little," I said. "Your well-disciplined rats understand the world better than I do."

⊶⊷

Mutano and I departed the warehouse in discomposed spirits. Sunbolt had disappeared after his victory and Mutano was pleased at the outcome but glum about the prospect of reclaiming his voice.

"That cat will never return it now," he said. "He has found it too valuable an instrument."

"That may be so," I said. "Yet you possess his voice, and perhaps it too can give advantages."

He shook his head. I knew that he was thinking of the woman he could not now beguile with ballades and canzoni and other intricate verbal nosegays.

I attempted to lure him into another line of thinking, saying,

"If Sunbolt had been killed in the fight, your voice would have died with him."

"'Tis as good as dead if I do not get it back."

"We shall work toward a better conclusion," I said. "Do you recall your observation of Sibylla's shadow as Veuglio made his way through our maze at the château?"

He nodded.

"Do you still hold that the shadow communicated in some fashion to the two of them?"

"Yes."

"Such a shadow, capable of thought and communication and of some degree of volition, would be most valuable in our trade."

Mutano agreed and added that he had been considering the subject, although he had lacked leisure to pursue the thought.

"What would Maestro Astolfo give to possess such an umbra?"

A great deal, he told me, for this speaking or signing shadow could be put to more uses than we could readily imagine. "A man might establish an army if he could command a company of intelligent shadows."

"How could he bend them to his will?"

"By threat of extinction. I can conceive no other way. They would not care for gold or any sort of object. They are independent of desires."

"Well, these thoughts are idle, like so many of our speculations upon the vitality and intelligence of umbrae. We have more pressing concerns. We need to resolve all this matter of the Baron Tyl Rendig and we must pursue the question of the relationship between the maestro and Veuglio and his ward."

"And we must reclaim my voice. It is accustomed to nobler purposes than frightening combative cats."

"Let us divide our labors. I will undertake to recover your voice whilst you search out information on the blind man."

"How am I to do so?"

"He was involved, perhaps allied, with the beggar guild of Tardocco," I said. "If you make search among that louse-rag company you are likely to discover the track of him."

"How do I inquire of them, seeing that they do not speak cattish?"

"Every task mounts difficulties—we must surmount 'em. How

am I to persuade Sunbolt to give up his human language, since I
have naught to offer in return?"

He smiled wryly. "That is a difficulty you must surmount. I
believe you already have a stratagem in mind."

"Truly? I do beseech you to reveal it to me."

"You are not one to make rash bargains," he said.

⤖〰◉〰⤙

In the tavern called The Double Hell I stationed myself at a table
where I could observe the thirsty come through the door with the
bright mid-afternoon light strong behind them. The fellow I awaited
would be called Quinias or Quinny or some such. He was the
brother of Maronda, she who at the cattery rival to Brotero's had
been so sharp-set against me. This Quinny—or Ninny, as I judged
him—I would recognize by his shadow. His sister had said of him
that he was hale and whole once more and this meant that he had
regained the shade that, as he told his sister, had been stolen from
him. I thought it more likely that he had acquired a shadow not his
own. If so, he had not got it from the establishment of Maestro
Astolfo, or I should have known of it.

No one likes to lose his shadow. It is not a mortal blow, but it is
a wearying trouble. If it is stolen or damaged, a man will seek out
a dealer in umbrae resupply and the difficulty is got around in a
hobbledehoy fashion. The fellow is the same as before, so he fancies, with a new shadow that so closely resembles his true one, no
one would take note.

That is not the case. His new shadow never quite fits him so
trimly, so conformably, so sweetly, as did his original. There is a
certain discrepancy of contour, a minor raggedness not easy to
mark but plainly evident to one versed in the materials. The
wearer never completely grows to his new shadow and goes about
with it rather as if wearing an older brother's hand-me-down
cloak.

Another change occurs also, not in the fitting or wearing, but
in the character of the person. To lose a shadow is to lose something of oneself. The loss is slight and generally unnoticeable, yet
an alert observer might see some diminution in the confidence of
bearing, in the certitude of handclasp, in the authority of tread upon
a stone stairway.

All these things I had been told or had read in books. I had never at that time experienced such loss myself and believed that I never would.

I am proud of my ability to find out these distinctions between original shades and acquired ones. I was confident that I would recognize this Quinny-Ninny when he entered, and I felt reasonably certain that enter he would. I had formed a picture of his character and I was content to sip ale and nibble at eggs in pickle until his arrival. The Double Hell is a tavern where gamesters repair and it is a superstition among this breed that to change place of play is often to damage luck. Even a modicum of success under a certain roof will lure the player to return again and again.

So I marked my man as soon as he slid slouch-wise into the room, shouldering against the heavy pine door with its carved flagon. He took a seat on the bench by the far wall. He signaled and a mug was delivered by a thin boy in a soiled shirt who showed no affection for him. He coppered the youngster and waved him away, looked about, then settled to his beer, awaiting his usual circle of fellow gamesters.

I rose and walked directly to him, unsheathing my shorter dagger. I buried it an inch deep into the table before him. "My name is Falco."

He gave the knife a quick appraisal before looking into my face. "That is interesting to know," he said. His tone was as suave as glove leather, but I heard the undertone of uncertainty.

"Know too that I brook no insult."

"No man should." He looked at my blade again.

"I am in the employ of Maestro Astolfo."

"Ah, the master shadow—"

"Take care you do not say *thief*," I said, "for that would compose an insult."

"Shadow merchant, I was about to say."

"You were about to say *thief,* and I would have had one of your eyes for it. I may yet pluck the left one, if you persist in untruth. *Thief* is a name I will not bear."

"Friend Falco," he said, "I never could call you thief. I never saw you until now."

"Another lie," I said. "I am not your friend."

"I hope that at some time it may be so, if I can make clear your confusion. I never called you thief."

"You have said to many that your shadow was stolen from you

here at The Double Hell. You complained broadly and bitterly. You applied to your sister for coin to regain it and she took pity and now she holds a deceived opinion of honest Falco. The truth is, you diced the thing away and were too cowardly ashamed to own to the fact. If you deny, you lie. I do not abide lies."

"It is true. I misled Maronda. She does not approve my gaming and calls me wastrel and good-for-naught. I was in close straits and must needs borrow. She was my last resort."

"Not for the first time, I'll warrant."

"She knows my brotherly affection. She understands that I will restore all in the near future."

"I should like to live so long as this near future," I said.

"Now I have said the truth. Now you are satisfied and will cease your threats."

"The threat holds until you confess in forthright words this mouse-heart shame to your sister in my presence."

He shook his head, frowning. "You demand too much."

I raised the end of the big table, edged its leg onto his toe, and plumped my bulk upon it. His face turned white before it purpled, but he made no outcry.

"Since you have laid your hand on the hilt of your sword, you can now hand it over to me."

He did so.

I took the blade, slid off the table, and grasped his elbow. "Now we shall journey to the slaughterhouse of Nasilia, where you will reveal to your sister Maronda your pitiable deception. You will avouch me an honest man who steals no shadow from a fumble-finger dicer. You will clear the name of Falco from your smutch till it gleams like a new eagle. This is your near future, is't not?"

He hung his head and breathed a grievous sigh.

"I do not relish the visit either," I said. "The smells of that cattery cause my eyes to stream and my head to burn. Nevertheless—*onward.*"

⊷⊨◉⊜⊶

I felt beset with these unpleasantnesses as soon as I glimpsed the low yellow-brick edifice and its thick, weathered door. I gestured and Quinias lifted and let fall the iron curl-tail knocker. Maronda opened the door, and it seemed to me that the scowl I saw on her face during our least meeting had never left it.

"Good day, Maronda," I said. "I have brought your brother to visit you because he has fresh and important news to report."

Standing half a hand span taller, she gazed down at him with weary distaste. "What is it now, worthless one?"

"I will step away," I said, "so that you may conduct your personal affairs in privacy."

Ten paces put me out of earshot, and I observed that their conversation was animated. Maronda was a statuesque and, might be, a handsome woman, but now her features were contorted with anger. Though I could not make out her words, I could hear the rising pitch of her voice, under the force of which her brother shrank and withered like a peony petal on sun-scorched stone. The conclusion of this recital was sharply percussive as she raised her good right arm and delivered her brother a slap on the cheek that sounded like a courtyard gate clapped to. He staggered and reeled backward.

At this point I advanced upon the pair to prevent Maronda from retiring. "Signorina Maronda," I began, and when she turned her gaze toward me Quinias furtively backed away. He was making an ungainly retreat, accompanied by unsisterly epithets.

"Signorina," I said, "I hold that you have done me an injustice. I am honest in the shadow trade and all otherwise. I do not ask for apology, for it is clear that you were deceived."

"Thou'rt no holy saint," she said, "and will receive no apology."

"Then that is settled and there is no reason we should not do business together."

"I suspect your business."

"I am in the market for a cat," I said. "If you can supply my need, I will pay the price you ask, within the bounds of reason. More coin, mayhap, than Nasilia has ever received for an animal."

"What sort of cat?"

"Let us talk a little and I will describe."

"Well then," she said, but her gaze was directed not at me but over my shoulder. I turned to see that Quinias was already far down Chandlers' Lane and now squirmed in weasel fashion around the corner into an alley. "Come inside."

"If you will oblige me, we can talk better here." Even outside, the musken air was working upon me. My eyes teared. I took a square of green silk from my cuff and dabbed at them. Then I spoke of the form of cat that I desired.

Mutano found me in the villa garden at twilight. I sat watching the late sun at play upon the high-billowed clouds, observing how tint mingled with tint, how the changing light altered the appearance of the cloud, and wondering how deeply into a mass of cloud a ray might penetrate and in what fashion the colors of the ray would change along its journey.

He came quietly toward me, unwilling, as I thought, to disturb my meditation. "You have found something out," he said.

"Naught of strong import as yet, but I have hope. I was pondering the way light intermingles with cloud and comparing that with the way shadow mingles with other substance. We are accustomed to improving the nature of wine, of cloth, of walls and corridors and gardens with our shadows. Silver, though, doth not acquire much tincture, nor does unglazed pottery. Pewter receives it only reluctantly and in slight measure. A lump of wax is not much affected."

"When wax is molten, it can receive as much umbra as we desire," Mutano said.

"And would this hold true of tallow also?"

"It would. . . . Ah, you have struck upon a corner of the truth."

"The baron is much troubled with frightening fancies. We hear that he dreams of being eaten alive by rats. He imagines that his head is aflame."

"His shadow has been taken and admixed with candle tallow," Mutano said. "It is easy to add shadow to things in liquid state."

"And the tallow divided into a number of candles."

"And those candles tumbled in with the ordinary ones to be used daily and nightly as required."

"And left about careless where they might be taken up and lit for any household purpose," I said.

"Or left about to be nibbled by rats," he said. "That is another unsettling thought, that a man's shadow may be the prey of rats. They would tear off a bit and then run in alarm away at a silly noise and return at uncertain intervals to gnaw again."

"Not one candle and one rat, but a dozen candles and numerous rats. Nibble-nibble now, nibble-nibble in an hour or half an hour."

"It would seem a fit defense," said Mutano, "to set an experienced and crafty cat as candle guardian."

"There is one called Sunbolt," I said, "who is clever enough to patrol the whole of a château, even if it be otherwise deserted."

"This Sunbolt hath many gifts. There is a principal one I should like to regain from him." Mutano's meowing had grown more irritated and irritating. I longed for him to purr.

"Be patient but a little longer. Meantime, how close were our surmises about Veuglio and Sibylla?"

"Each day discovers a new ignorance in me," Mutano said. "I had not imagined that in the company of the beggars there would be one acquainted with the feline language. Yet several there are who speak cattish and one who is master of three of the dialects. The beggars depend upon knowledge of the ways of the streets and alleys and nooks of Tardocco and none knows 'em better than the cats. 'Tis a familiar custom, their cat-talk."

"And what did your cat-tongued friends tell us?"

"Somewhat of Veuglio and Sibylla."

"And of Astolfo also?"

He was surprised. "Of Astolfo? No. How should he come into it?"

"Does he not seem to be everywhere? But then—was there any mention of a personage called Nomio or Mumio or something like?"

"Yes. Of Nomio a little was spoken, but since you name him, you must know already what was said."

"Not the whole of it. Let us confer now and decide how best to present our surmises and our designs for the future. A goodly table has been set for five and the best silver laid out."

"Veuglio and the girl are to be present?" Mutano asked.

"We shall make them welcome, but let us first trace out the thread of our tale. Tell me what you learned. Omit nothing."

We were long in conference. The first stars appeared singly and were soon gathered about by flocks of lights. Swallows flew to rest, taking their dainty scythe-shapes to dark corners. Bats began to tumble above the treetops. At last we went in to dress for the mealtime.

⟡

All were present, quietly chatting by candlelight.

As soon as we were seated I rose and raised my glass. "The custom," I said, "is to propose a toast to guests. And so I do. Live long and prosper smilingly."

We drank.

Then I said, "It is not customary to offer a toast to the ill health of anyone present or absent, yet I shall take opportunity to do so. My friends, I give you Baron Tyl Rendig, and may he lie gibbering while the rats of his phantasy chew his flesh and bone and spirit. May he sweat drenching gallons while he feels his head burning on his shoulders like a pitchy flambeau at a festival. May these two agonies light on him alternately and together by intervals as long as ever he shall endure and may their pains increase hourly. Is there anyone present who will refuse to join this salute?"

Sibylla looked at me, her haunted, haunting expression more sorrowful than ever. I thought I could remark, however, a glimmer of lightened mood upon Veuglio's features. Astolfo remained expressionless but slowly raised his glass and bowed his head in agreement. Mutano drained his glass in one swallow and Veuglio followed suit. The girl allowed herself a tidy sip.

I proposed another toast. "Although Mutano and I count ourselves members of this household, we sometimes take pleasure in regarding Maestro Astolfo as our host. And so let us toast his health and best welfare."

Veuglio and his ward joined.

"He is the most ingenious fellow to be imagined," I said, "for although the baron is a client in our present enterprise and Astolfo is bound by the courtesy of our trade not to betray his interests or to harm his person without dishonoring our house, yet he has found ways to make damage upon him without dishonor. I do not know all the steps and stops he followed to accomplish his ends, but I believe he has given you full satisfaction, friend Veuglio. Am I mistaken?"

The old man tasted his glass. "I can never grasp full satisfaction," he said, "but Astolfo has given me a very large measure."

"Were you in Veuglio's employ from the beginning?" Mutano asked Astolfo. "Or did you accept Tyl Rendig's commission and then lend your services to Veuglio?"

"My practice is scrupulous," Astolfo declared in the driest of tones. "The baron paid me to secure his château against thieves who might carry off what he deemed most precious in his estates. You and Falco laid those traps and pitfalls to thwart any who might come against the place. Did you not do your utmost to make the château secure?"

"We did our best," I said. "Our best was not sufficient."

"Was it not prudent of me to put your arrangements to the test?" Astolfo asked. "Should I not look to our client's interests and request Veuglio to inspect your efforts?"

"Yes," I said. "But the baron was no stranger to you nor to the other beggars and thieves and draymen and porters with whom you lived and caroused in your guise as the beggar Nomio. You were learning the ways of the under-life of the province in those days and you mingled with folk of every rank of society. I conjecture that you do so still in order to judge the currents of thought and heats of feeling of our citizenry. You would have learned all about the baron's brutal practices with women and about his peculiar viciousness toward young girls. You waited for opportunity to strike a blow against him."

"I am a man of affairs," Astolfo said. "I do not go about like the armored errants in the old children's tales dealing justice to those who need chastisement. My purpose is to amass gold and to mete it out for my amusement."

"But you do not flee unlooked-for occasion. When the baron applied to you, there appeared the chance to repay him somewhat for his savage iniquities."

"He never wronged me. I had no interest in his doings of whatever stripe. And I have fulfilled my commission to him. The château is safe from robbers, since none will possess Veuglio's exceptional skills. The house is so safe that the baron now intends to live there alone. He is convinced that no one can get at him through the maze you and Mutano installed. I have guided him through it, showing him a clear and easy path. I have drawn him a plan of the maze as you left it, just as he requested. He was pleased and offered to remunerate above the commission fee, but I refused. No other client of mine has been so justly served as the baron will be."

"As Nomio, you were friend to many a poor man," I said. "Veuglio was one of them. You knew, as did all that company, about the vile cruelties and the final murder that Tyl Rendig committed upon Sibylla, the daughter of Veuglio. When the baron approached you about the purchase of some shadow-stuff, you discovered your opportunity. For this project, you reclaimed one of your youthful skills. You found a way to steal the baron's shadow, or a part of it, and you stored it away for a later purpose."

"That is not true. How can it be? Here sits Sibylla at our table. She is not injured or mutilated. Much less is she murdered."

"That is not Sibylla. That is Dorminia, the daughter of the sad lace merchant. She fell victim to the sleeping sickness that afflicted so many young girls. When Veuglio began to restore her to herself, you attached Sibylla's shadow to her. Sibylla was murdered most cruelly in the upper room of an inn called The Dismal Fathom. She had been abducted by Rendig's men and delivered to the baron in that place. Her cries and screams were heard throughout the quarter, but the baron's men blockaded the lanes. Someone went to fetch Veuglio and the civil guard. Too late. When they led the blind physician up the stairs to the bloody room, it must have required every bit of courage—"

"Blind?" cried Veuglio. "I was not blind. My eyesight was blasted in my skull when I saw my Sibylla—"

I pray that I shall never again hear the sound of a voice so twisted with pain and piteous with grief. My flesh shrank and my neck hairs prickled.

Astolfo spoke. "Say no more. This is not proper matter to discuss at table."

"I will be circumspect. There are passages I cannot yet thread. Whoever was supposed to guard Sibylla failed in his duty. Or was bribed. Maestro Astolfo may know better than I. But what Veuglio saw there has given him cause to pursue the direst revenge he can devise. You are leagued with him in that design. I do not comprehend how—"

"Many things you do not comprehend," Astolfo said, "and never shall. Our cook Iratus is not patient of temperament. If we do not begin the repast, our breast of veal may be given to the hounds. Can you comprehend?"

"We would be foolish," I said, "to cross a person who has so many knives at hand." And so we passed to common gossip and speculations upon the nature of astronomy and the late lack of success of the fishing fleet because of some mysterious turmoil of the waters of the harbor bay and so the evening fluttered along until midnight fetched its terminus.

Our guests bade us good night and also farewell. Veuglio explained that they must be on their way well before daybreak. He had been summoned in his capacity as physician to attend the daughter of Count Ryzikus in the north of Tlemia. She was an-

other of the unaccountable examples of morose temperament falling into even blacker moods and now she had quit speech altogether
and would sit for hours looking into a space before her as if into a
different world.

"I have wondered," Veuglio said, "if the anxieties and incessant
troubles of our time do not burden the more sensitive spirits of the
young. Were they not formerly gay and carefree and passionate for
music and dance? That is how I recall them in my youth."

"Our youths often look brighter than they were in truth,"
Astolfo said.

"If a general dull pall has fallen upon them, would it affect their
shadows? But of course I know nothing of shadow-nature and the
fancy is idle."

"I have not studied the matter," Astolfo said, "but your conjecture intrigues me. Perhaps I may assign the study to Falco here. It
would give him business of his own to mind."

And so, with this sour little reprimand, off to bed.

❧

But not to sleep. As soon as I closed my eyes, the anguished voice
of Veuglio sounded in my head. The sight he looked upon had been
so horrific that it obliterated his power of seeing. From that moment he was blind. I recalled how Mutano's voice had been taken
from him when he shrieked—and the sight he looked upon had
been only a waxen effigy. What Veuglio had seen, I tried not to
imagine.

But if that had been his daughter Sibylla in the inn, how could
Dorminia have taken her place? Veuglio had sufficient skills to rid
her of her sleeping sickness, but why would her parents consent to
her companioning the old man? She must have been an orphan, I
thought, in the care of some priestly sisterhood. Astolfo would have
known of her circumstances and persuaded a friendly sister to
permit her to undertake the duty. Such as arrangement was not
uncommon and this one indicated the measure of respect Astolfo
held among certain of the clergy.

Even so . . .

I felt I was near to teasing an answer from this knotted mangle
of questions. Then, just as I thought I saw a glimmer of revelation,
sleep darkened my mind like a heavy shutter thrown closed upon a
window casement.

⊷══◉══⊶

So now I had come to the cattery again and was engaged in bargaining the fee, a minor task I had not expected. Already my nose began to drip.

"Four silver eagles," Maronda said. "I will not sell for less."

"That is dear," I said.

"I will not haggle. You agreed to pay the price I set."

"Within the bounds of reason, you will recall."

"For this cat and perhaps for none other, four eagles is a reasonable sum."

"Let me look upon this marvel," I said. "I shall count it a happiness merely to glimpse a cat rated at that price."

"Come round to the courtyard." She closed the clumsy door of the cattery and led me a few steps down the lane to an iron-barred gate. Through it I could see a fire-pit over which hung a large iron pot used, no doubt, for boiling down essences and creating other noisome exhalations. A mere whiff of the air here increased the pulsing of my brain and the blearing of my eyes.

There was a shady plane tree in the far corner and under it sat a long, low bench, and upon the bench reposed a cat. I could make out only a little from this distance, but its color was different from that of any feline I had ever before encountered. It was of the silver-blonde hue to be seen in the hair of fair women and nowhere else, a human color.

Maronda produced a key from the pocket of her gray smock and opened the gate. The cat was looking away from us and did not turn as we approached. When we were within ten paces, Maronda spoke the name *Asilia* and the animal slowly squared its head to gaze at us.

The eyes were startling, not only because of their color, a cool chicory-flower blue, though that was remarkable, but because of the intelligence that lay behind them. It was unmistakable, this knowingness; I felt the force of it instantly. It is one of my necessary skills to judge the relationship between character and appearance and I have met many a human person who showed much less intelligent aspect than did Asilia the cat.

She rose from her haunches, arched her back in a slow, graceful rainbow, and turned her front toward us. Her coat was silver-blonde all along her flanks and down her legs, but the tip of each toe was dusted with a frosty white and there was a narrow blaze down her chest, a marking that looked like a shiny, dainty dagger.

She seated herself again and faced us, like a queen granting audience from her throne.

"What think you?"

The cat looked directly into my eyes. I felt she was reading my thought. "A remarkable animal," I said. "How did you come by her?"

"That is none of your concern."

"For four eagles, it may be. Pedigree is important."

"So it is. That is why we shall keep it privy. You could not purchase the secret of the breeding for forty coins."

"Let me observe her movement."

Maronda raised her index finger. Asilia regarded her gravely for a long moment, as if she were deliberating whether to obey the suggestion, then rose again. She walked to the end of the bench, back to the other end, then repeated her march and settled again.

If water could walk in that shape, if the genius loci of a purling stream in the forest could take feline form, that is how it would move, not with one step and then the second, but with a flowing so smooth it appeared that no separate steps had been footed. Asilia moved slowly along the oak, but she *swept*.

"She has never been bred?"

"She is virginal, as you require."

"Hath she an ear for music?"

"Jollylegs the fiddler played a tune most merry and she seemed to listen. When he played the old, sad ballad 'Lament of Queens Departed,' she took close note and inclined her head most attentive."

"She did not join in the harmony?"

The woman with manly bones peered at me quizzically before grinning broadly. "She may have awaited an invitation unforthcoming."

I had formed an admiration for Maronda. If she had lived by a different means, I might have sought to keep her company for a time and learn her ways. But I could tie no amatory bonds with a female whose presence would make me sneeze, snivel, and stream from the eyes.

"I see that she follows your simple command to patrol the bench.

Has she been otherwise trained? Would she obey the signal of another person?"

"She will parade so at the crook of a finger, but that is all. She is no jongleur's pet, versed in trickery. Such training might mar the simplicity of her nature."

"I should not like that. But, please, do direct her to march again."

The sunlight had shifted a little and this time I was able to observe her shadow more closely. She was so sylphlike that she hardly cast one and its motions upon the bench-board were as gentle as those of a slight breeze dallying with a row of white lilies.

"Well, 'tis a bargain then," I said, and handed her the gold. "I shall return on the morrow with my comrade Mutano and we shall bring her away. You may be interested to know that she will be climbing high in the ranks of society and may possibly inhabit a château hereafter."

"Asilia cannot ascend higher than the station she now occupies," Maronda said. "She is a princess."

I would not disagree.

⊶⊨◎⊨⊷

Mutano was suspicious when I decorated one of the cook's thrush-cages with flowers and hung shiny toys about the bars. "I misdoubt me your bait will attract," he said.

"Only make certain," I said, "that the instrument with which you are to capture the voice is in working order. I will see to the bait. And do not neglect to bring the shadow."

We lifted the cumbersome curl-tail knocker again at the appointed hour and Maronda appeared. She gave Mutano a frank appraisal, from cap-feather to boot-toe. "This is the friend of whom you spoke?"

"This is Mutano. Troubled in his speaking, he is unable to greet you properly."

He doffed his cap and made a bow, only half jestingly.

"No doubt you make up for his silence."

I too bowed and exhibited the fanciful cage. "This is to transport Asilia," I explained. "She will not be long contained." I set it on the doorstep.

"Let us see if she consents," Maronda said, She turned and gave the finger signal, and Asilia came trotting forward toward the sunlight. At the doorway she stopped, took account of Mutano and me, and began sniffing at the cage with its flowerets and ribbons and spangles. She looked questioningly at Maronda, and when the woman nodded, she nosed her way into the cage. She sniffed at one bauble and another, then turned three times and sat.

"Take good care handling her," Maronda said. "Asilia belongs to you now, but if any harm comes to her through your agency or neglect, you will hear from me at close quarters."

Mutano handed me the cage, made another teasing bow to Maronda, and in rising stepped forward and kissed her full on the mouth.

Astonishment made her face an immobile mask. That expression remained in place for a count of five and was replaced by a frown of strong vexation. Again she resorted to the force of her arm, and the slap that resounded upon Mutano's cheek must have tumbled a lesser man. But he had braced himself for this reward of his insolence and stood steady, though with reddening face.

"Let me say amends for my friend," I said. "Since he cannot speak, he sometimes resorts to awkward measures to express his sentiments. He means no harm and our master Astolfo will chastise him severely."

Mutano sank to his knees and bowed his head. He was the very image of heartfelt abjection.

Maronda smiled despite herself and replied, "Your master must teach both of you the manners of gentlemen."

"We are eager to learn." I tugged Mutano's ear and brought him upright. Then I handed him Asilia in her cage and we boarded the cart that stood before the door and I took the reins.

⋅⊷⚌◉⚌⊷⋅

We arrived at the château in late afternoon. The western wall of the courtyard laid a shadow with an edge straight as a measuring stick over a third of the grounds. I carried the conveyance that held our precious Asilia. Mutano carried a black box something like a viol case. It contained Sunbolt's shadow.

We were to keep our part of the bargain and return the victor cat's shadow to him, but we wished to delay this moment for a little, so we made ourselves busy with buttons, latches, and other inconsequentials as we seated ourselves on the long bench by the wall.

After a few moments I opened the fanciful cage and Asilia trickled to the opening. Her first steps were tentative as she turned her head in one direction and then another, testing the smells and observing the spaces of the area. Then she shimmered out of the cage and flowed with her musical motion into the open. She investigated my hand, butting my fingers gently, and then took stock of Mutano's boot sole. I set the cage beside me on the bench and Asilia made her graceful parade march up and down before us when I lifted my finger.

Now Mutano withdrew from his wide belt a short wooden flute and piped four sweet, sad notes. Asilia drooped her head as if to listen. On the parapet above us rose the head and pointed ears of a cat. Sunbolt had been a-waiting us and now we were here.

The head disappeared. He was making his way down to the courtyard.

Mutano again sounded the flute, a long note to establish pitch. He followed the sound of the flute with the voice that was within him, rendering in the cattish tongue and musical idiom what I had learned was the ancient song "When I Was King o' the Cats and You Were the Farrier's Pet."

I am unfamiliar with this school of balladry and was not able to say whether Mutano was in tune or meter. I surmised that he was not in top form, because Asilia's reaction was unenthusiastic. Yet her innate politeness was such that she heard him out without scampering away, as I was strongly tempted to do.

When he finished Asilia took up the strain of the ballad Mutano had begun by sounding a wooden flute. The notes that the silver-blonde cat sang were flutelike, but the instrument was of purest silver, and there was a hint of tiny bells in the arpeggio passages, and the staccato notes sounded as if plucked on copper harp strings.

Sunbolt peered round the edge of a portal. He held this position, showing only his face and ears. Just before Asilia concluded her verse he stepped out but did not approach. Though he was deeply interested in our female, he was also apprehensive. She tugged at all his attentive faculties, but he was wary and determined to regain his shadow.

Mutano took up the black case and went to converse with the truculent orange cat. He squatted before him and there was talk I could not hear. Asilia leapt upon the bench to keep me company.

In a short time Mutano and Sunbolt went together through the portal into the long arcade. When they reappeared, they ambled side by side out into the sunlit area of the courtyard and I saw that Sunbolt's shadow, a muscular, commanding shape, followed him. The cat turned all about, inspecting the umbra from every angle. He seemed satisfied, even proud. He had been pining for it.

Mutano had kept his part of the bargain; Sunbolt's shadow was returned. But now Mutano went to the cart and came back with the voice-box mechanism and placed it on the ground a little way off. Evidently there had been some further negotiation while they were in the arcade. Sunbolt took several turns around the contrivance, with its large ear-trumpetlike horn and its convoluted tubing. He signaled agreement. Then they walked back into the arcade out of sight, Mutano carrying the voice-box.

Now I heard one of the loudest, most cacophonous mélanges of sound ever I had heard. First there was Mutano's voice issuing from Sunbolt: words of high anger, phrases of courtly lovemaking, speeches of cool deliberation—all the modes of speech Mutano had been capable of in former time. I could not make out the specific words, only their tenor and temper. This noise continued long enough that Asilia evinced boredom. She rose and stretched mightily, then resettled with an air of patient resignation.

We had a longer wait, for at this point began the yowls and screeches and threatening growls and peaceful purrs that had lodged in the gullet of Mutano. He was ridding himself of the feline vocabulary and sounded ardent in the doing of it.

So, if all had gone as planned, the exchange had been made. What had Mutano offered to get his voice back? Only the opportunity to acquaint Sunbolt formally with Asilia, a paragon female like no other he, or we, were ever like to encounter again.

Both voices had entered the contraption; each party inhaled his original from it.

This was the end of the episode, I thought. Mutano gathered the shadow-case and voice-box and handed the latter to me to stow in the cart. It only remained to find if Asilia wished to return with us to Astolfo's villa, where her welcome would be warm and her furnishings opulent, or to go back to Maronda at the cattery, or to stay here for the time being and lengthen her acquaintance with Sunbolt.

She appeared to be undecided. She gazed a good while at Sunbolt, taking in his figure and demeanor, weighing the possibilities. But then she turned, with some reluctance, and began to stalk deliberately toward the cage, which still sat there before the bench.

After four steps she halted and turned about again.

Sunbolt had begun to sing. He was rendering "When I Was King o' the Cats" the way it is supposed to be done—in a stout, strongly feline timbre, supple but well defined, and capable of innumerable grace notes and trills and gutturals. He was especially adept at the cattish art of wide intervals, leaping by eleven or twelve or thirteen from one tone to another. The feline musical system is dual, employing both tonal scales and free, unshackled tones, and these modes intermesh, sometimes *ad libitum,* to produce a music that is heard from no other mammalian creature and which is best appreciated by those who have troubled themselves to learn its rules, an educated group of musical connoisseurs that does not include Falco.

Asilia sat spellbound. She did not join in nor did she sing afterward, as she had done before, as if to correct Mutano's technique. She waited. We waited for her decision.

Sunbolt broke into another song very different in mood. This was a sweet, languorous melody with an intimate sadness, the ballade known—as I later found out—as "Lament of Queens Departed." Midway in its progress, Asilia joined her voice with his, softly at first, but then with a warming intensity that matched Sunbolt's. The song continued, rising in pitch, growing closer in its harmonies, until it seemed to vanish. If that love song had been a bird, I would have said that it soared out of sight.

> "The great queens sleep their longest sleep.
> O, where are the snows that once lay deep?"

Mutano and I exchanged glances, took up our gear, and came away.

⊷▬◉▬⊷

We found our maestro in the kitchen.

It should stand to reason that one renowned for sword skill would have little difficulty in overcoming an unarmed and insensate opponent. Yet here was Astolfo in a blood-smeared, greasy apron hacking with fumbling clumsiness at the defenseless carcass of a capon. He and Iratus had fallen into one of their broils and the testy cook had taken abrupt leave. He would return when his temper cooled, as was his custom. His length of absence was unknowable; it might be hours or even days.

The maestro stepped back from the big wooden block, looked at the mangled fowl, and wiped his forehead with his wrist. "In the matter of sentience, I cannot say. . . ." He paused, as if deciding whether or not to open his mind, and went to a near table and drank from a mug. "Yet I have seen a shadow that moved to attack of its own accord, and for a reason I could comprehend. It was the umbra of a young girl who had been raped, tortured, murdered, and then mutilated. It was a sight most harrowing. I sometimes must bend my will to the effort to recall. I entered the room with a lantern to find her body. Her shadow lay beside it on the floor. It quivered still. I could see that the shadow did not match the corpse, even in its haggled state. It was slightly larger. I recovered it and in later examination found that part of the umbra of another person had been attached to it or held in its grasp. At the time I was uncertain how it could have happened."

"Indeed, how could this very irregular phenomenon eventuate?" Mutano asked.

"Very irregular phenomenon eventuate," my roseate arse, I thought. Having gotten his voice back from Sunbolt, Mutano took pains to display its capabilities. For the past hours, he spoke as if a lexicographer had quartered in his mouth.

"The outrage upon the girl was so monstrous, her shadow must have tried to wreak some damage upon the shade of her destroyer," Astolfo said.

"That girl was the true Sibylla, Veuglio's daughter," I said. "In your guise as beggar you were with Veuglio when he burst into the room to be struck blind. You saw what the baron had done and saw instantly a means to repay. You sundered her shadow from her body and folded it into your beggar's robe. Veuglio could not see what you were doing. When you took her shadow, you gained part of the baron's, an advantage you had not expected."

Mutano looked at me in surprise. He had not followed closely the thread of the story, having his own concerns so sharply before him.

But Astolfo was not surprised. "It was unlooked for," he said. "I had never known of any shadow behaving so aggressively. There are accounts in old chronicles and histories, but those are not always reliable."

"And when the baron applied to you to install a shadow maze, you found your opportunity to avenge the girl and your friend

Veuglio. That was fortuitous, Tyl Rendig conceiving a desire for your protection. It gave you a way to work against him further by increasing his anxiety about the well-being of the candles."

"If he had suffered a burning of the brain and the sensations of being eaten by rats and wished to protect himself from the destruction of his shadow, then a maze would seem a sensible step to take," Astolfo said.

"Only if he had learned that pieces of his shadow had been admixed into tallow candles to be at the mercy of thieves and servants and rodents."

"Anyone who can read and write might send a message suggesting these things," Astolfo said. "You are capable and so is Mutano. . . . So, for that matter, is Iratus." He laid down the butchering knife alongside the three others and the pitiable fowl on the chopping block. He sighed and took another swallow from the mug. "I must learn something of the art of cookery," he muttered. "It is none so simple as I had thought."

"Now your avengement is assured. Will you set alight the candles or leave them for the rats to feast upon?"

He gave me his mildest and most placid gaze. "Why, I shall do neither. Our trade is honorable. I followed our agreement to the letter. I went with the baron throughout his house, showing him every trap, blind end, misstep, and pitfall that you two set out. I also gave him your plan showing all the dangers so that he could move into the rooms with a peaceful mind. When I had done these things, our agreement was completed. He paid over some coin and went to his other domicile to gather some goods he thought he would need. He was to return to the château just before dark and hide himself in one of those close rooms, protecting his precious candle ends."

"So there he will reside in safety with his precious lights about him, living a secluded life until old age."

"You have already reasoned that the girl who accompanies Veuglio, the one miscalled Sibylla, is one of the patients to whom he ministers for disorder of the mind and spirit. You know too that the shadow of the true, deceased Sibylla has been attached to this Dorminia and that it has learned the paths of the maze. Perhaps you had not thought that part of the baron's shadow still clings to Sibylla's, just as it did at the time of the murder. But if you had thought of that, you would know that Sibylla and Veuglio would be in communication and know every step that the baron now takes in his wanderings through his halls and passages. They share pieces of his single shadow, and what one part of it knows, so does the whole."

"That will be of small comfort to Veuglio," I complained. "Merely to know when and where the baron steps is no great thing."

"Yet he may receive some satisfaction from his missteps. He may rejoice at the final one."

"I do not—"

"The pair of you devised an intricate and ingenious maze," Astolfo said, "but there is no plan so ingenious it may not be improved upon. After our agreement with the baron was concluded and fulfilled to the last detail, I made a last visit to the château and effected a few beneficial changes to your arrangement. Here is a copy of the altered chart. The baron was supposed to have it already in hand, but in a moment of forgetfulness I neglected to pass it on."

"You never forget."

"In fact, he is in need of his new chart at this very hour as he makes his way through the maze. You two must take the cart and hurry to the château to deliver it. The time is near. Speediness is urgent."

"If 'tis so urgent, why do we not mount and ride?" Mutano asked.

"It may be that you will require the roll of canvas already loaded into the cart," he said. "The cart is slow, but it is best to be prepared for eventualities. I pray, though, that you do not arrive too late."

I studied the new plan of the maze. At first I could see no change. Then I passed it to Mutano.

He looked—and chuckled. "The true and utmost pattern of inventive simplicity." His every sentence had become an oration.

Astolfo reached down two mugs and filled them and we each accepted. "Better fortify yourselves before you go," he said. Then he took up the ruined bird and handed it to Mutano. "And on your way, please give this capon a decent burial in the herb garden."

We were weary of making again and again the journey to the château and back to the villa and since this was to be the end of it, we should have been glad. But we fell silent and spoke no more that night. Mutano took the reins and Mignonette, our little gray donkey, pulled our cart through the streets and out of the city. Only a few lights shone in the houses and taverns. Several of them winked out as the hours grew late.

The moon seemed to take up half the sky and once we were in the open fields it laid upon all the land a cool sheet of powdery silver. The double track of our road went forward like two furrows in a linen counterpane and Mignonette's hoofbeats were muffled, solemn as a dirge drum. At the end of the road sat the baron's house like a great sculpture cut from a salt block. It appeared to float above the ground in this whitest light and it was as silent as the moon that stood above it.

We tethered Mignonette outside and entered the silence of the courtyard. The battlements cast a black shadow here and in the middle of it were the shapes of two cats, shoulder to shoulder upon a parapet. We looked up to see them stark against the moon, Sunbolt and Asilia, watching us.

We paused, then went on into the arcade. Mutano bore a roll of coarse canvas across his neck. He wore a short cloak with a tall collar to protect his skin. I carried a lantern and the new chart of the maze Astolfo had entrusted to me. At the end of the arcade a stair led to the gallery above. Here I lit the lantern and held it up this way and that to make certain the light was strong enough to show where lay and leaned and arched and bent the shadows we had placed.

Then, onward.

I kept step with the directions on the map, though we were familiar with this first part of the maze. We followed along a corridor, then turned down one where the shadows crowded more thickly. At one point the lantern revealed a flight of stairs leading upward and I caught Mutano by the wrist. He looked at me. We consulted our diagram.

Our new chart was genuine. The space was empty. There were no ascending stairs, as indicated in the former map, but only a stepped series of shadows illusory over an abyss dim and deep and, at bottom, black as the sky behind the midnight.

Mutano nodded and we skirted the emptiness. A few paces brought us to a flight of stairs that we ascertained was true and solid.

Down we went. I held the chart to our light and we stepped carefully, tentatively.

On the stones we found the baron.

I had never seen the man before and now I never would. What lay there was no man. Most bones were smashed by his fall. His brains were dashed out, his face a wet and scarlet rag. His broken shadow lay beside him, an appalling mockery of his figure. There was a slip of paper in his hand, a maze-chart sopped with gore, and the remains of a lantern scattered around it. Three candle stubs lay on the flagstones in a pool of blood.

Mutano produced a small Sunderer and cut the ruined shadow from the corpse and secreted it in his cloak. He gave me a meaningful glance and then spread the canvas and we scooped the body onto it as cleanly as we could and rolled it over and tied it. I helped Mutano hoist it onto his shoulders and we started back. Mutano said nothing, but I knew he was pleased that the baron had been a man slight of figure.

I folded the chart and slid it into my sleeve. We did not need it. We knew our way from here.

We came out again into the great wash of silver light in the courtyard and breathed the nighttime gratefully. We brought our burden to the cart and I helped Mutano drop it in. Then, just as we were ready to mount the cart, those cats Asilia and Sunbolt began to sing a pure and intricate aria that climbed like a trellis of white roses into the moon and all the sky around. It was a lament, yet it held a note of happiness too, and I took pleasure in fancying that Veuglio and Sibylla might hear it above them in the nighttime wherever they were.

He would be a different person now, the wise and patient Veuglio. He never had possessed a vengeful spirit, however angry he had become in the most painful hours. But now vengeance had been done and the episode that had so darkened his soul had been resolved by the artful hand of Astolfo. Now the blind sage would walk with his soul at peace, a figure of enlightened existence, a person above the level of the mass of personages.

PART THREE

A Feast of Shadows

VIII

Shadow of the Past

The Feast of the Jester had come round again and was close upon us. It was a festival I disliked most thoroughly. Enough time had passed that Mutano had stopped deriding me, but I never forgot my earlier embarrassment and humiliation. During the Jester Feast, many of the citizenry dress in harlequin costume, and I was always reminded of the ridiculous outfit I had been duped into wearing when we had been involved with the jewel of the Countess Triana. That habiliment of silly ribbons and gaudy patchwork was one of the worst of the trials I had to endure during my apprenticeship to Astolfo. The return of the Feast brought the episode painfully to mind.

The parks and plazas and fairgrounds and avenues held throngs of citizens in Jester guise, making themselves ready for the riotous festivities of the celebration. There were other costumes and roles in plenty. The gracefully mournful clown Petralchio was a popular figure, as were the personae of Capitano Trionfo, that overly be-medaled miles gloriosus, and the females, Columbina, the large-eyed, flirtatious wife of the Captain, and Audacia, the gamine who lived by her wits in the company of spies, smugglers, dicers, and coin-clippers.

But the guise of Bennio was the favorite of everyone, from small boys to those tubby merchants who bulged out of the traditional harlequin costumes like porridges overflowing boiling pots. Not many were well suited for the role. Bennio was a legend from the earliest times of Tardocco, almost as established a symbol of the city as the harbor's Mardrake. He had been a surly, misshapen little man who conceived it his duty to chasten the excessively virtuous, robed in their pietistic airs, and to chastise the imperious wealthy, most of whom had amassed their fortunes by unscrupulous methods. He was despised by the haughty few and beloved by the unstudious many. His Feast had been initiated immediately upon his disappearance from the world. No one had recorded witness of his death and his final fate remained mysterious. Some there were who maintained that he was, in some unplumbable fashion, immortal and that some-day, while the Feast was being celebrated, he would reappear.

"Why is such a crabby, cross-grained, deformed figure so re-vered?" I once had asked.

"He is the obverse face of the aspect we like to present as our true selves," Astolfo had replied. "He is the truth that unmasks the fine and noble countenance that flatters us when we peer into our mirrors. His is the voice that sounds in our ears at midnight, say-ing, *This misdeed is your own; this was the crime you committed; your unrevenged wickedness is not forgot.*"

"He is a corrective?"

"A tonic—and a bracing one. You see with what pleasure the people celebrate his Feast."

"That is so," I said.

And now for the third time in twelve days, a seasonal Bennio was visiting our manse. This time Mutano and I were invited to confer with Astolfo and the Jester. The first two times they had met in private and the maestro had divulged nothing of the substance of their conversations.

He introduced him, saying, "You recognize our guest, Bennio the Jester?"

I nodded, and Mutano said, "And many another Bennio do I see all about in recent days."

"Our Bennio here is a member of the Society of Jesters and he comes to seek our assistance during the impending festival."

The Jester said, "I am also a member of the Civic Council and on their behalf, as well as that of the Jester Society, I do request your aid. We shall be grateful."

"Doth some fraction of this gratitude take the shape of coin?" Mutano asked. "My purse is as slender as a frostbitten pizzle."

I knew that Mutano had expended generously of late. He had so warmly exercised his newly regained voice in amatory pursuits that his funds had been exhausted before his desires were sated.

"We have arranged with Maestro Astolfo," the Jester replied.

He was the mildest version of a Bennio one might conceive. His voice was cultivated and not raucous, his manner polite, his gaze searching rather than mocking. His physique fitted well to the Bennio character, for his back was curled like a viol-head, his shanks were spavined, and his calves were crooked. But no scurrilous rhymes had he salted into his discourse and no fleering expression crossed his unassuming and ordinary countenance. During the festival, he would be constrained to wear a heavy mask with the wonted shaggy eyebrows, the ugly, painted grin, the curvature of red goatee that jutted toward the sharply hooked, enormous nose. Only with such a mask could he be credited as a Jester.

I took the fellow to be in daily life a man of affairs, a broker of grains, perhaps, or a skilled keeper of accompts. He must make a singularly modest clown, and I wondered how many of the other Jesters so prominent in our public spaces led lives equally unnoteworthy.

Astolfo spoke to him. "Mutano is anxious about payment just now," he said. "There is a lass with flaxen hair in Cobblers' Lane who is accomplished with the harp. She flatters him that he can sing."

Mutano shook his head glumly. There were no secrets from Astolfo.

"I accept your word that he is trustworthy," the Bennio said.

"I am warrant for him and for Falco." Astolfo indicated me with a nod. "And, come to that, your commission seems none so difficult. We are to construct the ritual coffin of the traditional materials and to the traditional specifications and accompany it in the general procession to the Tumulus. There we are to aid in interring it in the Jester's Boneyard. You are to be chief Ministrant at the burial, seeing that the likeness of the Jester in its coffin is settled into the earth and heaped over with clay and sod."

"Everything must be performed punctiliously," the Bennio said. "It is extremely important that the rituals are carried out according to custom. If there is a misstep or a gesture out of order, the consequences are unforeseeable but destructive."

"Why so?" Mutano asked. "Is it not so much mummery-flummery enacted to entertain crowds of gapers and japers? The Feast of the Jester is a time of confusion, of license and mockery, of swillage and careless tuppery. Why is this burial of an empty coffin so important?"

The Bennio looked at him with mild surprise. "But the coffin is not empty," he said.

"I have heard," I said, "that it contains only an effigy of the Jester, together with a specimen of the small stick-puppets called Dirty Benninos."

"Those are included in the coffin," he said. "I shall have them delivered to you. But the coffin also contains a shadow to be buried with the figures."

"Whose shadow?" I asked.

His tone was resigned. "In this case, mine own."

⁘

Astolfo explained.

We were occupying our accustomed seats in the small library, sipping at a voluptuous dark wine cool in an earthenware jug. A pleasing draught it was, but not strong enough to divert us from our thoughts.

"There is of course a Society of Jesters," he said, "and they take it upon themselves to perpetuate the Feast and preserve the memory of their great original. He was the first, they say, to make his vocation as a clown an accepted profession. Some claim he was the first of all Jesters, but that notion beggars credence. It is written that his gibes and mimes and epigrams and satires served to restrain the province councilors and the upper ranks of the military from grasping overmuch power and from abusing what they had already obtained. He kept watch upon their plots and stratagems and underhand processes. He gained the eyes and ears and then the hearts o' th' people and persuaded them to look with skeptical gaze upon all the doings of the leaders. He was the watchdog and the tocsin that made the citizens alert to—"

Mutano interrupted. "All this I have heard since the time I was an urchin with mine own Dirty Bennino clutched to my chest. I sang the song that all did sing:

> 'Crambo and crooked Bennio goes,
> But what the Jester knows, he knows.'

And I would laugh the snarling laugh that followed the rhyme."

He did so and I judged from his new-found voice that Mutano could fill the Jester role passably well.

"You remember clearly," Astolfo said. "I suspect that Falco too could spell out a familiar Jester's rhyme or two. Yet perhaps, in the interest of mercy, he will forbear."

I kept silent even though a couplet bubbled unwelcome into my brain: *This foolish world you hold so dear, Bennio bids to kiss his rear.* Then others crowded into my head, and I gazed out the open window into the late summer garden to drive them away. They were like those simple, repetitive tunes of childhood that burrow into the mind and buzz and chirp and will not silence.

"Still, it is all only ceremonious sham," Mutano said.

"Sham, flummery, vanity—if so, that matters not. It is custom and, as the ancient Plinius Secundus hath written, custom rules all behavior. A sentiment the larger populace clings to is that if we fail to revere and celebrate our Jester, we shall become always more susceptible to the deceptions and treacheries of those who hold authority over us. It would be like losing a certain power of judgment that helps to make us wary as citizens. And that in turn would make the city more susceptible to foreign attack."

"This description lays large responsibility upon a cap-and-bells, a curlicue spine, and some trite, scabrous rhymes," I said.

Astolfo blinked at me and asked, "Is my description of the importance of Bennio inaccurate?"

I considered. "It is accurate in the main."

"Then let us proceed, looking upon our task as our duty, as well as being to our profit. The Jester Society may gap its coffers for us, if we can fulfill its commission."

"You have told this Bennio that the task seems none so difficult. He must have laid down further conditions or warned you of some hindrances," I said.

"He and a few of his trusted colleagues believe that their Society is being undermined by foes of the Jesters or adulterated by the apostasy of some of its present members. He would enlist us, on behalf of his group of select associates, to discover who these impostors are and what their purposes might be. To be successful, we must do so before the ceremony at the Tumulus takes place. That is but a fairly short time from now."

"Why must this time limit be in place?" I asked.

"The Bennio who is our client had been chosen by lot, as is the custom, to be the Ministrant at the burial ceremony. It is not known to the city at large that the shadow of the Ministrant is taken from

him beforehand and laid in the coffin alongside the two other likenesses. It is the duty of the Ministrant to sacrifice his shadow for
the general welfare."

"He allows us scant time."

"He has no say. The third-phase moon is at the zenith in twenty
days."

"Ah," I said, recalling that a chief element of the Feast was that
the face of the Jester figured itself in the crescent moon at that hour.
The hooked nose, the low brow with its drooping, belled peak, the
glaring eye, and the up-jut goatee that almost touched the nose—
these features were most clearly visible during that point of the Feast.
It was a simpleminded form of apotheosis. Young children marveled
to see the Jester sailing the sky; their parents and the other adults
chuckled at the image. The features of the moon's surface that furnished this portrait of the Jester were always present when the moon
was visible and could be traced by anyone. But the crescent moon
at its zenith forced the imagination to construct a mocking celestial
countenance that smirked as it glowered down upon the follies of
us miserable mortals.

Mutano gave a rude snort to signify his disbelief. Then he said,
"I cannot conceive how the disruption of an empty ritual can cause
great harm. Still less can I conceive why anyone should want to do
so. What profit can there be in it?"

"That question our Jester could not answer," Astolfo said. "He
only had gained an apprehension that this disruption might be taking place. He had observed some peculiarities of behavior—some
scraps of talk, some knowing glances. And lately, he said, there had
been a large increase in the membership of the Society, though the
number of the citizens of Tardocco has not increased."

"What then is your surmise?" I asked.

"I can put no words to it. There are rumors abroad that the pirate Morbruzzo has designs upon the city, to bring his three-master
against us, to invade and then to attack and plunder and raze the
town."

"These rumors are ever-present," Mutano complained. "When
barbers run dry of scandal, they open their tattle-pouches to produce the name of Morbruzzo."

"There is talk also that the exiled husband of the Countess
Trinia, now lurking in the island of Clamorgra, has gathered a force
to bring against our province, as much for revenge as for plunder."

"That rumor too has grown threadbare," I said. "And dozens of others like these you can tally, but they remain baseless, insofar as we can know."

He nodded. "'S truth. Yet prudence suggests that we be ware of these possibilities."

"Even if one or t'other should prove more solid than vain, I do not understand how a misstep in the burial ritual could more endanger us," Mutano said.

"Well," Astolfo said, with a shade of impatience, "I shall admit I cannot see the consequence myself. We must question our Bennio more closely on the morrow."

⁘═◑═⁘

When he did appear shortly before the noon, our Jester was carrying a leather portmanteau of uncommon size and was accompanied by his dog. His name was Mars, we were informed, and certes no animal ever less deserved the name. He was small and white from muzzle to the stubby tail that he wagged continually. Even his spraggle whiskers gleamed steely, like the tines of a hayfork. But his eyes were largish black buttons that might have been cut from a basalt block and polished to a liquid sheen. He looked at the three of us as we stood out in the pebbled carriageway before the manse, turned as if to inquire of his master, and then, receiving a signal I could not perceive, scrambled over to sniff at our boots. Satisfied with a cursory investigation, he returned to his master's side and sat and regarded our faces each in turn.

"He seems an intelligent creature," Mutano said, "though none so bellicose as the name you have given him."

"He can defend himself well enough," the Jester said, "but his best value is as a jongleur. He can dance and prance, leap and tumble with the best of them." He cocked his hand leftward, lifted his thumb, and Mars leapt to the height of his shoulder and twisted twice in the air before finding the ground again.

"Well done," Astolfo said. "Shall we proceed to the instruction for our commission?"

The Bennio stooped to open his leather bag and brought out a roll of paper. "Here are the dimensions for the coffin, written out and with sketches," he said. "It would be better to look them over inside so that the breeze does not disorder the papers. And here is the mask I shall don before you cut away my shadow. I must be wholly in the character before it is taken from me. I shall bring the Jester effigy and the little Dirty Bennino when the coffin is ready."

"Let us advance to this procedure at once," Astolfo said. "The shadow separated will make measurement simpler and more accurate." He led us to the plastered brick wall that enclosed the kitchen garden. A large oblong of porous linen was affixed upon the plaster with brass nails.

We stood our Bennio before the cloth, adjusting his stance and posture until we were satisfied that he was casting the best umbra of a Jester we could obtain. The sunlight was bright and unhindered and the shadow was sharply defined at every edge and contour. It was the very Idea of a Jester: The hunched back curved like the belly of a goblet, the hands were elongate at the sides of the round stomach, the legs stood apart, knobbly and crooked. The large mask he wore threw a shape demonically mirthful, with aggressive eyebrows, great hooked nose, upthrust goatee, and a wide, feral grin. Over this countenance the peaked cap drooped a bell low upon the forehead.

"Now then, Falco," said Astolfo.

"Well, but let him speak as the Jester," I said.

"To what purpose?"

"To try to gain some sense of the nature of his shadow," I said, though my only true reason was curiosity as to the way this affable man might ply his role in public.

He spoke:

> "Crambo and crooked Bennio goes,
>   But what the Jester knows, he knows;
>   And what he knows the Jester will tell,
>   To set you a-laughing or rend you to hell."

Then he uttered the maniacal cackle that was the very soul of his sword-edge humor and even though I had expected to hear it, the hairs prickled at my neck. His voice was louder than in ordinary discourse and the timbre much changed. There was a metallic, harsh clatter at its center and a heavy breathiness around the syllables. I thought there must be an amount of space between mouth and mask, so that an indistinct echo was produced. Perhaps a metal contrivance had been inserted as a mouthpiece. His was an unsettling voice; I judged it might frighten children more than it would amuse them. Yet he would alter his performance to suit his audience of the hour, softening it for the very young.

I stooped and excised his shadow at the outer edge of his scallop-topped black shoes and Mutano and I rolled the cloth and laid it in the shade of the oak that grew by the garden gate.

While we were transporting the umbra, the little dog uttered a long and piteous howl. I would not have thought the small creature capable of such a houndlike cry. He stared at us with an angry accusatory gaze and I wondered if the minuscule warrior might rush to attack. A gesture from the Bennio quieted him, but he kept his black eyes fixed at me, whom he must have regarded as principal in the thievery.

"He does not like the new shadow—or, rather, the old one," the Bennio said.

Upon the space where the linen had hung stood revealed the man's true and present umbra. Of medium height, it was as straight and unremarkable as the shadow of any man. Indeed, one might suggest it as a representation of the upright life, the *integer vitae* that the ancient poet spoke of. I said of it, "Here is the shade of as honest a man as you might meet on any summer's day."

Mutano spoke the other thought. "This shape lacketh the savor of a true Jester. It is hard to picture so respectable a figure turning cartwheels, contorting into bow-knots, dancing fandangos with a dog, and spitting acrid rhymes."

"Yet it is the shadow of our Bennio," said Astolfo.

"His true name is not Bennio," I said.

"But that you knew already," our client said. "All members of the Society go by that name. It is the one people know. My birth name is kept secret so that my words can have the smart of the whip-snap and my private house and family may go unharmed."

"If this shadow is that of your true figure, the role of Jester must be onerous in the extreme. For it twists the actual person you are about its central axis like a well-rope around the winch," I said.

"The part of the humorist is proverbially a heavy one, is it not?" Astolfo said.

"Yes," I admitted, "but I had never expected to see the proverb so starkly illustrated."

"Well, 'tis a burden he must take up again," Astolfo said, "for Bennio has already chosen the shadow which is to replace the one we have severed. Shall we go into the hall of mirrors and try it on?"

"Yes," said the man in a tremulous whisper. But he did not move forward. He fell face-first to the ground, senseless.

·→══◎══←·

It required the better part of an hour and two cups of a fiery pear cordial brought from the cellar to restore our Bennio. Mars was dreadfully anxious, trotting round and round the chair in which we had deposited our Jester. He now professed gratitude for our bringing him into the cool dimness of the library, with its thick drapes and dark shelves. "Forgive me. 'Tis but a passing spell. I am sound."

"We might have warned you," said Astolfo. "Many there are to whom the sudden loss of his shadow brings on a fainting. Some are attacked by a vertigo; others suffer cold sweats and vomiting. It is no sign of a weakness within you."

He breathed quickly and unevenly. "For me, it was the onset of a too-swift exhilaration. I felt such a high elation, so sunbeam-quick a happiness, that I fell down dazed. It was the sudden purity of an immense relief."

"It may be you are ill suited to the Jester occupation," Mutano said. "If the shadow of Bennio weighs so heavy upon you, perhaps you should not put it on again."

"But I must," he said, "for the burial ceremony is urgent and if I do not fulfill the part, many evils will ensue."

"Evils of a kind you cannot describe," Mutano said. To show his impatience, he poured a thimbleful of cordial into a glass and drained it off.

"This much I know," the Bennio said. "The role of the Ministrant at the interment is supposed to be given out by lot. But there was no chance involved in the choosing of me. Because the steward who passed the box was clumsy, I saw that all the tokens were marked with my sign." He extended his right hand with a gold ring on the third finger. The red stone was marked with a gold symbol of Mars.

"Might you have been allowed to see the deception on purpose?" Astolfo asked.

He pondered. "I cannot comprehend why that should be."

"Do you know why you should be so singularly honored?"

"It is regarded as an involuntary honor—of a sort. But every Society member knows that this office entails the loss of shadow. That is the rule."

"Could this be at least in part a reason your name was made certain to be drawn? Might some one or two of the Society desire to see you shadowless?"

"Again, I can fathom no purpose in't."

"Nor can I. Let us go to the hall above where the shadows are stored and you shall choose one to replace the other."

"It must be in the figure of Bennio."

"Because you must act the Ministrant in that guise?"

"Yes."

"Well, we shall think upon that point. But let us go up. We have only a small stock of Jester umbrae, but there must surely be one to suit for the time being. Mars will come with us. The dog will be the ablest judge of what best fits."

⊷⊨⊜⊨⊷

Our plan of action required that we summon the aid of our crab-bish old acquaintance, Maxinnio the ballet master. I did not dote upon his company, but Astolfo enjoyed irritating the irascible fellow, goading him to heats of exasperation. We found him in his rehearsal hall.

"Go away," said Maxinnio. "Your breaths are unwholesome, your faces are ugly, and your bodies are clumsy beyond repair. Whoever admitted you into the house shall be dismissed upon this instant."

"Good morning, Maxinnio," Astolfo said. "I am pleased to find you in humor. The day is bright and inviting."

"How did you gain entrance?"

"My colleague, the rash Falco, offered to slice the gizzard of your porter if we were turned away."

"My 'porter,' as you call her, is a female of but fifteen years. I do not doubt he would show courage sufficient to attack her." He was seated at his desk in a small room adjoining the practice room of his dance studio. That space was deserted just now.

Whatever project Maxinnio had under way was in an early stage of progress. On the desk before him lay sheets of diagrams block-ing out the choreography of a new ballet. There were about a dozen of these sheets, most of them disfigured across their expanses with large X's. He was searching his way to a scenario.

"It is you who are so severe upon young girls," Astolfo said. "Falco is tender of heart on that head and would never threaten. A few polite words and a modest coin, and—lo!—she allowed us to enter. She smiled also, and that is a habit your Missana could not have learned under your tutelage."

"Missana? I had not heard her name spoken. I suppose that you will tell me she is my newest discovery, a future ballerina of great renown."

"I think not. She is plump and cheerful. You could not abide her presence."

"I cannot abide yours, but here you are. By what means can I get you gone?"

"Let us be more amicable," Astolfo said. "Did not the other girl I commended to your attention become a dancer of excellence? She too was a doorkeeper and hearth-sweeper, living here with her abilities unrecognized. I am of mind that you are in my debt for her discovery."

"She was troublesome and still is." He sighed dramatically and pushed his chair back. He gestured toward the papers strewn on his desk. "She hath conceived a grand new tragic role for herself as Queen Dido who dances many long, dolorous solo passages before she immolates herself at last."

"Yet are you not her dance master?"

"Go away."

"Thou'rt a lean and querulous creature," Astolfo said. "A physician might declare that you are distempered by an excess of the bilious humor."

Indeed, Maxinnio did appear changed since last we spoke with him. His face was drawn and more wrinkled than before and he appeared more restless in spirit.

"If I am peevish, thou'rt no palliative. Why have you not departed?"

"I desire your aid. Do you expect this new Dido piece to match the success of your 'Sorrows of Petralchio'? I recall those performances with pleasure."

"My 'Petralchio' had the advantages of surprise and variety. The setting was a traveling carnival with animals and acrobats and fire-eaters. The dancers mimed many different roles."

"Two clowns also were included," Astolfo said, "the long-faced Petralchio and the mischievous jester Bennio, who led Petralchio's lovely Columbina astray. That was a sequence filled with interest."

"What is it you desire of me? The last reserves of my patience? You are quickly draining those."

"I recall also the shadow-play upon the backdrop as your Bennio tumbled and cavorted. It seemed that in watching I could almost hear his imbecilic and insulting rhymes. Did your dancer cut those shapes or was the figure of a puppet behind the scrim brightly illuminated from the back? The staging was so adroit, I could not tell."

"That shadow belonged to the dancer, Cocorico, who was of great aid in designing his dance and its umbral counterpoint. In his narrowly limited fashion, he was a sort of genius."

"*Was,* you say?"

"So far as I know, he no longer performs. We had a falling-out and he departed my troupe in a fury and forever, or so he vowed. He vowed also to take revenge upon me, but all the principal males who leave make the same identical threat. They are a contumacious flock, these dancers."

"Why do they so cross thee? Certainly, you are a sweetly tempered man and as patient as a ten-year calendar."

"Yes, that is so, though I am much a-weary of thee and thy Boffo."

"Falco is my name," I said.

"Falco, Flotto, Farto. Begone and take thy names with thee."

"With whom has this Cocorico taken up in these latter days?" Astolfo asked. "There are some secrets of his craft I would learn of him."

"*Purloin from him* is the truer phrase. Thou'rt in ill luck. He has given up the ballet for some trade more suiting his disposition. Treason, mayhap, or assassination."

"Do you know of his whereabouts?"

"If I did, why should I tell you?"

"Why, to be rid of me. You make that out to be a happy state of existence."

Maxinnio blinked weary eyes at us, then rubbed each with the heel of his palm. He was tired of staring at his papers. I deduced that a new scenario that would satisfy his diva was not easy in the conceiving. He leaned into the back of his chair and stretched his arms before him. "Yes, that would be a blissful relief. Yet I do not know for certain where he may be. If he has given up performance, as he threatened, he shall have found an ancillary employment—as a director's assistant or in the design of costume or the placement of lights. He would never wholly forswear Terpsichore."

"If he is out of temper with you, he may hire out to your closest rivals. Which of the masters would that be?"

"There are none. My company is nonpareil."

"Yes, of course. But if some ignorant rustic were to imagine that you had a close rival, whom should he choose?"

"If he were devoid of proper judgment, he might alight upon the Draponi Troupe. If he were curious about the art, he would seek out the Signora Anastasia. It is not usual for a woman to lead a dancers' company and I doubt that Cocorico would encamp there. The Signora will brook not the slightest insubordinate gesture and Cocorico is of a surly and disputatious cast of mind."

"To the Draponi we shall march. I thank thee most prettily for your kindly aid and bid thee farewell. I hope you can forgive our hasty exit."

He flapped at us a languid, dismissive hand, as if we were flies that had settled on the drawings before him.

⋆⊷═◯═⊶⋆

Astolfo had no intention of visiting the Draponi. Knowing that Maxinnio would be pleased to discommode us, we found Buskers' Alley, leading off the waterfront, and halfway within it an old warehouse now partitioned into studio spaces. Herein the Signora Anastasia exercised her craft and art.

If she'd been a piece of cutlery, she'd have been a silver paring knife. Slight, small, compact, with bright gray eyes and hair, she seemed not to stand upon the floor of her studio but to come to a point upon it. I judged her to be well past her dancing years, but she showed the lithe strength and springy grace that the discipline confers. Her expression, a wry and quizzical smile, seemed never to change and I took it to betoken a lightness of heart that would be hard for a temperament like Maxinnio's to comprehend.

Two boys of about fourteen years were laying out squares of colored cloth on the floor as she directed them, turning one square that way to the angle of light from the tall windows and another square the other way.

She and Astolfo were old acquaintance.

"Tell me, Maestro," she said, "will a curtain of that shade of green suggest the depths of a forest? I have my doubts." She peered up at him as if she were testing, half in earnest, his judgment.

"My man Falco is ready to suggest such umbral tints and tinges as can lend it the cast of primeval creation," he replied.

She gave me an appraising glance, from toe to head, past to present. I felt I had been read like a letter delivered upon a salver. "I suspect he is a quickly suggestive fellow, but can he describe a color amenable to the furtive appearances of fauns and satyrs?"

I made a polite and silent bow.

"If there be nymphs to follow your satyrs, he is your man," Astolfo said.

"We shall have nymphs," she said. "The flute-notes shall draw them forth like roses trailing along the stones of a wall."

"You are reviving your happy production of 'Faunus's Waking Dream'?"

"For a brief period, while we prepare to mount a new piece involving Andromeda and Perseus and the Mardrake. That piece will cap our season, and I hold strong hopes of it."

"How can it fail?" Astolfo asked. "It is the favorite story told in Tardocco by means of dance, poetry, music, or painting. It is the signature of our city, with its attachment to local legends of the bay. And the Mardrake? That fearsome monster delights one and all. Who is to play that part? It is traditionally given to a Jester who enjoys the lascivious menacing of the maiden princess."

"I have assigned it to a Jester," she said. "You know of the renowned Cocorico?"

"We came seeking him. Your friend Maxinnio suggested—"

"Maxinnio would misdirect you," she said. "There is ill will between those two."

"Falco and I believed that this artful clown would delight in your productions over those of others. Maxinnio tried to misdirect, but we followed our own reasoning."

"He is absent just now. The mechanisms of the Mardrake occupy his thoughts. The monster must appear to be vast and our Jester is a small and crook-shaped man. He must look something like a giant black squid or octopus or some more frightening creature, with tentacles and other appendages, and yet he must move in time with viol and aulos, advancing and retreating, while coming ever closer to Tantalia, who is to take the role of Andromeda." She turned from Astolfo, looked in my face direct, and asked, "How do you think he might accomplish this task?"

I pondered. "He must construct a big puppet in the Mardrake form and place it behind a gauzy dim backdrop and illume it so that its enlarged shadow falls on the scrim from behind. Then he must move on the stage in front in precise concord with the puppet shadow. The two shapes will be seen to be one monstrous shape."

"How is he to sprout and extend tentacles and other aggressive organs that Tantalia shall cower from?"

"I cannot say."

"Nor can I. Nor can he. And so he has sequestered himself to study and devise."

"When he broke with Maxinnio, he brought all his properties and mechanisms and costumes with him," Astolfo said. "Does he keep them here in a safe place? I should like to look among them, if I may."

Now she turned shrewd eyes upon the maestro, speculating. "I am certain he would not like that."

"I believe that he might," Astolfo said, in his blandest manner, "for there is coin for him. If he keep and store in healthy condition some shadows of himself for use in Jester-roles, I would fee him for the borrowing."

"You would, yes, but I dare not allow you to examine anything of his without permission. It would not be wise for me to stand on his wrong side. He hath a temper and is not of a forgiving nature. He is also in a position to cause injury to the production, a harm so severe I could not right it."

"Perhaps I do not need to fumble through his effects," Astolfo said. "If you could describe certain of his illusions and stage deceptions, I could judge if any can be of use for my purposes. Does he keep in store a number of umbrae in his own shape?"

"Some dozen or so, I should say."

"Are these faithful to his own or has he added variation?"

She closed her eyes. "There are some shapes differing, but I cannot recall the small particulars."

"Doth he engage with other troupes or do else for hire of this kind?"

"With other troupes, no. We have an understanding very firm. What other ventures he may undertake with his stagecraft I know not, nor care."

"Has anyone besides ourselves made inquiry about him?"

"A trio of Bennios came seeking. They were a clumsy lot, ill fit to harlequin dress and without the natural grace that takes pains to seem graceless, as a Jester's part demands. I supposed that they desired instruction for their participation in some sort of event for the Feast, a guild dinner or a children's entertainment."

"And not finding him—"

"They went away a little downcast. They did not say they would return, so I surmise that they went in search of another Jester. At Feast time there are plenty to be found."

"Those expert in gamboling, as is Cocorico, must be much in demand," Astolfo said.

"For the while. Then they become again objects of indifference and derision. 'Tis like the onset of the Scarlet Pear season. At first everyone is avid to devour, but within four days they have eaten their fill and take the fruit for granted. It is the season of the Jester now, but after the coffin is buried in the hill, interest wanes."

"But Cocorico thrives also in the dull times."

"He possesses crafts that can be fitted to numerous endeavors," the Signora said. "He takes ordinary turns in the streets and plazas, amusing both child and elder. He is also something of a musician and can play pretty on the cithara and sing sweetly also. But for the most part he bawleth ranting rhymes in a cracked voice."

I could not but obey the impulse that came of a sudden upon me, and sang out:

> *"If those so-called truly were wise,*
> *They'd see themselves through Bennio's eyes,*
> *And thereupon 'twould come to pass*
> *They'd find out every sage an ass."*

The Signora and Astolfo stared at me in wonder. At last, Anastasia said, "Thou hast caught the words but not the tune," and Astolfo added, "You must strive more mightily, if you would make a passable clown of thyself."

⊷⚬⊶

"What a rout of Bennios!" Mutano said. He sat himself heavily upon the bench beneath the oak in the east garden and took without asking permission the flagon from my hand and swallowed a good half of the wine remaining. "I will see red and yellow harlequin dia-monds all through my dreams tonight. The people are readying for the Feast in thorough fashion."

"Where did you post yourself?" Astolfo asked.

"At Daia Plaza. It is the largest common gathering place and I thought to see the widest variety of all sorts of persons, as well as of Jesters. I would almost say the Jesters outnumbered the others all put together, but they were not quite so thick as that. There were scores of children playing at the role." He paused, knitting his brow. "It is a little disturbing to see young and fresh bodies trying to gnarl into deformed postures—an ugly sight. I think the young do not comprehend that a baleful disease twists some of our Bennios into figures-of-eight, that it is pain which makes them so bilious."

"I believe this is not generally known," Astolfo said. "It would be hard for some to conceive that the Jesters' mockery and ridicule is an outcry of agony."

I quoted:

> "Up my arse there spires a drill,
>   But it gives my soul no thrill;
>   In my gut there sits a stone,
>   A homely plaything but mine own."

"Falco has thrice besmutched this pleasant day with hoary Jester rhymes," Astolfo said. "I wonder if he envisions himself becoming one of that brotherhood."

"Nay, never," Mutano said. "Only look at him. He is too tall for the role, too well bulked, and he stands too straight. He never could sufficiently cramp himself."

"Our client too is tall and well formed, once he is rid of the Jester shadow," Astolfo said. "But when he puts the shadow on again, the physic of the clown replaces his own."

"And then his dog, Mars, goes quiet," I said. "It loves its master as crambo Bennio and distrusts him as an ordinary man."

"We shall visit the town together," Astolfo said. "The citizens are in a liberal frame of mind. We shall sup lightly here at the manse and then go abroad in Feast-days costume. We shall be of the crowd."

"We are to spy?" Mutano asked. "But who is it we are to spy upon? What do we seek?"

"I am uncertain," Astolfo said. "It may be useful—indeed,

urgent—to distinguish those of the brotherhood of true Jesters and those who are idly toying at the game."

"The custom of the Feast encourages the appearance of counterfeit Bennios," Mutano complained. "Ostlers, panders, smiths, nobles—anyone may don the motley and brandish the stick-puppet. They cannot all be bent upon disruption and the form of an invasion of Tardocco that you hint at."

"But if we can learn to distinguish the genuine Jester from the holiday-maker, we shall know something," I said. "For the guild was here beforehand and is being used by the intruders as a means to hide themselves."

"It is possible, yet we have to act as if the greater number are innocent of any plot," Astolfo said. "Otherwise, we shall have no point at which we can start to undo this tangle."

We stopped talking for a moment. Birds sang in the bushes and butterflies visited them, but we were immune to the blandishments of the hour.

I sighed. "A further difficulty is in the character of Bennio. Crambo and crooked, oppugnant to every gracious advance, alert to cause mischief when any chance arises—the Jester is not a willing purveyor of truths, even if these be to his advantage."

"And how are we to tell if one of the counterfeits has so practiced the tricks and songs and tumbling as to be as expert as any true Jester? Or if the true clown be not at the top of his form and so appeareth counterfeit?" Mutano said.

"The dog would know," I said. "It is unlucky for us that every Bennio does not keep a dog."

"The little white dog set up a howl because it thought we harmed its master," Mutano said. "It conceived that we had done away with him and another had taken his place."

"Maybe when Mars saw his Bennio in his actual state, the dog knew him to be unprotected and open to harm. Your actual Jester is a slight man, racked with ague, fit for no other occupation. He has made himself a Bennio as armor against the cruelties of the world. He is like those serpents which puff up and hiss fiercely. Even though they lack venom and are harmless, they keep attackers at bay."

"Are there any other creatures besides their dogs and the Jesters themselves able to detect impostors?" Mutano asked.

"Let us rest and consider and meet an hour from now in the

kitchen," Astolfo said. "We shall go on the town when the last streak
of sunset has darkened."

⊹⟫⊜⟪⊹

My costume was in the old fashion of the domino. I located it in an
armoire in a sewing room off our hall of blue mirrors. The slippers
lay in a drawer at the bottom. The hat was not so easy to find, but
a small black cock hat presented itself and I jabbed a white feather
into the velvet band. A mask of black silk completed my outfitting.

Mutano had desired, he said, to dress as a harlequin, the better
to fit into the crowd and observe, but finding the size too small for
him, had dressed in the coarse linen trousers and gray smock of a
tradesman. He hailed me: "Stout pewter mugs for two coppers each,
my friend. As warm a bargain as you'll find these Feast days. Come
buy my spoons and vessels!" He gave his phrases the lilt the vendors
gave them, but he had no implements to offer.

"Thou'rt too honest and love-passionate a fellow to imperson-
ate a tradesman," I said.

"My scheme is that I shall be taken for a noble disguising
himself in the garb of trade."

"And too honest for a nobleman also," I returned.

Astolfo had disdained costume and wore his ordinary doublet
and trunks, the soft leather boots with the floppy tops, the broad
belt with its fist-sized leopard's-head buckle. The sole unusual appurtenance was a sword in a black, silver-chased sheath. Customarily he went unarmed and I wondered as to his purpose, whether
the weapon was for costumery or for defense.

"Are you expecting that someone will mistake you for a pewter-
smith posing as Maestro Astolfo?" I asked.

"I have too honest a countenance to be mistaken for a shadow
merchant," the maestro said.

"Where do we post ourselves?" Mutano asked.

"There will be a throng at the Nuovoponte," Astolfo said. "The
fete-boats will be going up and down the Daia with their cargoes
of merrymakers and musicians and dancing girls. There will be
much to observe."

"A happy posting for me," he replied. "And I shall keep watch
o' the dogs. I think we may learn of certain signs from them."

Astolfo turned toward me. "In domino, you will be best posted
in the large park east of Daia Plaza. There are entertainment sites

spaced along the paths and carriageways. A number of guilds and brotherhoods are staging performances and tableaux, though the best of these occur on the night of the burial. Yet you will find much to observe. Many a Jester chooses these smaller places to tumble and trick, there being a closeness with their audiences."

"A good posting for me also," I said, "and as Mutano undertakes to keep watch o' the dogs, I shall eye closely all the cats."

"And where do you go?" Mutano asked Astolfo.

"I aspire to gain intelligence from among the guild of bellows-menders."

"There is no such guild," Mutano said.

"Well, I know a certain Sbufo," Astolfo said. "If there is no larger brotherhood, he must suffice."

"What news can one glean from a bellows-mender?" I asked.

"Whatever news the wind bears, they are bound to hear," he said, and this weak jest sent us on our separate ways.

⁂

Mutano mounted his Defender to journey to the bridge and Astolfo ordered his little roan brought round, but I chose shank's mare, thinking I might gain an impression of how the Feast was changing the complexion of the city. I had already felt a certain lack of gaiety and sprightliness in the common chat and prattle. The festivities were not impaired, yet they seemed none so joyous as formerly, none so carefree. Perhaps I might confirm or correct these piecemeal impressions with a walkabout.

My destination was Tasconi Park, a large area just below the upper crescent of the city. Here the servants of the wealthy houses were wont to take the air during their infrequent leisure hours—the valets and scullery maids, the grooms and footmen and handi-workers, the o'erdignified butlers and o'erfed cooks and bribable provisioners, the nursemaids and gardeners. Of this latter group there were many, for in these precincts stood the houses and grounds where many members of the Green Knights and Verdant Ladies Society inhabited. The men, women, and youths who labored in the great houses were always spilling over with gossip. Much of their store was mere fancy and much that contained some grain of truth was discolored by envy, jealousy, and the other adulterations that attend petty strife. These servants brought children to the park, their own progeny and those of their masters.

The children were of strong interest to me. Mutano's speculation that the Jesters' dogs might be useful in distinguishing those
Jesters inherently called to their craft from the pretenders to it had
intrigued me, though I thought that observation of the dogs would
be of limited use. Not all the Bennios owned dogs and the other
dogs about would have little interest in the clowns except as company to romp with when they were allowed.

The children were most closely attentive to the Jesters, choosing some as favorites and following their antics wide-eyed while
showing less interest in others. One set of Jesters brought forth a
particular reaction. These the children watched with fascination,
giggling nervously at their pranks; there seemed a kind of fearfulness in the way they watched them. When a Bennio sang out a
rhyme in his fleering cackle, the girls would hide their faces in the
folds of their nursemaids' skirts.

"Hi ho kadiddle, the cat and the fiddle,
Funny old Bennio has a new riddle:
What is the sight that all do like?
—The head of Morbruzzo set on a pike."

The name of the pirate was often dropped and the name of a by-
standing boy substituted. "The head of Tommaso set on a pike"
would cause the lad to break into proud laughter.

And now that the sky had drained to a lush, warm purple, I trod
along the pathway that led to the entertainment plot set aside for
the Green Knights and Verdant Ladies. There the rehearsal of the
set of tableaux and dances in which Andromeda was rescued by Perseus would draw a number of children, for they loved to see frightening monsters onstage and the Mardrake promised to be delightfully
horrible, a first-rate squeal-raiser. Mutano and I had come to this
place earlier when we delivered a half dozen of our shadow-eating
plants that Anastasia was using in her climactic scene.

The performance was already well in progress when I arrived
and I was pleased to see that my conjecture about the mechanics
proved correct. There was a large Bennio-puppet mounted behind
the scrim in the background and it imitated exactly the motions of
the black-clad Bennio onstage, so that the two entities appeared as
a single large one. The actor playing this role was not Cocorico; he
lacked the mocking savagery of movement that made the Mardrake

not only dangerous as a predator but lickerish as an aggressor. He had not the favored Jester's finesse. Cocorico himself was probably hidden among the spectators, taking note how to improve the performance.

Then, as the music became more excited, the monstrous appendages—tentacles with toothy maws, eyestalks, and a massive outsized pintle—grew from the beast like plants bursting suddenly from the earth. I could not see how this illusion was arranged; the footlights kept the mechanical operation in dark shadow. It was neatly done and elicited squeals and squeaks from the children scattered in the crowd. A few of the nursemaids giggled and blushed.

I began to move closer to the stage for a better vantage when my left elbow was taken in hand and a gruff voice said in my ear, *"Step this way, Master Falco."* I felt the point of a blade in a right-side rib.

I could sense two of them, at least, so I followed the order without protest, allowing the hand to pull me along into the edge of the bordering grove.

"I fear you are to have a rude awakening," the voice said. I recognized the rural, southern-province accent and the voice too seemed very familiar, though distorted by the Jester-mask.

"Who—"

Then a heavy piece of the purple sky fell hard upon my head and I unwittingly buried my face in the grass.

⊷⊜⊷

As the voice had promised, my awakening was rude. Someone dashed a dollop of stinking liquid into my face and, as the world began to emerge from the darkness of my brain, I was grasped by the scruff of my neck, lugged across a small, dim room, and dropped into a chair made of iron slats. My mask was torn from my face.

Seated across from me in an oaken chair with a thin leather cushion was a loutish, large man with coarse features, a nose broken in long time past, enormous hands that gripped the chair arms, and stiff blond hair unkempt. His voice sounded like the rattle of dried peas in a gourd. "Papa is dead," he said.

I failed to comprehend. "Papa?"

"Yours," he said, "and mine. Our father is dead. . . . For forty days and nights."

"Nights?"

"I count the nights because I laid awake thinking."

"Thinking?"

"You never credited I could, did you? Thought I was a slow-wit or un-wit. But I found you out, and didn't take long about it."

"Osbro?"

"I am your brother Osbronius, the one you struck down from behind with a spade as we were digging turnips. It felt good to thwack you down there in the park. Felt the best in a long time. I never forgot, just waiting out the time. I knew the hour would come and ho-ho it did. I could have struck you down dead."

"Why didn't you? You must be angry enough to do so." I rubbed my face, trying to wipe away some of that foul liquid.

"We have plans for you. No good if you're dead."

"We?"

He gestured and I turned my head, painfully, to gaze upon two others in Jester motley, equally as large and menacing as my brother. These would be his associates who had waylaid me. Looking at them, I decided that this had not been their first experience in mayhem.

"Where are we?"

"Just where I want us to be."

"How did you bring me here?"

"What do you care?"

I did not care. My head was in such hurt that I babbled without purpose. Here he sat before me, as big and rough as a stunted tree, yet I could not grasp the fact. He had come from a past time that existed only as a dull memory and from a place that was now as a foreign country to me.

"Our father, how did he die?"

"You don't care about that either."

"I would like to know."

"He wore out, is what I guess. The years kept piling on him till all he could do was tell me to do this chore and that one. About used him up, I guess. Died during the night. I found him in the morning and went to the magistrate. Then I went back to the house and got all the silver and copper I could locate and came the road to 'Docco. It had been in my mind for a long time to search you out, Todo."

"No one calls me Todo anymore."

"Falco—that's what you go by. I know that. Thirty-two days I been watching you and asking. I know a lot. And you can call your-self King of the Islands, but you're still Todo who walked away and left me to look after the old man and plod the furrow and boil the cabbages. Back in Caderia we heard a little about you and the fortune you were piling up by stealing shadows. I made my vow: Todo won't enjoy that wealth forever. Part of it is mine. A big part. Maybe all."

He fell silent and breathed heavily. It was a long speech and he must have composed it again and again in his head. I was surprised he had not decorated it with spurious poetry and muddled philosophy, as he used to do.

"I have no wealth," I said. "I am only a household servant."

He raised his finger. The large Jester nearest my iron chair stepped over and slapped me smartly across my eyes.

"We know what you are and where you live and what you do and where you go. When you lie, you are only asking me to break your bones. I don't mind doing that."

My eyes had teared and I wiped my face again. My ears rang, but it seemed to me I heard the steady wash of tide below the floor. Smells of all sorts abounded—salt fish, tar, raw hemp, spices, all mingled with sandalwood, moldy lumber, and canvas. This little room served, or had served, as a counting room. We were in the rear of a warehouse on the harbor.

"Broken bones have yet to make me rich," I said. "If you have observed me for a time, you will know that."

"You deal in shadows with your master. There is profits in these shadows. You will share some of these profits."

"With you—and how many others?" I asked.

"The others is no concern of yours."

Osbro's manner of speaking suggested that he did not refer to the hirelings with us now. Persons of higher station and of broader connection were involved. Astolfo had suspected that a strategy was in play to disrupt the Feast of the Jester as a beginning and from that point to sow disorder throughout the city, making it vulnerable to threat. From what quarter and from whom the threat issued he did not know.

"You demand some share of the profit of Maestro Astolfo's enterprise," I said. "Are you proposing to enter into a partnership? If you have services or intelligence to offer, he may well consider the notion; he welcomes new opportunities for trade. But you will have to negotiate with him, and he is accustomed to tight bargaining."

"You are our advantage," Osbro said. He grinned. "I think he will come to terms if we send you to him piece by piece."

"You believe he holds me in such fond regard? He is not soft of heart."

"If he was to receive one of your hands, or only an ear, his heart might soften."

"A hand or ear might be got anywhere," I said. "Mine are not so peculiar that he would recognize them. He would not believe you have me in your keeping. If I wrote a message and signed it in a certain particular way, he would understand our situation and might be willing to meet with you. He would of course demand certain conditions."

"In your message you would put some cypher to give us away."

"I will give you my assurance that I would not."

"Guido," Osbro said, and raised his finger and again the big one stepped up and boxed my ear most heartily.

"What can I give away?" I cried. "I do not know your associates or what they desire. I do not even know where I am. Come to that, I do not even know where the maestro is at this hour."

"How then would you send him a message?" Osbro asked.

I had the impression that he hoped my response would be sufficiently inadequate that I must be pummeled again. "My colleague would deliver it," I said. "He would await the maestro at our villa and acquaint him with the situation. A reply would return shortly."

"This man—'colleague,' you call him. Where is he?"

"You will find him at the Nuovoponte, dressed in the garb of a minor tradesman. He is a large—"

"Your Mutano is not so large that he may not be taken down," Osbro said. He observed my expression. "Did I not tell you that we kept watch? We know your ways. We know who Mutano is." His smile was a little too complacent, methought.

"Why did you not also follow the maestro? Since he is the one useful to your purpose, you could have spared me blows."

"Why should I spare you? I am of mind that we have but started. We would have the three of you here together now, only Gracchio lost track of the old man." He gave the silent one an unfriendly glance.

"I am at a loss," I said. "If you desired to confer with the three of us, you had only to come to the manse and knock at the gate. We are agreeable to trade and to new custom."

"We do not know the inner defenses of the house, only that it is well guarded. We like to maintain the ruling hand."

"There may be easier ways to pursue your desires. What is it that you aim at?"

He nodded at the one called Gracchio, and as he approached I saw that he intended to kick my knee. I moved it slightly so that his toe struck a good part of the iron slat on which I sat. He did not cry out, and the Bennio mask hid his expression.

"A great lot of questions you ask," Osbro said. "These are things you do not need to know."

Well, I would have to know, if he was going to obtain answers. But his retort implied that he himself did not know what was to be divulged. Astolfo's conjecture was beginning to be borne out. Some broad, dark strategy of large consequence was under way. My brother was connected to it, but he did not understand how he was being used. He was engaged in a game too complex for a digger of turnips.

"Bring writing materials," I said. "I will write out the message and you may con it over to see if I have betrayed you. You can examine the private sign by which he will know me."

Osbro pondered. His brow wrinkled and his gaze unfixed. At last he said, "We have nothing to write with."

"There is a tottery old desk there in the corner," I said. "Some clerk must have cleared the bills of lading in this room. Perhaps some implements remain."

Guido and Gracchio walked over to the dusty desk and rummaged about. The top was cluttered with detritus: ends of rope, broken locks, broken glass, a black boot with the heel missing. The high top of the desk was furnished with two ranks of small compartments, one of which yielded a clutch of frazzled quills. From a side drawer Gracchio produced a stone inkwell encrusted with dried ink. He raised his mask and spat into the stone to dampen the ink. They brought these implements to Osbro and he waved them toward me.

"Paper?" I said. Guido must have disapproved my pronunciation of the word. He delivered my forehead a straight blow with the heel of his palm.

Gracchio found a length of rotten canvas on the floor. He held it up and tore off a square.

"I will try," I said, "but with these materials the words will be difficult to make out."

"Write," Osbro said.

I picked up a grainy board end that lay on the floor by my chair, spread the canvas out, and dipped the nearly useless pen. As I wrote, I spoke aloud: "Maestro Astolfo. I am held by some who threaten my life. They demand to confer with you and will do you no harm. Follow the bearer of this message. You will recall our secret sign." With exaggerated motion, I made a series of intricate loops.

Guido passed the scribbling to Osbro. He looked at me for a long moment, then accepted the writing and began to study. He held it up and pointed. "This is the sign between you?" I assented, and he nodded gravely.

Here was a crucial point. I had taken no pains to make the words fully legible and the crude canvas blurred their contours, but Astolfo ought to be able to make them out. *The complot you feared is under way. Guard yourself. Prepare.* The secret sign was a meaningless scrawl.

If Osbro could read, I was in for a long and bloody time of it.

He raised his head from his examination. "You say your Mutano is at the Nuovoponte?"

"Dressed as an ordinary tradesman," I said. "He is half a head taller than me—"

"We know what he looks like," said Osbro. "And these two will meet him and force him to take them to your master and bring both of them back here and we'll settle up on our ground and on our terms. No lackeys sneaking around secret passages to knife us. That's why you wanted us to go to your big house. In this place I will set the rules."

"You mean to have all advantage," I said.

"Yes I do, yes." He turned to the duo of Jesters and gave orders.

When they left on this errand, he leaned back in his seat and regarded me anew. "You don't look like I thought you would."

"You've been watching me. My appearance cannot surprise you."

"I mean, when I first saw you. Different then."

"I must say that I admire your espial," I said. "We are a wary crew. If someone is keeping watch, we always know. Many there are who thirst after the maestro's secrets."

"You still think me witless. It is not so hard to spy."

"I do not call you witless. Perhaps I have too much vaunted my own wit. Perhaps my brain is none so keen as I believed."

We fell silent for a long space, each feeling the strangeness of meeting after so long a time.

"Do you remember our mother?" I asked.

He would not answer. I listened to the tide, trying to picture where the piers stood that it washed against. I tallied smells in my head; there was one odor unusual but almost familiar. I tried to recall and then *Sandalwood,* I thought. Where had I met it before?

At last he spoke. "I blame the old man. Like she was a donkey, how he treated her. Working her like a donkey. Beating and cursing. She broke down early, but I remember her quiet and kind. She wept much."

"Yes. I saw you weeping once along with her."

"Well, I didn't cry when the old man died. Glad he's gone. I could have made things easier for him in the last times, but I didn't."

"He beat you too."

He looked at the wall behind me. "Sometimes."

"Often."

"Yes. But there came a time he had to stop, if he wanted to live."

"I thought about it too, doing him in."

"You have no nerve for it."

"You beat me more often than he did. I took courage to strike back."

"To sneak from behind. I whipped you because it was your fault I got so many welts. He was always harder on me."

"We're both free of him now. Why need you come against Astolfo? I could find a place for you in Tardocco where you might learn things that would be helpful for many years to come."

"I want what you have. By rights, the greater part is mine."

"I have little. But Mutano and I could teach you—"

"Enough of this," he said. "I am too old to be learning magic shadows and such trickery. Easier to take what you gave gathered. Now I am going to tie you to that chair and wait hidden outside to see who arrives. If my men are followed by Astolfo's men, I'll see 'em before they get here."

He took down a length of chain hanging on the wall and brought it three times about my chest and locked it behind me. He had come prepared with a lock. That meant that he had visited this place and chosen the room in which to imprison me. He was not trusting to improvisement but was keeping to a plan. I could not decide if the plan was his own.

I struggled but the chain was tight upon me and the links pinched my flesh when I moved. "I need to piss," I said.

"No you don't," he said. He closed the door tight when he left but did not lock it, there being no lock.

I sat still, trying to lessen the cruelty of the chain, and thought. There was much to try to comprehend. The loss of my father was not burdensome because I had taken for granted he had died long ago. Osbro I had pictured as taking a wife or a hire-wench to do for him as he farmed the small patch of land for half its produce, the other half going to Lord Merioni—or by this time to the lord's heir. I had imagined my brother as becoming accustomed to his lot, thinking of me only in idle moments, if at all. It did not occur to me that he could have designs upon me in my station. I had dissevered that time of my life and thought it swallowed by oblivion. But here was Osbro, and in a position to do me ill. His rise in fortune was swift.

Yet he had arrived in the city in the same predicament as I—ignorant of cultured life and with no local family or friends through whom to make acquaintance and lacking most of the skills required to make a living. I had formed a scheme, based solely on a tissue of improbable rumor, to burrow myself into the trade of shadows, and I had chosen the rashest of ways to do so. Great good fortune had been my ally—and the fact that Astolfo perceived that the umbrae might become for me a vocation, a labor of love, and not a profession or, at worst, a means of conversion to petty crime. I had possessed an advantage without knowing of it.

Osbro would have none. He too would have arrived friendless, hungry for advancement and profit, but without a specific ambition. He would present himself at a hostel or a tavern like The Iron Coulter where exiles from plough and pasture sought refuge in Tardocco. At one of these sites he would have loitered, watching and listening as his silver dwindled, hoping to fasten upon some method to search me out. He said that talk about me had reached Caderia. What he had heard would be only speculative exaggeration, but plausible to his ears.

He would not have thought that many a pair of eyes would be

watching him, as they watched all new-arrived rustics. We straw-chaff ploughmen were raw materials, ready to be turned to mostly dark purposes, to be made into footpads, housebreakers, arm breakers, tavern-brawl quellers, and slaves condemned at the wharves to labors even harsher than farmland had thrust upon us. A few vain promises and a spare coin or two from a glib and easy-mannered fellow clad in silk—and the bargain was made and the unwary undone. Soon the rustics accumulated debt that would keep them in low station and impecunious circumstance for years on end.

Some such thing had happened to Osbro. He had drunken too deeply with a handy and specious gabbler and ensnared himself in he knew not what sort of scheme as a pawn or cat's-paw. Coin had been promised in heaps and, once the business was completed, the considerable pleasures of the city would be open to him. These fancies were the stuff of his dreams, but the outcome would prove bitter for him.

To me he seemed nearly useless as an instrument. Only his connection to me, and thus to Astolfo, was of value, unless his ignorance and bumptiousness counted as assets. There was one way in which they might. If the grand scheme that involved him were discovered or if it failed through ineptitude, he could be discounted as a participant, as being too naive to be able to carry out any part in it.

He must have done a deal of talking, Osbro with the grape in him, for his suborner had learned of his connection to me and of mine to Astolfo. If that last alliance were already known, then those who had deceived Osbro were known to Astolfo and me and probably to Mutano also. Our opponents would be known to us from time past and we would deal with them according to our histories.

Time drew on as my bladder grew tighter and the chain links more irritating. I could not think that Osbro's emissaries could carry out their mission in a way to please him. Mutano, even though wearing only a tradesman's short sword, would disarm the two of them in brief order, and bring them to Astolfo as captives. I judged these fellows burly but bumbling. The next move was the maestro's, and he held the upper hand.

After what seemed a very long time, my brother returned, freed me from the iron, and led me to a filthy corner of the great space outside the little room to relieve myself. Then he brought me back to the disused office, laid down four thicknesses of ancient canvas, and bade me lie down. He chained my right foot to the iron chair. I remonstrated, saying that I had no desire to escape, that negotiations must be under way, and that we would all be rewarded by the results.

For answer he gave me a gloomy, halfhearted kick in the ribs. "They should have come back by now," he muttered, and went off to find, I expected, a bed much softer than mine.

No matter. I disposed my chain as comfortably as I could and slept as soon as my eyelids closed.

⊶═◯═⊷

The daylight was bright in the cracks and crevices of the walls and roof when voices in the warehouse woke me. Osbro and Mutano were talking, but I could not make out the words. The tones were easily readable: Osbro spoke loudly and with some heat; Mutano spoke softly and with a touch of humor.

I sat up when my brother kicked the door open and exhibited me to Mutano. My colleague showed no surprise and barely glanced my way.

"What is this damned toy?" Osbro demanded. He flung it down on the canvas beside me.

"This is Maestro Astolfo's belt with the leopard's-head buckle," I said. "It is his customary wear. Everyone recognizes it. How did you come by it?"

"I brought it to this person at Astolfo's request," Mutano said. "He sends it to identify himself to you and as a surety of his good faith in negotiation with our amicus here."

"So then, Guido and Gracchio are inexpert swordsmen?" I said.

"I have met nimbler," Mutano said.

"If you hold them, I care not," Osbro said. "For all I care, you may reap their gizzards. I have this Falco, as you call him. You come unarmed, so you cannot take him from me."

"Yet what can you do with him? He is of no value to you now."

"I shall question him and find out all the defenses of your house, all your comings and goings, and where you store the treasure you have gathered for so many a year."

Mutano made a smiling half bow. He was dressed in his most splendid finery, with salt-white lace collar, black silken trunks and hose, red slippers with applied gold flowerets, and large gauntlets of flocked, stiff linen. His purpose in this dress, methought, was to cause Osbro to feel lowly and uncertain. "Then our intentions are in balance, for we shall closely question the two Jesters under our sway."

"They can tell you nothing, for they know nothing."

"They know more than they think they know, more than you suspect. They can describe, for instance, the appearance of at least one of those who have paid you to do certain things of which you cannot comprehend the results."

"What say you now? Speak plain."

"You are a fool in hire. You do not know to whom you are in hire or for what reason. With a little trouble, Astolfo can find out. What he learns from you will be to your good. Let us deal openly."

"What terms?"

"It is no use my asking you to release Falco, for you will refuse out of hand. But you must keep him safe and without abuse. We will hold your two men until our bargain is concluded, then we will let them go at the same time you release Falco. Astolfo values him as a bodyguard and is willing to pay a reasonable ransom, provided that you agree to his other condition."

"What other condition?"

"He will meet with you in person and question you about your new friends and acquaintances, the men you met and had commerce with when you first arrived in the city. He suspects them as his rivals in trade who are out to undermine his enterprises and drive him into poverty. If you answer satisfactorily, he will supply you with gold enough to make a start in the city in some enterprise of your own."

"Where would this meeting take place? I will not come to his big house with its entrapments."

"We shall seek out another place. You may examine it beforehand to inspect its safety."

"That place too may be a trap."

Mutano pretended to brush dust from his sleeve. "We have allowed you to keep Falco. Take him with you. If you suspect trickery, you may kill him. Your two ungainly fellows shall be allowed at your side and they will be allowed arms."

Osbro rubbed his chin, his scalp, and the back of his neck. "Where is this meeting point?"

"That is undetermined. We are trying to find a place you will accept, some place out of the city where none of our associates might hide. A lonely place that is secure."

"I do not trust you and your master."

"Astolfo's word is his bond, as everyone avers. His familiar belt is the sign of it. All Tardocco knows."

Osbro picked up the belt and turned it over, inspecting it with indifference. Shrugging, he passed it to me. "I must think upon these things," he told Mutano.

"I will return in four hours. The meeting place will have been chosen and I can lead you to it for your inspection. After four hours, the agreement no longer holds. We are pressed for time—as I believe you know."

Osbro gave him a keen glance, then dropped his head, as if to ponder. Then: "Well," he said.

Mutano came to me and clasped me on the shoulder. "Be of good spirit," he said. "And take good care of the maestro's belt." He turned and went out the door and I heard his footsteps echo through the warehouse. The outer door opened and closed. He had departed.

Osbro waited, listening intently. He went into the warehouse and peered out through a broken board. When he came back, he unchained me quickly and said, "Come along. We are going to another place. If we stay here, I shall be set upon."

"You have Maestro Astolfo's word," I said.

"Yes, and as useless it is to me as that childish belt that you are buckling on. It does not suit with your domino outfit. In fact, it makes you look even more ridiculous."

"I shall wear it because it is a sign of the maestro's earnest promise." I said. "He will keep faith with you in whatever agreement you both arrive at."

"Wear it, then, to look the fool you are. But come along. We go to another place." He appended to his command a resounding slap to my ear. It recalled vividly the days of my early youth.

IX

Gathering of Shadows

Osbro was correct in asserting that Astolfo's belt with its heavy buckle sorted ill with my domino costume. The cincture hung loose upon my hips and the leopard's head bobbed up and down, annoying my codpiece. I was overtired of the black-and-white livery; I had worn it for three days now and it was soiled and stinking. The mask had been destroyed and the cock hat with white feather had been knocked from my head and booted to lie forgotten in some foul corner. Osbro, fearing that Astolfo and Mutano would rescue me from his control, had now moved me four times within the jumble of storerooms and warehouses that brooded over the tides of the harbor. With each change of place my clothing and corpus grew dirtier.

I was heartened then when my brother announced that a site for negotiations had been agreed upon and that my exchange for Guido and Gracchio was arranged for this same evening. I looked forward to returning to the comforts of our villa, to its baths and beds and to the prideful dishes of Iratus. The crusts and orts that Osbro had allowed me to eat gave me gut-gripe and a sharp temper.

"Where is this happy event to take place?" I asked.

He paused before replying, wondering perhaps how I might use the intelligence. Then: "At a château north'ard of the town a little."

"You have inspected the place and are satisfied?"

"I am not wholly at peace, but in the main they have met my demands. It is not the big house you live in where I could not discover all the traps. It is not here on the wharves where Astolfo can count on so many friends and allies unknown to me. For the same reason, I said no to two places in the middle of town. The château is set off alone in the fields and there is just one road going to it. I have somebody already watching that road. No one can get there without being seen."

"You must have looked over the interior also."

"From top to bottom, through every passage and corner. Nobody is staying there, unless we count a brace of cats."

"A large house needs skillful mousers," I said.

"A deserted house? The man that owned it has died and no blood-kin has come to put a claim on the place."

"All the more reason."

"The cats mean nothing," he said. "They are but cats."

"Are the rooms and corridors well lit and open?"

"As open and bare as a desert plain."

"Then you have struck a good bargain," I said, thinking that Mutano must have removed our maze of shadows and made the site seem as harmless as a mug of fresh cow's milk. For this was the site of the château of the baron Tyl Rendig. Astolfo was in process of petitioning the provincial magistrates for the property as our reward for revealing the crimes of the murderous monster. The maestro told the judges that the Fates had punished the man, bringing him to fall by accident to his death. This tale was credited and we thus avoided years of legal delays and entanglements. It would be long before a final decision was forthcoming; the magistracy was not friendly toward Astolfo. They who deal in shadows are always suspected by high-minded civic leaders.

Where Osbro had procured his mount I could not say, but mine was familiar. It was Defender, Mutano's habitual transport, and his lending of it to me was a signal favor. He had supplied a comfortable saddle too, one of my own. I took the stirrups and reins well contented.

The half moon that hung over our lonely track was of a reddish-gold color and when I gazed at it I thought how in the lunar last quarter fell the hour that the ritual burial of Bennio's coffin must be performed. We must conclude this business with Osbro in haste. Astolfo would say, *Well-ordered haste*.

The land on both sides of our road was mostly level, but there were shallow declivities here and there from which we could be watched by a prone onlooker. Osbro was taking all the precautions he could, but he knew he was vulnerable, not least because he was unwilling to reveal the identities of his superiors in the confederacy. That secret he thought his best advantage at this point. In this present exchange of prisoners his position was favorable to the extent that Astolfo desired to have me back in sound health while Osbro was not greatly concerned to regain Guido and Gracchio. His position was unfavorable because when the names of those with whom he was complicit were spoken, Astolfo would know more of them and of their histories than my brother knew, he being lately come to Tardocco. The maestro would then be nearer to glimpsing our opponents' complete design.

Tired as I was, I still had to be wary and ready to act upon the instant, whatever the situation. When we arrived at the château and entered into the courtyard where the exchange was to take place, I gave the area a quick glance-over. It was as Osbro had desired. The moon stood directly above and cast no shadow from walls or battlements. The space was empty except for the well mouth, a knee-high rude structure of stone. In our previous reconnoiter of the château, Mutano had let me down into this well by a rope. There seemed no place for Astolfo to make use of his sciomancy and the order of exchange was to be the simplest possible: Guido and Gracchio were to amble their horses to one side of the courtyard. Once they halted and were examined by Osbro, I would urge Defender toward Astolfo and Mutano. This part was most awkward for me, for if my brother desired to betray me, he could plant a knife in my ribs and gallop away with his henchmen and spur out of reach in moments.

So when the two sheepish knaves had made their way to our side and I began my approach to my colleagues, I felt my hairs prickle and the flesh rise on my forearms. Something was out of order.

The sky had darkened and the light of the reddish moon was uncanny and unrevealing. Except for the slow plod of Defender's hooves, there was no sound, and the silence emphasized the strangeness of the light. Another light was in play, I realized as I passed the well mouth. From that cavity issued an intermittent yellow glow. The glow came from the chamber I had found earlier at the bottom of the well, but the passage of the light was hindered by some moving object.

I reined Defender to a halt and watched as a black creature emerged slowly into the courtyard. One part of it curled over the edge of the well curb on my side. Another part oozed over the stones directly before it. Defender snorted and stamped and his nervousness underlined the surrounding silence and the gradual, dark advent of the creature.

Then there were sounds of alarm from behind me where Osbro and the other two stood. Guido it was who uttered a curse, but stopped off in mid-phrase. Gracchio groaned. I heard nothing from my brother.

The emergence of the thing continued, tentacles and pseudo-pods lapping over the stones onto the sandy arena, and then the bulky black central body lugged its way out of the hole. With the light streaming from beneath, the dreadful thing cast a great, mis-shapen shadow in every direction around itself. Now I could hear its breath, a low raspy wheezing. There was something mournful in the sound, some quality that suggested the black creature regret-ted the reality of its own existence.

Onward it came, slowly making its way toward Osbro's group.

I looked to Astolfo and Mutano. They watched the beast with interest but without apparent fear. I nudged Defender toward them, then reined him round so that I could observe from a middle distance.

The monster was almost wholly unearthed now, and it tumbled the curbstones down in its progress. It made a huge moan, a garbled roar that sounded something like an angry lion's threat mingled with the neigh of a terrified horse. This savage trumpeting was enough to cause Gracchio and Guido to wheel their horses about and gallop out of the courtyard gateway into the broad dark-ness of the outer world.

Osbro stood his ground. After a brief time of indecision, he trotted toward the monster, unsheathed his sword, and began chopping at various appendages. He swore a number of mighty oaths, like those I had heard him utter many years ago when a cow stepped on his foot or a pig escaped the sty and ran away into the woods.

Mutano burst out laughing and Astolfo allowed himself a broad smile. I urged Defender toward them and then reined in and we stood as a trio.

Then, with a long and sorrowful sigh, the monster died a flabby death and collapsed upon itself to reveal its true nature of cloth and canvas, hog bladders and silk bladders, its armatures of wire and cable.

This revelation of the creature as an elaborate puppet set Osbro into a fury. He rushed at us to attack, but then, seeing that the three of us stood ready at defense, reined in and came to a standstill. "What mummery is this?" he cried. "Do you think me a child to be frightened by such a deception? What are you about?"

"Child or man, you were deceived," Mutano said, "for you fell upon the puppet with might and main. I doubt there is enough whole cloth left to fashion a nose-rag."

"I did not expect to be tricked so stupidly. We had made a bargain. Your false monster served no purpose."

"Well, as to that," said Astolfo, "you are now in our hands and without your henchmen to aid you. We have regained Falco in sound health, though a little mishandled, I should judge. And you shall find it much to your good to respond to our inquiry."

"Break my bones, then," Osbro said, "but I will reveal naught."

"The breaking of bones is an unfriendly sport," Astolfo said. "A polite colloquy over cold fowl and a passable wine offers a more civil entertainment. I do hope that you will accept our invitation. We can go at once and be at table within the hour."

"I mistrust your big house," Osbro muttered. He gave me a straight, black look.

"And what if you mistrust?" Mutano said. "You are our prisoner and any invitation is but a polite formality."

"Let us leave now," I urged. I was tired, hungry, thirsty, and befouled. I much desired the refuge of the villa.

"We must await Sbufo," Astolfo said, "but now I see he is with us already."

A small, plump man was pulling himself out of the well, stepping from a ladder or some other support onto the firm sand. With a rueful countenance he examined the ruin that Osbro had made of his large toy. The complicated contrivance must have cost him many an hour of intricate labor. Then he turned to greet us with a brief bow and a happy grin.

"Your Mardrake performed well," Astolfo said. "It will be the most memorable part of the tableau wherein heroic Perseus rescues Andromeda from its gruesome clutches."

"It will perform more ably there than here," Sbufo said, "for Cocorico conforms better than I to the apparatus. He has the Jester's gift of gesture that I have not."

"You have done excellently," Mutano said. "I believe that Falco too was taken in, along with his straw-wit brother."

"I was deceived," I said, and Sbufo bowed and grinned and bowed once more.

"I was not," said Osbro. "Whatever kind of thing it was, I knew it would fall to my attack."

"And so it did," I said. "You braved your dread foe and now the puppet is no more. Perhaps you shall fare as well if ever you battle Dirty Bennino." Another rhyme rose unbidden and I gave it voice:

"Lo, the conquering hero's come
With a pimple on his bum
And with gore upon his blade
Stained with lopping a cabbage head."

"No more!" cried Mutano. "The lanes and avenues are filled with clumsy Jesters cackling out infantile rhymes. We need not add our clamor to the rabble's."

"I shall desist," I said.

Sbufo brought a donkey cart from outside the western wall of the courtyard, piled his broken engine into it, and we returned to Tardocco in contented silence. Osbro contributed to the silence but not, methought, to the contentment.

⊷⟞◎⟝⊷

I made a thorough but hasty toilet and joined the company out in the garden. The servants had hung lanterns and set other lights about a large table covered with yellow oilcloth. The viands were the afore-promised cold hen, together with sallets, peppered beans, and wines red and white. Upon this stalwart repast I made quick inroads and listened as Astolfo unfolded his plans to Osbro.

"You need not name Pontoso, Arachnido, and Cherrynose as your confederates," he said, "for of them we know already. And understanding that we know so much, you may well comprehend that we shall find out further intelligence without your aid. But we are under the constraint of an approaching hour by which time our commission must be resolved. Thus, it is to our advantage that you tell us all you know. We shall make it to your advantage also."

Osbro denuded a thighbone and pitched it into the dark grass. His eyes gleamed bloodshot in the flickering light and a gauze of sweat stood on his forehead.

He was afraid. But Astolfo had offered him no violence. I was willing to bestow a healthy kick or two upon him in the interest of fraternal regard, but those blows he would not fear.

"You are apprehensive," Astolfo continued, "that those whom you betray to us will come against you in quest of your life when your treachery is known to them."

"They will do so," Osbro said.

"But now you will be under our protection," Astolfo said. "They will not come against us. We shall be well prepared, and we have the civil authorities on our side."

"They care nothing for your authorities, and you are but three men. You have others to call to your aid, yet in the end you can count yourselves but a small company. And they will not be frightened by any play-toy this bellows-mender can invent."

Sbufo grinned and raised his glass in salute. He must have felt he had bested Osbro, for all my brother's bluster.

"You speak," Astolfo said, "as if you knew a great deal about these persons you have leagued with. You speak as if they had taken you into their innermost circle."

"They have told me little. I have made some findings in my own interest."

"You have spied upon them. Do you trust your findings so wholly?"

"Spying is not hard to do," Osbro said. I recalled that he had uttered that thought before. He was always slow to learn.

"Perhaps not," Astolfo said. He was careful to keep amusement out of his voice. He, who had all the resources of umbrae, had found some of our commissions difficult. One of his familiar proverbs ran thus: *When the watching is not troublesome, the watcher is being watched.* Osbro seemed not to comprehend that his hireling confederates had abandoned him, that though treated like a guest he was our captive, and that his only way forward now was to join with us and divulge all that he knew. He had been visibly startled when Astolfo named certain of his associates. Pontoso, Arachnido, and Cherry-nose were overseers between them of a half dozen storehouses and lading docks. This trio was best known about the wharves for their bullying manners and not for their honesty.

I too was somdel surprised that the maestro had this knowledge. There had not been sufficient time for him and Mutano to unearth those names through inquiry.

"A spy must possess certitude of memory," Mutano said. "What is the state of yours?"

"There are things I know I won't ever forget," Osbro said. He gave me a long, sharp look.

"Well, you have heard my proposal," Astolfo said. "Think upon it tonight and give me your answer in the morning. You are to repose here as our guest and your needs will be supplied. Let us now turn to subjects of lighter import. Tell us, Sbufo, of the most entertaining of the Feast spectacles that are to be shown. You have been working with the stagers and dancers and musicians and artists, have you not?"

Sbufo took a thoughtful sip of wine and began a long and humorous account of the trials and triumphs of the various performances. His husky voice rose barely above a whisper, but it drew from us loud laughter.

⊷═◉═⊷

I left them there in a while and made my way to my room, undressed, and lay down in bedraggled disposition. My ribs and thighs ached from the blows and kicks I had gained as my brother's captive and my eyes yearned for sleep. I lay on my right side, facing a small table at bed-head. This position brought my face level with Astolfo's belt buckle. I had put it there and forgotten to return it to him. As I reached over to snuff the candle one of the eyes of the leopard's head seemed to follow my movement.

This motion was illusory, a consequence of wavering candlelight, but the eyes of the buckle caught my attention. The belt was familiar to me—and to many others, as we had told Osbro—but I had never had occasion to examine it closely. Now as I did so, the greenish eyes of the countenance seemed to be misaligned, one set a little lower than the other. I picked it up and on impulse pressed with my thumb on this eye and with a click the buckle opened.

Inside lay a diamond as large as the nail of my great toe. It was not perfect; it shone yellowish and with a pronounced flaw in the center. Seeing it, I recalled our commission with Countess Triana and how her shadow had been sealed into a precious stone by one who schemed against her. This stone in Astolfo's belt also contained a shadow. I felt certain of my conclusion, though I could see little, turning it this way and that in the unsteady light.

Whose shadow had he enclosed here?

Its value to him was great, for he kept it close at all times, except for this present nonce. He had sent it to me as a sign of his identity and a token of reassurance. So Mutano had said.

But neither of these reasons would be adequate, since Mutano's presence guaranteed the maestro's association and Astolfo would not take pains to reassure me, knowing that I could guard my own safety.

The most valuable umbra he could possess would be his own. As a shadow dealer, he needed to make certain of the security of his own shadow. If it fell into the hands of another, that person would have power over him. If it were known that he had lost it, he would be without credit in his profession.

Of course, he cast a shadow as I did and as all others did who walked in light, but the ones he cast from day to day would not be the primaries. They would be secondaries and tertiaries that he put on each daybreak like clothing to go abroad in. The primary was too precious for daily wear.

With my own hand I had carved the admonition into the oaken headboard of the bed I now lay in: *Bumpkin lad, Protect thy shade.*

Astolfo protected his shade by setting it in stone and hiding it away in the prominent buckle. A thief who managed to purloin from him the shadow he cast would acquire only a secondary object, one that would provide little means to harm the maestro.

An ingenious defense, I thought, but had to wonder why he would entrust it to Mutano and me to handle with less than perfect care in the company of Osbro and the others. He was leaving much to the risks of seizure or mischief. What if Guido decided he liked the look of the toy or Osbro tossed it into the harbor waters in a fit of pique? These possibilities must not have concerned him.

It came to me that he did not fret about the loss of his umbra because he knew where it was located at all times. We all communicate with our shadows, though we do so generally without specific awareness. We simply know that our shadow is before or behind, aslant to the left or right of us. We have the same knowledge if it is detached from our body, though we must train ourselves in this particular awareness, sharpening our instinctive sympathy with philosophical exercises.

And that was how Astolfo could name the names—Pontoso, Arachnido, Cherrynose. I had carried his umbra from one storehouse to another. The overseers and managers of these sites were commonly known. The places to which Osbro had bundled me identified at least three of the number of those who were leagued against the city. Their friends and associates could be traced also, figures with whom my brother had made no acquaintance, personages kept dark from him.

Weariness was overcoming me like a sheepskin robe pulled up about my ears, but before I gave over to sleep I made a solemn resolution. The portable shadow offered an invaluable means of espial. Reduced in size by the agencies of lenses and mirrors and subducted into a convenient container, it could be made secure and locatable at all times. True, I possessed no diamond in which to place it, but something . . .

⊹⊷●◗⊶

. . . something no dream divulged to me.

I awakened with my conception sharp in mind, but the image of a shadow-container had not come.

I rose and washed my hands and beard and repaired to the kitchen. I had risen late. No one was about but a sulky potboy scrubbing at a big copper kettle, rubbing and rinsing and looking at the reflection of his face. Without speaking, I set out bread and cheese and ale and made a healthy breakfast of them.

Then, as the morning brightened and promised a fair day, I gathered materials and set up the same arrangement we had made for our apprehensive client. I laid a sheet of coarse cloth against the plaster of the western garden wall and positioned my body before it. I had my silver demilune ready, using my left hand, since I would have to face northward to be able to sever my shadow.

The easiest of all ways to appropriate a shadow is by *surrender,* when a subject willingly gives over his or her shade to the blade. The reasons to do so are numerous. For females it is often a matter of fashion; some of them dislike having no choice and are willing to take off the primary in exchange for the variety of secondaries to be worn on different occasions. Balls and festive dinners and attendance at rhapsode performances and so forth require shades with some gaiety and lightness of style; more sober occasions—funerals and annual memorials—call for a stylish severity, with darkness enough to mark the event but not so much as to obscure physical attractiveness. Men of affairs choose shadows of firm outline and well-defined tint, believing these qualities to suggest honest forth-rightness. And so forth.

I was surrendering my shadow; there needed no sleights of art to take it. My purpose was to imitate the maestro's warrant of security and range of intelligence-finding that the shadow embedded in the diamond gave him. To own a transferable shadow must be something like having an animal, a tracking hound, say, that I could communicate with. All sorts of other uses began to tease my imagination.

To cut my shadow away I would have to stoop and sever it on the left side of my boot sole. When I straightened up, the umbra, though then separate from me, would straighten also its shape on the cloth and stand as I stood. Mutano's game with the shadows of cats had demonstrated how the movement of separated shadows still followed the movements of the absent casters.

The sky was blue, the sun bright. My shadow lay stark upon the cloth. My blade was keen. I bent to my task—and remained in that position for so long a time that my knees began to give way. My hand trembled and the blade-edge came not a-near the edge of my umbra. I desired to cut away my shadow and place it in one of the blue mirrors in the long hall of the third story of the manse. But my arm would not obey my will. I could not bring myself to perform the deed.

What sensation would I feel when my shadow was severed? How would I change in that moment and how would I be different thereafter? I was uncertain what I would gain and what I must lose.

In a few moments I stood erect. I could not do the deed, and could not say why. For the first time in my life I reproached myself for cowardice.

⊷≡◉⊜≡⊶

Now we were four. While I sat in my room disconsolate and troubled in spirit, Osbro spent the greater part of the day in private conference with Astolfo. Mutano was nowhere on the grounds and I expected that he visited the flaxen-haired female in Cobblers' Lane, though lately he admitted that his commerce with her had not been going well. I could only surmise, but I suspected that his interest in her grew less ardent daily. In fact, there seemed a hint of distaste in his infrequent remarks about her. More and more these recent days he had reverted to his feline mannerisms. I began to think he longed to keep company with cats, as in time past.

In the mid-afternoon he returned to the villa and he and I spent a dry hour in desultory converse in the small library. He was not in a divulging frame of mind and I was pleased when at last Osbro appeared in the hallway outside the open door. We hailed him, adjusted his borrowed clothing to suit our taste, had mounts brought round, and rode away with him into town.

Our destination was a tavern newly favored by Mutano. It was called The Cat o' Nine and offered strong country ale served in an adjoining rose-trellised beer garden. We sat at an oaken table wherein rhymes and initials were plentifully dug and ordered bumpers.

"In the ventures we undertake, we must have utter confidence in our colleagues," Mutano intoned. "We must trust their loyalties, depend upon their abilities, and know their capacities. Therefore, while Falco and I sip this cup of ale in the manner of gentlefolk, we shall oblige you to drink it down in a single swallow."

Osbro was nothing loath. He raised the pewter mug. "Salute, Mutano and Todo." Down it went.

"Who is this Todo you address?" Mutano said.

"He intends myself," I said. "Our father named me Todigliano after a miserly noble who was the brother of our landlord, Merioni. He hoped with this naming to get into the lord's good graces. That did not happen, so I was called Todo for vain reason. After I fought with Osbro to gain my freedom from the farm, I made my way to Tardocco to join with Astolfo. On the journey hither I made myself Falco, a personage more likely to impress the maestro."

"*Fought,* my brambly arse," Osbro said. "You sneaked from behind like a coward and laid my head open with a spade. . . . Ough!"

This last interjection resulted from the kick I delivered his shin beneath the table. "You are under our strict discipline now," I told him, "and you will learn never to contradict the statements of your superiors."

"The world can never see the day when you are my superior," he said. "Let's stand and settle for good the question. I will drub your worthless carcass like a washerwoman beating clothes on a rock."

Mutano, sitting beside, gave him a casual backhand slap. "Our

Falco is too valuable a commodity to be drubbed by a new recruit. Keep your mouth shut except to guzzle."

A new bumper had arrived and Osbro attacked it manfully.

"*Osbro,*" I explained to Mutano, "is the truncated *Osbronius,* another cousin or nephew or bastard son of the landlord, his name another useless obeisance on our father's part."

"Osbro and Todo," said Mutano. "In my mind's eye, I see you both standing beside a brace of mules and matching them fart for fart. Doth not such an amusement pass for a chivalric tournament there in Caderia?"

"It is more honorable than lurking behind people to steal their shadows. . . . Ough!"

At the same time, Mutano and I had kicked the monosyllable from him.

"You have been in company some four or five hours with Maestro Astolfo," I said. "Does he impress you as one who sneaks and thieves, as one without substance and honor?"

He paused, wiping foam from his lips. In a more serious tone he said, "No. There is more to him than I thought. There are rumors he is a magician, a sort of trickster charlatan, who makes folks believe he has power over them through their shadows. That is what I heard back home."

"And now?"

He mused. "He has powers, but they are not magical."

"He scorns all talk of magic," Mutano said.

"He spoke to me of skills I might gain," Osbro said. "He was kind toward me."

"Did you tell him what he wished to know?"

"I cannot say. Seemed to me I told him little, just chatting as I might at a beery table like this one. Yet he seemed to glean something from my words I did not wot of."

"He asked about some who might have designs upon the wealth of the city?" Mutano asked.

"No. He asked if any of those with whom I bargained spoke with out-country accents or used strange words. He asked if any of them smelled peculiar to me. Just chat like that."

"Drink up," I commanded. "Did he speak of the disciplines you must undergo to be well trained in our vocation?"

"He promised that you two would take me in hand and lead me onward."

"Did he speak of the rewards you might gain?"

"I did not ask and he did not say. He gave me two silver eagles for expenses I might run into."

"No," I said. "He did not. You do not have any silver. You never had any."

"Indeed I do." He reached into the cuff of the blouse Astolfo had lent him and brought forth a pair of coin-sized tin buttons. He glared at them. "These were silver when Astolfo gave them to me."

Mutano boxed his ear—too gently, I thought—and said, "We call him Maestro Astolfo and from this moment so shall you. Do you understand?"

"Yes."

"Say the words."

"Maestro Astolfo."

"What answer did you return to his question about the accents and vocabularies of your associates?" I asked.

"I told him that many of the accents here in Tardocco are strange to me. I have lived all my life on a farm in the country and don't hardly know one kind of speech from another. But there is a man they call Digitus with an odd way of talking through his nose. To me he sounds like a foreigner."

"Say some words that he used."

He frowned and closed his eyes. Over by the rose trellis a seated lutenist was singing a soft and melancholy ballad which he seemed to address to a handsome woman with magpie hair, velvet black with a silky white streak along the part. At a well-lit table to our right three youths were casting dice and giggling. The warm night wind swayed the leaves of a tall fig in the center of the garden. Finally Osbro said, "Foo-gus?"

Mutano look at me.

"Perhaps *fougasse*," I told him. "It's a kind of bread they eat on the western coasts."

"Drink again, Arsebro," Mutano said. "Ale is a great restorer of memory."

Though he appeared to doubt the truth of that statement, Osbro complied.

"What question did he ask that most surprised you?" I said.

He shook his head wonderingly. "He asked if I had any maritime experience, particularly in the matter of piloting ships or riverboats."

"And when you told him you had none?"

"He said that was regrettable but not crucial. He asked if I could swim and I said yes."

"Where did you learn to swim?"

"In the stream we call Dove Creek a little way out from the farm."

"Who taught you?"

"That woman they call La Pluma. She taught me some other things too." His smile was a little tipsy and happily reminiscent.

"How did you come to know her?"

"She used to visit our father after Mother died. I want my silver eagles back."

"What are you speaking of?"

"You took my coins and put buttons in their place."

"I did?"

"You or him."

That statement earned a pinch that would leave a purple patch on his thigh. "I do not relish being called a thief," Mutano said.

"You are unwise in your drinking custom," I said. "Too much ale confuses the memory. I would expect that your silver, if it ever existed, will be just where you placed it in your blouse."

He dug the coins out and laid them in his left palm. He blinked at them as if he had never seen them before.

"Drink up," Mutano ordered. "You are falling behind. Falco and I are into our tenth round."

He shook his head. "That cannot be true."

"Down the gullet," Mutano said. He pushed a new bumper to Osbro. "Drink up. Be merry. I feel a song rising to my throat."

"I regret this piece of news," I said.

"So do I," said Osbro with a hiccough.

I pulled his nose. "You must never disrespect your superiors," I said. "That results in sore punishments, especially if you disparage their musical abilities."

Mutano launched:

> "When I was King o' the Cats and you were the farrier's pet,
>   Things were as they ought to be and may be yet Again."

"Lubly," Osbro mumbled. "Byoofl."

"It is good that you say so," I said. "It argues a modicum of taste. Now it is your turn."

"To sing?" He looked at me with an expression of terror. "I have no voice for song."

"You are too modest by far," Mutano said.

"Stand and give throat," I said.

He lurched to his feet and grasped the table edge with flattened, white fingers. With a timbre like falling rock, he began:

"Hog drovers, hog drovers, hog drovers are we,
  A-tuppin' the women wherever they be—"

"Quiet that braying!" "Stop his mouth!" "Silence!" The sentiments of our neighbor tipplers were clear to us. The lutenist made a derisive brangle upon his strings.

"Barbarous!" said Mutano. "Sit down and bring no more shame upon us. Thou'rt not fit company for onagers."

Osbro hung his head. "Tol' you so." He sat; it was an unsteady movement.

"Why did the maestro ask if you were a boat pilot?" I said. "He knows the greater part of your history and knows you to be no seafarer."

"I don't know."

"Drink up," said Mutano. "Maybe an answer will come to you."

He tried but could get down only a petite sip.

"Be more manly," Mutano said, and slapped him on the back.

An expression of bewilderment crossed Osbro's face. "He asked if I could see well in the dark."

"See in the dark? What did he mean?"

"Don't know. Tol' him I could if I had a light and he smiled."

I raised my hand to cuff him but desisted, unsure what result might follow. "A silly thing to say."

"He smiled at it."

"The maestro is a generous man," Mutano said. "A less good-hearted person would have set the dogs on you. Lame jests are the lice of social intercourse."

"No dogs, not him. He would set shadows on me."

"What do you mean?" I asked.

"To suck my soul and leave me a husk. Ever'body knows. That's how he came wealthy. Sucked the souls from people and stole their gold. Ever'body in Caderia talks about it."

"Ignorant mud-choppers," Mutano said. "What do they know of the ways of the learned?"

In a subdued, unhappy voice Osbro said, "I wish I could read. 'Deed I do." He set his hands flat on the table, laid his head on them, and closed his eyes.

"You do not have our permission to sleep," Mutano said.

For reply Osbro began to snore.

"We have lost a cup-companion," I said to Mutano. "What do you make of him?"

"I think him honest enough, yet I cannot fathom why Maestro Astolfo shows interest. He has no skills useful to us."

"What was this matter of ship piloting? Is the maestro taking us to sea?"

"We must assume that he gathered intelligence from Osbro we cannot recognize."

"Yes."

We were silent for a space, then Mutano proposed a topping-off of our drinks. We would arrange for the tavern to lay out a sleeping space for Osbro in the cellar. He could make his way home in the morning. We would return to the manse now and be prepared. We had tasks to accomplish.

Astolfo had never mentioned the name of our Jester-client to us, so Mutano and I had taken to referring to him first as il signor Misterioso, and then as Sterio. But the specifications he had delivered as to the ritual coffin were not mysterious. They were meticulous and set out in old-fashioned language, suggesting how deeply rooted in tradition was the Tumulus rite. The shape required was hexagonal, the upper sides slanting to modest angles at the shoulder-points; the length was two and one-half cubits, the breadth three hand-widths at the shoulders, tapering to two and one-half at termination. The wood was cedar, prepared to take the bright red, yellow, and blue lacquers of the harlequin costume.

I proposed giving over this preparation to our groom, who was a clever hand at carpentry, but Mutano said that he and I had better do the construction ourselves. "It is all false shamming," he said, "but if something goes wrong with the ritual, we must bear our part of the responsibility. We should not appoint the groom. He has no notion of what might be at stake."

His caution won me over and we set to sawing, planing, sanding, joining, and mixing colors. There were finicky instructions about how the design of the diamond-shapes should overlap the edges of the box and we took close pains with that detail and the tedious others.

When finished, the small coffin presented a gay appearance, yet there was an air of melancholy dignity about it too; it seemed a fitting resting-container for an effigy, a stick-puppet, and a shadow. The sight of it inspired Mutano to recall:

> *"The world will still go round and round*
> *When Bennio slides into the ground."*

He essayed the accompanying cackle of laughter but could not find the right intonation.

I capped the antique chant:

> *"When the Jester stands again uprose,*
> *The world its revealing shadow throws."*

We set the coffin on a platform in an upstairs storeroom for the first coatings of lacquers to dry and went about outfitting our cart for the transport to the Tumulus.

Astolfo was to drive the cart, with Defender serving as dray horse. "This once and ne'er again," said Mutano. We did not wish to be outdone by any other household or individual in the matter of equipage, so we applied colors red and yellow and white to the sideboards. The wheel spokes were black with gold-and-white arrow designs. This labor consumed the better part of a day, but we were gratified by the look of the conveyance when we were finished.

"A satisfactory cart," Mutano said, "but at the last, the whole affair is only a falsity."

⋅⊷⊜⊷⋅

Osbro returned from his beery initiation and was steady enough that Mutano continued to train him in our necessary arts and disciplines.

I was to take no part, Astolfo ordained, because the temptation for me to enjoy too energetically the wrestling bouts and wooden-sword encounters would be always present. Nor would have my brother received instruction from me with the warmest enthusiasm.

Other tasks busied my hours. We had counted on a number of days of brisk umbral trade, as the folk prepared costumes, exhibits, tableaux, and dances for the Feast. Those requests had slackened lately; the preparations in the households had come pretty far along and latter orders would be mostly for the sake of finesse.

But the maestro had assigned me a laborious study. We needed— he emphasized *necessity*—our maps of the city brought up to date. Our library was well stocked with charts of the thoroughfares and parks and commercial establishments, but the harbor area had sustained a goodly amount of construction in latter years. Trade was increasing; new sources of supply had opened in the eastern islands; new markets arose along the western coastline. New shippers were opening warehouses; workers from our northern provinces flocked to the harbor, along with laborers from other points of the weather vane. Dwellings sprang up within and around this area, as did auxiliary and ancillary enterprises. Wealthy Tardocco was becoming wealthier.

Still the town lacked defenses. We hosted no standing military, only a Civil Guard to keep domestic peace and a separate dozen or so private armed groups allied with the Guard and chartered by the Council. These groups could count five or six members at most. All these forces were adequate to quell street brawls and conflicts between drunken sailors, to dampen thievery and abduction and the myriad other rogueries that infest a port city, but they offered scant protection from large, well-armed outside forces of the kind Astolfo suspected might now threaten us.

A sage civic leader of ancient time had pronounced in oracular fashion that Tardocco should protect itself with "wooden walls." He succumbed to age before he could unfold his meaning and debate flared as to whether or not he had intended that the city should be walled all about. That idea made little sense for a town open to the sea on one side. The opposing faction declared that Arisius must have believed that the town should build ships and mount a navy. This latter was the logical alternative, but it entailed great expenditure as well as an array of skills then unavailable.

In the end, nothing was done, and we lay vulnerable.

So I pored over the dusty-musty maps in the old leather port-folios, making notes on sites I knew had changed and listing other spots I must visit now in order to rectify the existing charts and re-describe the present sites.

These tasks must be done quickly.

The maestro himself had several projects under way, some of them unrevealed to Mutano and me. But we were aware that he was undertaking one part of Osbro's training himself. He was teach-ing him the workings of the villa—how it was provisioned, how the operations were maintained: the servants, animals, mechanisms, tools, gardens, various shelters, and so forth. We wondered at that; he had hardly spoken to us of these subjects at all. Osbro was avid to learn of these matters and was well suited, since he had observed such management for a long time from beneath, as a supplier of farm goods to noble houses.

⋯≡◦═⋯

When I could no longer bear sitting at a table turning over crack-ling parchment charts, I rose and rode into town. I stalled the small, gray mare called Patience at a livery stable near Daia Plaza and made my way about on foot. The lanes and public squares were less crowded than they had been last time I was here, as if the citizens were holding down their highest spirits until the Feast proper.

Even so, there was hurly-burly aplenty. Mutano had reported earlier that his perambulation had turned up a great number of Bennios, and that number must have increased. Jesters were everywhere—small and large, dexterous and clumsy, ebullient and taciturn, musical and decidedly unmusical. The air of subdued gloom I had noticed before still held, but it was a little abated because of the larger number of clowns.

In the park greens impromptu tournaments took place and little boys and beardless youths clattered at one another with wooden swords and shields made of discarded tin salvers. Greased-pig chases were proving popular among similar groups. Spontaneous wrestling matches broke out and soon turned into earnest fights that loosened teeth and blackened eyes. Football games were in progress every-where, so that one could hardly walk a hundred paces without hav-ing to toe a ball or two out of the way.

My plan was to return to the Nuovoponte, take the slick stone steps down to riverside, and follow along the Daia to the harbor area, noting the new establishments springing up and the old that slumbered in desuetude, numbering the piers and landings, and studying the currents. The old establishments were of interest because they were infrequently overseen or inspected and so were available as hiding places for thieves and other malefactors. The closer I came to the harbor the more buildings I saw of this nature. Along the wharves the buildings in constant and profitable use stood side by side with edifices deserted and crumbling, dens for smugglers, rats, and fugitives.

Astolfo seemed to expect that Tardocco would be set upon by pirates—by Morbruzzo, renowned for savagery in pillage, or by others almost equally feared. A greater fear was that some of the brigand bands had leagued together for a concerted attack. It was hardly unheard of that port cities fell prey to pirate fleets. Reggio, a fat island city to our southeast, had fallen to pirates four times in a dozen years. At last, as if its spirit were exhausted, the whole town crumbled in ruins in a series of earthquakes.

An irony attending our fear of pirates was that Tardocco itself, according to some historical accounts, had been founded as a safe haven by pirates, a place for their ships to load off plunder and to repair damages sustained in battle. Astolfo threw doubt on the legend, saying that our comfortable commercial town liked to give itself rakish airs, "like a chaste maiden cherishing a hidden tattoo of an arrow-pierced heart." I preferred the legendary origin to the staid conjectures written by scribblers pedantic from birth. I liked also the myth of the Mardrake that inhabited the bay; that legend implied a long and eventful history largely unknown in our more humdrum time.

Trudging along the loading piers at waterside, I recognized a familiar door, the side entrance to the great, gloomy warehouse that sheltered the offices of the merchant Pecunio, the old man whose commission had occasioned my introduction to the business of shadow-trading and its accompanying perils. This stretch of buildings looked more disused than any other I had passed. No lights showed between the board sidings of the structures and the planks of the piers were slick with algae. Pecunio's front was the exception; the main entrance had been opened recently, though the trackings were unclear, especially in this fading, violet light. But the white stone sill of the side door bore boot marks, though no light shone out from any crevice.

I slipped to the door and laid my ear against it and heard nothing. But the silence was not somnolent; it was like the silence of a man holding his breath. I waited, holding my own breath, and in a while I thought I heard sounds muffled by the thick pine door— steps as of several persons pacing about, a rumbling as of a handcart being trundled over the floor. I stood in this posture for a long time but could learn nothing else.

＊＝◉◲＝＊

My circuit now brought me to Rattlebone Alley, a narrow passage that led to Chandlers' Lane and thence to the broad avenue northward to the parks and the upper crescent of the city. An ill-favored tavern on my right-hand side emitted a soft dribble of voices and I stepped within to a low-ceilinged room with four bare tables and a long plank counter supporting five large casks. Upon tall chairs along the counter perched three querulous old men, being served with seeming reluctance by a sallow woman. She had seen better days but evidently took no pleasure in recalling them.

I stepped to the splintery board counter and asked for ale.

"Rum," she said. "Rum only." Her voice was of a timbre to alarm ravens.

"Rum then."

"Show your copper. Copper first, then rum."

I laid a silver coin on the wood. "Rum for all."

If she was glad of the sale, she did not exhibit unbridled joy. Nevertheless, she brought forth fresh wooden cups and poured four.

I tasted mine and pushed it back to her. "Silver deserves better. For the barmaid too."

She managed a glimmer of a smile, pushed her slate-gray hair back, brushed the front of her smock with a hasty hand, and began again, producing a large brown jug from a shelf below the counter.

"Better," I said, after a small sip. "I thank you." I raised my cup and the old fellows returned my salute.

"Your health," one said, the only one to return my gaze. His accent marked him from the Molvorian hills.

"Worked up a little thirst," I said, "walking down from the Nuovoponte. I was to meet a friend, but he never arrived." I went on chatting in this vein, making inane observations and telling flaccid jokes. In a while the quartet warmed to my sallies and a meandering, pointless conversation began.

"The city is eager for the Feast to begin," I said. "Never have I counted so many Jesters. There's a Bennio here, there, and everywhere—except in this part of town. Not a single Jester have I seen along the wharves."

They considered in silence until the affable one said, "You have come too early."

"How is that?" I signaled for another round.

"Late in the night, you might see a dozen or more just outside the door."

I turned to the other two. "Have you seen so many Jesters?"

They shrugged. They did not care to pursue the subject.

I asked the woman. "You see 'em?"

"I do not like the Jesters," she said. "They order rum, they drink it down, they run away, singing some poor rhyme or other about Bennio's privilege during his Feast."

I recited:

> *"Come pour Bennio his mite of drink*
> *That gives him fuel with which to think;*
> *Then fill his empty cup again*
> *To stay the raging of his brain."*

"That's the one," she said, "or one very like. They all sound the same to me, and they all result in my loss."

I laid down another small silver. "Custom rules all," I said. "I'll stand for the Jester's score this once. Does he—do they—often come in here?"

"Too often," she said, picking up the coin.

"They come ashore at night in cockleboats," my conversationalist said.

"From what ships?"

"Those we never see. There are only three at anchor now, not counting the *Tarnished Maiden*."

"The *Maiden*?" said the sullen one "That is no vessel at anchor. That is a hulk that Ser Arbolo has let lie to rot. Time the hull was stove in and the hulk sent to the bottom, say I."

"But men go out to it or past it," said the other. "Some got up as Jesters."

"How do these new Jesters perform as clowns?" I asked.

"Like serpents trying to play lutes."

I saw that the remarks of this informant unsettled his companions; they shifted apprehensively in their seats.

"The plazas are filled with unfunny Jesters and stumble-foot acrobats. Few are suited to the roles. It is well they follow other trades to earn their bread," I said.

The third man broke his silence. "I followed the sail for nigh forty years. Many a first mate racked my hide who should have been tending sheep on the mountain. What calling do you follow?"

"My father wanted me to be a thief," I said. "My mother desired me to become a celibate priest. And so I ended by doing naught, wasting my days with ale and female."

"That is the best way to live," said the ancient tar. "How do you furnish it?"

"The unwary are my benefactors. Listen! I seem to hear one besotted prospect calling from Daia Plaza for me to come deliver him of his o'erweighty purse. I must bid you good night." I swallowed my last and left.

--->=◎=<---

I entered Chandlers' Lane in a bemused state of mind, thinking on my encounters in Rattlebone Alley. If the intelligence I had gathered was even partially accurate, Astolfo's fears were justified. Under the confusion of the Feast a strategy was going forward that involved the Society of Jesters, the ritual of the coffin burial, and the safety of the city.

It was dark now, but the windows and doorways of the workshops were open and brightly lit. In time past, all the candle-makers had set up in this street, and though new ventures had lately found quarters here, there were still a score or so of candlers, some of them of a third or fourth generation in the trade.

Now, though, these artisans were turning their hands to another kind of facture. This was the season of masks, and Tardoccan masks were objects widely sought after. These were not the flimsy wooden masks layered with white plaster so common elsewhere. These were constructed with a linen foundation to which pitch was applied. Then the interiors were waxed with one ply of wax and the outside with as many waxen layers as desired, dyed and sculpted to the buyers' directions. After the hardening, the candlers applied thin glazes to which our firm contributed shadow-tints. In broad daylight our tints were invisible to most eyes, but in the flickering candles of the Feast, they yielded expressions that charmed or alarmed.

If logic applied, the tradition of the mask must seem ridiculous. The purpose of the mask is first of all to conceal the wearer's identity; the second purpose is to signal that the wearer is engaged in the festivities, eager to share in the pranks and counterfeits and amatory antics and satiric frolics to which the season gives license. During these days nobles turned into draymen, young maidens donned the faces of slattern hags, women changed into men and men into women, and men-women changed into women-men. No stigma attached, not only because of the customary practices of the Feast but also because the masks sufficiently hid identities. Why then would one commission a mask whereon the features were tinted with his or her own shadow, teasing strangers and acquaintances with hints about who one was?

Astolfo had offered his thoughts. "The most of our clients do not intend to hide themselves within or behind shadows. Their purposes are cosmetic, to emphasize and augment certain physical attractions or facets of personality. The tall woman who fancies she bears some aura of mystery will have a light shadow applied to her face and upper torso. It serves the usage of a veil without the awkwardness and obviousness of draped cloth. She thus underlines her attributes."

"But misapplication is ruinous," I replied. "The loose-lived bravo who wishes his fellows to think him dangerous and more foolhardy than he truly is will shroud himself in an umbra so ominously black he looks like he has fallen into a well."

"Thus, like the woman, he gives himself away by hiding himself."

"But the one instance is by design and the other, stupid one is not."

"And so," Astolfo concluded, "one of the first principles of our craft is illustrated. *The shadow reveals by concealing.*"

That principle of the trade might well apply to most of the practices of Feast time, I thought. This carnival gives opportunity for individuals to open apertures upon some other self which in part they naturally already are. He who has but one self has no self at all, saith ancient Q. Curtius, and I may add that his adage is doubly true of females. Is there any woman anywhere who is not in some

large or small part of her nature a cat or a willow tree? And breathes
there a man who is not also a dog?

⊷═◉═⊷

As I made my way back toward the center of town, I saw that the
number of revelers had increased, though there was not an oppres-
sion of bodies, as there would be later on. Torches lit the way and
various strains of music filled the cooling air. I quickened my pace,
for I wished to visit again the site of the entertainment of the Green
Knights and Verdant Ladies, the narrative of the monstrous
Mardrake and the heroic Perseus. The last time I came here I was
rudely reintroduced to my long-disregarded brother, an unpleasant
encounter.

I was surprised when I arrived at the garden guild's entertainment area to find only a few onlookers watching, without keen
interest. The scene in play was the most exciting one, with the
Mardrake advancing to menace Andromeda. Here was a different
and more frightening monster than before, more voluminous, darker
in aspect, with motions of tentacles and pseudo-limbs strongly convincing. The movements were languorous as the appendages rolled
outward, the tentacles waving slowly at their tips; it was such a kind
of movement as one would envision to take place underwater. Out
came the Mardrake from the waves—which were suggested by the
undulating shadows of vines and broad-leaved saplings—and it unscrolled itself toward the rock where the princess was chained.

But no princess stood there. The players were only rehearsing
the scene, trying to get the apparatus to operate satisfactorily. The
unfurling-refurling of the beast was superior to that of my earlier
experience and I surmised that Cocorico had arrived and was ma-
nipulating Sbufo's bladders and levers, playing out his part.

There was another difference also. The shadows the monster
cast were not stable in outline. As one round tenebrous mass rolled
forward, its edges were torn away, leaving fluttery rags that seemed
to writhe in agony. In the main body of this shadow holes appeared,
small at first but slowly enlarging until the mass of it presented the
appearance of a great, coarse mesh. These debilitations slowed
the progress of the Mardrake toward its goal; it did not halt, but
every forward motion it made seemed to pain it harshly. Then the
interior mass was eaten all away and the scene stopped before its
conclusion.

"A thousand, thousand curses on these plants!" a voice cried out. "Can we not learn to regulate their appetites?"

This would be Cocorico, vexed nearly to his patient limit by our shadow-eater plants. We had warned the wise ballet mistress Anastasia that these plants were perhaps not sentient, or at least not completely sentient, beings. They could not be trained as dogs and monkeys and novice dancers might be trained. We had warned her too of the dangers of them and I had described at length what would happen if one of them fastened upon the shade of one of the actors or stagehands. I told her, "Only imagine what would happen if they got free into the audience. You can almost hear the shrieks of men and women and children whose shadows are being devoured."

She had listened in solemn silence but was determined to acquire the effect that the hungry ravaging produced for the performance. In that regard she was canny. I could see that those writhings and fervid surges would add wild mood to the scene.

Yet it was a perilous decision. Mutano and I had set up a small square tent of black velvet behind the stage in which the plants were kept dark and watered when not active onstage. We had carefully explained how to transport them from spot to spot and had warned one and all of the danger.

Cocorico was execrating the plants at length as I departed. I judged that the rehearsal was stalled, perhaps for hours, and I was a-weary of footing about. I trudged to the livery stable, mounted, and rode back to the manse and put me to bed supperless.

When Sterio, our shy client, told us he would never again put on the harlequin costume, that he was finished with the Society and the Tumulus ritual and all that it entailed, his little black-eyed dog seemed to regard him mournfully, as if he had lost his true master. He had arrived driving a cart with the effigy and stick-puppet to be buried. The puppet, Dirty Bennino, was tucked into the left hand of the effigy.

"Do you fear for your life?" Astolfo asked.

It was the mild mid-afternoon and the four of us stood by the paddock fence, watching as the groom forked orchard-grass hay into the feed troughs. The season was too early for foddering with hay, but the horses had been put up here so long they had denuded the enclosed turf of grass. A wisp of hay rode the breeze to where we stood and Sterio plucked it from the air and slid it into a corner of his mouth. "I am fearful," he said, "but I think they dare not take my life. My role in the Feast ritual is too prominent. As the Ministrant, I am central to the proceedings."

"Is not the purpose of our antagonists disruption?" I asked.

"Yes," he replied, "but if the disruption comes from an outside force, the agents would give themselves away. It must appear to be missteps of my own or of the others involved."

"Well then," said Mutano, "we must make them show themselves. Let no fault of ours be used as excuse. Would you like to inspect the coffin and cart?"

Sterio followed us to a shed on the upper side of the paddock, where Mutano peeled away the canvas wrapping. He looked over the coffin, paying close attention to where the angle of the harlequin diamonds met the edges of the oblong box. With the coffin he seemed content, but the cart brought a hint of frown. "Is this not a little overdone?" He pointed to the design on the wheel spokes.

"We wanted to stand out from the others," Mutano muttered. He was disappointed that his artistry was challenged.

"It will do well," said Sterio.

"Perhaps it would be good to make sure that you have settled in mind all the proper steps of the ritual," Astolfo said. "We must not let the blame fall upon you. Let us watch your progress through them."

"If you insist," he said. "So . . . The approach must be made in this fashion." He breathed deeply, then took a slow step forward and after a hesitation carried on as he had been taught the tradition commanded. It took no longer than the third part of an hour for him to complete his role, but then Astolfo requested him to repeat the whole, and then again several small passages within it. He answered to every suggestion, though obviously puzzled about the maestro's reasons.

"I thank you for your patience," Astolfo said. "You have provided us with a safeguard against our carelessness. We shall be able to know if you have gone amiss at any point."

"I shall be watched closely by many sets of eyes, if I were to perform. But I think I shall avoid that danger. I have hoped that I might hide myself here with you until the Tumulus hour has passed."

"If you do so," Mutano objected, "the ritual will not take place and our opponents have won the day. The Feast will fall into confusion and the people's discontent may well turn into riot, as happened in ancient time when the traditional Saturnalia was forbidden by a new cult of overly ascetic priests. The invaders would love to see that happen."

"I did not accept the assignment at risk of my life, only of my shadow."

"You will be protected," Astolfo said. "Mutano is there beside the cart; Falco is in the forefront of the crowd at the site. They are both armed and ready to defend you. I too shall be nearby, taking stock of the spectators, looking for anything untoward. Osbro must stay to watch the villa, but he can be called for if necessary."

"You must judge me a craven," said Sterio. "Yet if I meet a foe face-to-face, I bear my part without qualm. In this affair, I do not know whom to trust or from what quarter attack may come."

"We shall be doubly, triply alert," Astolfo said. He turned to Mutano and me. "Shall we be prepared?"

"We shall," Mutano said, and I nodded.

"If so you say." The tone of his voice betrayed Sterio's doubtfulness.

"Let us go apart," Astolfo said to him. "I will give further assurance and you can demonstrate again certain steps of the ritual I may already have misremembered. While we do so, Mutano can unload the effigy and stick-puppet from your cart."

⊷≡◉≡⊷

Next morning the four of us sat at table in the kitchen, Osbro being admitted to our group. He was accounted one of us now, fully a colleague.

"Time is narrowing," Astolfo told us. He sipped at an herbal brew steaming in a clay mug. Each of us was consigned by the maestro to this drink, with which we nibbled little oatcakes sweetened with honey. "We must set out our purposes; we must plan how to achieve them; we must act."

"Our worst difficulty is that we are fighting cobwebs and moonbeams," I said. "Who are our foes? What do they want? How are they to advance against us?"

"If we act upon my small set of premises, our endeavors may be wholly useless. Yet if we do not act at all, we are certain to lose the struggle," Astolfo said.

"How do you define this struggle?"

He gave me a glance, mildly questioning. "What would result if the ritual were disturbed and the face of Bennio were not discerned within the moon?"

"Nothing of consequence," Mutano declared. "It is all empty show. The vulgar crowd would be angry at first and then only out of sorts. Survival is not at stake."

"The people would be dispirited and confused," I said. "They would be unwilling to join together in any concerted plan of action."

"The city would be unsecured?" Astolfo asked.

"For a short time," I replied. "For five, six, seven days, perhaps. Then all would return to the state it is now—except that the usual grumbling would be louder and more acerbic."

"I will propose that during that time, in the dark of the moon, a pirate force will advance upon the town and be aided by those they have implanted here. Once it is taken, they will use this city as marching armies use small villages—seizing treasure, killing the men and youths, raping, murdering, and enslaving females, usurping the Council duties and taking hold of the governance of the town, despoiling the urbs entirely, and leaving it to the mercies of kites and crows. That is why the ritual performance must fail."

"Fail?" Mutano and I spoke in concert. Osbro shook his head.

"I shall make certain that it does fail," Astolfo said.

"But maybe our Misterioso can bring it off correctly," I said.

"Please be attentive, for the projections I lay before you are intricate, difficult to grasp in the whole, and uncertain of even a partial success. If our schemes prove vain, the result is disaster. I do not request your approval; I count you as already enlisted in the effort. Knowing what you know, you are now active players. The dangers are acute and the plan, I say again, is complex in all its parts."

Osbro, Mutano, and I looked at one another like men ordered by a trusted mentor to leap from the edge of a tall precipice into an abyss of mist.

Mutano and I signaled our readiness. Osbro hung back a little, then took a breath and said, "I am willing."

"Very well," Astolfo said. "Now each of us must take up separate tasks and responsibilities, but all efforts must knit together at the appointed times. Here is what I envision. . . ."

He was meticulous, even tedious, in his explanations, but we were grateful for every detail he outlined. He had convinced us of the magnitude of the peril and of the urgency of our separate duties.

⊷⊶

My first duty, which I had to attend to by myself, was to seek out allies and cement relationship with them. It was to my old friend Torronio that I turned. We had kept in contact with each other as best we could. He was still hiding in exile, and this meeting had been difficult to arrange.

"It has been a long time since we took the plants from the Dark Vale. I had thought you would communicate before now," Torronio said. He tossed the twig with which he had been toying into the small fire we sat beside. The flame responded with a lick of black smoke. The fire was not for heat; this night was warm, its breezes welcome. We only desired illumination out here at forest edge, away from the trail. Our horses champed the long grass, their brown eyes orange with firelight. An owl sent its challenging halloo across the darkness.

"How so?" I asked.

"The rumors of unrest are abroad. Even an exile like me hears mutterings. And you were seen gathering gossip in Rattlebone Alley."

"If you have spies in the town——"

"Not spies. Only observant acquaintances."

"Observers, then. I recognized the Molvorian accent of the old sailor in the tavern in Rattlebone Alley. This conference with me means that you maintain hope of regaining your former station."

"I am not averse to returning to society. I tire of contemplating the objects of nature. The poets may have all my share of the crags and ferny glades and limpid springs and triumphal rainbows."

"Does your band of robbers share your distaste for the natural world? Are the Wreckers thinking of becoming potboys and horse traders and gutter-muckers?"

"The Wreckers are no more. You remember that the man you named Goldenrod fell victim to those soul-snatching plants. Since that time Sneakdirk, as you called him, took a fall from a precipice as he was gathering samphire. There remain only Squint and Crossgrain."

"And Torronio."

"And myself, yes. But three can hardly make up a band, especially as we have little contact nowadays." He found another trifling twig and laid it on the fire.

"Could you gather them to you to join in a task that entails some danger and good hope of reward?"

"Coin?"

"In abundance—and also a pardon from the Council for all crimes and malfeasances of which the band has been accused."

He showed surprise. The shifting light on his features gave him an apprehensive expression. His time of exile had worn his spirit ragged. "Do you have the promise of the Council that we are to be forgiven?"

"No. But Astolfo is confident that if our venture succeeds, you and your comrades shall have the freedom of the city, along with handsome emolument and the comforts of female comradeship."

"You mentioned a danger."

"In the secret transport and directed igniting of oils and other flammables. We shall face an enemy force unknown in quantity. But you and Squint and Crossgrain have faced perils before and have come off well. All necessary equipage shall be supplied, for there must be digging of fosses also."

He passed his hand along his forehead as if to relieve the pressure of uncertainty. "When would this action begin?"

"In a few days." I handed him the little pouch. "Here is coin for present expenses. If you accept it from me, that means you have accepted the offer."

He paused a long moment, then took it in hand. "Now the night is less friendly than before," he said. "I seem to feel enemy presence about us in the darkness. It is only my fancy, I expect."

"It is a fancy worth heeding," I said.

The owl had quieted. We listened to the silences gathering in the forest until I rose and we stamped out the puny flames. He mounted and rode slowly into the woods and I came back to the villa the long way round.

⌗

In the morning Mutano and I were giving cart and coffin a final, slow inspection. All was perfect, as far as we could tell. We spoke guardedly about our roles in the impending conflict. We needed to know in a general way what each was doing, Astolfo had said, but the particulars were best known only privately. If one of us was captured, he could give up only partial intelligence.

Now Mutano was complaining about the arrangement. "By whom are we to be captured? What could they learn from us? Nothing from me, for I have but the flimsiest speculation of what the whole of our strategy is."

"You have been practicing to regain your cattish tongue of late," I said. "Are cats to take part in our defense of the town?"

"The maestro assigned me to inquire among the beggars' guild and the cats that gather to 'em about strangers that have come to town and in particular about newcomers to the harbor area. He has convinced me that the invasion is to take place a little at a time. That those who have dispersed themselves within Tardocco will join with others at the harbor near the mouth of the river, and that at a certain signal a ship anchored in the bay will dispatch trained and armed groups to meet with others and overwhelm us all. It will be all of a sudden, a lightning strike. Astolfo desired for me to estimate how large is the number among us already."

"Have you made a guess?"

He brushed invisible dust off the coffin and replaced the wrapping. "They are fewer than we feared. No more than a hundred, perhaps. These are to be joined by another forty or fifty from shipboard."

"So few?"

"They are trained and bloodthirsty. If we were not forewarned, this town would be easy prey."

"Yet Astolfo did not forewarn the Civil Guard or the private guard forces of the nobles and the wealthy."

"He is uncertain how many are trustworthy. Maybe these groups have already been seeded with turncoats."

"I do not understand this strategy," I said. "We are a puny number. There must be schemes in place you and I are ignorant of."

"Well, look for the *Tarnished Maiden* to play some part in the fray," Mutano said. "I tell what I was enjoined to keep secret."

"The *Tarnished Maiden*? That derelict has lain in the harbor for years, awaiting its destruction by the owner. If Ser Arbolo had not died and his sons were not still at quarrel, it would be in pieces at the bottom of the waters. It is not fit for action—for anything."

"So I would have thought also. . . . What is that sound?"

I listened and finally heard shouting and wild music a long way off. "Revelry. Some Feasters are impatient."

"'Tis yet but a few days. They will tire themselves and sleep through."

"Unlikely," I said. "The antics and entertainments will begin in earnest now. I am looking forward to the gardeners' guild presentation of Perseus and the Mardrake."

"You may be somdel disappointed," Mutano said, "for Cocorico is not to perform the Mardrake role."

"Why not?"

"The maestro has made him and Sbufo associate with me in our defensive maneuvers."

"What can a dancer and a puppeteer do in the way of mounting a defense?"

"I cannot say, but maybe Astolfo will reveal his mind to you. Do you not confer with him in private today?

"In about an hour from now."

"And I confer with you and Osbro afterward. The maestro is very secret in this business."

⸱⊷═○═⊶⸱

I was to speak with Astolfo in the small library, but when I arrived the door was closed. This was unusual, for it was heretofore left open always as an invitation for Mutano and me to come study the lore of umbrae. Here stood shelves with every knotty, grime-laden text on the subject that had emerged since the invention of writing. Or so the weariness of my eyesight had often suggested.

I knocked and heard him invite me in and entered.

He was not visible. A long rank of lit candles sat on the table to my right and the curtains were drawn to let in light on that side. I closed the door, supposing that privacy was in order, and stopped some eight paces into the room.

There I halted, suddenly overcome with a sensation like nothing I had felt before. A dizziness powerful enough to cause me to totter struck upon me and I experienced a paralyzing bewilderment. It was something like rushing up a flight of stairs to come to the top and find that the steps ended and there was nothing there, nowhere to plant one's feet, so that one had to hold back by the balance of the toes alone. It was almost to plunge into the blue depths of empty sky. My breath flew out of my chest, and I gasped to bring it back. The room pitched and yawed like a vessel in choppy tides.

Such were the physical sensations. But there was another feeling too, a dreadful loss of some sort, as when one learns of the sudden death of a dear friend or relative, of an event so unforeseen it seems incapable of taking place in the world you know. Yet it does take place. It has already taken place. Some part of yourself has been subtracted, some aspect of your person has been canceled. At this moment and always afterward, you are a different being from what you had been and what you might have been.

Astolfo spoke from behind me. He had hidden behind the door as it opened. "Your shadow is safe," he said. "It has found its place in the mirror."

One of our large blue mirrors stood at his left-hand side. The servants must have brought it down from the hall on the third floor. I looked into it but in this light could discern nothing. "If I do not sit, I will fall," I said.

He grasped my elbow and led me to the chair at the end of the table. "Compose yourself." He took up the decanter there and poured a glass of ruby wine. "To restore you."

I sipped and sipped again. The taste was different from any wine of my experience. I sniffed at it.

"No," he said. "It is a vintage familiar to you. But as your spirit has altered, your senses too have already altered and many things you will now begin to know in a new ways."

I took another sip, tasting. "I feel as if I just now forgot something important to remember."

"You will find that you have not. Yet you will always feel that you have."

I coughed. "Why did you steal my shadow?"

"You must not go into this impending combat wearing your primary shadow. Its loss in that way could mean death, or worse. Now your umbra is in the protection of the house. You must choose from our stock the one you will wear in the struggle."

"It will not be the same. I have lost something of great value. I do not know why I say so."

"It is a loss, but it brings advantages. You will find your nature more changeable, more quickly adaptive to fresh circumstance. You will gain facility with other languages; you will have a surer sympathy with other people and with animals. Witness Mutano, how

cleverly he learned the feline dialect and how he communes with
cats—with dogs too, if he so desired to learn. He could not do these
things if he were still chained to his primary."

"Then I shall be less myself than before."

"Less a Falco in some indefinable measure, yes. But not less
a man."

"Mutano told me that he had given up his shadow because you
advised him to do so. For a thief of shadows, or a dealer, to retain
his primary left him vulnerable, you told him. He did not speak of
these advantages you name."

Astolfo smiled. "He does not know of them—or at least he has
not thought about them. He *surrendered* his shade, and his mind is at
peace with the exchange. Your shadow was *severed,* and so you have
a sense of violation. The results shall be similar in the end."

"Why did you sever mine? I would have given it up willingly."

He shook his head. "You would not. You thought to sever it
yourself but could not bring yourself to do so."

"How come you to know that?"

"It is written into the history of the shade. I have examined these
umbrae for many years. They retain the marks of intention as well
as of deed for those who can distinguish the signs. Have you not
deduced the characters of men from their shades? This ability is but
a refinement of that one."

"Then you may know many other things about me I would not
wish known."

"I am almost certain that I do, but I know not which ones they
may be. You have attempted to read my shadow time and again.
What have you learned that I would keep concealed?"

"You do not wear your primary. You store it safe away in
the jewel in the leopard's-head buckle. If I read your present
shadow closely, I only read the history, a small bit of it, of another
person."

"Your thought is largely true, but the umbra of another changes
when it is attached to me—and the history of that person is changed
also."

I took a swallow of the wine, then drained the glass. I was becoming accustomed to the new taste of the familiar vintage. "You
claim, then, that you can transform the past life of another simply
by assuming his shadow?"

"Transform, no. But an alteration occurs. And it is not *the* past life in singular number. We all have innumerable past lives and wear them the way we wear innumerable shadows."

"I must find time to study these matters."

"I urge you to do so. Meanwhile, you must choose an umbra to keep you company in the combats near upon us. You know your tasks assigned and when they are to be fulfilled. Choose accordingly."

I rose, placed my hand on the table to steady myself, and spoke softly. "Very well."

As I was leaving, Astolfo began to extinguish the candles.

⋆┅◉┅⋆

I mounted the stairs. Tall lancet windows on the other side of the hall let in a mellow late summer light. No shadow companioned me. I was strongly aware of the fact. Even though I am engaged in the complex trade of umbrae and think upon them unendingly, I am usually not much more attentive to my own than are most other people. I take it for granted, knowing, without knowing, its position nigh to me and the general look of it. It is like a part of the body, unobtrusive as long as nothing ails it.

Now I had none. I did not feel unclothed. One's shadow often mingles with other shadows, as when one walks through woods or stands in the shade of a wall, and then it is unseeable; there is no feeling of nakedness then because the knowledge that it still exists and will make its presence known in the light is constant.

This sensation was more like a kind of loneliness that settles upon the spirit at a certain marked time. Some episodes of our lives close forever; the experiences we had felt during those times we shall never experience again. So it is when friends or siblings or pet animals die or when a lover bids one farewell forever or when we forget the sound of a piece of music but longingly recall our former fondness for it.

Having never before been without a shadow, I had never desired to have one. But now I did, and this sensation too was novel. It was not like hunger or the spur of lust. Perhaps many of us wish for a friend, a silent confidant who knows our desires and fears without our having to confess them, a respectful but impartial other whose otherness is not a separating quality. Perhaps that friend is and has always been our shadow, an amicus whose absence is the first palpable sign of its past presence.

The shadow is one's other that is not another.

⊶⊷

For my role in the invasion defense I needed, I thought, a dark shadow, black but not conspicuously so, with the ability to move furtively. Our battle was to be nocturnal. Yet it had to be able to withstand a sudden onslaught of light as a necessary part of our counteroffensive tactic. I recalled such a one as being stored in the fourth mirror in the row and I went to it, to stand and peer.

To look into those dark blue mirrors where umbrae are stored is like looking into an empty concert chamber to see what echoes remain. It is as much a matter of projection as of perception. At first nothing is there. Then, as eyes accustom, hazy shapes appear—or almost appear. In time these shapes acquire characteristics, partly seen and partly remembered from the first encounters. One may say as much of acquaintances newly met after years have passed. "Is that truly you, Jacopo?" we say, descrying features half recognizable beneath the changes time has wrought upon them.

Minutes drew past as I stood, trying to sort out one half shape from the others. When I fastened at last upon the entity I wanted to call forth, I discovered my gaze could not steadily fix upon it. The shade I sought seemed to avoid my attentiveness, drifting behind other umbral figures. The chore was something like trying to hold in mind one certain passage of smoke from a campfire as it ascended into the nighttime.

Something was distracting me, and finally I comprehended. A shadow I did not desire to wear was making itself known to me, standing unmoving while the others wavered and slipped into the depths or sidled toward the edges of the glass.

I rested my eyes upon it and was at first not impressed. It was not as dark as the one I had sought, nor had it the other's force of presence. It was a dark gray-blue hard to make out in the glass and its outlines were more sinuous than martial. I fancied it not the most proper for the warrior-personage I must become.

But as my examination continued, I began to see these characteristics in more useful terms: *discretion, gracefulness, judiciousness, persistence,* and *alertness.* These were qualities that Astolfo and even

Mutano had remarked as lacking in me at times. It seemed that this shadow sensed those weaknesses and designed to repair them.

I turned the mirror sidewise to the light from the windows and stood straight and still before it. *"Friend,"* I said, and after slow moments the shade came from the glass, passed through my body, and took its place on the floor, joined to my right foot-sole. In its course it touched my *vis* like the quick dust-brushing of a moth wing.

X

The Absent Shadow

I had well understood that Astolfo had regarded our present mission as being of utmost importance, but when he severed my shadow, he forcibly impressed upon me the ominous urgency of our undertaking. He must foresee and comprehend certain future emergencies that I could not glimpse. Otherwise, he would never have taken my umbra in so abrupt a fashion. Born in Caderia, I could not easily sympathize with the Feast of the Jester, nor understand its importance to the townspeople. Mutano, of a severely skeptical turn of mind, dismissed it as sham. Astolfo viewed it in his usual unhurried, thoughtful way: It was an established custom, and not to be perverted to base ends or used as a disguise for violence upon Tardocco. The custom must be protected.

So I attacked my separate duties with fresh resolve, even those that entailed some amounts of confusion and tedium—as did this immediate task of training my brother for his role in the impending conflict.

I had not expected that Osbro would be able to read a map. He could not read written words; "quill droppings," he called them. Even so, I had drawn a map of the city, using for a general scheme old maps we had at hand, newly revised by my recent, hasty investigations, and he was able to keep the plan of the town orderly in his head. We sat side by side at the table in the small library and I reviewed the sheet with him. It was not necessary to gain a detailed picture of the river Daia, I said, in order to know its banks and piers and jetties, its depths and shallows, swift stretches and obstacles. He followed my instruction in patient silence, tracing with his finger on the page the courses and features as I described them. When he failed to understand he would give me a questioning look.

He did so now, tapping one section of the stream with a well-tended fingernail. "This?"

"Yes, here beneath this pier, a drain empties into the river. Bear well away from the pier or the inflow will turn your boat sidewise to the current. Then it would be difficult to straighten again. Are your navigational skills improving?"

He sighed. He would rather not have been sitting by lamplight during this jolly blue morning with its birdsong and sunbeams delighting the jolly outer world. From afar we heard the muffled, rag-tag sound of revelry. It would soon be time for the Tumulus ritual celebrators to reach our grounds and he would fain be among the masqueraders. He was to accompany Mutano in the cart.

"I navigate the best I can," he said, "but I don't know the ways of boats. I think the one I've been given is not much of account. The what-you-name-it, the rudder, is clumsy and hard to turn. The flimsy thing seems hardly stuck together."

"Sbufo rebuilt the boat according to the plan that he and Astolfo drew up. He is considered a good craftsman."

"It looks like it'd fall apart if a gull lit on the front."

"On the prow, you mean. If the boat falls apart, it is designed to do so. You have boasted of your swimming prowess. La Pluma taught you well, you claimed."

"She did not teach me how to swim in rivers. We swam in a pool of Dove Creek under the willow trees. There were daisies in the grass along the bank."

"I hope you will not tell me that she twined them into your hair."

He reddened a little and returned his gaze to the map. "How about this place here?"

"A sandbar that is not always there. You need not fret about it. In fact, if you keep to the main current, in the middle of the stream for the most part, you need fret about little on the seaward course. When you enter the harbor it will be difficult to reach your object. The tide will be with you, but you will have to push hard to reach the ship."

"If it is there."

"As the maestro said, we must act as if it will be. We must act as if all his guesses were certain facts. Otherwise, we have no procedure at all."

"I would like to know many things more."

"As would I. Now, as you enter the harbor the dilapidated hulk called the *Tarnished Maiden* will be on your left-hand side. On the starboard lies the stretch of inner shore where the water is too shallow for ships to anchor. From that shore the great firelight will come. As soon as you see the flames leap up, you are to attack the pirate vessel, abandon your craft, and swim to the *Tarnished Maiden*. Do not be frightened by the appearance of the hulk but get you aboard where you will be safe."

"All this I've been told already. Why should I fear what the old derelict looks like?"

"Because Astolfo says it may present a fearsome appearance. That is all I know."

"And then?"

"Then your part in the fight is concluded until you row to the wharves. There is a dinghy for you and the others."

"What others?"

"I do not know. Perhaps it is best not to."

He rubbed his neck. His doublet held at the neck a collar of fresh, stiff linen, and this fashionable dress was uncustomary to Osbro. He was used to the countryman's open collar and spacious smock. "There is much we don't know. It is like gathering roses in the dark o' th' night."

"Astolfo says—"

My sentence was interrupted by Mutano, who, after a casual knocking of the doorframe, entered to tell us that the procession was drawing nigh to our eastern gate. It was nearing time to join with it.

I turned to Osbro. "We will discuss the map and the plan of action again if you desire."

"If a question comes to me. But I reckon I got it in mind."

We followed Mutano. He was striding along eagerly.

⋅→━◉━←⋅

The cart stood just outside the gate, looking trim and handsome in the cool light. In the bed lay the coffin; it should contain, according to ritual protocol, an effigy of the ancient Bennio; the small stick-puppet Dirty Bennino that was Bennio's mascot; and the shadow of the Ministrant that custom decreed must be buried in the Tumulus when the crescent moon stood in its zenith.

Defender waited in harness. When we arrived he turned his head to give Mutano a most reproachful look. He was no work-horse to plod along, trailing a cumbersome, humble cart; he was a proud mount, lively in spirit and courageous of heart. He did not understand why he had been consigned to this drab duty or why Osbro, Mutano, and I were dressed all in black trunks and doublet and with a short black cape lined with green. Astolfo had ordered this livery because it would stand out from the great display of har-lequinades the revelers would wear. We would be able to recognize one another with ease.

"All must be dependable," Mutano had said. "We cannot pre-dict what will happen." For that reason, Defender had been uncom-monly well foddered and curried for the past few days. This was another of the numerous cautionary measures the maestro had set forth, many of them superfluous, as he had admitted. But he quoted the proverb, *"A lace untied—and woe betide."*

We had laid a board across the front of the sideboards for a seat and on one side sat a fat cushion of harlequin cloth red and blue and yellow. This was for the driver, Mutano said.

"Why none for me? Why must I sit on bare oak?" Osbro asked.

"Defender declared he would not pull the cart with a plough-boy perched on a cushion like one of the grand," Mutano replied. He had to speak loudly, for the procession was drawing closer upon us.

Osbro let the weak jest pass.

It was time for me to find a space across the roadway from which I could enter into the crowd as it passed, while keeping close to our conveyance, alert for possible trouble.

Now, as the procession passed around the slow, sweeping curve of the roadway that joins with the Via Daia, we heard more brightly the piping of flute and aulos. Drums rattled. Dogs barked. Pipes squealed. The noise of the trudging clogs and wooden-soled boots upon the cobbles was like the sound of a great rain hurtling upon a hard-baked plain. Now and again a trumpet or sackbut would bray, recalling the Jester's mocking strain:

"Crambo and crooked Bennio goes,
  But what the Jester knows, he knows."

They were well in sight, the flautists and pipers, the brasses and the drums, and after them came the populace of the city, so motley in dress, station, and degree that they resembled in total aggregate the idea of a bedraggled Harlequin, a communal personification. Yet they were different individuals. Nobles were borne forth in chairs and litters; wealthy burgers rolled along in gaudy two-wheeled carriages. But even the well horsed could go at no faster pace than the crowd afoot allowed. Scolding mothers and tipsy fathers, flustered nursemaids, one-eyed beggars, and wide-eyed scullery maids jostled against one another, each hindering the passage of each, some shouting, some singing, some silent and sullen.

Following this crush came the mountebanks. The Jester representation was the most popular, but there were Pantaloons and Columbinas and Petralchios by the dozens, walking upon their hands, or skipping, cartwheeling, tumbling, and leapfrogging when space afforded. The prettiest Columbinas found opportunity to strike poses—and to strike the faces of loungers who offered ungallant addresses.

Then came the trades—the cobblers, millers, weavers, carters, wheelwrights, potters, tinkers, seamstresses, locksmiths—workmen and their masters and apprentices, striding, sauntering, lolling, strutting, essaying what gait soever their feet might fancy. I saw the household of the cattery mistress, Nasilia, all in a group and observed that the crowd thinned about them, avoiding the smell they bore.

Varied bands of young folk followed, their dress parading some of the causes and factions of Tardocco. The charities for the crippled and wounded and leprous sent maidens with baskets of blossoms to strew; the guild of Green Knights and Verdant Ladies sent a quartet of lads and lasses decked out in foliage that served as scanty clothing; the Red Fletch Society of Archers lent the procession a line of tall sharpshooters, so attractive of feature as to make maidens blush at their own fancies.

At the last trailed those of grave visage: the savants and pedants, the scriveners and keepers of documents, the philosophers natural, moral, logical, and cosmological. Some of these were robed and wore the pomegranate-shaped hats peculiar to their academies; others affected for modest purpose the homespun garb of carpenters and smiths. Among them trod the priests of colorful deities and mystic tenets in silks and velvets and bleached linens, barefoot or shod in homely sandals.

This latter flock was raucously attended by a rabble of grinning urchins and querulous dogs. Many of the urchins were pebble-pelters, and they recalled Bennio's old cry:

"Pay no reverence to the graybeards old;
  Their pizzles are puny and their brains are mold."

The crowd parted on the other side of the roadway, allowing Mutano and Osbro to insert our cart into the procession. When we joined the progress and our cart was known as the vehicle for the harlequin coffin, a shout went up and a nearby trumpeter sounded a tucket. Then the procession went forward again at its uncertain pace.

I could see nothing amiss, no Jester-figure poised to leap aboard the cart and tumble out the coffin or to seize the reins from Mutano and speed the cart away from the rout, ruining the necessary, pre-scribed ritual Such a gambit would not be possible, anyway; the crush was too close-packed.

So I walked along, watching Defender as he nosed ahead. I took careful note of the members of the march. Two housemaids were gossiping about a Bennio of their neighborhood and finding that they differed in estimate of his character. The tall one with the high-crowned hat of white felt recounted how this local Jester had com-forted a lad during his long illness and, by causing him to smile at his jollities and japes, had restored his appetite so that the medico then was able to bring him to health. The shorter, portly one in black bombazine complained that this same Bennio had filched a ring from her sister and given it to her rival for a certain Giacomo's affections.

"Giacomo the smith's prentice, you mean?"

"Yes. That is the one."

"Who received this ring from Bennio?"

"A hussy named Cecilia."

"She of the house of Masilio?"

"Yes."

"Then the Jester but returned the ring that belonged to her al-ready. She was betrothed to Giacomo, only he claimed to change his mind. 'Twas a shame upon her. But when Bennio returned the ring the shame was on her betrayer. Giacomo has now repented and sues to win her back. It was a good deed of the Jester."

I stepped away from this chattering pair and fell in behind a piper who was at the moment not tootling but making repair to the mouthpiece of his instrument. The remarks of those two women were typical of the accounts of the Jesters that were always abroad during Feast days. Some saw the Bennio as an instigator of mischief; others knew him as a purveyor of helpful deeds. They were glad to forgive his coarse and fleering ways, his pinching and poking and playful buffets. For every face he presented to the gaze he had also an obverse, and both of his faces were widely witnessed and consistently contradictory. Astolfo had voiced a thought about the original Jester that I did not comprehend: "Every jest at which you laugh is also one at your own expense."

The maestro was nowhere to be seen. All Mutano and I knew was that he would be close to us during the burial ceremony, looking on, like myself, to forestall whatever tribulations might befall. He would be disguised, I suspected, as another of the Bennios who infested the late afternoon landscape. Our cart was to join the Ministrant at the Tumulus, there to be unloaded by four dark-robed members of the Jester Society.

The brief rite would then take place, with the Ministrant uttering the traditional phrases and making the traditional gestures. There would be chanting and dancing by torchlight and then the torches and all other lights would be extinguished. The coffin would be thrust into the ground and sod laid over it. At the moment the final clod thumped down upon the small harlequin coffin, the moon would be at its zenith and upon its face would appear the features of the original Bennio—his cocked supercilious eye, his hooked nose, his sneering grin and up-jut goatee, the cap with its jaggedly cut headband low on his brow.

This visage of the Jester anyone might sight any time of year in clear weather with the moon in crescent phase. Only the ritual of the Feast brought the image to fall sharply upon the eye, to the wonderment of children and the amusement of their parents, and to the fond reminiscence of the old folk. The Jester was at home in the moon once again: Let Autumn come with his cornucopia; let Winter follow, shivering in his white, beggarly rags. Clown Bennio will have put his humpy shoulder to the wheel of the year and nudged it onward in its course.

My most pointed attention I gave to the many Jester figures. Our client, il signore Misterioso, had caused us to believe that the counterfeit Jesters were part of the forces bent upon the seizing of Tardocco. I watched as many as I could, noting which ones were accompanied by dogs and subtracting them from suspicion. A false Jester would not have had time to train an animal. I kept a careful eye on the children as they watched the Jesters at their antics. If any hint of fearfulness appeared in their eyes, I subtracted those Jesters also, having concluded that the true Jesters had something of a sinister cast to their characters which would alarm children, however slightly. Most of the remaining clowns were ordinary citizens no more skilled at the role than I was. Among this cram of folk the infiltrators would be hard to distinguish and I tried to think of details that might single them out. Astolfo had asked Osbro about accents and vocabularies, but the general hubbub obscured much of the talk. The Jesters whom I took pains to walk among were mostly silent, except when the impulse rose strong within them to burst into one of the old refrains:

> "Once he stands in the moon uprose,
> The world well knows what Bennio knows."

The procession was enlarging in number. From parkways and side streets and alleys celebrants poured into the press. The day was growing late—the western sky was purpling, the eastern going silver-gray. The moon was visible, a sliver like a toenail paring, but it was not yet at zenith. The noise of the people had grown quieter, though horns still bleated now and again and an indecent rhyme or two burst forth at intervals like shooting stars into a twilight sky. It would be yet a while before solemnity took hold, but I began to feel its imminence.

I edged toward the cart, needing to take a place close by it before we reached the Tumulus. As I made my way across, I saw one of the Jesters who was following a swaggering bravo produce from his busker's shoe a dainty scissors and neatly clip away the purse that hung by a thong from the youth's embroidered linen belt. I pretended to lurch into the thief, excusing myself clumsily. "Mi spiace, signor. Scusi." "Per n'ente," he replied, revealing with his dialect that he was no native. I could not place the origin of his accent. Now I looked to find other Jesters close by who would be associated with him, but I could spot none with certainty. He may have been no more than an ordinary thief, come to the Feast for the rich pickings.

As I brushed by the young man who was the victim, I turned and pointed at the Jester and made a scissors-sign with my fingers. The hero felt for his purse, then grasped the Jester by the wrist and demanded the return of his silver. As this altercation continued, two other Jesters came forward to take the thief's part, shouting angry words in that same dialect. The conflict broke off when the thief dropped the purse to the cobblestones and dodged into the crowd and his confederates disappeared.

I could not decide. Were these four men among the force of infiltrators? Their outland accents would seem to furnish evidence. Yet why would an invading band risk making its presence known with petty thievery? Also, this incident took place so far from our cart that the false Jesters could offer it no threat.

We are still battling cobwebs, I thought.

⋆═◉═⋆

Now the Tumulus came into sight. Here was the grassy pyramid, about one story in height with two smooth, well-grassed, small terraces built into its sides. Upon one of the terraces was mounted an earthen platform where the Ministrant stood with two black-robed aides beside him. He was robed in a violet-blue silk the color of the darkening sky above us. A hood covered his head and below it hung a Jester-mask different from all the others present. It was Bennio's form, but the face was of shiny white, a polished lacquer, while the mouth and eyebrows and daggerlike goatee were not red but of the darkest black. Around the eyes were large black circles and the mouth too was black, not shaped in the fleering grin but downturned in a deeply mournful expression. The Ministrant moved his head slowly from side to side and the mask made it seem that he was searching through the crowd to sight specific individuals.

This was not the traditional aspect and its effect upon the press of people was powerful, though not immediate. Some few minutes were required, but little by little the rhymes and singing quieted, the horns and harps silenced, and the babble halted.

Mutano stopped Defender and tied the reins to his seat-board and then he and Osbro stepped back into the bed of the cart. They moved with grave deliberateness and their black livery emphasized the slowness of their motions. The two aides who had stood beside the Ministrant now left their posts and descended the molded sod steps to level ground. They marched slowly, slowly, to the cart. Mutano and Osbro delivered the coffin into their hands.

When they received the box they turned it crosswise so that its head rested on the shoulder of one and its farther end on the other's shoulder. Then they marched back to the Tumulus and began the ascent, taking each step with utmost care. But even with this cautious slowness, the right-hand aide made a misstep and the coffin slipped off his shoulder. There was an intake of breath from every person in the crowd. The sound was like the hiss of a great sea wave as it rushed against a cliff side.

The aide reached around and caught the box. If it had fallen, it would have tumbled all the way to level ground. The two of them paused to readjust, then climbed again to reach the platform where the Ministrant stood looking out of his Tragedy Mask.

Cut into the hillside behind him was a grass-covered door and he pulled it slowly open to reveal the darkness of a crypt the size of a shepherd's hut. He stood to one side and intoned in a voice that echoed hollowly from the interior of the mask words that I could not understand. Maybe they were sounds that were not words.

The silence of the crowd was broken by a single despairing female voice: "No!" She understood that the ritual was being disordered. The worst kind of fortune must ensue for all the citizenry. Such things she would have heard from her grandmother and mother. No variance was allowable.

A dread moan ran through all the ranks of celebrants, wordless but with a music such as a dying windstorm makes.

His wordless roar sounded again from the Ministrant's sad mask.

From below rose the voice of an old man: "No!" He began to sing the ritual rhyme the ceremony demanded: "Crambo and crooked Bennio goes—"

The Ministrant's chant grew louder. It was like the crackling of lightning strokes along a mountain crest. The elderly man fell silent. All were silent, even the children and dogs.

The aides brought the coffin to the Ministrant. He made passes above it, fluttering his hands in a silly, meaningless fashion. Then he stepped aside.

The aides carried the coffin into the earth-crypt and the Ministrant slowly closed the sod door, sealing them inside. He turned about to face us in the crowd below and removed his Tragic Mask to reveal a face painted in the likeness of the original Bennio. This image served momentarily to reassure the people, but I discerned features familiar to me beneath the clown makeup.

Here stood Maestro Astolfo before the multitude. He had assumed the role of the Ministrant. He who always shunned the plaza, the market square, the harbor-side or any other public place now exposed himself to the gaze of all. Few would recognize him, I thought, because most of his traffic with clients was through Mutano and me and the direct encounters were conducted in an easy and modest manner in private. He was ever a mild and affable man in his dealings and took pains not to make himself notable.

Still, there were bound to be some present here who would recognize him.

He raised his arms to shoulder height and the copious sleeves of his twilight robe unfurled like the wings of a great sea-ray, fluttering silently. His voice, though hardly stentorian, would be audible in every corner as he began to chant:

> "You witness now, my friends, the night
> When all is wrong within the rite.
> When celebration of the Feast
> In th' ancient fashion must be ceased,
> For now there hangs upon our town
> A doom that shortly shall come down."

As this strain was concluding Mutano had already unhitched Defender from the cart and brought him forward to the foot of the Tumulus. Osbro accompanied him and I made my way to the pair, trying to draw no attention to myself.

Astolfo concluded:

> "Look to yourselves, your families;
> Lock your doors and guard your keys;
> Find your sword and keep it nigh,
> Lest the enemy happen by;
> Trust no man, no woman, or beast,
> In this dark hour of the Jester's Feast."

Now the three of us ascended the Tumulus, stepping slowly up the sod-plots, and watching for any threatening advance toward us

by a band of false Bennios. Closely as I looked, I could find no aggressive actions. The crowd was in a state of dazed confusion; some
of the servants and others looked on openmouthed as Astolfo sang
his mocking song of warning. Those individuals of higher station
murmured to one another; they were trying to comprehend whether
Astolfo's performance was a serious warning or only another
jesting prank that might suit the occasion in some newfangled
manner.

We had feared, when planning our strategy for this hour, that
some spectators would be so enraged by the disorder, the perversion,
of the ceremony that they might attack our pseudo-Ministrant. So
now we formed into his bodyguard and stepped to the second foot-
hold below, placing our hands on our hilts but not withdrawing
our blades.

> "Heed the warning that I give:
> Defend yourselves to keep alive;
> Find your homes, depart this throng;
> The hour grows late, the time is wrong.
> The Jester sits not in the moon—
> Look you above: It sails alone!"

He raised his hand and pointed and everyone look to see the
truth of this words. The Feast had failed. The moon stood directly
overhead, but no features of a mocking face were to be seen. It was
a moon like any other in crescent phase—reddish, familiar, and
leprous-appearing in its patchiness. The ancient Bennio had scorned
his Feast and turned his hunched back on Tardocco and on all the
world.

Astolfo again opened the door to the crypt. The light was nigh
leached from the sky now, but the crowd was able to see that the
Ministrant's two aides appeared before them in ordinary dress, no
longer robed. They came out, bearing the gaudy coffin. They held
it between them and slowly and officiously removed the lid to
disclose—nothing.

The coffin was empty.

No Dirty Bennino, no Jester effigy, and, though the onlookers
could not see what was missing, there was no shadow of a Ministrant.

Two black cats ambled out of the crypt and sat down on either side of Astolfo and looked down upon the crowd with disdainful gaze. It was as if they usually inhabited this hole in the hillside and were mildly annoyed at being disturbed by a sullen mass of human beings.

For the folk had indeed become sullen. Discontent showed plainly in their postures, and groups of them moved restlessly, shifting their feet. They looked to one another. Their Jester-masks turned left and right; the small children clung to their parents, sniffling; the elderly muttered oaths. The general mood was testy and could quickly become violent—as we had feared.

Astolfo descended hurriedly to the level of the roadway, we three flanking him, though still with blades undrawn. Mutano grasped Defender's reins and handed them to Astolfo as the maestro mounted. Then Osbro lifted the tongue of the cart from the ground and gave our colorful conveyance a backward push. The men and women behind scrambled to avoid its crush, jostling and cursing. One old woman fell to the ground and was pulled out of the path of the cart at the last moment by an alert chambermaid. A number of the brawnier men ran to slow its progress, grasping the sideboards. Others gathered and, straining from behind, brought it to a standstill.

It was a brief distraction, but it afforded all the time Astolfo needed to put his heels to Defender's flanks and canter away out of the crowd into a side path and then away into the darkness of the grove that surrounded the Tumulus.

In this failing light the confusion was such that Osbro, Mutano, and I were able to lose ourselves in the moiling crowd. Harsh cries of protest rose and scuffling broke out. Parents sought after their children. Some of the elderly wept, while others looked about hollow-eyed. Fury and black melancholy reigned among the skeptical, as well as among the faithful.

Mutano had claimed that the Feast was a spurious, vain, and contrived celebration, empty of any content but its own tradition. Perhaps he was correct from the logical point of view, but logic was not in force now. Unaccountable feelings held the people in sway. Emotion ruled, as it did during wrestling matches, horse races, and other heated competitions. The people of the crowd discarded their individual identities and the whole mass of them became a single entity with a confused and powerful *vis* and without the capacity for orderly thought.

Ill will would fetch the populace to fiery violence if they could locate a blamable victim. But the disarray was thorough. Most of them did not comprehend what had taken place; they only knew what had *not* taken place. The ceremony was ruined; the lunar Jester did not show his face; the peace of Tardocco was despoiled. The city stood in danger from some source it could not name.

◈

It was long past midnight before we made our separate ways back to the manse. I walked with wary caution, fearful I might be recognized as one of the four men who had undermined the climax of the Feast. I need not have been so apprehensive, for the citizens I observed were preoccupied with their own thoughts and injured feelings. They gathered in muttering groups at lane intersections and around the doors of crowded taverns. No trumpets rent the silence and no flautists embroidered its dense fabric. The folk eyed one another with suspicion and spoke abruptly each to each and not at all to those unknown.

When I came into the house I heard the sound of earnest voices in the small library and found there Astolfo, Mutano, Osbro, and our Misterioso client seated at the table. Their late refreshment was again herbal tea and oatcakes.

Astolfo gestured me to sit and hearken to Mutano's complaints.

"I see what we have done," Mutano said, "but my intellect does not stand so tall as to enable me to comprehend why we have done it." There was a hint of whining in his tone, almost cattish.

Astolfo, mildly: "What have we done?"

"We have mocked and sucked dry of meaning an ancient tradition."

"One that you did not believe has any meaning," I said. I set the mug before me beside the clay urn and Osbro filled it with the steaming tea.

Mutano waved my remark aside. "I had thought it was our duty to preserve the ritual from interruption or abuse by those who would harm us. Now we have accomplished what we feared from them—the dispiriting of the populace and the confusion of their purposes."

"And nothing else?" Astolfo asked.

"Now they are forewarned," I said. "In your changes on the Jester's rhymes, you have proclaimed to one and all of the dangers that lie before us."

"The enemy is also forewarned," Mutano said. "The infiltrators could hear your strains as clearly as I."

"And so?"

"You have forced their hand," I said. "The Civil Guard has been alerted, the houses will bar their doors, the old and defenseless will fly to those who are armed and prepared. Our foe had not counted on preparedness. Now they must act swiftly. Maybe they will have to act before they are ready."

"Well—and are we ourselves ready?" Astolfo asked. "The moon will be dark for a very short space now. Within that time the attack will come upon us under cover of the deepest darkness and our enemies shall have the advantage of the weakened power of will of the whole citizenry."

"I am prepared," Mutano said. "I can play out my part on the *Tarnished Maiden* along with Sbufo and Cocorico."

"I am prepared," Osbro said. "I have been working with the boat and believe I know how to control it."

"I have rehearsed my duties," Sterio said. "I think I shall be credited."

"What are your duties?" I asked. "I have not been told of them and do not know how they fit with those of my band of defenders."

"You are not involved with Sbufo's part of our activities," Astolfo said. "But let me introduce our valuable Misterioso client at last. Now that the Feast is done, there is no harm in your knowing his name. He is Signor Alfredo Tristia, a privy councilor to the magistracy of the city. He serves with us. His duty now is to return to his fellows of the Jester Society and inform them of everything that has occurred between him and us."

Mutano slapped the table sharply. "We know of infiltrators in the Society! Why do we tell them of what we have done?"

"Might be, to smoke 'em out," Osbro said. "The ones that are angry about what we did will act unfriendly toward the signor. The ones that wanted the ritual disrupted won't say anything. They will be the foe."

"A distinction that lacks clear definition," I said.

"But I know these men," Signor Tristia said, "and their reactions will either confirm or disarm my previous suspicions. I shall be able to gain a reliable tally and I will report the number to Maestro Astolfo. And then my role is played out. I shall join my family in a village in the mountains for the time being. I cannot safely stay in Tardocco."

"And so we only carry out our plans as before," Mutano said, "with the added small advantage that we now have some vague notion how many false Jesters are leagued with the pirates. But also there is also the disadvantage that they know who we are and how many—or, I should say, how few."

"And how vulnerable," I said. "So they will hasten their attack before our numbers can grow."

"How are our numbers to grow?" Mutano returned. "Except for the maestro's warnings in Jester-rhymes, the populace has no inkling of the struggle that impends."

"Is that not a favorable circumstance?" Astolfo asked. "If we had to repulse a well-planned attack with an undisciplined citizen force, ill armed and untrained, the result would be a limitless carnage. To chop down beardless youths, braggartly bravos, enfeebled old men, and foppish nobles would be a merry pastime for Morbruzzo and his minions. Tardocco would suffer the fate of Reggio and all the other port cities that have fallen to sea-invaders. The only hope I can envisage lies in the strategy we have laid out."

"Which must go exact at every point," I said. "If one of us fail in any one detail, we are lost—and the town destroyed."

"Well," Astolfo said, "all here have signified their readiness except yourself. Are you prepared for the exercise?"

"I should like to speak to you alone on that score," I replied.

He gave me a look which betrayed some surprise, a most unusual expression for the maestro. "In this matter, what touches one touches all. You may voice your concern here and now."

I spoke firmly. "I think not."

"Then you and I shall retire to the kitchen for a space while Mutano talks through our strategy once again."

He rose. I followed.

―――◦◦◦―――

A low rushlight was burning in a small, homely lamp in a shelf beside the sink, so that the room was gloomy. Astolfo sensed as much and said, "Let us take something a little more martial in spirit than tea." He reached down a bottle of wine spirits from the cupboard and poured two little glasses. He set one atop the big butcher's block in the center of the room and hoisted himself up backward beside it. I pulled a leather-strap chair to a near table and sat.

"I do not believe that your courage fails," Astolfo said.

"I mistrust Osbro's capabilities. He knows nothing about boats and currents and such."

"Little is required to know."

"I would be better placed in his part."

"You cannot swim."

"If all proceeds as it ought, I would have no need."

"You risk your life pointlessly."

"It is no great risk."

He bethought himself a space, then said: "You wish to supplant your brother in the greater danger?"

"Yes."

"After this long time you have discovered a reservoir of fraternal affection. A season past, you might have called that sentiment an infirmity."

"Perhaps so, but my argument stands. I am better fitted for these duties."

"That may or may not be so. How comes it that Osbro knows how to swim and you do not?"

"He is my elder. While his tutoress, La Pluma, was teaching him to swim, she was teaching me to read."

He chuckled and sipped daintily at the powerful liquor. "She was an instructress of varied talents."

"And of joyous appetites." I raised my little ruby-colored glass etched with a grape design and matched his imbibing in polite daintiness. This bit of a drop held a touch of heat.

"Well, it is true that the part you first took upon yourself is less difficult and much less dangerous than the venture with the boat. And in that other effort you would have your friends by you."

"Torronio and Squint and Crossgrain, yes. They are indeed our friends. They are taking a large risk also. If the pirates are victorious in this struggle, they will execute the Wreckers when it is done."

"The Wreckers?"

"So they call themselves after being falsely accused of drawing ships to wrack with deceptive signals."

"They have been in hiding. How did you communicate with them?"

"I left a cipher message at two taverns. Torronio has paid observers about the town to keep abreast of affairs. He harbors hopes, I believe, of vindicating himself and returning to his former station in society." I tasted the liquor again. Along with its dark heat there hinted fruit; cherry, perhaps.

"If we are victors, his family will welcome his return and Tardocco will proclaim its gratitude," Astolfo said. "After the event he can reclaim his life of old."

"That is why he is prompted to this action."

"And what shall you do after it is over, assuming that we are successful?"

"Why, shall we not take up again our former lives also?"

"In the shadow trade, you mean?"

"Yes. What else might we do?"

He drank off his glass and leaned forward, elbows crossed on his knees, and spoke in a firm tone different from any I had heard him use before. "It has always been of secondary—nay, of accidental—importance to me, this business of umbrae. I am beginning to think I have given to it a sufficient amount of my lifetime."

"You mean to give up shadows?"

He looked at me steadily, his expression mild as always but earnest in a new way. "My passion was at first and ever afterward to speculate upon the nature of the world—the truth, if there is one, that lieth within or beside or beneath or above the order of everything that is and is not."

"You will pursue philosophy?"

"I began my investigation not with things, which are only materials, after all, but instead with shadows, which are commonly viewed to be but insubstantial hints, the dim echoes, of things. By thinking upon shadows, I hoped to make, as 'twere, a flanking sortie upon the riddle. If shadows are but the hints that objects and personages trace against the light, shall not the hint whisper more of *essences* to us than the objects themselves reveal? . . . So ran my thoughts at first."

I reflected. "This seems a most roundabout method of proceeding. It is like studying the life of a spider by examining her web. If you never laid eyes on the spider itself, you would have an inaccurate and probably an exceeding strange notion of the animal. Her handiwork can tell you little."

"Spiders perish by the thousands, leaving often their webs behind. The web is their essence, their signature upon the spaces of the world. The spider is a thing of parts—eyes, legs, mandibles, gut-pulp. The web is one single thing, beginning to end, no matter how complex the pattern it holds."

"And so?"

"It required some little time before I understood the principle: Things composed of separate elements must pass away and discompose. A human person is made up of flesh, bones, blood, organs, and of mind and spirit. When a woman dies, her corpus becomes again those separate parts, and each of the parts, and the smaller parts of those parts, rejoin with the elements of earth and sky to which they are most closely related. Even stone, under the press of weather and the wear of time, can come apart to particles finer than the whitest flour."

"But—"

"But the woman's shadow is a unitary and undiscomposable entity. It may change in shape and tint and size and in details, but the material of which it is made is always consistent with its essence. Its soul and body are one and the same. The shadow therefore is eternal. That thing we call its *caster* is temporary and accidental. What is eternal is real. All else is transitory falsity."

"Now I gain importance in my own estimation," I said, "as one who trades in eternals."

He sighed at my impertinence and signaled that we should try the liquor again. I was agreeable and wished my dainty glass larger, particularly because I comprehended that the maestro was bent upon talking at length in this vein. I listened attentively; I supplied him with questions. Though the matter of his talking had nothing to do with the crisis at hand, I did not interrupt and tried to follow the train of his thought. It was as if he had kept these notions in the dark bottle of his mind and now released the stopple and poured them out in a heady winelike stream.

At one point, he spoke of shadows as being possibly sentient entities and said that if that were the case, we could no longer treat them as insensible objects. "That is why I wish to make a more conformable arrangement with shadows before time harvests my weary flesh. I must rid me of my proprietary habits of mind and observe more closely, in case the shadows desire to communicate more fully than I have understood. When I relinquished my own umbra, my sympathies and comprehensions broadened and deepened. The same thing happened when I took your shade."

"How now?"

"You have resolved to adopt your brother's more dangerous part in the coming fray. Answer me this: Do you believe you would have done so if I had not nipped away your shadow the other day? Does its absence not exert you toward a warmer sympathy with Osbro— and with others also, perhaps?"

"I cannot say."

"Think upon it."

I set my little glass on the table and pushed it from me with the tip of my finger. "I will consider these matters after the conflict. The dangers at hand occupy all my mind. I take it that you approve of our exchanging roles?"

"Yes, if you explain to Osbro carefully his new duties. And you must send word to Torronio that a substitution has been made."

"I shall do these things. What else must I attend to?"

"I know of naught else now, but leave me alone with my thoughts."

"Good night," I said.

I went into the library, where the others sat in conference at the table with maps and lists spread out before them. I tugged Osbro aside and began to acquaint him with his newly acquired role.

XI

The Shadows Among Us

We could afford no longer delay. The night following my private meeting with Astolfo and the subsequent hour with my colleagues, I walked to the Daia. I took obscure byways alongside the parks and plazas. The houses I passed in this midnight hour were silent and dark and I fancied there were eyes upon me behind curtained windows—but then I smiled at my apprehensions. I knew these domiciles by daylight as the ordinary houses of shopkeepers, lesser officeholders, ship owners, and the like. It was only foolish little fears that made the back of my neck feel so unprotected.

I reached the river unmolested and, I assumed, unobserved.

The sky was full of stars, but they were more distant than ever and the night was one of the darkest I could recall. I could see no lights as I shoved off from Sandpoint Landing a little distance above the upper park. The lanterns and torches that had brightened the Jester's Feast were quenched and the tents and pavilions and re-viewing stands taken down. Only the barking of two restless dogs marked the silence. Tardocco was still under the pall of its disappointment with the failed festival.

Feelings had run high at first and rumors arose that violence might beset Maestro Astolfo; his hand in the disaster was widely suspected. But the occasional loud outbursts had now given way to a general discontented muttering, a surly public mood from which no reprisal would emerge. Even so, the maestro kept close to his studies and strategies in our villa and did not show himself outside the house.

These studies and plans required his keenest attention, and ours as well. Mutano, Osbro, and I were at his side from the beginning,

and in the later development the puppet masters Sbufo and Cocorico were to join us, as were Torronio and his associates, though
always under cover of darkness. Our strategy was intricate, composed of several parts that must fit closely, and I was to be the principal agent of action. This was the role I had requested, distrusting
Osbro's ability to carry it through. Astolfo ascribed my taking the
role to fraternal affection. If this were true, his surmise was justified by premises I did not understand.

At any rate, here I was, determined to guide our little craft down
the Daia into the harbor bay. It was a balky vessel, some twelve feet
long by five across, with only a rudimentary rudder to point her
and a flimsy pole to keep her off the banks and some infrequent
silted shoals. Osbro had tried his hand at piloting her and had named
her the *Reluctant Maiden,* playing upon the name of the deserted hulk
in the harbor called the *Tarnished Maiden.*

It was not so imposing a boat as to deserve any name at all,
though she was indeed reluctant to obey her tiller. She had been
made over to look as if she were adrift, an orphan escaped from her
moorings. Such wayward vessels were not rare, particularly during
the times of festival when owners flushed with wine or overly eager
to impose themselves upon women were careless of their duties.

She was to be unremarkable, to attract not even casual notice,
insofar as that were possible. And she was to move and otherwise
appear as if unmanned, and so I had to lie prone on her bilgy
bottom for much of the length of my journey. I was required also
to raise my head above the gunnels to find my bearings and to ascertain the positions of stars, but for the most part I must drift blindly
down the river, trusting to instinct and my preparatory study of the
currents—and to fortune.

If the *Reluctant Maiden* nudged her prow against a pier or any
other obstruction, she would come all apart to separate pieces. I
would be boatless in the swift reaches of the upper river—I, a man
who could not swim.

If she ran aground or cracked sidewise against one of the moored
boats scattered along the irregular banks, I might well be discovered by agents of our enemy. The hour of attack upon the town
was nigh. We hoped it would not come this night, for we must strike
first. This suddenness would be one of our few advantages, we
being so pitiably few in force. If I were found out, that would be
mortal for our strategy—and for me too. I was armed only with

my short sword and a brace of daggers. Beside me in the boat lay a pike with a rusty old lancet blade; it would be of little use in defense; the barge pole might make a more effective weapon.

A crude, short paddle lay by the pike. If I had not gathered enough momentum to reach my objective when I got into the bay, I would employ it—to little effect, I thought. Stuffed beneath the box that housed the tiller was an inflated oilskin bladder Sbufo had fashioned as a flotation pillow for me when the boat disjointed itself.

With the thought of reducing my visibility, I cloaked with the shadow that had made itself my comrade. Its gray sinuosity might be less conspicuous than a sharply black blot against the starlight. In a night so deep as this, if I made my motions gradual and kept close to the inner shadows of the sides, I should go unseen. The umbra I wore had another use also, one even more important to my well-being.

The length of the vessel from the stubby little bowsprit to about one-third of the way to the stern was covered over with black cloth, part painted canvas and part worn and damaged velveteen. This covering had been patched together from various sources, principally from the small tent that had enclosed the shadow-devouring plants during the Green Knights and Verdant Ladies' presentation of the story of Perseus and Andromeda. The covering served now the same purpose as before, shielding from the light as many of the umbra-eaters as Mutano and I had been able to crowd into the space. If an unhappy accident occurred and the plants found a way to come at my shadow it would be perhaps more difficult for them to discern than one of velvet black. A paltry protection, I thought. I was in danger as much from the plants inside my boat as from the enemy outside it.

Now that I was upon the Daia our offensive was under way. Osbro would be in the company of Torronio and his crew, Squint and Crossgrain and the others, on the western beach of the bay. There a narrow stretch of silvery sand lay in a crescent along the water in front of a grove of palms and its line of tall, thick undergrowth. Double trenches had been dug from one end of the beach to the other. The bottoms of the trenches were lined with gunny and old canvas and over this covering were laid stooks of long rushes that had been soaked in oil. To top off his preparation, Torronio had flooded the trenches with all the flammable liquids he could lay hands on.

All this lighter together ought to make a sizable and surprising conflagration. Torronio only awaited my signal to spark it. Osbro should now be at his station there with Torronio, watching for the first entrance of my *Reluctant Maiden* into the bay waters. We must act in concert; the double watch at the trench sites should make us a little safer.

The most bothersome difficulty was that I had no way of keeping an exact time; an approximate timing would have to suffice. I had a shuttered lantern of the kind we used when tending the shadow-eater plants in the converted stable and the candle it contained was graduated with bits of scarlet string tied round to mark off some of the important points I must pass. But I could open it only now and again to snatch a brief glimpse of the taper for fear its flicker would give me away. I must resist the temptation to open the shutter more often than completely necessary.

Too much the success of our enterprise depended upon guesswork. Where had I drifted to by now? I could hear only the silken murmur of water sliding seaward and its gentle push against the sides of the boat. I would not cover enough distance in my voyage to make use of the stars to determine landward points, but I could keep the boat fairly well aligned with the aid of star positions.

Now I smelled something different in the Daia water, an odor of fetid orts and slops, of the carcasses of spoiled meat and fowl, and the leakage of jakes. I was at the spot where the large drain from the rows of the great houses rolled into the river beneath its surface. The complaints of the larger populace against this noisome adulteration were continual and not modest in volume. The Council had taken no steps to halt the poisoning and to protect the Daia because they could not think how to do so. "We lack imagination," Ser Vennio Colluccio said, confessing the truth. Maestro Astolfo had offered a plan to the Council which they had rejected on the grounds that none of them could understand what he had proposed.

This drain was a landmark. I was now a little less than a quarter of the way. I ventured a glimpse of the candle and found it shorter by that correct amount. Soon my ungainly boat would gather speed as small tributaries—streams and pebbly creeks and runoff from springs—fed into the river. To prevent my having to raise my head above the gunnels, the tiller had been fitted to protrude into the boat through the stern, and this arrangement made the handling of the rudder clumsier than it would otherwise have been, for the slot through which it was allowed to move back and forth was but a short two feet. In my practice attempts that had been sufficient room, but I had doubts upon this matter when it came to the hour of action.

I had doubts upon many matters, doubts upon doubts redoubled. Sbufo and Cocorico were the cleverest puppet masters, contrivance-builders, and originators of stage effects that Tlemia Province ever had seen, but the project that the maestro had envisioned and laid upon them was large in conception and onerous of construction. Mutano was with them as guard and overseer on the *Tarnished Maiden* and if the enemy boarded that decrepit hulk he could fend off the intruders for a good long while. Pirates or no, they would rarely have met Mutano's equal with weaponry.

Still, if the old ship had not been refitted properly, or if some pulleys and linchpins and blocks and hinges did not move at will, my colleagues would be helpless to prevent all of them from meeting a damp destiny at the bottom of the bay. The crux of the action was in the timing of its parts.

For the pirate ship had now arrived and was lying at anchor toward the seaward mouth of the harbor. The *Tarnished Maiden* sat only three ship's-lengths aft of it toward the wharves. The pirate crew would see no danger in this invalid derelict—which had recently listed more than usual, as if slowly taking on water, and so our enemy had anchored closer than prudence normally would suggest. Mutano had first sighted their presence and reported it to Astolfo. The seemingly careless position of the pirate vessel was encouraging.

But that was the intelligence of yestere'en, and it was the present moment that pressed upon me. If I were not occupied with the toil of directing the boat, I might have fallen prey to a palsied fear.

A particularly difficult stretch confronted me at this point, where two streams poured in from the left bank and another, slightly southward, from the right. The conflicting currents created a sort of slow, wide whirlpool that might turn my *Maiden* in a circular path. If the stern got pointed downstream, I would be unable to square it about before the swifter flow of the Daia caught me. I needed the force of the river full at my stern when I reached the bay, for our plan was to ram the pirate vessel and it would require all the strength I could gather to propel me across the calm water. There was no thought of an impact powerful enough to inflict damage on the big ship, but a direct, head-on contact was necessitous. Any different contact would be in vain.

So when the currents on the stern from portside began to force the bow to port, I strained on the tiller with all my might. I glanced into the river, trying to see the flow of the currents. I caught my breath and managed to stifle a startled oath. The water was scattered with faces, faces everywhere, bearing the crooked nose and unbalanced grin of Bennio the Jester.

It took a short moment for me to comprehend that these were masks. The revelers of the Feast had pitched their masks into the river and streams, disgusted by the collapse of the ceremonies. The masks thumped gently against the sides of the *Maiden* and there was a disheartening moment when the boat stalled and the Daia began to tug it about. I was able to hold fast, though, and then the opposing current took hold and the prow righted and came around toward the big yellow star, Egeria, that drooped over the harbor, a familiar guide for all mariners who sailed the coastline.

The *Maiden* was now moving quickly and steadily and Tardocco slipped by me on both sides, a great unconscious presence in the nighttime. I could smell the odors of the town: the dusty-grass smells of the racetracks, the beery, stale fumes of taverns and stews, the aromas of fresh bread from the bakeries that must labor in the night, the unmistakable musks and eye-watering perfumes of Nasilia's cattery, the faint whiff of salt in the mild breeze from the open sea. These smells were guideposts that told me in loose terms my positions on the river.

The cattery smells reminded me of Mutano's stratagems. My cumbrous comrade had conferred with Sunbolt and reached an agreement. The great orange cat, perhaps as a gesture of gratitude for the gift we had given him of his new mate Asilia, had agreed to gather to our cause a brief alliance of the cats of harbor-side. These were to be our spies, taking note of the beggars and broken-down sailors and ship-jumpers and escaped slaves, relaying what intelligence they might. It could not be completely reliable intelligence because the feline race, and the wild and independent males in particular, have little interest in the deeds and motions of human

beings, except as these affect their dietary situations. Even so, Mutano had been able to collect some details and had made some
plausible surmises and had relayed them to Astolfo. The arrangement still held; those cats even now observed activity and gave
disordered and often confusing reports.

Any fact or rumor Mutano could glean might be of use to the
maestro, for it was the duty of his post to try to find out the number and placement of those agents who had already infiltrated Tardocco. They would be in hiding all along the wharves, most of them
waiting inside the great, dark warehouses. I had felt presentiments
of them when last I visited the precincts of Rattlebone Alley. The
foe was among us; we could not doubt it. When the pirates came
ashore, the traitors would welcome them and the two forces would
join and advance with naked blades upon the helpless avenues and
sleeping houses.

⊷═◉═⊶

I risked taking a look abroad. The boat was now in the heart of the
city, where the streets ran like wheel spokes into the plazas and
where the civic buildings sat. The squat barracks of the Civil Guard
huddled between a small slot-windowed gaol and the grander, brick-
faced Hall of Justice. There the magistrates and their clerks, the
attorneys and their scribes, spent long days trying to keep solemn
faces and accurate, current accounts of complaints, grievances, petty
crimes, and the occasional gruesome felonies. I barely made out the
shapes of these structures against the western horizon before I pulled
in my head again and concentrated on the tiller.

I had expected that some inn or other would keep late hours
for the bibbers in their gardens, but there was no sound of revelry
or of the quiet, amorous plaints of lutes and citharas beneath the
casements of comely females. Eros had withdrawn his unpredict-
able persona from the midnight. It was not merely as if the Feast of
the Jester had failed and the original Bennio had refused to impress
his features within the moon, it was as if the ancient clown himself
had been found dead in some prominent square of the city and now
the world wore its mourning black and suffered its sorrowful de-
spondence in a silence as deep as a ravine.

If the time was gloomy, if the hour was deserted, if all movement ceased and all activity stalled, this was how Astolfo desired
the state of things to be. Tardocco lay torpid; it seemed to invite a

dire fate to fall upon it. It lay apparently undefended, as ripe for the taking as Psyche awaiting Eros or, perhaps more appositely, as Andromeda powerless before the Mardrake.

Though now a Mardrake was to be our ally.

So we hoped.

For sixteen seasons now I had depended upon the resourcefulness of Astolfo. I had learned to trust his knowledge and skill and to hold fast to his counsels. Times when I thought his strategies fanciful or impossible of fulfillment, I was proved mistaken. Plans difficult to picture, much less to fathom, resulted in happy outcomes, usually with coin in their wakes. But our assault as laid out this night seemed so knotted in conception and so circumstantial in its details that I allowed misgivings to tickle my mind. To keep them at bay I tried to imagine what our lives would be like if our schemes succeeded. There would be a large change in the way we kept ourselves, but I could not foresee its character.

If we succeeded, the city fathers would show their gratitude. How could they not? They would reward us with coin and perhaps at last the commerce of shadows would be recognized as legitimate and shed the unsavory reputation that tacitly clung to it as its unwelcome umbra. I would walk abroad as a partner in our enterprise, as respected as any overseer of a lord's estates.

I recalled my private conference with Astolfo. He desired to give up the trade of shadows. If I understood correctly, he was determined to devote himself to the study and rigors of philosophy. He would not engage, however, in the pursuit of logical corollaries and cloudy theorizing. The maestro was in search of some sort of entity that embodied an absolute purity of reality, a being so completely unsullied of spirit and body that its shadow would be . . . What?

I could not envision the thing he tried to describe when I sat by his side and fortified my powers of comprehension with cherry brandy. It had characteristics belonging to shadows, but it partook of an ideal I could not limn in my mind. If it was an Ideal Shadow, what could it look like? Would it even possess physical attributes? I certainly could not picture this entity while lying soggy is a disintegrating boat with my life in continuous peril.

But now the muting of the sounds of the river dispelled thoughts of Astolfo and his strange ambition.

The *Maiden* was entering the harbor waters, and at a rate of speed that propelled me a fair distance into the bay toward my goal. But soon my progress slowed, for even with the tide in my favor the current was quickly dissipated. Only a few Jester masks floated along here.

I opened the lantern shutter. The candle was half consumed. Now was a moment of great risk, for I must raise the lantern and show a light visible to Osbro and Torronio on my starboard side and to Astolfo back on the wharf I had just slid past. I held it aloft, keeping its enclosed, blind side toward the pirate ship, and turned it three times the other way, counting to five on each turn. From the beach came a brief answering flicker and then in a moment a soft knell, much like the sound of a bell buoy, came from the wharves. That would be the reply from Astolfo's set of recruits. There was no signal from the *Tarnished Maiden,* but Mutano at his post there would have noted the two signals I received.

The pirate vessel lay directly before me. She appeared to be some distance away, but she also seemed immensely big. Perhaps the darkness enlarged the image of its bulk, for it looked mountainous to me in my shabby little boat, and the notion that I was on the attack against the big three-master struck me as the foolishest conceit the maestro or anyone else of sound mind could ever entertain.

My *Reluctant Maiden* was small, but she was well named. Her drift had slowed more than we had counted upon. The only means I had to make way forward was the short, crude paddle that I must use directly from the stern, working as best I could around the rudder. Oars were out of the question, their lengths too easy to remark by sound and sight. The paddle was a desperate expedient, the only thing we could think of. We were landlubbers, Osbro, Mutano, and I, and even Astolfo's grand store of general knowledge was scanty in regard to matters maritime.

When I confessed my ignorance and complained of it, the maestro replied that the task must be undertaken and that if we were better versed in the ways of water, we would be too knowledgeable to allow ourselves to make the attempt. "We would realize it as impossible?" I asked. He quoted the old saw, *"Fortune may favor fools,"* and added, "And we know that we are fools. That is why we have made such careful plans."

And so I paddled onward, straining and formulating vile, silent oaths. Yet I must have made better progress than I had thought, for when I twisted about to look, I found I was quite close upon the big ship. I had passed the *Tarnished Maiden,* now abaft to port, and bobbed within the shadow of my objective. I estimated her distance to be an approximate sixty-count forward, and then I opened the lantern. The candle was short, but from within the mirrored interior it threw enough light to be seen ashore. I turned it first to shine toward Osbro's beach site and then wharf-ward, where again my light was answered by a soft belling.

⋆┈═◉═┈⋆

The response from the beach was not so modest. The flare of a torch rose skyward and then swooped to earth. A file of yellow-white flame ran along the length of the whole strip of sand. The flames shot up to the height of the palm trees behind them, from one end to the other. Accompanying the flames was a loud clatter of metal on metal, a frenzied drumming, and I heard the excited shouting of hoarse voices.

Lights came alive on the pirate ship, one by one by one, and I heard the oaths of startled men, spoken in various tongues, and the bawling of sharp orders. I did not understand the words but knew the import to be for every man to occupy his battle station. But discipline aboard pirateers can be loose, and a large number forsook their duties and rushed to the stern taffrail to see what was taking place on land.

Here was the moment upon which all depended. I pulled the covering off the array of shadow-eaters and wrapped myself in it, making sure to enclose every inch of my body in the black fabrics. I dared not peep out, but I could hear the plants sway and writhe as they felt the presence of shadow-prey. I reached about me under the covering to take hold of the oilskin bladder Sbufo had sewn together. It was supposed to enable me to float to the *Tarnished Maiden*. I felt all around but could not touch it. It must have got kicked aside as I struggled with the tiller and now lay outside my protection of canvas covering. I dare not put my hand out to search, for I would cast a shadow the plants would immediately attack. The light from Osbro's fires was powerfully bright. The sailors on the ship that hung above me were caught in the glare.

The only food the plants could find was the shadows of the pirates on the decks above. The eaters would begin their onslaught the moment my *Reluctant Maiden* touched the looming hull. The ravenous vines would be able to scale those weathered strakes without impediment, but some would yet cling to the *Maiden*. We had to make certain they never got back to the city, where they could turn upon the shadows of the populace. There had already been one serious injury when one of the Verdant Ladies' careless gardeners had stepped between a plant and the light.

To prevent this possible calamity Sbufo and Cocorico had made of my boat an invention I must now employ. I put little faith in it; in fact, I mistrusted it entirely. My stubby little bowsprit was a dowel which served as the linchpin of my vessel. They had found this old, disused, and apparently abandoned boat in the corner of a shipyard, and, after acquiring it on the cheap, had taken it apart board by board. Then they had put it back together without the use of nails, holding its shape with shroud-line, twines, and thin iron wire.

The bowsprit was the key to the undoing. When it ran against the pirate hull, that pressure caused it to retract, and when it did so, the tensions that held all the parts of the boat together relaxed at once and the *Reluctant Maiden* came all apart instantly.

I had not believed it could perform as Sbufo described.

"Think you," he said. "Have you not often seen those familiar toys, the ships-in-bottles that the elderly tars with lost limbs or other disfigurements enjoy to put together? You know how they insert all the small pieces that have been joined to a single string and then pull that string tight so that the bottled ship stands erect? That is what we have done with this dumpish boat, only it will work backward. When the time comes, when this dowel touches the pirate hull, your boat will fall to pieces. When that happens, you must embrace this oilskin bladder and hold fast to it and never drown while you strike out for the *Tarnished Maiden*." He had handed me the bladder in the shape of a bolster. All black it was, and he bade me keep it near.

But it was lost. I felt about for it desperately and when the boat began to come apart to pieces—a change that happened rapidly—I looked all about and finally saw it in the bay waters an unhappy distance away. How it had got loose I did not know, but it could be of no aid to me now. The cold bay water roared suddenly over my head and I flailed my arms about, but only in blind panic, not trying to swim, for I had no conception of the skill. I thwacked my forearm sharply on a board that floated by. I struck it so sharply that I broke a bone, or so I thought, as pain coursed through my arm and shoulder.

I was able, though, to crook my elbow over this length of wood, and it supported me for a time sufficient to collect another of its kind and transfer it under the same arm and thus gain enough buoyancy to stay afloat. I began paddling with my other arm and one leg toward the *Tarnished Maiden*. The diseased old hulk lay a ship's-length away, but I felt confident I could attain to its safety, despite my painful arm and the unhealthy draughts of bay water I was imbibing.

To most other men the decrepit hulk would have appeared to be no safe haven. It would seem instead a terrible peril—or a grisly, certain doom.

A confusion of loud voices rose from the pirate ship behind me. Most of the sounds were screams of those whose shadows were being ingested. Shouts of amazed consternation clamored also. Some of the crew must have looked out at the *Tarnished Maiden* and seen there what I saw in brief glimpses as I fought to hold on to my wood and keep my head above water.

⊷═◉═⊶

The old ship lay three-quarters sidewise with her prow pointed toward shore, exposing her stern to the pirates and me. Over the taffrail came again the Mardrake, the foul monster that my brother Osbro had once defeated heroically at the château of Baron Rendig, hacking its fabrics to ribbons and patches with his fierce sword.

But here now was no frail, small puppet flopping out of a well-head. This Mardrake was of a grand size, its tentacles as thick as my thighs for most of their prodigious lengths. The bulk of the thing caused the vessel to list heavily. A precarious position this was, for the *Maiden* seemed barely to keep afloat on her best days. If the ship foundered, I would probably drown in the wash.

Slowly the monster came over the stern. I could hear even in my watery exertions the squealing of pulleys and I pictured Sbufo and Cocorico scurrying from one set of levers to another, pulling, jerking, turning, and straining to make the huge machine perform its functions.

I made my way toward it, but my arm pained me severely and I had grown tired in the struggle with the boat and with battling the waves. I had to rest for a moment and so dog-paddled for a space with my flotsam-support under my armpit.

This brief respite afforded me a view of our circumstances. The fire-pits that Osbro, Torronio, Crossgrain, and the others

were tending on the shore still flamed gloriously, and so high did
the fire leap that it touched off the crowns of the palm trees behind
and they caught one by one, like lamps being lit along a nighttime
street of brothels. This grand illumination shed a wild, yellow glow
upon the whole scene. I saw the soiled harbor water with its Jester-
masks, the *Maiden* and its threatening Mardrake, the wharves and
sullen structures at the river mouth and all round it, and the pirate
ship now in the grip of a struggle with the voracious plants. It looked
also as if the crew members had set to against one another. Caught
in the glare of the pit fires, the attacking plants must soon perish,
for they could not survive light, but before they turned to gray and
harmless ash, they would tear away to oblivion the shadows of many
a cutthroat aboard the ship.

But other pirates crowded to the rails, fearing more a monster
in the water that they could well see and understand than ebony
plants aboard ship that they could not comprehend at all. They now
lofted arrows at the Mardrake and some of these fell into the water
around me. One of the arrows speared through the forehead of a
floating mask of Bennio, and this sight brought home to me the danger
that I was in from the pirate archers.

All the bay was black and yellow-white and red and smoky and
loud with shouts and shrieks.

I started thrusting toward the *Tarnished Maiden* again. The pirate crew, if they spotted me in the water, must have considered me
a man whose senses were deranged. The Mardrake was a formidable
object, even to me who knew its risible secret. It was continually
growing in bulk, the tentacles thickening. It was no octopus, for at
least a dozen or so tentacles had sprouted from it now, thrashing
furiously. The sound it made was nigh deafening, nothing like the
leonine roar of its small forebear. It emitted a high-pitched hooting
that carried over the water and echoed from the waterfront fa-
cades. That call descended in pitch, sliding its note like the tin
whistle a child blows upon. It must have wakened the people of
Tardocco in fright, if the pulsing of the fires in the pits had not
already roused them.

The waves the false Mardrake created pushed against me so forcibly I feared I must lose arm-clutch of my floating lumber. Mutano
was supposed to find me in the water and bring me safe aboard, but
I doubted whether he could locate me in the commotions of the
surface. I had to make a quarter circuit away from the stern; the

power of the backwash close to the monster was greater than I could overcome.

Then I distinguished my colleague's outline on the deck where a piece of the structure had broken off. His shape was unmistakable, and he had already dropped a rope ladder that knocked against the hull loudly enough to draw my eyes to it. I strove heartily in the water. Live or die, I thought, even though my exertions this night had left me scant strength.

When I reached the ladder I let go my makeshift raft and clung to the first rung above the water with my right hand. But I could not climb. Mutano realized my predicament. He began to haul me up. I scraped along the hull, thumping against it, and could barely keep hold. But up I went until he grasped my wrist and grappled me aboard.

I lay gasping and heaving. He loomed over me like an uncouth monolith against the sky. "Identify yourself," he said. "We allow no lubbards aboard this vessel."

I coughed weakly and he nudged me with the toe of his boot. "Speak."

"I am . . . Falco . . . late of . . . the *Reluctant Maiden*."

"Take my advice," said he, "and never put faith in the word *maiden*."

What fool would follow Mutano's advice in the matter of women? I did not say these words, instead coughing up a cupful of bay water by way of reply.

"Your hand." He pulled me to my feet, but my knees had no more strength than a brace of sickly puppies. I fell against his chest. He allowed me to rest there for a moment, then made me stand. "You must tax yourself," he said. "The Mardrake will soon launch. We must away from the ship. See the dinghy forrards there? Go sit you in it and restore. We four must flee this derelict on pain of drowning." He supported my staggering steps to the boat he had lashed tight against the side at mid-ship and I collapsed onto its stern bench. "Stay you here. We will join you ere long."

I sat shivering with ague and my carcass felt as if it had served as the clapper in an iron bell, beaten against the metal until it was only a suffering spirit and no body at all, the very soul of aching. I felt so weak I wondered if I could curl my fingers, and it, having done so, I could straighten them again. I tried this exercise and found with a touch of surprise that some parts of my body could still obey the impetus of my mind. But when I felt for my sword I found it missing—at the bottom of the bay, no doubt. I felt in my boots; the daggers too were lost.

Our Mardrake now spat smoke from its many-toothed maw, black clouds pouring out of the beast like ink from an overturned bottle. To give *vis* to this overgrown mechanism Sbufo had applied the use of a small oven with attached bellows, probably several of them. The conceit of a fire-breathing monster that lived underwater seemed illogical to me, but our purpose was to instill panic in the minds of the pirates, not to test their powers of reasoning. Morbruzzo could not have gathered his crew of murderers and rapists from among scholars and natural philosophers. The oven warmed by the fire was attached to the whistle that uttered that unnerving howl of the mechanism.

Now at last I would get to meet this Morbruzzo with my blade drawn, I thought. In fact, I desired simply to lay eyes upon him, to compare the man in his flesh with the dire picture that rumor had formed in my mind for so many seasons. He had attained in popular imagination the size and ferocious aspect of the man-eating giants of children's tales.

I turned toward the ship and saw that the plants had done what work they could before the shore's firelight demolished them and that the crew remaining—a surprisingly large number—were launching small boats. They would be trying to reach the waterfront, evading the Mardrake and deserting their ship before the creature attacked it.

Despite the battered condition of my body and its cruel aching, I began to smile. Astolfo had founded his plans upon the notion that our enemies were ignorant, no more reasonable or knowledgeable than children, and his surmise was proving correct.

Now Sbufo and the celebrated Cocorico came scrambling from belowdecks and ran with Mutano to the pilot boat in which I sat. Mutano slipped the knots and freed the boat. He motioned me out and the three of them swung the craft over the side. It hung swaying from the pulleys and when it came back again against the hull Mutano pushed me into it. Then they clambered in and down we went, to light awkwardly upon the surface of the bay.

Wasting no time, Mutano slashed the cables with his sword, and we were free. Sbufo and Cocorico took up the oars, fitted them into the locks, and rowed as hard as they could.

Mutano stood behind them to call direction. "We must away quickly," he told me. "The *Tarnished Maiden* will go the way of the *Reluctant Maiden*. The joinings have been disjoined. She will fall apart."

"You design to cause the pirates to believe the Mardrake destroyed the ship," I said. "Astolfo had not divulged this thought to me."

"Best to keep the plan divided. If one of us happened to let slip some knowledge about his part, a spy still could not put all parts together."

"No more explanations. My head is overfull." I do not know whether I said those words or not. Maybe I only groaned.

XII

The Shadow Not a Shadow

To this point of our designed defense all the twines had knotted together to form a net. By now Osbro, Torronio, and their band should have deserted the beach and made their ways to the waterfront, or nearly. There they were to join with Astolfo and the townsmen confederates he could trust. Theirs would be but a small troop, we expected, waiting in the shadows along the wharves for the infiltrators and their allies within the city to expose themselves when the remaining pirate crew reached the meeting site.

At that time a bloody, pitched battle must take place, but our prospects for victory at this moment seemed better than before. Much of the pirate force had been depleted by the shadow-eaters and most of the rest were distracted by the Mardrake, as it now advanced toward their ship. The *Tarnished Maiden* sighed her last breath as her joinings gave way and all the sections disparted. She sank slowly at first and then with a loudly hissing swiftness. The wake of that sinking thrust the great, hollow puppet onward toward the pirates. They showered it with ineffectual arrows.

At the same time, the marauders launched from their warship three tenders which already were skirting westward around our Mardrake, heading toward central harbor-side. We were in a race with these boats, speeding to reinforce Astolfo and Osbro on shore before the pirates arrived. The firelight was darkening now, the entrenched flames subsiding, and the palm trees only smoldering. Even so, I could see against the afterglow the pirates' cockleboats and tried to count the number of men in them. No more than three dozen, I judged, but we could not know how many traitors would join with them ashore.

⊷⊨⊙⊜⊨⊷

Then all of us—defenders, pirates, and the citizenry snug in their homes—heard a sound we never shall hear again. It was a roar of towering, insensate rage, as of fury loosed that had been confined for ages in the heart of its host's whole being. It was at the same time a cry of undying grief and unendurable longing that was the soul of that incomprehensible being. I felt the pressure of the anguished cry against my skin the way that I would feel the buffeting of a hot, savage wind. It proceeded from every direction at once. Painfully, I turned to look all about—to find the pirate ship behind me in its last throes of struggle with the plants, then toward the western shore with its dying firelight, and then forward toward the wharves, where torchlights now flared, one after another.

Our *Tarnished Maiden* had gone down at the center of the bay. There it had released our contrived Mardrake seaward toward the pirates. Could our makeshift beast have uttered the outcry that caused my spirit to shudder so violently? I knew it could not, but I could conceive no other source.

Then we all saw, all of us.

⊷⊨⊙⊜⊨⊷

There rose from the waters a being that thrust toward the sky like a sea-engendered tower. Larger than the three-master, this creature cut off my sight of that ship. It was like a great, animate battering ram of liquid basalt. It kept on thrusting upward, upward and outward.

The surface, or tegument, of the thing shed a cascading detritus as the being attained an ever-greater height. Rusted anchors fell from its body, along with ship fittings of all kinds, iron and brass tumbling down again into the bay. Live swordfish and huge squid, bones of great fishes, skeletons of men, shells of giant conches, streams of black mud and yellow sand, costly ornaments of gold and silver, masts and spars covered with algae, broken clusters of reef fell away from its bulk.

All things this water had ever received the creature brought with

it to the light, and then this gathering of broken metal and mineral
tumbled from its bulk into the waves. It held a beautiful Andromeda in its clutch and shook her savagely back and forth. When she
too toppled down this primeval Mardrake's flank, I made her out
to be the figurehead of a sunken vessel, long since drowned. She
had been tugged from the prow by savage currents and thrust into
the howling winds once more.

I saw its eye.

I was certain I saw its eye, small as it was, amid all those resur-
rected objects the beast was shedding from itself. It was not like the
eye of a fish or a serpent. It was a human eye, and I was certain beyond
doubt that the creature saw me. I felt the power of it seeing me; I
felt the pressure of its gaze upon my soul.

It saw the four of us, rocking violently in our tiny boat. It saw
but disregarded us and fell upon the false Mardrake.

Large and ingenious as Sbufo's handiwork was, it still was only
a mechanism of stagecraft, a trifle of canvas and pulleys and hempen
lines and inflated bladders. He had shaped merely a great, sea-borne
doll. The Mardrake that burst from the primal waters demolished
it with a single blow. The parts of our false contrivance scattered
across the surface of the bay, except for the heavier center, which
sank at once.

Our boat lurched in the towering surges and almost capsized. If
there had been not an even more powerful current beneath its
bottom, we would have gone over. But the wave beneath propelled
us wharf-ward at a great rate and we were driving headlong toward
the pilings of the piers. Sbufo and Cocorico dropped their oars and
clutched the gunnels.

I heard Mutano's harsh, despairing cry. No standing man
could keep his place when the boat pitched upward so sharply.
My friend was catapulted into the murderous waters and swept
away. I could not glimpse him.

I gripped the bench on which I sat with both hands and buried
my chin in my chest.

Higher and higher the surge carried us.

Many a time before this moment I had imagined my death. A
valiant ending I pictured each time, but none of my fancied demises
were watery; they were always delivered by swords, and always by
half a dozen expert opponents at once. I had fancied too that I
would be mourned by various women, whose fair faces would

appear before my mind's eye in my final moment. Their names I would not be able to recall. Now I must submit to a miserable, unheroic drowning.

But—the harbor was not to be my grave. The immense wave transported our boat to such a height that it flew in an arc over the pier-edge and dropped bottom-downward square onto the drenched planking. It was as if we had been cast like a die upon the lumber by a blind, immortal hand.

It was not a comfortable docking. My bones tumbled so violently I felt they must each have unjoined. My upper jaw cracked my lower jaw. The base of my spine felt as if the planet had swung upward to hammer it into my skull.

The boat did not shatter. We were shaken and battered like a bell buoy weathering a tempest, but we had escaped drowning and the purposed wrath of the ancient Mardrake.

Mutano was not in our company. I looked but could find him nowhere in the tumult of waves.

With a hard-breathed effort I loosed my hands from the bench and made my body stand. I had to steady, bracing my legs apart before I could turn to look backward into the bay.

The Being was there, vaulting against the dome of the sky and its every star. Now I could not find its eye. It was faceless, featureless. Without a mouth it gave voice again to the woes with which eon after uncountable eon had tortured its spirit. The sad, angry howl gained in burden of sorrow until I could bear no more. If it had continued, I might well have plunged into the waters, willingly to drown. It was the voice of a more sorrowful universe than the one in which I lived.

Then the howl died to a heartbroken lament and the lament died to silence and all other sounds now quieted and went dumb.

⊷═◉═⊶

Astolfo had once proposed a conundrum. "Suppose, Falco, that all the utterance of all animate beings that have sounded since the beginning of the world were given voice in a single, unbroken breath. Would it be a cry of terror, a moan of despair, or a shout of jubilation?"

I could not answer. And now that I had heard the utterance he described, or something very like it, I still could not answer. But I could report that the Mardrake was not jubilant.

The Being sought the deep again, casting off this upper world that must have offered insult or done it injury no human being shall ever comprehend. Its entry into the water was silent, but the tall, smooth swells it mounted spread across the width of the bay, roiling the debris scattered on the surface and pushing westward the tenders the pirates had launched. Those marauders would have to beach and march to the wharves to reach their goal. They would lose time and we would be prepared for their advent.

Their galleon was beleaguered. The backwash from the Mardrake's sounding heeled it over so far I doubted it could right itself. After a space it did come upward again, with heavily streaming decks. But only a few sailors stood to their posts; most had been sluiced overboard. Not enough crew remained to man the ship and turn about.

If we could attack the pirateer now, we would have it in hand, I thought.

But our pressing concerns were ashore.

The town had awakened. All along the docks were scores of half-dressed citizens, confused, bewildered, and frightened. They milled about, glaring at one another suspiciously, desiring to place blame on this one or that one. Our enemy now was dispersed among this crowd, but there was no way to distinguish friend from foe.

Osbro and Torronio, Squint and Crossgrain with four others of their group I knew only by sight had arrived from their fiery beachfront, and I saw them slipping into the crowd. Eight members of the Civil Guard, their red tunics now protected by breastplates, moved to companion them. Here again was an arrangement I had not been told of, that the Civil Guard was allied with us in the defense of Tardocco. These men moved by pairs to both sides of the tall warehouse entrances, waiting to see which of these would open to bring swords against them.

I scanned the scene from left to right, trying to glimpse Astolfo and whatever small band that would be accompanying him. He was not to be seen.

Now I urged my body with sore and limping gait to pier-edge to seek in the bay waters for Mutano. He must have drowned, I thought. Our venture at this site had been distasteful to him, for he distrusted water as a cat distrusts it. He had even complained, requesting Astolfo to make out a strategy that would allow us to combat our enemy on dry land. The maestro voiced misgivings. "They will not challenge us on land until they have made the harbor secure for their reinforcements—or for their retreat, if we gain the upper hand."

There was no sign of my colleague in the unruly waves, only spars and broken oars, shrouds, splintered decking, arrows and spears tossed this way and that in the currents, along with the sardonic faces of Bennio. But it was too soon to mourn my friend; he was well practiced in escaping perils whole-skinned.

The pirate tenders now had beached on the smoking westward strip of sand and the blackguards that manned them had no way to make a concerted attack of the wharf. They started marching along the waterline in groups of six, readying for fight. They would link with their waiting allies.

⊸═◑═⊶

After the manifestation of the Mardrake, after its entrance into our familiar world from its abyss of primal eons and cloudy myth, how could our petty conflicts over property and ownership, about material goods and shadow goods, of personal vengeance and individual honor, appear to be anything else than childish trifling? The immemorial shadows of ancient histories known and unknown lie over our brief and sunlit days, but rarely do they reveal themselves with physical intrusion. When they do so, our present existences diminish in our estimations to their true, insignificant statures.

What had drawn this entity to display to the upper world something of its immeasurable vastness, of its immortal, tortured solitude? What occurrence here above could disturb its indifference to all that took place in other zones of existence?

I have speculated that it was the shadow of the false Mardrake. Osbro's fires were bright enough to cast the shadow of the puppet from where it lay on the surface of the bay to the very bottom. Perhaps the creature thought to defend itself from a rival; perhaps it was enraged that a graceless parody of its form presented itself against the firelight. But that made no sense. Revenge and hope and love and regret and all those human suasions could not touch it. It did not exist in a zone where such terms held meaning.

So it was more with bemusement than with apprehension that I watched the shrunken pirate band trudge along the sands in our direction. On they came, leaderless as far as I could tell, and weary were their steps. They were still a good hundred fifty yards away, but I could begin to make out details.

They were not extraordinary. These would be dissolute sailors ready to follow any master who promised coin and salt beef. A tar whose luck at dice had deserted him, or one whom rum held in its aromatic embrace, or another on the dodge from justice or an angry spouse would join with these crews. I had met the like of them many a time in Stinking Lane and Rattlebone Alley. Some of the faces looked hazily familiar.

They came to the edge of one of the small streams that branch off from the Daia as it pours into the bay. A large clump of twisted dwarf willows shrouded the stream mouth. They entered into this leafage and disappeared. They did not emerge to the packed sand strip on this side of the stream. I kept my gaze upon that spot but saw nothing.

They will advance another way, I thought. They will come upon the waterfront from behind. They will gather their comrades-in-arms from the inner warehouses and deserted accounting chambers and try to surround us by filing through the narrow alleyways along there. It was a feasible plan as long as they went unnoticed, but those passages were so narrow that two men, or even one, could halt their progress. So, any presence they showed in the alleyways would be a feint. The real attack must begin in another quarter.

The round figure of Sbufo and the slender one of Cocorico stood by my side, watchful and ready. They drew their swords. I would have to fight weaponless.

⇥═◉═⇤

One of the alleys did yield surprise. A hair-prickling screech sounded, a yowling as of a forest tree-tiger with its tail caught in a trap. Everyone was startled, including my comrades and myself, though I thought I recognized the squalling as delivered with familiar intonation.

Out of the alley-shadow stepped Mutano. His hair was plastered to his forehead and water dripped from every inch of the angry man. His face was contorted with frustration and a barely controlled ferocity animated his actions. In the crook of his left arm he wrestled the head of a pirate. A bald and ugly object it was, scarred and tattooed and bloody-bearded, and Mutano's pummeling was not improving its appearance. It was attached to a body of considerable musculature that my colleague subdued with difficulty—mainly by dint of pounding the face regularly and with meaningful emphasis. If he enjoyed the pastime, his expression gave no hint. All fury it was.

The he flung the man down and gave him a generous kick in his rib cage. "They have arrived," he announced, looking about at our confused assemblage. "The pirates are in the buildings. They came up underneath in boats and then through the floors." He paused to award his victim another kick. "We have seen that prank before, have we not, Falco?" He gestured at the rows of warehouses on either side of us. "They will rush out of this rank of doors together at once. All we have to do is to cut them down as they come. We only have to take our places and stand our ground. They are none so many as we feared."

I called to him. "I thought you drowned."

"Falco," he said, "so long as you live, never speak to me again of water."

I shouted as loudly as I could. "Guards and watchmen! Stand your stations! Our foemen are hiding in the warehouses, like rats in their holes. When they gain courage to attack, the archers must loose a first volley and then stand aside to let the lancers through."

No archers or lancers were present among the puzzled multitude that crowded the wharves. My words were intended for the ears of the traitors listening inside their gloomy shelters. If they disregarded my empty threats and tumbled out to make a battle of it, the outcome might not be to my liking. In numbers we were now superior, but the townsmen were untrained and not given to organized bloodshed. They might well flee at the first assault and the traitors within the press would not spare to puncture them as they retreated.

I concluded my speech. "Now let them come to us, my friends, and meet their miserable fates. Let them hail their confederates in the town for the last time, for those too shall die."

⊷━◐━⊶

After these foolhardy words a silence fell upon that part of the crowd nearest me. I almost hoped the pirate force would spring out upon us with thirsty weapons and soul-shriveling shouts and blood-crazed eyes. I was weary to the marrow of my bones, but I was also tired of the continual threat. Season after season the town whispered, muttered, and grumbled of Morbruzzo and his legions who would descend upon us like boiling brimstone poured from the polestar. It would be soon and fiery, said the old codgers. They hunger for my maidenhead, said the silly girls. They will take my gold and spoil my wife and daughters, said the plump and roseate men of business. They cannot harm my indomitable soul, claimed the shoals of philosophers, who could barely heap together enough *vis* to supply one soul among them all.

So we stood ready, Mutano, Cocorico, Sbufo, and I, for our fates to meet us face-forward.

⤙══◈══⤚

The crowd had fallen silent. For a long, uneasy moment, nothing stirred. Then the pair of doors of the largest building that stood before us swung slowly inward. Out of the cavernous darkness of that shelter and into the graying predawn light stepped Astolfo. He was dressed in his usual outfit, except that he wore the red tunic of the Civil Guardsmen and over that garment a steel breastplate. This piece of armor I judged ceremonial rather than battle-ready; it was engraved with the leopard's-head figure of his customary belt buckle. He carried no sword.

He held, though, a length of shiny chain with thick, heavy links. To this weighty iron was attached a slender figure of medium stature. This personage wore a Bennio mask, along with the ordinary doublet and short cape that many courtiers and bravos habitually donned. Astolfo jerked the chain, but his captive did not stumble, moving forward with a fluent gracefulness.

Astolfo dropped the chain onto the planking and came to stand beside his prisoner. "Fellow citizens—here is your dreaded Morbruzzo!" He swept off the mask with an exaggerated, theatrical gesture.

I blinked my eyes four times. I did not comprehend.

"Morbruzzo?" cried the woman. "Long time past, I rid me of that witless, un-human devil."

Now I recognized her. The passing years had been gentle upon the physic of Fleuraye. Her figure had changed little since that long-ago hour she had bested me in swordplay. All too often have I recalled that shameful episode: the miserly Pecunio cowering from the duel, Astolfo flinging a shadow about Fleuraye to obscure her vision as I lay helpless upon the floor, awaiting the thrust of her blade through my heart. I recalled too the promise she made upon departure, that she looked forward to another encounter with the maestro, at a time when she would reap a rich retribution.

Her figure had grown more muscular than lissome, but it retained its swift gracefulness. Her carriage was as haughty as before and her gaze as challenging. But her former piquancy had soured; it had acquired a superciliousness. Her expression and her bearing suggested that she had found her life a banal passage through violent years. There was a vacancy about her that I have observed in soldiers who'd survived brutal campaigns. Part of her center had been taken away.

And now Astolfo had outgamed her once more and destroyed all the prospects of the petty pirate empire that she had envisioned. This dream must have been her best, last hope. Now only a bitter rage would animate her spirit.

Her minion murderers, two hundred or so, were being led from the warehouses by about four score armed citizens, Civil Guardians, fathers, and young men of substance. Astolfo's warnings in his role as Ministrant had not gone unheeded. Volunteers must have gathered to put themselves under his command. His martial armor showed that he had foreseen this moment and that he relished adopting this persona of the glittering hero. He would frolic in the role like an otter sporting in the ripples of a stream.

It was another of his serious, or partly serious, games. Mutano, Osbro, and I had not known that our faction had gathered supporters among the populace; Astolfo kept the fact to himself. Maybe he feared we would let slip intelligence we should not, but it was more likely that he enjoyed surprising his allies as well as his opponents.

I reflected again that the maestro was many times the plaything of his own humor, that he could no more resist the opportunity to confound expectations than the cat can resist pursuit of a mouse.

And of felines here and now the number was redoubtable. Following our plans, Mutano had petitioned Sunbolt to our aid. That authoritative cat had gathered a company of Maulers, Worriers, and scar-flanked amateur battlers from the under-story of Tardocco. Information about newcomers to the area had been passed from these cats to the members of the beggars' guild and thence to Astolfo. He still maintained connection with that guild from the days of old, when he and his mentor Veuglio walked among them to gather an understanding of their ways of life.

These veteran cats would doubtless expect to be recognized for their efforts in foiling the invasion. Perhaps they anticipated an award of a great yellow wheel of communal cheese or an avenue-long trough of fresh cow's milk. They were evidently expectant of some event, for they lined the rooftops of storerooms and warehouses and looked down upon the scene of Fleuraye's surrender with unwavering attention. In the light of the emergent dawn their eyes glowed greenish-orange, like eyes of topaz set in stone statuettes.

"You tell us you rid yourself of Morbruzzo," Astolfo said, "and that is so. You were his consort and you betrayed him, just as you betrayed Bellarmo, your first pirate consort, during the time of Pecunio. You drained the old miser's fortune into your own coffers and used the gold to bribe Morbruzzo's hirelings to turn upon him when the hour of your revenge came round."

"My revenge? I do not comprehend you."

"You had a sister named Solana. Morbruzzo abducted her, and what was done to the unhappy girl needs no recounting. But when you heard of it, you devoted all your remaining life to her memory and her avengement."

"How might I bring this about?"

"You had Pecunio's fortune in hand. You were willing to demean and degrade yourself in any way that would sway Morbruzzo's men to your cause. Pirate crews are not famous for loyalty."

"You must explain to me how I accomplished this grand scheme. I seem to have forgotten the devious, bloody steps I took."

"All that will be revealed to all at your trial before the magistrates. Tardocco would not have been averse to your destruction of Morbruzzo. But after his murder you decided to carry out the plans he had laid to subjugate this city and use it as your base for a pirate empire. These are the crimes the magistrates and the citizens will hold against you."

"A trial, is't? My blood is up for a jig on the gallows-tree. And if you will mount a trial, then you and the world shall hear my story. Why should I not bind this smug, fat Tardocco to my subjection? It is a port easy to take by force. It would be in my grasp even now, if not for that great, black waterspout that intruded upon the battle. Fortune favored you."

"If I say that our city holds its harbor Mardrake in reserve as a weapon of war, you cannot refute me. If I say it appeared at my bidding and I can bid it do so again, the word shall pass to any other pirate fleet that regards our town as helpless prey."

"It was an accident of nature," she said. "You possess no such power of command."

He ignored her denial. "The Civil Guard will of course commandeer your ship. Not enough of the crew is left aboard to be able to sail such a galleon. She must remain in the harbor, for the time being."

"The *Vengeful Maiden* is yours, for all the good she may do you."

"Your reinforcement, the two-master we spied on the horizon hanging half a league off—she did not come to your aid but went about into the open sea."

"The *Sly Handmaid* is well out of your reach. Perhaps she shall return with her friends at another hour when you will still be busy puffing yourself up like a smithy's bellows."

"We shall be pleased to encounter her," Astolfo said. "Our Tardocco is a hospitable port. And well defended."

Her voice did not tremble or waver: "We shall see."

"The sun is just rising," he continued, "and our cats are restless. Much remains to do, though we are all tired, cold, wet, and thirsty. Mutano must take a few seasoned colleagues in a pilot boat out to your *Vengeful Maiden* and secure the vessel. Osbro and Torronio are to march back to their sandy fire-pits and make certain that all coals are quenched. Falco is to take charge of our prisoners, who, for the near future, shall be chained together in these two adjoining warehouses. I shall escort you to our small, stoutly barred gaol close by the Hall of Justice. There you may meditate upon your misdeeds till time of trial."

"Your cowardly city begs for pillage," she said.

"And after we have finished our chores?" I asked Astolfo. I was tired of talk—of everything.

"Then all this present company of defenders shall meet upon this selfsame spot at twilight this evening," he said. "We shall go into the town and open every bottle and cask where they stand. If any tavern keeper try to halt our progress, he shall share a gaol room with the pirate queen Fleuraye. The prospect of such a shelter will instill in him a proper gratitude."

We looked at one another, all of us weary, bloody, sooty, begrimed, and aching, and agreed that Maestro Astolfo's agenda of celebratory duties was sound and sensible and must be followed to the smallest detail. I was determined to bear my part, even if I had to be held standing by three strong men.

⊶⊷◉⊷⊶

These, then, were the occurrences of that long, dark night.

XIII

A Shadow All of Light

In these dull latter days the Feast of the Jester meets with nearly indifferent regard. Clowns still perform in the plazas and amid the park greens. They tumble, juggle, and sing out raw rhymes, but their reception is marked more by fond reminiscence than by fresh enthusiasm. The legend of the original Bennio has dimmed; his satiric functions have been taken up by court poets and by the antics of ordinary tumblers. His visage still can be seen in the waning moon, but children must be carefully instructed on how to make it out. Many of his ancient chants are no longer found acceptable in polite circles.

But in our own small circle the Feast is celebrated in jovial fashion. On the fourth cycle of the festival's return, Astolfo and I were making the annual journey to Tardocco on a matched pair of tar-black horses, both of them as gaily leathered and richly furnished as any highly prized and nobly sponsored courtesan. Telluria and Gabriel rode beside us in a two-wheeled carriage decorated lavishly and, methought, not entirely artfully. Telluria's taste had not quite caught up with her new position.

She is my spouse, this blue-eyed, blonde, curly-tressed woman, and the daughter of a county farmer. She was brought by Astolfo to his household as a maid-of-all-work. One morning when I came to his great farmhouse centered in the acreage to make report and receive direction from the maestro, I found her washing milk jugs at the large kitchen basin and humming a gay ballade. I threw a casual embrace about her waist.

She turned on me swiftly. "Thou'rt called Falco?"

"I am so."

She eyed me up and down and crosswise. "Well, thou'rt a jack well formed. Many a lass would quickly rattle the straw with thee. But I did not come to this world to drop bastards on the face o't. If you'd have the good o' me, you must consult first my father and then my three brothers and then the magistrate in his house at the crossroads."

I considered these words an unpromising beginning, but after a certain hungry period of restless longing, I did consult with her father and her brothers and found them to be affable and sensible men with lump-muscled forearms and knotty cudgels. The silver-haired magistrate too was a complaisant sort, helpful in every respect my future kinsmen made mention of.

Our child of six months she calls Gabriel after a generous bachelor uncle. I call him Stolfino to honor Master Astolfo. This name I keep private to myself. Telluria knows the maestro only as my former employer in a trade she distrusts and comprehends but dimly. She did suggest that we might confer the pet name of Falchino, but I do not want our babe to follow my troubled path through the wildwood of this world. Better for him to study the sages, to learn the science behind whatever art or trade he may pursue. Better for him to acquire politic manners and cheerful aplomb than to go lumbering about ale-muddled with sword in hand through the Tardocco midnights. Better to be Astolfo the honorary uncle than Falco the foolish father.

＊━━◎━━＊

We dwelt in Caderia now, the place where I was born and lived until I left to pursue my fortune in the port city. We were traveling now from Caderia upon a warm, late summer morn abundant with butterflies. The road was empty except for Telluria, Gabriel, the cheerful red-haired lad who drove the carriage, Astolfo on his mount, and myself. The fields of barley and oats lay ripening on all sides. Now and again a low rock wall rose and then left off at knee-height, as if the farmer had lost interest in construction. The sky was blue and sweet. The world smelled of sunlight.

Astolfo had purchased the Caderian land upon which Osbro and I were reared, and another small estate adjoining. His prediction that he might forswear the shadow trade had come to pass. "I intend to seek for a certain ideal entity I have long conjectured of. I seek the purest and most spiritual of objects that ever existed, the physical thing that is itself wholly, or almost wholly, a spirit. I would welcome your company in this venture, but I do understand that a wife and child may discommode your participation. A corner of the farmland shall be at your usage, but if you would prefer to stay with your brother Osbro at the town villa, I shall content myself."

"How did you come by the farmland?" I'd asked. "Lord Merioni has the reputation of being one who never relinquishes his acres."

"He has left our sphere of existence. His heir is a lady named Lisensia," he replied. "This is what she said to me: 'I am a frivolous woman. A farm depresses me—all mud and horse droppings. The dumb beasts of the field bore me and the insects that fasten to them vex me. I care only for finery and for foppish young men useless to society—if they be comely of face and figure. Should you buy from me my father's land, I shall waste the whole recompense, down to the last copper.' She being so free-spirited, I received the land at a good price."

"Did not the town council lend, or award, you the coin to do so? They owe to you the preservation of Tardocco."

"They too have been generous," he said, "but mostly in other respects. I wanted to make sure our title was free here and so employed my own resource."

"I should like to meet this openhanded Lisensia."

"Thou'rt too old to be of her interest," he said, "and perhaps of a temper too settled. She will prefer the peach-cheeked young bravo who cannot cypher without the aid of his fingers."

"Your tutelage has ruined me," I returned. "You have misspent my youth upon vain studies of tepid sages."

"It was my pleasure to do so. Now, what say you? Will you partner with me in this quest for the purely spiritual physical thing that I have spoken of to you aforetimes?"

"I cannot fathom what we are to be in quest of," I said. "To my ear, it smacketh too much of philosophy; I have had my fill of weevily old treatises smelling of spiders. I am well acquainted with your library and do not care to revisit it."

"The library is no more. I have distributed the whole of it to the schools and hermitages."

"Are these heavy tomes well received among 'em?"

"The scholars love nothing so much as the mystifying phrases of Hermes Trismegistus, the o'erstretched syllogisms of Teteles, and the dull observations of Lullius. They scramble to these texts like ants to the carcass of a rotting rat and find great sweetness therein."

"I wish them each and all a hearty feast. I found those pages none so toothsome."

"Yet are you not now wiser than you were before you undertook such lavish perusal?"

"I have become wise enough to avoid all philosophy."

"For a Falco, that *is* wise," he said.

⁘

For the most part our arrangement has worked comfortably. I live with Telluria and Gabriel in a log-walled cottage set at the edge of an oat field. A tributary of Dove Creek called Reedy Run bubbles close by our humble door; a well in the yard supplies fine water; a wide-spreading hawthorn sports in its season clusters of reddening berries to which birds of every hue flock in tuneful parliaments.

This life is a gift not entirely free, for I am still subject to the maestro's orders and to his mild suggestions also. My compliance pays for my rent and for much of my keep. The duties are not onerous; Astolfo is no longer in trade. He is sought out, however, to consult with artists and architects, dressmakers and stage-players, perfumists, writers of commercial agreements, drapers, and others. He advises those who inquire upon the craft of shadows and cares not whether they pay in coin or in empty promises. This almost desultory activity entails errands and other small tasks that I cheerfully take up. I ride almost every other day to his large house in the center of the estate, Casa Indolenza, and receive a listing of these minor duties.

The city elders were less generous to Osbro and me than to Astolfo, but we do not complain. We possess as much wealth as we can gracefully bear. Our friend and ally, the erstwhile bandit Torronio, gained pardon for himself and for his Wrecker associates, and his family has taken him back into its fold. Those citizens who answered the call to arms that Astolfo sang out in his role as Ministrant during the Feast of the Jester have been recognized and officially commended. Those who did not respond have been questioned and some unsettling discoveries have been revealed.

"Now the citizens shall be less self-satisfied and more vigilant," Astolfo said. "For a while, at least."

So we rode toward the city in contentment. Now and again Tel-

luria would sing childish verses to Gabriel, who occupied her lap.
The driver of the carriage, a tall fellow with hair the color of polished brass, would occasionally join in:

> *"In the land where leopards leap,*
> *A lonely shepherd tends the sheep,*
> *When the night begins to fall,*
> *The leopards eat 'em one and all."*

It is an old nonsense lullaby. I had heard it often as a child, and
it has always proven to give the little ones exciting dreams. In response, I sang out a verse that drifted into my recollection:

> *"O when the winter snows do fall,*
> *Covering hillocks, mantling all,*
> *And desp'rate hunger attacks the leopard,*
> *He may in turn eat up the shepherd."*

Torronio had begged off attendance at the manse for this occasion, pleading family affairs. He was engaged in trying to find place
among the various enterprises of his tradesmen-kinfolk for Crossgrain, Squint, and the others who had fought with him against the
pirates at the fire-pits. Old grudges die hard in families, and the
older the family line the more fiercely are the grudges held. Torronio's diplomatic skill had borne little fruit, but he is an optimist.
Sooner or later they must come round, he said. He now had friends
among the town elders, who could impose special taxes upon
certain ungrateful individuals who might be pointed out to them
by that valiant defender of the city, Torronio. He denied any suggestion that this form of diplomatic persuasion was extortionate.

⋅⇥○⇤⋅

Mutano would be present at the feast. "You cannot prevent me,"
his jesting letter said. "Nor can tempest, plague, nor the armies of
the East. For we have our hearts and cannot be overcome." The
best I could cypher out of the incomprehensible word were by the
letters m, w, x, r, u, and perhaps n. It was a term borrowed from
the feline tongue that I took to signify something like "fortitude"
or "nerviness."

Often nowadays Mutano leant toward feline usages. This was

no great wonder, for with his share of our reward he had purchased the cattery of Nasilia and had transported all her animals to his new property, the great château that had once belonged to Tyl Rendig. Astolfo, on his behalf, had petitioned the Council and the elders and the respectable nobility who were connected in any way with the vile baron to grant for a nominal sum a perpetual lease on that forbidding edifice.

Now the turrets and battlements, the corridors and long halls were populated by cats of every shape, color, breed, and temperament. They were not slaughtered for their musk, although the Château Felis, as it was now called, did still supply the perfumists. But Mutano had collaborated with the Green Knights and Verdant Ladies to produce a rose attar that had the strength and something of the olfactory qualities of cat-musk. The Lady Aichele had been successful in crossing one of the few remaining shadow-eater plants with an exotic musk rose and this base for scent had become a favorite. She and Astolfo had other experiments in progress together, but I was not privy to their goals.

The description of Château Felis I was forced to gather at second hand, for my violent aversion did not allow me close acquaintance. Even when Mutano was away from his domicile, the feline miasma that hung upon him was sufficient to cause my nose to flow and my eyes to tear. I was disappointed, because I had become fond of his consort, Maronda, the straightforward woman who formerly oversaw the cattery for Nasilia. She had softened in address, no longer being so ready to answer a forward remark with a slap to the head or a blow to the chest. She doted upon Mutano. Her green eyes followed his every motion, her gaze was as attentive as that of a cat watching a hummingbird. Maronda allowed Mutano a latitude she would allow to none other. I was careful of my manner in her company.

I had prepared a question, designed to annoy, that I put to Mutano on every occasion of these commemorative feasts. I had asked it four years running, but I never had courage to ask with Maronda standing by. If I found him standing alone, I would ask it this year again. That promise I made to myself and would not break it.

Sunbolt too would not be present at our reunion, nor would his consort Asilia. They served, Mutano had told me, as liaisons between himself and his staff of attendants and all the cats who dwelt at the château, a large number of whom were their progeny. Sunbolt's office was to instruct the males in the martial arts of spitting, howling, arching the spine, and the traditional techniques of out-right combat. Every instruction for combat exercises began with his giving an elaborate account of his victory in the legendary duel with the great Mauler, Uccisore. His charges heeded with rapt attention. He was not so nimble as formerly and his belly swayed as he marched to and fro before his recruits, reciting his epic for half the length of an hourglass. Asilia stretched out forward at the side of the assembly, regarding her big orange mate with a cool, proud gaze.

So, our company was not complete for this year's celebration, but we were sufficient to form a merry group and there would be food, drink, song, and a tiresome amount of gushery over the infant.

Yet there was a heavy sadness to surmount. Astolfo had sent word to me by messenger that the blind sage Veuglio had died. His end, as the master described it, was peaceful and had taken place in the farmhouse, where the frail old man had lodged during his final days, cared for by his charge, Dorminia, the girl who played the role of his daughter Sibylla in the maestro's avengement upon Tyl Rendig. Astolfo was weightily saddened by Veuglio's death. The saintly old man had served as his mentor in his youth, and the attachment was almost filial. In his turn, Veuglio was devotedly grateful to Astolfo. The young shadow adept had looked to the welfare of the old man and his daughter ever since one of the pe-riodic Island Fevers of so many seasons ago carried away his wife, Sophia.

⊷≡◉═⊷

We arrived at the villa in the late afternoon. The day had cooled only slightly and a few smears of cloud glowed pearl-pink in the west, as the late sunlight suffused them like red wine dripped into water. The breeze was easy.

A short, bustling steward let us in through the front gate. He gestured to a brace of brawny servants and they trotted to look after the needs of Astolfo. The steward relieved our driver and pointed out to him where his quarters stood, then led the carriage to the front door of the manse. Two other servants came out, took up our baggage, and hurried away.

The steward showed Astolfo to his room, the modest bed-chamber he had occupied when in residence, and settled him, while Telluria and I stood in the hall. He came out again and said, "This way, if you please," and we followed.

"Where is Osbro?" I asked. "I expected him to greet us."

"He had to attend to a household detail," the man said. "I will show you to your room."

We followed him a while along the corridors, Telluria bearing Gabriel in her arms. Then I halted and said, "Are you certain this is the way? I am familiar with this house."

He went on a few paces, then stopped to open a door on the left-hand side. "For your inspection."

The little room had not changed. Empty except for washstand, rude chair, clothes-hooks, and bed, it was as barren as it was when I'd inhabited it. In those youthful days I would lie on the bed to daydream of a golden future or bend to examine my features in the water of the basin to see if the dissolutions of the previous night had taken too evident a toll. The straw mattress was as lumpy as before and the gray blanket as threadbare. The thick headboard taunted me once again with the admonition I had been ordered to cut into it: *Bumpkin lad, Protect thy shade.*

Telluria came to stand beside me in the doorway. "'Tis a little cramped, but I'm sure your brother has done his best. Falco, you can stretch out on the floor while Gabriel and I take the bed tonight."

"It will not come to that," I said. "This is Osbro's little jest. Or Astolfo's. They are reminding me that I am not to forget my origins." I addressed the steward. "Is that not correct?"

"The master did not tell me his mind—only to bring you here first and then show you into a larger chamber. If you will come this way, please. Your belongings have been installed."

He led. We followed. Telluria sighed with relief.

⋇═◦═⋇

She had labored for an hour to make herself ready for her appearance at dinner. I thought Telluria looked comelier than ever, but when I said so, she gave me an impatient frown and began to take her persona apart to refashion it from the inside out. Then she spent a good measure of the sandglass trifling with her presentation of Gabriel. He was very proper in his little white dress and beaded red bootlets.

When I asked her opinion of my new apple-colored tunic and green trunks, she gave me a hasty glance and an indifferent shrug. "How am I to judge o' thee? Thou'rt a man and may appear as you please. For a woman . . ."

This was not a novel theme between us.

"Tonight you will be compared only with Maronda," I said. "She stands as stiff as a sentry and carries the brawn of a stone-mason."

"And I am no petite and honeyed pastry," said she. "And you shall not speak so of Maronda. She is a handsome woman. You would not say such things in her presence."

"Indeed I would not. She would strike me down and kick my ribs in."

"And serve thee justly." She gave little fussy pattings to her blonde locks. "Let us go down, if you have done with mocking our friend."

⁕═◉═⁕

We met in the larger dining hall where Astolfo had first introduced to Mutano and me the girl he had called Sibylla. It now was lit by wall sconces and by a battery of candles on all sides and by another rank of them upon the table. Trophies rescued from our sea-battle with Fleuraye's forces were mounted along the walls: lengths of broken spars, bits of sail, a rusty lance, several short swords, and the clumsy rudder that guided my ramshackle *Reluctant Maiden*. There were a dozen or so water-mottled Jester masks disposed in asymmetrical order. Their expressions seemed more benign than sarcastic, an effect of candlelight.

Astolfo must be surprised at the transformation of his hall.

We sat here in this space much too large for us. We were seven, but the table was laid for eight. Astolfo was to sit at the head, and on his right-hand side a full service was set out. It was different from those before the rest of us. Our dishes were of stoneware painted white and our napery upon which the knives and spoons rested were as white as sea foam. But the linen for the empty place was black and the wine cup was of silver.

This was the place of Veuglio, had he been here to occupy it.

Astolfo had not yet appeared, but the footman seated us, presumably at the maestro's direction, though the manse now belonged

to Osbro. He was placed on Astolfo's left-hand side, and then in order downward Telluria with gurgling Gabriel in her lap and me at
her side where I would be subject to her reprimands.

Across from me was Maronda. There was space enough between
us that her cat-scent did not ignite my usual fiery sneezes in her presence. On her left sat Mutano and on his left, next to the head, was
laid that setting for Veuglio.

As we waited for Astolfo, I seized the moment to snatch a large
green olive out of a yellow bowl and cast it at Mutano. It thumped
off his forehead onto the table. So then he shied a lump of bread at
me and missed. It fell to the floor and a servant picked it up.

We were rewarded, me by a sharp pinch on my thigh from
Telluria and him by a swift finger-poke in the ribs by Maronda.

⋆⇥▄◉▄⇤⋆

Then the corridor door opened and Astolfo appeared. He was
dressed in one of his military costumes, the one he had worn when
he staged my arrest for attempted theft within the grounds of the
Countess Triana. That was when we secured the safety of the gem
for some time to come. Here again was the sea-colored caftan, the
cloth-of-gold sash, and the red cloak. He had found it not proper to
wear the large, white-plumed hat.

Had he donned this costume to remind me of my embarrassment in that episode? I could not doubt it.

He was accompanied by Dorminia. We all recognized her at
once, though she was much changed from the young girl with the
white hair and perplexed expression. She had gained in height at
least two inches and held herself with almost military bearing, her
spine straight and her broad shoulders squared. Her clothing was in
violent contrast to Astolfo's. A robe of grayish dun fabric something
like sackcloth hung to her ankles. A length of linen rope was looped
around her waist. Her sandals were such as any tradesman might
wear. White her hair had been before; now it was of a moonlight
tint. Her expression was serene as she took in our company with a
series of observant gazes. She did venture a hint of a smile when
she looked upon Gabriel squirming in Telluria's embrace. When the
babe saw her his agitation settled and he looked at her as he might
have upon a camelopard.

Brushing away the footman, Astolfo pulled out her chair and
handed her the black napkin from her setting. Then he slipped out

of his cloak, handed it off, and eased into the fancifully carven oak chair at table head.

Without permission or preamble, I rose to propose a salute to my brother. "How the lowly are risen!" I said. "It must seem to you but a sennight past that you were muddying the waters of Dove Creek with La Pluma teaching you to dog-paddle—and to perform other doggish tricks. Now you are installed in a great manse prominent in Tlemia Province, overseeing the tillage of your fields and gluttoning on the fat o' th' land, if I may judge by this table you have set out."

It was a plenteous array, too lavish to inventory at a glance, although I noticed that Mutano was eyeing purposefully a large poached tench laid out on watercress on a crystal salver, a morsel I would strive to gather first to myself.

I continued my salute: "And here is to the well-being of Mutano and Maronda. Long may they prosper and may they enjoy as many lives as those of all their cats added together. That would reckon up to two or three eternities, at least."

I drained my glass and sat and my conclusion was the signal for the rest of the party to offer salutes. Each of them made short speeches equally as inane as my own.

Astolfo rose, raised his glass, and said only, "To remember absent friends." Then he sat.

The ensuing conversations then fluttered about one subject and another, never resting long enough to invite serious discourse, and when the chat about families and crops and passing indispositions and the erotic propensities of the priesthoods sank to murmurs and expired, the reminiscences began.

I expect that we shall be talking to the end of our days about the attack of the warship upon Tardocco and about our defeat of the pirate queen Fleuraye. This fiery female was still alive, having beguiled a council of magistrates to spare her life. She was, however, put to a task that she could little relish. Her great three-master, the *Vengeful Maiden,* had been dismantled, taken apart timber by timber and sheet by sheet, and the parts brought to land. The ship was being remade into a bridge over one of the muddy tributaries of the Daia. The pirate crew served as the workforce, and Fleuraye oversaw their labors with a keen severity. Other, more severe, punishments awaited her after the completion of the bridge—a task that she was taking a very long time to accomplish.

Our talk this evening followed the course of that taken by veterans of campaigns since warfare came to its bloody birth. Mutano told his heroic tale with, methought, an immodest amount of embellishment. To my own account I added augmentation sufficient to match his. If Cocorico and Sbufo had been present, the saga might have continued for days and nights together. Maronda and Telluria listened indulgently to episodes that must by now have become all too familiar to them, but Gabriel grew pettish and began to fret. Telluria unsheathed and silenced his complaints with an abundant mammary.

It is traditional in the retelling of one's martial exploits to admit to a moment of fear. In accounting the overcoming of fear, one adds glory to glory. I spoke of the genuine terror that struck my soul when I looked upon the Mardrake's eye at that moment when the Being broke skyward out of the bay.

"Halt you there," said Mutano. "I gazed upon the thing. It had two eyes—and not like those of fishes or serpents. Like human eyes."

"I saw one eye. It saw me. It stared like en evil moon set in a towering pillar of pitch."

When we appealed to Astolfo, he said, "Falco saw but one, perhaps because he expected to. It is the habit of poets to paint their monsters with one eye. Their depictions stand so strong in the mind, it hinders accurate observation." He then recited about two ells of Latin verse that none of us paid attention to.

"I do not heed the inky tribe," I said. "I have tried to fathom from what I saw with my eyes the nature of the creature. I can gain no hint of what it might be."

"My thoughts can be but surmises," Astolfo said. He spoke slowly, as if thinking upon the matter afresh. "The lore names the Mardrake immortal, but I think it can be only nearly immortal, surviving in a sort of dream-state in the black waters. Long ago I read a passage in an anonymous treatise that I now begin to give some credence to. The long-dead scrivener wrote that the Mardrake is a shadow that inhabited an immeasurably ancient primal age before shadows gave up corporeality. In the beginning, said he, shadows inhabited the two states, the substantial and the insubstantial. They still retain some characteristics of their earliest form of organism, or we could not so physically handle them as we do, sundering, positioning, and sculpting. But in the major part of his being, the

Mardrake is still a living creature, lying within the depths of the bay in a trancelike sleep."

"Mutano suggests that it attacked our large puppet-monster out of annoyance, the way a sunfish will attack lures of owl feather or wisps of horse tail," I said.

"Perhaps. Yet have you not in the grip of a vivid dream struck out with your arm against a wall or pillow or the headboard of a bed? It may be that the false Mardrake disturbed the sleep of the real one and it responded unthinkingly."

"And you suppose that this being may be only half corporeal? If it does possess a greater bodily nature than what it showed during the battle, its dimensions must be immense."

The maestro bit his lower lip, considering. "It may be that we saw only the smallest part of him. The legends draw him of a size incomprehensible. As for his nature being half substance and half nonsubstance—well, many a graybeard has described the nature of humankind in the same terms."

"And many a poet has seen mankind as no less a monster than the Mardrake," I said.

Mutano said, "If he be half of substance and half of spirit, then his corpus will die. What then of his nonsubstantial half?"

"No one ventures to say, though the poet describes his dream-enwrapped existence as a troubled one, down in the oceanic darkness. You will recall:

"There hath he lain for ages and will lie,
  Battening upon huge sea worms in his sleep,
  Until the latter fire shall heat the deep;
  Then once by man and angels to be seen,
  In roaring he shall rise and on the surface die."

The creature must be aware that in some future a final cosmic hour shall end its existence."

Telluria spoke up softly. We all looked at her in surprise. "Mutano called the sea-beast 'he.' Could it not be female? Maybe it saw the puppet and thought it a child, maybe her own grandchild."

Astolfo took a long moment to respond. "None can say. It has been most often suggested that the Mardrake is a single, unique individual without siblings. It has been thought the only one of its kind."

"Was it not born?" Telluria said.

"No one knows. It has been written that—"

She disengaged our babe from her breast and wiped his mouth. Then she nodded in agreement with herself. "Whatever the creature is, it was born of a mother," she said. She smiled at Gabriel as his eyelids drooped and closed.

⊷⊨◉⊜⊨⊶

We feasted, we drank, but we were not the roisterers we were of old. Perhaps the presence of infant Stolfino gave cause to quiet our high spirits. Certainly the presence of Dorminia and the recollection of Veuglio weighed upon us. When Mutano rose to sing his favored ballad of love, "When I Was King o' the Cats and You Were the Farrier's Pet," Maronda plucked him by his blue-and-gold gored sleeve and he sat.

Astolfo spoke to her. "You do not allow Mutano to caterwaul at us and for that we are grateful. All the more so, since the opportunity is open for you to sing. We all know of your pleasant skill with a song."

She frowned and declined, but then after lengthy amounts of pleading from the rest of us, she rose to render a doleful ballad of a foolish young blade who falls into evil ways and meets a bad end, leaving his mother and sister to grieve. By the time she had finished, tears stood undropped in her eyes. I had heard talk that her brother Quinias had once more strayed from the path of virtue and was at odds with the authorities. There was a whisper he might have befriended the pirate invaders, but I put no faith in it. He was a fellow with no murder in him, only petty betrayal.

We divined the private burden of Maronda's lay and were glad when it was finished.

Astolfo allowed a space of silence to ensue before he began.

"I will speak of the passing of Veuglio. I had not seen him for two seasons and had received only vague tidings. He had reestablished relations with the beggars' guild. He also was a frequent visitor to the leper colony in the foothills, making the journey afoot with Dorminia at his side—he now called her Dorminia and never again Sibylla. She followed him as his ardent disciple and helpmeet. She had left the comforts of her wealthy family to cleave to my old friend and look to his well-being.

"When they came to my door I recognized that Veuglio was in

his last days and that he counted upon me to see to his end. We laid him in the bedroom in the west wing and administered to him as best we could. Dorminia never abandoned his bedside.

"I saw him take his wordless, final breath and then lose it to the aether. His form was still, his features were peaceful. The setting sun cast his shadow beside him on the bed linen. When Veuglio died, his shadow changed its nature. It had been lying dark, like any other umbra. And then it became like no other.

"At that moment his shadow rose up from the bed. Within the red sunlight I could no longer make it out. I could not say if it were in the room.

"Dorminia stood up. She bent over Veuglio and kissed his forehead. She turned and took up Veuglio's staff where it leaned in the corner. Then she gave me a long and mournful gaze. And then, with pouch and staff, she departed. I did not know if ever I would lay eyes upon her again."

He paused and put a knuckle to his right eye. If he wept then, I did not see the tear.

"But here she is with us tonight, in answer to my most earnest request. I am grateful, as I think you will be also. . . . Let us raise a glass. She does not indulge in wine, so we must taste for her tonight."

We followed his welcome direction.

He continued. "Her presence allows me to exhibit to you the realization of an idea—nay, a dream and a hope—I have held to for long and long. I have spoken of it to Falco and to Mutano also, though I think they paid little attention, thinking it a foolish fancy.

"But let us try to discover if our best hopes are always false."

At his signal two servants came to the table. They bore between them a screen such as those who entertain crowds at fairs with shadow-puppets employ. These are made of a close-woven linen that has the capacity to register the smallest details: the jagged cap of a Jester-puppet, the delicate curls of a Columbina-puppet. The servants placed this screen behind the chair in which Dorminia was seated.

Then they went around the walls, extinguishing the torches and candles installed there.

All the room was dark except for the illumination upon our table. Astolfo gathered the table candles into a phalanx in front of Dorminia. She rose and pulled aside her chair.

Now she stood sidewise to the light so that her umbra would be cast upon the screen.

It was a long and silent time before her form appeared, and when it came to sight it was difficult to make out. The umbrae we normally observe are alterations of ambient light caused by material objects or phenomena. Whatever presence casts a shadow composed of light is not of a material substance. A shadow whose shape is formed all of light is not easily perceived.

I have thought that it must be the shade of the *vis,* the outline of the life force of someone the pains and sorrows of the world have scraped clean of every mark a human fault could lay upon it. Only moon-bright purity can cast a shadow made of light.

Yet it was not the shadow of Veuglio—or not entirely. It was intermixed with other shapes besides, for Dorminia's form was an inseparable and almost undistinguishable part of it, and so was Sibylla's; it was a shadow that chose to accompany Dorminia because in our world she had become the thing nearest its own nature.

I looked around at our party. We had all risen to our feet without realizing that we had done so. Mutano, Maronda, Osbro, and Telluria gazed wonder-struck. Gabriel opened his eyes and beheld and smiled and fell asleep again still smiling.

"We are ever in your debt, Dorminia, for consenting to make the journey here," said Astolfo.

The screen was removed. She gave each of us a grave, smiling bow and walked from the room, her bright shadow now unseeable.

Astolfo explained. "She returns now to the leper colony in the foothills."

He drank the last of his brandy and upended his glass on the table. We did likewise.

And went quietly to our chambers and their restorative beds.

⊷━◉━⊶

I rose at an unwontedly late hour in a room without other occupants. Telluria and Stolfino would already be breaking their fast in the dining hall with fruit and barley groats. I gathered myself and allayed my hot thirst with the water jar and rubbed six handfuls of the basin water into my face and hair and then berated Falco yet once more in repentant tones: "Thou'rt too far along in years for such night-work, fellow. Thou'rt no longer the reckless bravo of the alleyways."

I hurried to find our company. I did not want to omit making my manners to Osbro and voicing once again my gratitude to Astolfo and I had my singular matter to put to Mutano.

The opportunity was lost. The steward informed me that Osbro and Astolfo had gone to the mid-city to search out the artist Petrinius and inspect his mural. He had at last finished his great work, now called *Humanity Most Inhumane,* and was hiding away from the raging wrath of some of the personages portrayed therein. Telluria and the babe were finished at table and now stood in the sunlight of the courtyard, watching as servants packed our belongings into the conveyance that had brought Mutano and Maronda hither.

Mutano stood there too, observing with care how the task proceeded. Maronda had stepped aside to speak to Telluria and to coo over the babe. My old colleague gave me a quizzical, amused glance as I approached.

"I have a thing to ask of thee," I said.

He smiled knowingly and nodded.

"It may be that you already foretell the import of my question."

He grinned.

"But I am in earnest and I must have your promise that you will tell the truth, wholly and without deception."

He nodded acquiescence.

"Are you, at last, the King o' the Cats?"

He closed his eyes, as if to consider, then opened them to gaze seriously into my own. He spoke calmly and volubly for a longer space of time than I had supposed he might. But whether he answered affirmatively or negatively, my narrow acquaintance with the feline language has still not allowed me to know.